COUSIN PHILLIS
AND OTHER TALES

MRS GASKELL was born Elizabeth Cleghorn Stevenson in 1810. The daughter of a Unitarian, who was a civil servant and journalist, she was brought up after her mother's death by her aunt in Knutsford, Cheshire, which became the model not only for Cranford but also for Hollingford (in *Wives and Daughters*). In 1832 she married William Gaskell, a Unitarian minister in Manchester, with whom she lived very happily. Her first novel, *Mary Barton*, published in 1848, was immensely popular and brought her to the attention of Charles Dickens, who was looking for contributors to his new periodical, *Household Words*, for which she wrote the famous series of papers subsequently reprinted as *Cranford*. Her later novels include *Ruth* (1853), *North and South* (1854–5), *Sylvia's Lovers* (1863), and *Wives and Daughters* (1864–6). She also wrote many stories and her remarkable *Life of Charlotte Brontë*. She died in 1865.

ANGUS EASSON is Professor of English at the University of Salford. He has edited Dickens's *The Old Curiosity Shop* and Gaskell's *North and South* and published a study of Elizabeth Gaskell.

THE WORLD'S CLASSICS

═══

ELIZABETH GASKELL
Cousin Phillis
and Other Tales

═══

EDITED WITH
AN INTRODUCTION AND NOTES
BY ANGUS EASSON

Oxford New York Toronto Melbourne
OXFORD UNIVERSITY PRESS
1981

Oxford University Press, Walton Street, Oxford OX2 6DP

London Glasgow New York Toronto
Delhi Bombay Calcutta Madras Karachi
Kuala Lumpur Singapore Hong Kong Tokyo
Nairobi Dar es Salaam Cape Town
Melbourne Wellington

and associate companies in
Beirut Berlin Ibadan Mexico City

Introduction, Notes, Bibliography,
and Selection © Angus Easson 1981
Chronology © Oxford University Press 1981

This selection first published as a World's Classics paperback 1981

British Library Cataloguing in Publication Data
Gaskell, Elizabeth
Cousin Phillis and other tales. – (The World's classics)
I. Title   II. Easson, Angus
823'.8   PR4710
ISBN 0-19-281554-7

Printed in Great Britain by
Hazell Watson & Viney Limited
Aylesbury, Bucks

CONTENTS

INTRODUCTION

'My dear Scheherezade', is the flattering opening of one of
Charles Dickens's letters to Elizabeth Gaskell. Scheherezade
charmed her husband night after night to keep her head and if
Elizabeth Gaskell, under lesser compulsions, was not so
prolific, she proved from her earliest efforts that she was a
natural story-teller. Dickens's flattery was not in any way a
condescension to her art, even though part of an attempt to
placate Gaskell after she had accused him of stealing and
writing up one of her stories. It was sincere enough, for
Dickens greatly valued Elizabeth Gaskell as a writer of fiction
for his weekly magazine, *Household Words*, and knew she could
spin tales as cunningly as the Sultan's wife in the *Arabian
Nights' Entertainment*. In her turn, though she might resent
his editorial interference, Elizabeth Gaskell knew the value of
a man who paid well and promptly for what she wrote and who
admired her talents enough to think her worth flattery when
other writers were ignored or had their work unceremoniously
altered, revised, and rewritten in the editorial office. Although
never dependent upon her writings for a livelihood, Elizabeth
Gaskell's range and art in her short stories alone would
establish her professionalism.

Married in 1832 to William Gaskell, a Unitarian minister,
Mrs Gaskell's family and duties in Manchester always came
first. The late 1830s, though, saw the beginnings of a literary
production which was to make her famous on publication of
her first novel, *Mary Barton* (1848), and that lasted until her
death in 1865, when she left her greatest novel, *Wives and
Daughters*, not quite complete.

Her earliest independent piece, a contribution to William
Howitt's *Visits to Remarkable Places* (1840), though a description of Clopton Hall in Warwickshire, includes story-shaped
elements, as when she describes her schoolgirl self and a friend
wandering round the old house:

There was a curious carved old chest in one of these passages, and
with girlish curiosity I tried to open it; but the lid was too heavy,
till I persuaded one of my companions to help me, and when it was

opened, what do you think we saw? – BONES! – but whether human, whether the remains of the lost bride, we did not stay to see, but ran off in partly feigned and partly real terror.

Oral tale-telling is strong in the jump at the audience on 'BONES!', while the terror that is 'partly feigned' and 'partly real' shows that psychological understanding, which underpins all of Gaskell's best fiction, putting us here in touch with real girls.

Elizabeth Gaskell found it natural to tell stories and she told them well because she was a natural (not an artless) story-teller. A friend, Susanna Winkworth, testified to her power and her art: 'No one ever came near her in the gift of telling a story. In her hands the simplest incident – a meeting in the street, a talk with a factory-girl, a country walk, an old family history, – became picturesque and vivid and interesting.' The selection in this volume aims to show that range and that craft, for though the attraction of ghosts and witchcraft has kept a small number of the stories in print, Elizabeth Gaskell's achievement in this form is comparatively little known and yet remarkable. In a busy life, apart from her novels and the *Life of Charlotte Brontë* (1857), she produced about thirty short stories, some of considerable length. As a novelist her career between *North and South* (1855) and *Sylvia's Lovers* (1863) is a blank, yet apart from the outstanding biography of Charlotte Brontë, she produced thirteen stories, two of them novellas, in this time. Even her earliest fictions, 'Sunday School' stories combining instruction with entertainment, show her knack for detail and humour.

As well as delighting in storytelling, Elizabeth Gaskell found that the time she could spare for writing from being wife, mother, and controller of a household was often best expended on the shorter forms of fictions. Stories also sold well and money towards household expenses was no mean consideration. The market for shorter fiction in magazines was expanding and once enough stories had accumulated through periodical publication they might be collected in volume form and paid for twice over. In 1858, in Germany, planning to extend a family tour but without the cash to do so, Elizabeth Gaskell wrote two stories for Dickens and was paid £40 by return. Such was her value to Dickens and his to her. Despite all coolnesses and a sense on her side of never quite trusting him, it was to Dickens for his magazines *Household Words* (1850–59) and *All the Year Round* (1859–70) that Gaskell sent most of her work. The first five stories printed here went to him; the other two appeared in the *Cornhill Magazine* (founded 1860), managed by George Smith of the publishers Smith, Elder, with whom Elizabeth Gaskell was drawn into association by the writing and publication of the *Life of Charlotte Brontë*. For Smith she wrote her greatest short fiction, 'Cousin Phillis', but as the stories in this collection show, her contemptuous disparagement of work as 'good enough for Dickens' was rather a humorous knock at the man than a selling short on artistic worth.

'Lizzie Leigh', like Elizabeth Gaskell's first great success, *Mary Barton*, is set largely in Manchester. In it, Gaskell explores the possibilities in two ways of life meeting and reacting when Mrs Anne Leigh, impelled by love of her lost daughter, dead to her through the duty she owes her husband, comes from the country to the town. The story is partly a quest and partly a mystery in its interlinking of Susan and the foundling child, of Will's love and Lizzie's recovery. The death of Lizzie's child may seem harsh: it is, though, not only the price Lizzie must pay for restoration to her family but also the penalty of James Leigh's grim judgement on his daughter. If the use of the Palmers to knot together both plots – Lizzie's discovery and Will's love – is a little contrived, the connecting links are expertly placed and the chastened reunion in love and sorrow of mother and daughter is balanced by the happy union of Will and Susan, while Gaskell infuses the whole with a sense of acute observation that shows how intensely she saw what she wrote. When Susan produces the child's things, there 'was a little packet of clothes – very few – and as if they were made out of its mother's gowns, for they were large patterns to buy for a baby'. Through such detail Elizabeth Gaskell authenticates her world.

Like many of her contemporaries, Elizabeth Gaskell delighted in ghost stories. She tells how one night, when Charlotte Brontë was visiting her, 'I was on the point of relating some dismal ghost story, just before bed-time' – though Charlotte, her nerves strung up, 'shrank from hearing it'. A

'dismal' ghost story: because when we want to be frightened
we want to be frightened as thoroughly as possible. When in
1852 Charles Dickens asked Elizabeth Gaskell to contribute
to the special Christmas number of *Household Words*, a ghost
story was very much in order and 'The Old Nurse's Story' the
result. At the beginning, when the Nurse feels no terror at the
ghostly organ music, thinking rather it was 'pleasant to have
that grand music rolling about the house', the story has the
strength to dare to laugh at its own terrors, but this early
reaction is modified and first awe and then terror predominates from the Nurse's discovery that the organ plays despite
being empty inside. The threat to the child menaces more and
more, while past and present meet in the hall where the
lighted chandelier gives no light and the blazing fire no heat.
Hatred and jealousy are re-enacted, proof of how real is the
threat to Rosamond. There is no cheating on the ghosts nor
on the destructive nature of human passion.

The Old Nurse herself comes from Westmoreland. The Lake
District was well known to Elizabeth Gaskell from family
holidays and more memorable by being the scene of her first
meeting with Charlotte Brontë. It was too the home of
Wordsworth, a poet to whom Gaskell responded deeply.
'Half a Life-Time Ago' and 'The Crooked Branch' both show
how Elizabeth Gaskell drew on and transformed Wordsworth.
If she does not employ Wordsworth's challenges to our
response nor his exploitation of language and romance con-
ventions of storytelling in poems like 'The Idiot Boy', yet the
characters' relations to each other and environment, as in
Wordsworth, display 'the essential passions of the human
heart'. Susan Dixon, in 'Half a Life-Time Ago', is torn between two loves, that for her brother and that for her pros-
pective husband. Her vow at her mother's death-bed to care
for her brother is unaffected by his subsequent mental collapse,
so when Michael, her betrothed, makes Willie's consignment
to a lunatic asylum the price of their marriage, Susan breaks
with him. But the sacrifice is not one of those that mean giving
up what we do not want. Michael's charm is made clear in the
episode when Susan finds, after quarrelling with him for hitting
Willie, that her brother is easily won to devotion again by
Michael. Susan's hunger for that love which Michael alone

can give finds concrete expression in her vigil beneath the wrecked yew tree, while the struggle of the way she has chosen in faith to her vow and duty to Willie, who offers no comfort or reward by return of love, is deftly expressed by the intermittent physical wrestling with her brother's fits, compelling her at the worst times to 'sally out to taste the fresh air, and to work off her wild sorrows in cries and mutterings to herself'.

If Susan Dixon yet has the consolation of helping Michael Hurst's widow, her end happier than seemed likely, the ending of 'The Crooked Branch' is starkly tragic. In its original form, one in a sequence of tales for the 1859 Christmas number of Dickens's new periodical, *All the Year Round*, the title was 'The Ghost in the Garden Room'. With nothing directly supernatural, 'The Crooked Branch' is a story of the return of the dead. Benjamin's haunting of his parents is the more horrible because he is still in the body when he stages the resurrection so long wished for by his mother, so terrible in its manifestation and outcome. In setting the devotion of the old couple's adopted daughter, Bessy Rose, against the warping of their son, Gaskell develops a favourite contrast between the man who with all worldly opportunities turns them to corruption and the woman who employs what talents she has to make rich the lives of others.

Another part of Gaskell's romantic inheritance appears in 'Lois the Witch', published earlier in the same year as 'The Crooked Branch'. The witch-hunts of seventeenth-century New England have in this century powerfully served Arthur Miller in *The Crucible* to parallel Macarthy's UnAmerican Activities Committee. An eighteenth-century writer might have viewed the events with scepticism and made their perpetrators hypocrites. Yet Gaskell, though she does not believe in witchcraft, recognizes the terrifying fact that most of those involved, both prosecutors and victims, believed and trembled. Her romantic recognition of man's inner darkness, of the shaping power of the imagination, helps her depict the psychology of hysteria both collective and individual in a community shut off from the world, turned in upon itself, where fear, jealousy, superstition and literal belief all tangle; where panic, once started, cannot be halted until it has worked out its fury in destruction, leaving the community aghast, like those self-betrayed, at the evidence of their own turbid passions. Gaskell enters imaginatively into the minds of those who believe in witches. Orphaned and exiled, Lois is trapped, by her circumstances and by the Hickson family, headed by its proud matriarch, Grace, prepared to humble herself only when her unlovely yet beloved son's tottering sanity is threatened. Belief in witchcraft is a force that feeds upon the entwined desires of those in community, township, and family, feeds too upon the individual heart, which is powerful for wickedness as well as for love, and the story insists upon the tragic consequence for Lois. Only at the end, when it is too late, does the story open out into the light of reason with the community's confession and plea for forgiveness, brought to us by Holdernesse and Hugh Lucy, who stand in the mental and physical freedom that so contrasts with the dark depths of imagination and society that destroys Lois.

Imagination predominates too in 'Curious, If True', yet the ambiguity of the title enforces the joke of the story. For this is a world viewed through the literal eye of a puritan (Whittingham stresses his descent from Calvin), while the author's imagination plays with the effect of time upon the timeless creations of fairy and folk tales. Only an adult who has delighted in fairy tales could enjoy the story: a child would be too innocent and an ignorant adult merely bored. Part of the fun is in spotting the figures distorted by time and by Whittingham's oblique vision, while the power of these creations to delight through the ages is suggested when, as Whittingham ascends the stairs, he almost fancies 'that I heard a mighty rushing murmur (like the ceaseless sound of a distant sea, ebbing and flowing for ever and ever), coming forth from the great vacant galleries that opened out on each side of the broad staircase'. It is, though he doesn't know it, the constant and eternally new repetition of 'Once upon a time'.

Sleeping Beauty is among the guests at the Chateau and it might be easy to suggest her story as the pattern of 'Cousin Phillis'. Phillis Holman, though, is not merely waiting to be woken by a kiss. She is a girl passing naturally through adolescence into full maturity, coming violently into the passional life through her love for Holdsworth. She is not asleep, but growing, a process often painful even as it is inevitable. Change is hinted at in her progress from childish pinafore to a woman's apron and the story explores change both in Phillis and in the larger society of which she and Holdsworth are part. The Holman family's world of Dissent, inherited from the seventeenth century, with a continuity of values on one hand from Virgil and Horace and from Christianity on the other, is faced by the new world of railways and political change. Phillis learns Italian so she can read Dante, but Holdsworth, who thinks she reads Dante to learn Italian rather than to seize hold of a sublime poet, suggests she read Manzoni's great historical novel, *The Betrothed*. Manzoni's novel not only challenges the values of the world of Dissent by being a fiction, it belongs also to the new world of Italian nationalism, a world of political change that goes hand in hand with the mobility of society and ideas that the railways bring. Such change is not necessarily bad, though it may be regretted.

And yet even within Phillis's world, life is not static. There are indeed moments when Phillis seems held, unchanging – when for instance Paul and Holdsworth watch her after she has been shelling peas, framed by the window, or later when Holdsworth sketches her. Each time, though, Phillis moves, embarrassed once she is aware of the watchers, unable to have her portrait drawn because her feelings are so changed by Holdsworth. Change in the larger world may be inevitable; change in the individual is unavoidable. Even the cycles of the farming year underline this, for the two hay harvests, alike yet not the same, are times of crisis in Phillis's relationship with Holdsworth; and yet how different is the situation between one year and the next.

Holdsworth is not a villain. He does not jilt Phillis, he is free to love and marry in Canada, though he shows how Gaskell's men may feel less deeply, are less devastated by love than her women. His sphere of activity is large, physically spanning Italy, England and North America, where Phillis's is turned upon herself, in suffering. As the title reminds us, it is Phillis's story and though we never learn from Paul what happens to her later, one thing seems certain: that her final hope for a return to the old ways is a vain one. She cannot be a child again, for the transition from pinafore to apron was more than a change of garments. 'The same kind of happy days never return', and whether Phillis is to love again or not, whether she marries or remains single, she cannot go back into the past. The idyllic elements of the Holman farm do not conceal the rigours of agricultural life nor do the idyllic elements of the story conceal the changes that Phillis has undergone. Along with loving creation of detail, Gaskell reveals a toughness that characterizes all her best work, whether comic or tragic.

NOTE ON THE TEXT

The text of each story is that of first volume publication: publishing details are given in the notes at the end of the volume. Obvious errors have been corrected, while the spelling of a few words (e.g. 'sate' for 'sat' and 'grey' for 'gray') and certain features of punctuation have been made consistent. The use of inverted commas conforms to the style of the World's Classics. A very few textual emendations have been silently made. On proper names, Elizabeth Gaskell could be very off-hand; in 'The Old Nurse's Story', for instance, the servant Agnes is also called Bessy. With one exception the first name used by Gaskell is adopted throughout: in 'Cousin Phillis' the ladies where Paul lodges are here called the Misses Dawson, not the Misses Brown, and their brother consequently called Mr Dawson instead of Hunter. The brief explanatory notes at the end of the volume are keyed into the text.

SELECT BIBLIOGRAPHY

THERE is no complete edition of Elizabeth Gaskell's works: the most comprehensive, both now out of print, are *The Works of Mrs Gaskell*, ed. A. W. Ward, 8 vols. (Knutsford edition, 1906), which excludes *The Life of Charlotte Brontë*, and *The Novels and Tales of Mrs Gaskell*, ed. Clement Shorter, 11 vols. (World's Classics, 1906–19), which includes *The Life of Charlotte Brontë*. Oxford English Novels included *Cranford*, ed. Elizabeth Porges Watson (1972) and *North and South*, ed. Angus Easson (1973) with introductions and annotations: both since issued as paperbacks and *Cranford* issued in the new World's Classics. Penguin English Library have published *Mary Barton, North and South, Wives and Daughters, Cranford and Cousin Phillis*, and *The Life of Charlotte Brontë*, with introductions and annotations: these are good, except that *Wives and Daughters* has a corrupt text. The novels and a selection of the short stories are available with modern introductions in the Everyman Library.

The Letters of Elizabeth Gaskell, immensely readable as well as providing much biographical material, are edited by J. A. V. Chapple and Arthur Pollard (1966), while a selection of them, with linking biographical narrative, *Elizabeth Gaskell: A Portrait in Letters*, is edited by J. A. V. Chapple and J. G. Sharps (1980).

The biography by A. B. Hopkins (1952) is largely but not entirely superseded by the new material of the letters, of which Winifred Gérin was able to take advantage (1976), though she does not always take sufficient account of Gaskell's Manchester background.

Studies that include biographical information but are more concerned to use background material to illuminate a reading of the work are J. G. Sharps, *Mrs Gaskell's Observation and Invention* (1970) and Angus Easson, *Elizabeth Gaskell* (1979). An excellent short critical introduction is Margaret Ganz, *Elizabeth Gaskell: The Artist in Conflict* (1969) and on the novels two useful studies are W. A. Craik, *Elizabeth Gaskell and the English Provincial Novel* (1975) and Arthur Pollard, *Mrs Gaskell: Novelist and Biographer* (1965).

Not much has been written on the short stories. Edgar Wright has some discussion in *Mrs Gaskell: The Basis for Reassessment* (1965) and the studies by Easson, Ganz and Sharps give consideration to them. John Lucas has a chapter on 'Mrs Gaskell and the Nature of Social Change' in *The Literature of Change* (1977), which includes 'Cousin Phillis'.

A CHRONOLOGY OF ELIZABETH GASKELL

Age

and 'The Crooked Branch' in *All the Year Round*. Visits
Whitby where she collects material for *Sylvia's Lovers*.
Takes her daughters Meta and Florence to Germany,
returning via Paris

1860   *Right at Last and other Tales* published. 'Curious if True'   49–50
        in *The Cornhill*. Visits to France

1861   'The Grey Woman' in *All the Year Round*   50–1

1862   Visits Paris, Normandy, and Britanny with Meta and a   51–2
        friend, returning to London for the Exhibition. Back in
        Manchester she over-exerts herself in relief work among
        the workmen, and has to recuperate. Writes a Preface to
        Vecchi's *Garibaldi*

1863   'A Dark Night's Work', 'An Italian Institution', 'The   52–3
        Cage at Cranford', and 'Crowley Castle' in *All the Year
        Round*. 'Cousin Phillis' in *The Cornhill*. *Sylvia's Lovers*
        published by Smith, Elder. Visits Mme Mohl in Paris,
        going on to Rome with three of her daughters. Her
        daughter Florence marries

1864   'French Life' in *Fraser's Magazine*. *Wives and Daughters*   53–4
        begins to appear in *The Cornhill*.

1865   *Cousin Phillis and Other Tales* and *The Grey Woman and*   54–5
        Other Tales published. Visits Dieppe, and Mme Mohl in
        Paris. Buys a house, The Lawns, nr. Holybourne in
        Hampshire, and dies there suddenly on 12 November

1866   *Wives and Daughters* published posthumously

LIZZIE LEIGH

*

CHAPTER I

WHEN Death is present in a household on a Christmas Day, the very contrast between the time as it now is, and the day as it has often been, gives a poignancy to sorrow, – a more utter blankness to the desolation. James Leigh died just as the far away bells of Rochdale Church were ringing for morning service on Christmas Day, 1836. A few minutes before his death, he opened his already glazing eyes, and made a sign to his wife, by the faint motion of his lips, that he had yet something to say. She stooped close down, and caught the broken whisper, 'I forgive her, Anne! May God forgive me!'

'Oh my love, my dear! only get well, and I will never cease showing my thanks for those words. May God in heaven bless thee for saying them. Thou'rt not so restless, my lad! may be – Oh God!'

For even while she spoke, he died.

They had been two-and-twenty years man and wife; for nineteen of those years their life had been as calm and happy, as the most perfect uprightness on the one side, and the most complete confidence and loving submission on the other, could make it. Milton's famous line* might have been framed and hung up as the rule of their married life, for he was truly the interpreter, who stood between God and her; she would have considered herself wicked if she had ever dared even to think him austere, though as certainly as he was an upright man, so surely was he hard, stern, and inflexible. But for three years the moan and the murmur had never been out of her heart; she had rebelled against her husband as against a tyrant, with a hidden, sullen rebellion, which tore up the old landmarks of wifely duty and affection, and poisoned the fountains whence gentlest love and reverence had once been for ever springing.

But those last blessed words replaced him on his throne in

her heart, and called out penitent anguish for all the bitter estrangement of later years. It was this which made her refuse all the entreaties of her sons, that she would see the kind-hearted neighbours, who called on their way from church to sympathise and condole. No! she would stay with the dead husband that had spoken tenderly at last, if for three years he had kept silence; who knew but what, if she had only been more gentle and less angrily reserved, he might have relented earlier – and in time!

She sate rocking herself to and fro by the side of the bed, while the footsteps below went in and out; she had been in sorrow too long to have any violent burst of deep grief now; the furrows were well worn in her cheeks, and the tears flowed quietly, if incessantly, all the day long. But when the winter's night drew on, and the neighbours had gone away to their homes, she stole to the window, and gazed out, long and wistfully, over the dark grey moors. She did not hear her son's voice, as he spoke to her from the door, nor his footstep as he drew nearer. She started when he touched her.

'Mother! come down to us. There's no one but Will and me. Dearest mother, we do so want you.' The poor lad's voice trembled, and he began to cry. It appeared to require an effort on Mrs Leigh's part to tear herself away from the window, but with a sigh she complied with his request.

The two boys (for though Will was nearly twenty-one, she still thought of him as a lad) had done everything in their power to make the house-place* comfortable for her. She herself, in the old days before her sorrow, had never made a brighter fire or a cleaner hearth, ready for her husband's return home, than now awaited her. The tea-things were all put out, and the kettle was boiling; and the boys had calmed their grief down into a kind of sober cheerfulness. They paid her every attention they could think of, but received little notice on her part; she did not resist – she rather submitted to all their arrangements; but they did not seem to touch her heart.

When tea was ended, – it was merely the form of tea that had been gone through, – Will moved the things away to the dresser. His mother leant back languidly in her chair.

'Mother, shall Tom read you a chapter? He's a better scholar than I.'

'Aye, lad!' said she, almost eagerly. 'That's it. Read me the Prodigal Son.* Aye, aye, lad. Thank thee.'

Tom found the chapter, and read it in the high-pitched voice which is customary in village-schools. His mother bent forward, her lips parted, her eyes dilated; her whole body instinct with eager attention. Will sate with his head depressed, and hung down. He knew why that chapter had been chosen; and to him it recalled the family's disgrace. When the reading was ended, he still hung down his head in gloomy silence. But her face was brighter than it had been before for the day. Her eyes looked dreamy, as if she saw a vision; and by and by she pulled the bible towards her, and putting her finger underneath each word, began to read them aloud in a low voice to herself; she read again the words of bitter sorrow and deep humiliation; but most of all she paused and brightened over the father's tender reception of the repentant prodigal.

So passed the Christmas evening in the Upclose Farm.

The snow had fallen heavily over the dark, waving moorland, before the day of the funeral. The black storm-laden dome of heaven lay very still and close upon the white earth, as they carried the body forth out of the house which had known his presence so long as its ruling power. Two and two the mourners followed, making a black procession, in their winding march over the unbeaten snow, to Milne-Row Church – now lost in some hollow of the bleak moors, now slowly climbing the heaving ascents. There was no long tarrying after the funeral, for many of the neighbours who accompanied the body to the grave had far to go, and the great white flakes which came slowly down, were the boding forerunners of a heavy storm. One old friend alone accompanied the widow and her sons to their home.

The Upclose Farm had belonged for generations to the Leighs; and yet its possession hardly raised them above the rank of labourers. There was the house and outbuildings, all of an old-fashioned kind, and about seven acres of barren unproductive land, which they had never possessed capital enough to improve; indeed they could hardly rely upon it for subsistence; and it had been customary to bring up the sons to some trade – such as a wheelwright's, or blacksmith's.

James Leigh had left a will, in the possession of the old man who accompanied them home. He read it aloud. James had bequeathed the farm to his faithful wife, Anne Leigh, for her lifetime; and afterwards, to his son William. The hundred and odd pounds in the savings'-bank was to accumulate for Thomas.

After the reading was ended, Anne Leigh sate silent for a time; and then she asked to speak to Samuel Orme alone. The sons went into the back-kitchen, and thence strolled out into the fields regardless of the driving snow. The brothers were dearly fond of each other, although they were very different in character. Will, the elder, was like his father, stern, reserved, and scrupulously upright. Tom (who was ten years younger) was gentle and delicate as a girl, both in appearance and character. He had always clung to his mother, and dreaded his father. They did not speak as they walked, for they were only in the habit of talking about facts, and hardly knew the more sophisticated language applied to the description of feelings.

Meanwhile their mother had taken hold of Samuel Orme's arm with her trembling hand.

'Samuel, I must let the farm – I must.'

'Let the farm! What's come o'er the woman?'

'Oh, Samuel!' said she, her eyes swimming in tears, 'I'm just fain to go and live in Manchester. I mun let the farm.'

Samuel looked, and pondered, but did not speak for some time. At last he said, –

'If thou hast made up thy mind, there's no speaking again it; and thou must e'en go. Thou'lt be sadly pottered* wi' Manchester ways; but that's not my look out. Why, thou'lt have to buy potatoes, a thing thou hast never done afore in all thy born life. Well! it's not my look out. It's rather for me than again me. Our Jenny is going to be married to Tom Higginbotham, and he was speaking of wanting a bit of land to begin upon. His father will be dying sometime, I reckon, and then he'll step into the Croft Farm. But meanwhile –'

'Then, thou'lt let the farm,' said she, still as eagerly as ever.

'Aye, aye, he'll take it fast enough, I've a notion. But I'll not drive a bargain with thee just now; it would not be right; we'll wait a bit.'

'No; I cannot wait, settle it out at once.'

'Well, well; I'll speak to Will about it. I see him out yonder. I'll step to him and talk it over.'

Accordingly he went and joined the two lads, and without more ado, began the subject to them.

'Will, thy mother is fain to go live in Manchester, and covets to let the farm. Now, I'm willing to take it for Tom Higginbotham; but I like to drive a keen bargain, and there would be no fun chaffering* with thy mother just now. Let thee and me buckle to, my lad! and try and cheat each other; it will warm us this cold day.'

'Let the farm!' said both the lads at once, with infinite surprise. 'Go live in Manchester!'

When Samuel Orme found that the plan had never before been named to either Will or Tom, he would have nothing to do with it, he said, until they had spoken to their mother; likely she was 'dazed' by her husband's death; he would wait a day or two, and not name it to any one; not to Tom Higginbotham himself, or may be he would set his heart upon it. The lads had better go in and talk it over with their mother. He bade them good day, and left them.

Will looked very gloomy, but he did not speak till they got near the house. Then he said, –

'Tom, go to th' shippon,* and supper the cows. I want to speak to mother alone.'

When he entered the house-place, she was sitting before the fire, looking into its embers. She did not hear him come in: for some time she had lost her quick perception of outward things.

'Mother! what's this about going to Manchester?' asked he.

'Oh, lad!' said she, turning round, and speaking in a beseeching tone, 'I must go and seek our Lizzie. I cannot rest here for thinking on her. Many's the time I've left thy father sleeping in bed, and stole to th' window, and looked and looked my heart out towards Manchester, till I thought I must just set out and tramp over moor and moss straight away till I got there, and then lift up every downcast face till I came to our Lizzie. And often, when the south wind was blowing soft among the hollows, I've fancied (it could but be fancy, thou knowest) I heard her crying upon me; and I've thought the voice came closer and closer, till at last it was sobbing out

"Mother" close to the door; and I've stolen down, and undone the latch before now, and looked out into the still black night, thinking to see her, – and turned sick and sorrowful when I heard no living sound but the sough of the wind dying away. Oh! speak not to me of stopping here, when she may be perishing for hunger, like the poor lad in the parable.' And now she lifted up her voice, and wept aloud.

Will was deeply grieved. He had been old enough to be told the family shame when, more than two years before, his father had had his letter to his daughter returned by her mistress in Manchester, telling him that Lizzie had left her service some time – and why. He had sympathised with his father's stern anger; though he had thought him something hard, it is true, when he had forbidden his weeping, heart-broken wife to go and try to find her poor, sinning child, and declared that henceforth they would have no daughter; that she should be as one dead, and her name never more be named at market or at meal time, in blessing or in prayer. He had held his peace, with compressed lips and contracted brow, when the neighbours had noticed to him how poor Lizzie's death had aged both his father and his mother; and how they thought the bereaved couple would never hold up their heads again. He himself had felt as if that one event had made him old before his time; and had envied Tom the tears he had shed over poor, pretty, innocent, dead Lizzie. He thought about her sometimes, till he ground his teeth together, and could have struck her down in her shame. His mother had never named her to him until now.

'Mother!' said he at last. 'She may be dead. Most likely she is.'

'No, Will; she is not dead,' said Mrs Leigh. 'God will not let her die till I've seen her once again. Thou dost not know how I've prayed and prayed just once again to see her sweet face, and tell her I've forgiven her, though she's broken my heart – she has, Will.' She could not go on for a minute or two for the choking sobs. 'Thou dost not know that, or thou wouldst not say she could be dead, – for God is very merciful, Will; He is, – He is much more pitiful than man, – I could never ha' spoken to thy father as I did to Him, – and yet thy father forgave her at last. The last words he said were that he forgave her. Thou'lt not be harder than thy father, Will? Do not try and hinder me going to seek her, for it's no use.'

Will sate very still for a long time before he spoke. At last he said, 'I'll not hinder you. I think she's dead, but that's no matter.'

'She is not dead,' said her mother, with low earnestness. Will took no notice of the interruption.

'We will all go to Manchester for a twelvemonth, and let the farm to Tom Higginbotham. I'll get blacksmith's work; and Tom can have good schooling for awhile, which he's always craving for. At the end of the year you'll come back, mother, and give over fretting for Lizzie, and think with me that she is dead, – and, to my mind, that would be more comfort than to think of her living;' he dropped his voice as he spoke these last words. She shook her head, but made no answer. He asked again, –

'Will you, mother, agree to this?'

'I'll agree to it a-this-ns,' said she. 'If I hear and see nought of her for a twelvemonth, me being in Manchester looking out, I'll just ha' broken my heart fairly before the year's ended, and then I shall know neither love nor sorrow for her any more, when I'm at rest in the grave – I'll agree to that, Will.'

'Well, I suppose it must be so. I shall not tell Tom, mother, why we're flitting to Manchester. Best spare him.'

'As thou wilt,' said she, sadly, 'so that we go, that's all.'

Before the wild daffodils were in flower in the sheltered copses round Upclose Farm, the Leighs were settled in their Manchester home; if they could ever grow to consider that place as a home, where there was no garden, or outbuilding, no fresh breezy outlet, no far-stretching view, over moor and hollow, – no dumb animals to be tended, and, what more than all they missed, no old haunting memories, even though those remembrances told of sorrow, and the dead and gone.

Mrs Leigh heeded the loss of all these things less than her sons. She had more spirit in her countenance than she had had for months, because now she had hope; of a sad enough kind, to be sure, but still it was hope. She performed all her household duties, strange and complicated as they were, and bewildered as she was with all the town necessities of her new manner of life; but when her house was 'sided,'* and the boys come home from their work, in the evening, she would put on her things and steal out, unnoticed, as she thought, but not without many a heavy sigh from Will, after she had closed the house-door and departed. It was often past midnight before she came back, pale and weary, with almost a guilty look upon her face; but that face so full of disappointment and hope deferred, that Will had never the heart to say what he thought of the folly and hopelessness of the search. Night after night it was renewed, till days grew to weeks, and weeks to months. All this time Will did his duty towards her as well as he could, without having sympathy with her. He stayed at home in the evenings for Tom's sake, and often wished he had Tom's pleasure in reading, for the time hung heavy on his hands as he sate up for his mother.

I need not tell you how the mother spent the weary hours. And yet I will tell you something. She used to wander out, at first as if without a purpose, till she rallied her thoughts, and brought all her energies to bear on the one point; then she went with earnest patience along the least-known ways to some new part of the town, looking wistfully with dumb entreaty into people's faces; sometimes catching a glimpse of a figure which had a kind of momentary likeness to her child's, and following that figure with never-wearying perseverance, till some light from shop or lamp showed the cold, strange face which was not her daughter's. Once or twice a kind-hearted passer-by, struck by her look of yearning woe, turned back and offered help, or asked her what she wanted. When so spoken to, she answered only, 'You don't know a poor girl they call Lizzie Leigh, do you?' and when they denied all knowledge, she shook her head, and went on again. I think they believed her to be crazy. But she never spoke first to any one. She sometimes took a few minutes' rest on the door-steps, and sometimes (very seldom) covered her face and cried; but she could not afford to lose time and chances in this way; while her eyes were blinded with tears, the lost one might pass by unseen.

One evening, in the rich time of shortening autumn-days, Will saw an old man, who, without being absolutely drunk, could not guide himself rightly along the foot-path, and was mocked for his unsteadiness of gait by the idle boys of the neighbourhood. For his father's sake Will regarded old age with tenderness, even when most degraded and removed from the stern virtues which dignified that father; so he took the old man home, and seemed to believe his often-repeated assertions, that he drank nothing but water. The stranger tried to stiffen himself up into steadiness as he drew nearer home, as if there were some one there for whose respect he cared even in his half-intoxicated state, or whose feelings he feared to grieve. His home was exquisitely clean and neat, even in outside appearance; threshold, window, and window-sill, were outward signs of some spirit of purity within. Will was rewarded for his attention by a bright glance of thanks, succeeded by a blush of shame, from a young woman of twenty, or thereabouts. She did not speak or second her father's hospitable invitations to him to be seated. She seemed unwilling that a stranger should witness her father's attempts at stately sobriety, and Will could not bear to stay and see her distress. But when the old man, with many a flabby shake of the hand, kept asking him to come again some other evening and see them, Will sought her down-cast eyes, and, though he could not read their veiled meaning, he answered timidly, 'If it's agreeable to everybody, I'll come, and thank ye.' But there was no answer from the girl, to whom this speech was in reality addressed; and Will left the house, liking her all the better for never speaking.

He thought about her a great deal for the next day or two; he scolded himself for being so foolish as to think of her, and then fell to with fresh vigour, and thought of her more than ever. He tried to depreciate her: he told himself she was not pretty, and then made indignant answer that he liked her looks much better than any beauty of them all. He wished he was not so country-looking, so red-faced, so broad-shouldered; while she was like a lady, with her smooth, colourless complexion, her bright, dark hair and her spotless dress. Pretty, or not pretty, she drew his footsteps towards her; he could not resist the impulse that made him wish to see her once more, and find out some fault which should unloose his heart from her unconscious keeping. But there she was, pure and maidenly as before. He sate and looked, answering her father at cross-purposes, while she drew more and more into the shadow of the chimney-corner out of sight. Then the spirit that possessed him (it was not he himself, sure, that did so impudent a thing!) made him get up and carry the candle to a different place, under the pretence of giving her more light at her sewing, but, in reality, to be able to see her better; she could not stand this much longer, but jumped up, and said she must put her little niece to bed; and surely, there never was, before or since, so troublesome a child of two years old; for though Will stayed an hour and a half longer, she never came down again. He won the father's heart, though, by his capacity as a listener, for some people are not at all particular, and, so that they themselves may talk on undisturbed, are not so unreasonable as to expect attention to what they say.

Will did gather this much, however, from the old man's talk. He had once been quite in a genteel line of business, but had failed for more money than any greengrocer he had heard of; at least, any who did not mix up fish and game with greengrocery proper. This grand failure seemed to have been the event of his life, and one on which he dwelt with a strange kind of pride. It appeared as if at present he rested from his past exertions (in the bankrupt line), and depended on his daughter, who kept a small school for very young children. But all these particulars Will only remembered and understood when he had left the house; at the time he heard them, he was thinking of Susan. After he had made good his footing* at Mr Palmer's, he was not long, you may be sure, without finding some reason for returning again and again. He listened to her father, he talked to the little niece, but he looked at Susan, both while he listened and while he talked. Her father kept on insisting upon his former gentility, the details of which would have appeared very questionable to Will's mind, if the sweet, delicate, modest Susan had not thrown an inexplicable air of refinement over all she came near. She never spoke much; she was generally diligently at work; but when she moved, it was so noiselessly, and when she did speak, it was in so low and soft a voice, that silence, speech, motion, and stillness, alike seemed to remove her high above Will's reach into some saintly and inaccessible air of glory – high above his reach, even as she knew him! And, if she were made acquainted with the dark secret behind, of his sister's shame, which was kept

ever present to his mind by his mother's nightly search among
the outcast and forsaken, would not Susan shrink away from
him with loathing, as if he were tainted by the involuntary
relationship? This was his dread; and there upon followed a
resolution that he would withdraw from her sweet company
before it was too late. So he resisted internal temptation, and
stayed at home, and suffered and sighed. He became angry
with his mother for her untiring patience in seeking for one
who, he could not help hoping, was dead rather than alive.
He spoke sharply to her, and received only such sad de-
precatory answers as made him reproach himself, and still more
lose sight of peace of mind. This struggle could not last long
without affecting his health; and Tom, his sole companion
through the long evenings, noticed his increasing languor,
his restless irritability, with perplexed anxiety, and at last
resolved to call his mother's attention to his brother's haggard,
care-worn looks. She listened with a startled recollection of
Will's claims upon her love. She noticed his decreasing
appetite, and half-checked sighs.

'Will, lad! what come o'er thee?' said she to him, as he sate
listlessly gazing into the fire.

'There's nought the matter with me,' said he, as if annoyed
at her remark.

'Nay, lad, but there is.' He did not speak again to contradict
her; indeed she did not know if he had heard her, so unmoved did he look.

'Would'st like to go back to Upclose Farm?' asked she,
sorrowfully.

'It's just blackberrying time,' said Tom.

Will shook his head. She looked at him awhile, as if trying
to read that expression of despondency and trace it back to its
source.

'You and Tom could go,' said she; 'I must stay here till I've
found her, thou know'st,' continued she, dropping her voice.

He turned quickly round, and with the authority he at all
times exercised over Tom, bade him begone to bed.

When Tom had left the room, he prepared to speak.

CHAPTER II

'MOTHER,' then said Will, 'why will you keep on thinking she's alive? If she were but dead, we need never name her name again. We've never heard nought on her, since father wrote her that letter; we never knew whether she got it or not. She'd left her place before then. Many a one dies in – '

'Oh my lad! dunnot speak so to me, or my heart will break outright,' said his mother, with a sort of cry. Then she calmed herself, for she yearned to persuade him to her own belief. 'Thou never asked, and thou'rt too like thy father for me to tell without asking – but it were all to be near Lizzie's old place that I settled down on this side o' Manchester; and the very day at after we came, I went to her old missus, and asked to speak a word wi' her. I had a strong mind to cast it up to her, that she should ha' sent my poor lass away, without telling on it to us first; but she were in black and looked so sad I could na find in my heart to threep it up.* But I did ask her a bit about our Lizzie. The master would have her turned away at a day's warning (he's gone to t'other place; I hope he'll meet wi' more mercy there than he showed our Lizzie, – I do, –), and when the missus asked her should she write to us, she says Lizzie shook her head; and when she speered* at her again, the poor lass went down on her knees, and begged her not, for she said it would break my heart (as it has done, Will – God knows it has),' said the poor mother, choking with her struggle to keep down her hard, overmastering grief, 'and her father would curse her – Oh, God, teach me to be patient.' She could not speak for a few minutes, – 'and the lass threaten-ed, and said she'd go drown herself in the canal, if the missus wrote home, – and so –

'Well! I'd got a trace of my child, – the missus thought she'd gone to th' workhouse to be nursed; and there I went, – and there, sure enough, she had been, – and they'd turned her out as soon as she were strong, and told her she were young enough to work, – but whatten kind o' work would be open to her, lad, and her baby to keep?'

Will listened to his mother's tale with deep sympathy, not unmixed with the old bitter shame. But the opening of her heart had unlocked his, and after a while he spoke.

'Mother! I think I'd e'en better go home. Tom can stay wi' thee. I know I should stay too, but I cannot stay in peace so near – her, – without craving to see her, – Susan Palmer, I mean.'

'Has the old Mr Palmer thou telled me on a daughter?' asked Mrs Leigh.

'Aye, he has. And I love her above a bit. And it's because I love her I want to leave Manchester. That's all.'

Mrs Leigh tried to understand this speech for some time, but found it difficult of interpretation.

'Why shouldst thou not tell her thou lov'st her? Thou'rt a likely lad, and sure o' work. Thou'lt have Upclose at my death; and as for that I could let thee have it now, and keep mysel by doing a bit of charring. It seems to me a very backwards sort o' way of winning her to think of leaving Manchester.'

'Oh mother, she's so gentle and so good, – she's downright holy. She's never known a touch of sin; and can I ask her to marry me, knowing what we do about Lizzie, and fearing worse? I doubt if one like her could ever care for me; but if she knew about my sister, it would put a gulf between us, and she'd shudder up at the thought of crossing it. You don't know how good she is, mother!'

'Will, Will! if she's so good as thou say'st, she'll have pity on such as my Lizzie. If she has no pity for such, she's a cruel Pharisee, and thou'rt best without her.'

But he only shook his head, and sighed; and for the time the conversation dropped.

But a new idea sprang up in Mrs Leigh's head. She thought that she would go and see Susan Palmer, and speak up for Will, and tell her the truth about Lizzie; and according to her pity for the poor sinner, would she be worthy or unworthy of him. She resolved to go the very next afternoon, but without telling any one of her plan. Accordingly she looked out the Sunday clothes she had never before had the heart to unpack since she came to Manchester, but which she now desired to appear in, in order to do credit to Will. She put on her old-fashioned black mode bonnet, trimmed with real lace; her scarlet cloth cloak, which she had had ever since she was married; and always spotlessly clean, she set forth on her unauthorised embassy. She knew the Palmers lived in Crown Street, though where she had heard it she could not tell; and modestly asking her way, she arrived in the street about a quarter to four o'clock. She stopped to inquire the exact number, and the woman whom she addressed told her that Susan Palmer's school would not be loosed* till four, and asked her to step in and wait until then at her house.

'For,' said she, smiling, 'them that wants Susan Palmer wants a kind friend of ours; so we, in a manner, call cousins. Sit down, missus, sit down. I'll wipe the chair, so that it shanna dirty your cloak. My mother used to wear them bright cloaks, and they're right gradely things* again a green field.'

'Han ye known Susan Palmer long?' asked Mrs Leigh, pleased with the admiration of her cloak.

'Ever since they comed to live in our street. Our Sally goes to her school.'

'Whatten sort of a lass is she, for I ha' never seen her?'

'Well, – as for looks, I cannot say. It's so long since I first knowed her, that I've clean forgotten what I thought of her then. My master says he never saw such a smile for gladdening the heart. But may be it's not looks you're asking about. The best thing I can say of her looks is, that she's just one a stranger would stop in the street to ask help from if he needed it. All the little childer creeps as close as they can to her; she'll have as many as three or four hanging to her apron all at once.'

'Is she cocket at all?'

'Cocket, bless you! you never saw a creature less set up in all your life. Her father's cocket enough. No! she's not cocket anyway. You've not heard much of Susan Palmer, I reckon, if you think she's cocket. She's just one to come quietly in, and do the very thing most wanted; little things, maybe, that any one could do, but that few would think on, for another. She'll bring her thimble wi' her, and mend up after the childer o'nights, – and she writes all Betty Harker's letters to her grandchild out at service, – and she's in nobody's way, and that's a great matter, I take it. Here's the childer running past! School is loosed. You'll find her now, missus, ready to hear and to help. But we none on us frab* her by going near her in school-time.'

Poor Mrs Leigh's heart began to beat, and she could almost have turned round and gone home again. Her country breed-ing had made her shy of strangers, and this Susan Palmer appeared to her like a real born lady by all accounts. So she knocked with a timid feeling at the indicated door, and when it was opened, dropped a simple curtsey without speaking. Susan had her little niece in her arms, curled up with fond en-dearment against her breast, but she put her gently down to the ground, and instantly placed a chair in the best corner of the room for Mrs Leigh, when she told her who she was. 'It's not Will as has asked me to come,' said the mother, apologetically, 'I'd a wish just to speak to you myself!'

Susan coloured up to her temples, and stooped to pick up the little toddling girl. In a minute or two Mrs Leigh began again.

'Will thinks you would na respect us if you knew all; but I think you could na help feeling for us in the sorrow God has put upon us; so I just put on my bonnet, and came off un-knownst to the lads. Every one says you're very good, and that the Lord has keeped you from falling from his ways; but maybe you've never yet been tried and tempted as some is. I'm perhaps speaking too plain, but my heart's welly broken, and I can't be choice in my words as them who are happy can. Well now! I'll tell you the truth. Will dreads you to hear it, but I'll just tell it you. You mun know,' – but here the poor woman's words failed her, and she could do nothing but sit rocking herself backwards and forwards, with sad eyes, straight-gazing into Susan's face, as if they tried to tell the tale of agony which the quivering lips refused to utter. Those wretched, stony eyes forced the tears down Susan's cheeks, and, as if this sympathy gave the mother strength, she went on in a low voice, 'I had a daughter once, my heart's darling. Her father thought I made too much on her, and that she'd grow marred staying at home; so he said she mun go among strangers, and learn to rough it. She were young, and liked the thought of seeing a bit of the world; and her father heard on a place in Manchester. Well! I'll not weary you. That poor girl were led astray; and first thing we heard on it, was when a letter of her father's was sent back by her missus, saying she'd left her place, or, to speak right, the master had turned her into the street soon as he had heard of her condition – and she not seventeen!'

She now cried aloud; and Susan wept too. The little child looked up into their faces, and, catching their sorrow, began to whimper and wail. Susan took it softly up, and hiding her face in its little neck, tried to restrain her tears, and think of comfort for the mother. At last she said, –

'Where is she now?'

'Lass! I dunnot know,' said Mrs Leigh, checking her sobs to communicate this addition to her distress. 'Mrs Lomax told me she went –'

'Mrs Lomax – what Mrs Lomax?'

'Her as lives in Brabazon-street. She told me my poor wench went to the workhouse fra there. I'll not speak again the dead; but if her father would but ha' letten me, – but he were one who had no notion – no, I'll not say that; best say nought. He forgave her on his death-bed. I dare say I did na go th' right way to work.'

'Will you hold the child for me one instant?' said Susan.

'Aye, if it will come to me. Childer used to be fond on me till I got the sad look on my face that scares them, I think.'

But the little girl clung to Susan; so she carried it upstairs with her. Mrs Leigh sate by herself – how long she did not know.

Susan came down with a bundle of far-worn baby-clothes.

'You must listen to me a bit, and not think too much about what I'm going to tell you. Nanny is not my niece, nor any kin to me, that I know of. I used to go out working by the day. One night, as I came home, I thought some woman was following me; I turned to look. The woman, before I could see her face (for she turned it to one side), offered me something. I held out my arms by instinct; she dropped a bundle into them, with a bursting sob that went straight to my heart. It was a baby. I looked round again; but the woman was gone. She had run away as quick as lightning. There was a little packet of clothes – very few – and as if they were made out of its mother's gowns, for they were large patterns to buy for a baby. I was always fond of babies; and I had not my wits about me, father says: for it was very cold, and when I'd seen as well as I could (for it was past ten) that there was no one in the street, I brought it in and warmed it. Father was very angry when he came, and said he'd take it to the workhouse the next morning, and flyted* me sadly about it. But when morning came I could not bear to part with it; it had slept in my arms all night; and I've heard what workhouse bringing-up is. So I told father I'd give up going out working, and stay at home and keep school, if I might only keep the baby; and after awhile, he said if I earned enough for him to have his comforts, he'd let me; but he's never taken to her. Now, don't tremble so, – I've but a little more to tell, – and maybe I'm wrong in telling it; but I used to work next door to Mrs Lomax's, in Brabazon-street, and the servants were all thick together; and I heard about Bessy (they called her) being sent away. I don't know that ever I saw her; but the time would be about fitting to this child's age, and I've sometimes fancied it was hers. And now, will you look at the little clothes that came with her – bless her!'

But Mrs Leigh had fainted. The strange joy and shame, and gushing love for the little child had overpowered her; it was some time before Susan could bring her round. Then she was all trembling, sick impatience to look at the little frocks. Among them was a slip of paper which Susan had forgotten to name, that had been pinned to the bundle. On it was scrawled in a round, stiff hand, –

'Call her Anne. She does not cry much, and takes a deal of notice. God bless you and forgive me.'

The writing was no clue at all; the name 'Anne,' common though it was, seemed something to build upon. But Mrs Leigh recognised one of the frocks instantly, as being made out of a gown that she and her daughter had bought together in Rochdale.

She stood up, and stretched out her hands in the attitude of blessing over Susan's bent head.

'God bless you, and show you His mercy in your need, as you have shown it to this little child.'

She took the little creature in her arms, and smoothed away her sad looks to a smile, and kissed it fondly, saying over and over again, 'Nanny, Nanny my little Nanny.' At last the child was soothed, and looked in her face and smiled back again.

'It has her eyes,' said she to Susan.

'I never saw her to the best of my knowledge. I think it must be hers by the frock. But where can she be?'

'God knows,' said Mrs Leigh; 'I dare not think she's dead. I'm sure she isn't.'

'No! she's not dead. Every now and then a little packet is thrust in under our door, with may be two half-crowns in it; once it was half-a-sovereign. Altogether I've got seven-and-thirty shillings wrapped up for Nanny. I never touch it, but I've often thought the poor mother feels near to God when she brings this money. Father wanted to set the policeman to watch, but I said No, for I was afraid if she was watched she might not come, and it seemed such a holy thing to be checking her in, I could not find in my heart to do it.'

'Oh, if we could but find her! I'd take her in my arms, and we'd just lie down and die together.'

'Nay, don't speak so!' said Susan gently, 'for all that's come and gone, she may turn right at last. Mary Magdalen did, you know.'

'Eh! but I were nearer right about thee than Will. He thought you would never look on him again if you knew about Lizzie. But thou'rt not a Pharisee.'

'I'm sorry he thought I could be so hard,' said Susan in a low voice, and colouring up. Then Mrs Leigh was alarmed, and in her motherly anxiety she began to fear lest she had injured Will in Susan's estimation.

'You see Will thinks so much of you – gold would not be good enough for you to walk on, in his eye. He said you'd never look at him as he was, let alone his being brother to my poor wench. He loves you so, it makes him think meanly on everything belonging to himself, as not fit to come near ye, – but he's a good lad, and a good son, – thou'lt be a happy woman if thou'lt have him, – so don't let my words go against him; don't!'

But Susan hung her head, and made no answer. She had not known until now, that Will thought so earnestly and seriously about her; and even now she felt afraid that Mrs Leigh's words promised her too much happiness, and that they could not be true. At any rate the instinct of modesty made her shrink from saying anything which might seem like a confession of her own feelings to a third person. Accordingly she turned the conversation on the child.

'I'm sure he could not help loving Nanny,' said she. 'There never was such a good little darling; don't you think she'd win his heart if he knew she was his niece, and perhaps bring him to think kindly on his sister?'

'I dunnot know,' said Mrs Leigh, shaking her head. 'He has a turn in his eye like his father, that makes me –. He's right down good though. But you see I've never been a good one at managing folk; one severe look turns me sick, and then I say just the wrong thing, I'm so fluttered. Now I should like nothing better than to take Nanny home with me, but Tom knows nothing but that his sister is dead, and I've not the knack of speaking rightly to Will. I dare not do it, and that's the truth. But you mun not think badly of Will. He's so good hissel, that he can't understand how any one can do wrong; and, above all, I'm sure he loves you dearly.'

'I don't think I could part with Nanny,' said Susan, anxious to stop this revelation of Will's attachment to herself. 'He'll come round to her soon; he can't fail; and I'll keep a sharp look-out after the poor mother, and try and catch her the next time she comes with her little parcels of money.'

'Aye, lass; we mun get hold of her; my Lizzie. I love thee dearly for thy kindness to her child: but, if thou canst catch her for me, I'll pray for thee when I'm too near my death to speak words; and while I live, I'll serve thee next to her, – she mun come first, thou know'st. God bless thee, lass. My heart is lighter by a deal than it was when I comed in. Them lads will be looking for me home, and I mun go, and leave this little sweet one,' kissing it. 'If I can take courage, I'll tell Will all that has come and gone between us two. He may come and see thee, mayn't he?'

'Father will be very glad to see him, I'm sure,' replied Susan. The way in which this was spoken satisfied Mrs Leigh's anxious heart that she had done Will no harm by what she had said; and with many a kiss to the little one, and one more fervent, tearful blessing on Susan, she went homewards.

CHAPTER III

THAT night Mrs Leigh stopped at home; that only night for many months. Even Tom, the scholar, looked up from his books in amazement; but then he remembered that Will had not been well, and that his mother's attention having been called to the circumstance, it was only natural she should stay to watch him. And no watching could be more tender, or more complete. Her loving eyes seemed never averted from his face; his grave, sad, careworn face. When Tom went to bed the mother left her seat, and going up to Will, where he sate looking at the fire, but not seeing it, she kissed his forehead, and said, –

'Will! lad, I've been to see Susan Palmer!'

She felt the start under her hand which was placed on his shoulder, but he was silent for a minute or two. Then he said, –

'What took you there, mother?'

'Why, my lad, it was likely I should wish to see one you cared for; I did not put myself forward. I put on my Sunday clothes, and tried to behave as yo'd ha' liked me. At least I remember trying at first; but after, I forgot all.'

She rather wished that he would question her as to what made her forget all. But he only said, –

'How was she looking, mother?'

'Will, thou seest I never set eyes on her before; but she's a good, gentle-looking creature; and I love her dearly, as I've reason to.'

Will looked up with momentary surprise; for his mother was too shy to be usually taken with strangers. But after all it was natural in this case, for who could look at Susan without loving her? So still he did not ask any questions, and his poor mother had to take courage, and try again to introduce the subject near to her heart. But how?

'Will!' said she (jerking it out, in sudden despair of her own powers to lead to what she wanted to say), 'I told her all.'

'Mother! you've ruined me,' said he, standing up, and standing opposite to her with a stern white look of affright on his face.

'No! my own dear lad; dunnot look so scared, I have not ruined you!' she exclaimed, placing her two hands on his shoulders, and looking fondly into his face. 'She's not one to harden her heart against a mother's sorrow. My own lad, she's too good for that. She's not one to judge and scorn the sinner. She's too deep read in her New Testament for that. Take courage, Will; and thou mayst, for I watched her well, though it is not for one woman to let out another's secret. Sit thee down, lad, for thou look'st very white.'

He sate down. His mother drew a stool towards him, and sate at his feet.

'Did you tell her about Lizzie, then?' asked he, hoarse and low.

'I did, I telled her all; and she fell a-crying over my deep sorrow, and the poor wench's sin. And then a light comed into her face, trembling and quivering with some new glad thought; and what dost thou think it was, Will, lad? Nay, I'll not misdoubt but that thy heart will give thanks as mine did, afore God and His angels, for her great goodness. That little Nanny is not her niece, she's our Lizzie's own child, my little grandchild.' She could no longer restrain her tears, and they fell hot and fast, but still she looked into his face.

'Did she know it was Lizzie's child? I do not comprehend,' said he, flushing red.

'She knows now: she did not at first, but took the little helpless creature in, out of her own pitiful, loving heart, guessing only that it was the child of shame, and she's worked for it, and kept it, and tended it ever sin' it were a mere baby, and loves it fondly. Will! won't you love it'? asked she beseechingly.

He was silent for an instant; then he said, 'Mother, I'll try. Give me time, for all these things startle me. To think of Susan having to do with such a child!'

'Aye, Will! and to think (as may be yet) of Susan having to do with the child's mother! For she is tender and pitiful, and speaks hopefully of my lost one, and will try and find her for me, when she comes as she does sometimes, to thrust money under the door, for her baby. Think of that, Will. Here's Susan, good and pure as the angels in heaven, yet, like them, full of hope and mercy, and one who, like them, will rejoice over her as repents. Will, my lad, I'm not afeard of you now, and I must speak, and you must listen. I am your mother, and I dare to command you, because I know I am in the right and that God is on my side. If He should lead the poor wandering lassie to Susan's door, and she comes back crying and sorrowful, led by that good angel to us once more, thou shalt never say a casting-up word to her about her sin, but be tender and helpful towards one "who was lost and is found,"* so may God's blessing rest on thee, and so mayst thou lead Susan home as thy wife.'

She stood, no longer, as the meek, imploring, gentle mother, but firm and dignified, as if the interpreter of God's will. Her manner was so unusual and solemn, that it overcame all Will's pride and stubbornness. He rose softly while she was speaking, and bent his head as if in reverence at her words, and the solemn injunction which they conveyed. When she had spoken, he said in so subdued a voice that she was almost surprised at the sound, 'Mother, I will.'

'I may be dead and gone, – but all the same, – thou wilt take home the wandering sinner, and heal up her sorrows, and lead her to her Father's house. My lad! I can speak no more; I'm turned very faint.'

He placed her in a chair; he ran for water. She opened her eyes and smiled.

'God bless you, Will. Oh! I am so happy. It seems as if she were found; my heart is so filled with gladness.'

That night Mr Palmer stayed out late and long. Susan was afraid that he was at his old haunts and habits, – getting tipsy at some public-house: and this thought oppressed her, even though she had so much to make her happy in the consciousness that Will loved her. She sate up long, and then she went to bed, leaving all arranged as well as she could for her father's return. She looked at the little, rosy, sleeping girl who was her bed-fellow, with redoubled tenderness, and with many a prayerful thought. The little arms entwined her neck as she lay down, for Nanny was a light sleeper, and was conscious that she, who was loved with all the power of that sweet, childish heart, was near her, and by her, although she was too sleepy to utter any of her half-formed words.

And by-and-by she heard her father come home, stumbling

uncertain, trying first the windows, and next the door-fastenings, with many a loud, incoherent murmur. The little Innocent twined around her seemed all the sweeter and more lovely, when she thought sadly of her erring father. And presently he called aloud for a light; she had left matches and all arranged as usual on the dresser, but fearful of some accident from fire, in his unusually intoxicated state, she now got up softly, and putting on a cloak, went down to his assistance.

Alas! the little arms that were unclosed from her soft neck belonged to a light, easily awakened sleeper. Nanny missed her darling Susy, and terrified at being left alone in the vast, mysterious darkness, which had no bounds, and seemed infinite, she slipped out of bed, and tottered in her little nightgown towards the door. There was a light below, and there was Susy and safety! So she went onwards two steps towards the steep, abrupt stairs; and then dazzled with sleepiness, she stood, she wavered, she fell! Down on her head on the stone floor she fell! Susan flew to her, and spoke all soft, entreating, loving words; but her white lids covered up the blue violets of eyes, and there was no murmur came out of the pale lips. The warm tears that rained down did not awaken her; she lay stiff, and weary with her short life, on Susan's knee. Susan went sick with terror. She carried her upstairs, and laid her tenderly in bed; she dressed herself most hastily, with her trembling fingers. Her father was asleep on the settle down stairs; and useless, and worse than useless if awake. But Susan flew out of the door, and down the quiet, resounding street, towards the nearest doctor's house. Quickly she went: but as quickly a shadow followed, as if impelled by some sudden terror. Susan rung wildly at the night-bell, – the shadow crouched near. The doctor looked out from an upstairs window.

'A little child has fallen down stairs at No. 9, Crown-street, and is very ill, – dying, I'm afraid. Please, for God's sake, sir, come directly. No. 9, Crown-street.'

'I'll be there directly,' said he, and shut the window.

'For that God you have just spoken about, – for His sake – tell me are you Susan Palmer? Is it my child that lies a-dying?' said the shadow springing forwards, and clutching poor Susan's arm.

'It is a little child of two years old, – I do not know whose it is; I love it as my own. Come with me, whoever you are; come with me.'

The two sped along the silent streets, – as silent as the night were they. They entered the house; Susan snatched up the light, and carried it upstairs. The other followed.

She stood with wild, glaring eyes by the bedside, never looking at Susan, but hungrily gazing at the little, white, still child. She stooped down, and put her hand tight on her own heart, as if to still its beating, and bent her ear to the pale lips. Whatever the result was, she did not speak; but threw off the bed-clothes wherewith Susan had tenderly covered up the little creature, and felt its left side.

Then she threw up her arms with a cry of wild despair.

'She is dead! she is dead!'

She looked so fierce, so mad, so haggard, that for an instant Susan was terrified – the next, the holy God had put courage into her heart, and her pure arms were round that guilty, wretched creature, and her tears were falling fast and warm upon her breast. But she was thrown off with violence.

'You killed her – you slighted her – you let her fall down those stairs! you killed her!'

Susan cleared off the thick mist before her, and gazing at the mother with her clear, sweet, angel-eyes, said mournfully, –

'I would have laid down my own life for her.'

'Oh, the murder is on my soul!' exclaimed the wild, bereaved mother, with the fierce impetuosity of one who has none to love her and to be beloved, regard to whom might teach self-restraint.

'Hush!' said Susan, her finger on her lips. 'Here is the doctor. God may suffer her to live.'

The poor mother turned sharp round. The doctor mounted the stair. Ah! that mother was right; the little child was really dead and gone.

And when he confirmed her judgment, the mother fell down in a fit. Susan, with her deep grief, had to forget herself, and forget her darling (her charge for years), and question the doctor what she must do with the poor wretch, who lay on the floor in such extreme of misery.

'She is the mother!' said she.

'Why did not she take better care of her child?' asked he, almost angrily.

But Susan only said, 'The little child slept with me; and it was I that left her.'

'I will go back and make up a composing draught; and while I am away you must get her to bed.'

Susan took out some of her own clothes, and softly undressed the stiff, powerless form. There was no other bed in the house but the one in which her father slept. So she tenderly lifted the body of her darling; and was going to take it down stairs, but the mother opened her eyes, and seeing what she was about, she said, –

'I am not worthy to touch her, I am so wicked; I have spoken to you as I never should have spoken; but I think you are very good; may I have my own child to lie in my arms for a little while?'

Her voice was so strange a contrast to what it had been before she had gone into the fit, that Susan hardly recognised it; it was now so unspeakably soft, so irresistibly pleading, the features too had lost their fierce expression, and were almost as placid as death. Susan could not speak, but she carried the little child, and laid it in its mother's arms; then as she looked at them, something overpowered her, and she knelt down, crying aloud, –

'Oh, my God, my God, have mercy on her, and forgive, and comfort her.'

But the mother kept smiling, and stroking the little face, murmuring soft, tender words, as if it were alive; she was going mad, Susan thought; but she prayed on, and on, and ever still she prayed with streaming eyes.

The doctor came with the draught. The mother took it, with docile unconsciousness of its nature as medicine. The doctor sate by her; and soon she fell asleep. Then he rose softly, and beckoning Susan to the door, he spoke to her there.

'You must take the corpse out of her arms. She will not awake. That draught will make her sleep for many hours. I will call before noon again. It is now daylight. Good-bye.'

Susan shut him out; and then gently extricating the dead child from its mother's arms, she could not resist making her own quiet moan over her darling. She tried to learn off its little, placid face, dumb and pale before her.

> 'Not all the scalding tears of care
>   Shall wash away that vision fair;
> Not all the thousand thoughts that rise,
>   Not all the sights that dim her eyes,
>   Shall e'er usurp the place
>   Of that little angel-face.'*

And then she remembered what remained to be done. She saw that all was right in the house; her father was still dead asleep on the settle, in spite of all the noise of the night. She went out through the quiet streets, deserted still although it was broad daylight, and to where the Leighs lived. Mrs Leigh, who kept her country hours, was opening her window-shutters. Susan took her by the arm, and, without speaking, went into the house-place. There she knelt down before the astonished Mrs Leigh, and cried as she had never done before; but the miserable night had overpowered her, and she who had gone through so much calmly, now that the pressure seemed removed could not find the power to speak.

'My poor dear! What has made thy heart so sore as to come and cry a-this-ons?* Speak and tell me. Nay, cry on, poor wench, if thou canst not speak yet. It will ease the heart, and then thou canst tell me.'

'Nanny is dead!' said Susan. 'I left her to go to father, and she fell down stairs, and never breathed again. Oh, that's my sorrow! but I've more to tell. Her mother is come – is in our house! Come and see if it's your Lizzie.' Mrs Leigh could not speak, but, trembling, put on her things and went with Susan in dizzy haste back to Crown-street.

CHAPTER IV

As they entered the house in Crown-street, they perceived that the door would not open freely on its hinges, and Susan instinctively looked behind to see the cause of the obstruction. She immediately recognised the appearance of a little parcel, wrapped in a scrap of newspaper, and evidently containing money. She stooped and picked it up. 'Look!' said she, sorrow-fully, 'the mother was bringing this for her child last night.'

But Mrs Leigh did not answer. So near to the ascertaining if it were her lost child or no, she could not be arrested, but pressed onwards with trembling steps and a beating, fluttering heart. She entered the bed-room, dark and still. She took no heed of the little corpse, over which Susan paused, but she went straight to the bed, and withdrawing the curtain, saw Lizzie, – but not the former Lizzie, bright, gay, buoyant, and undimmed. This Lizzie was old before her time; her beauty was gone; deep lines of care, and alas! of want (or thus the mother imagined) were printed on the cheek, so round, and fair, and smooth, when last she gladdened her mother's eyes. Even in her sleep she bore the look of woe and despair which was the prevalent expression of her face by day; even in her sleep she had forgotten how to smile. But all these marks of the sin and sorrow she had passed through only made her mother love her the more. She stood looking at her with greedy eyes, which seemed as though no gazing could satisfy their longing; and at last she stooped down and kissed the pale, worn hand that lay outside the bed-clothes. No touch disturbed the sleeper; the mother need not have laid the hand so gently down upon the counterpane. There was no sign of life, save only now and then a deep sob-like sigh. Mrs Leigh sate down beside the bed, and, still holding back the curtain, looked on and on, as if she could never be satisfied.

Susan would fain have stayed by her darling one; but she had many calls upon her time and thoughts, and her will had now, as ever, to be given up to that of others. All seemed to devolve the burden of their cares on her. Her father, ill-humoured from his last night's intemperance, did not scruple to reproach her with being the cause of little Nanny's death; and when, after bearing his upbraiding meekly for some time, she could no longer restrain herself, but began to cry, he wounded her even more by his injudicious attempts at com-fort: for he said it was as well the child was dead; it was none of theirs, and why should they be troubled with it? Susan wrung her hands at this, and came and stood before her father, and implored him to forbear. Then she had to take all re-quisite steps for the coroner's inquest; she had to arrange for the dismissal of her school; she had to summon a little neigh-bour, and send his willing feet on a message to William Leigh, who, she felt, ought to be informed of his mother's where-abouts, and of the whole state of affairs. She asked her mes-senger to tell him to come and speak to her, – that his mother was at her house. She was thankful that her father sauntered out to have a gossip at the nearest coach-stand, and to relate as many of the night's adventures as he knew; for as yet he was in ignorance of the watcher and the watched, who silently passed away the hours upstairs.

At dinner-time Will came. He looked red, glad, impatient, excited. Susan stood calm and white before him, her soft, loving eyes gazing straight into his.

'Will,' said she, in a low, quiet voice, 'your sister is up-stairs.'

'My sister!' said he, as if affrighted at the idea, and losing his glad look in one of gloom. Susan saw it, and her heart sank a little, but she went on as calm to all appearance as ever.

'She was little Nanny's mother, as perhaps you know. Poor little Nanny was killed last night by a fall down stairs.' All the calmness was gone; all the suppressed feeling was displayed in spite of every effort. She sate down, and hid her face from him, and cried bitterly. He forgot everything but the wish, the longing to comfort her. He put his arm round her waist, and bent over her. But all he could say, was, 'Oh, Susan, how can I comfort you! Don't take on so, – pray don't!' He never changed the words, but the tone varied every time he spoke. At last she seemed to regain her power over herself; and she wiped her eyes, and once more looked upon him with her own quiet, earnest, unfearing gaze.

'Your sister was near the house. She came in on hearing my words to the doctor. She is asleep now, and your mother is watching her. I wanted to tell you all myself. Would you like to see your mother?'

'No!' said he. 'I would rather see none but thee. Mother told me thou know'st all.' His eyes were downcast in their shame.

But the holy and pure did not lower or vail her eyes.

She said, 'Yes, I know all – all but her sufferings. Think what they must have been!'

He made answer low and stern, 'She deserved them all; every jot.'

'In the eye of God, perhaps she does. He is the judge; we are not.'

'Oh!' she said with a sudden burst, 'Will Leigh! I have thought so well of you; don't go and make me think you cruel and hard. Goodness is not goodness unless there is mercy and tenderness with it. There is your mother who has been nearly heart-broken, now full of rejoicing over her child – think of your mother.'

'I do think of her,' said he. 'I remember the promise I gave her last night. Thou shouldst give me time. I would do right in time. I never think it o'er in quiet. But I will do what is right and fitting, never fear. Thou hast spoken out very plain to me; and misdoubted me, Susan; I love thee so, that thy words cut me. If I did hang back a bit from making sudden promises, it was because not even for love of thee, would I say what I was not feeling; and at first I could not feel all at once as thou wouldst have me. But I'm not cruel and hard; for if I had been, I should na' have grieved as I have done.'

He made as if he were going away; and indeed he did feel he would rather think it over in quiet. But Susan, grieved at her incautious words, which had all the appearance of harshness, went a step or two nearer – paused – and then, all over blushes, said in a low soft whisper, –

'Oh, Will! I beg your pardon. I am very sorry – won't you forgive me?'

She who had always drawn back, and been so reserved, said this in the very softest manner; with eyes now uplifted beseechingly, now dropped to the ground. Her sweet confusion told more than words could do; and Will turned back, all joyous in his certainty of being beloved, and took her in his arms and kissed her.

'My own Susan!' he said.

Meanwhile the mother watched her child in the room above.

It was late in the afternoon before she awoke; for the sleeping draught had been very powerful. The instant she awoke, her eyes were fixed on her mother's face with a gaze as unflinching as if she were fascinated. Mrs Leigh did not turn away; nor move. For it seemed as if motion would unlock the stony command over herself which, while so perfectly still, she was enabled to preserve. But by-and-by Lizzie cried out in a piercing voice of agony, –

'Mother, don't look at me! I have been so wicked!' and instantly she hid her face, and grovelled among the bedclothes, and lay like one dead – so motionless was she.

Mrs Leigh knelt down by the bed, and spoke in the most soothing tones.

'Lizzie, dear, don't speak so. I'm thy mother, darling; don't be afeard of me. I never left off loving thee, Lizzie. I was always a-thinking of thee. Thy father forgave thee afore he died.' (There was a little start here, but no sound was heard.) 'Lizzie, lass, I'll do aught for thee; I'll live for thee; only don't be afeard of me. Whate'er thou art or hast been, we'll ne'er speak on't. We'll leave th' oud times behind us, and go back to the Upclose Farm. I but left it to find thee, my lass; and God has led me to thee. Blessed be His name. And God is good too, Lizzie. Thou hast not forgot thy Bible, I'll be bound, for thou wert always a scholar. I'm no reader, but I learnt off them texts to comfort me a bit, and I've said them many a time a day to myself. Lizzie, lass, don't hide thy head so, it's thy mother as is speaking to thee. Thy little child clung to me only yesterday; and if it's gone to be an angel, it will speak to God for thee. Nay, don't sob a-that-as;* thou shalt have it again in Heaven; I know thou'lt strive to get there, for thy little Nanny's sake – and listen! I'll tell thee God's promises to them that are penitent – only doan't be afeard.'

Mrs Leigh folded her hands, and strove to speak very clearly, while she repeated every tender and merciful text she could remember. She could tell from the breathing that her daughter was listening; but she was so dizzy and sick herself when she had ended, that she could not go on speaking. It was all she could do to keep from crying aloud.

At last she heard her daughter's voice.

'Where have they taken her to?' she asked.

'She is down stairs. So quiet and peaceful, and happy she looks.'

'Could she speak? Oh, if God – if I might but have heard her little voice! Mother, I used to dream of it. May I see her once again – Oh mother, if I strive very hard, and God is very merciful, and I go to heaven, I shall not know her – I shall not know my own again – she will shun me as a stranger and cling to Susan Palmer and to you. Oh woe! Oh woe!' She shook with exceeding sorrow.

In her earnestness of speech she had uncovered her face, and tried to read Mrs Leigh's thoughts through her looks. And when she saw those aged eyes brimming full of tears, and marked the quivering lips, she threw her arms round the faithful mother's neck, and wept there as she had done in many a childish sorrow; but with a deeper, a more wretched grief.

Her mother hushed her on her breast; and lulled her as if she were a baby; and she grew still and quiet.

They sate thus for a long, long time. At last Susan Palmer came up with some tea and bread and butter for Mrs Leigh. She watched the mother feed her sick, unwilling child, with every fond inducement to eat which she could devise; they neither of them took notice of Susan's presence. That night they lay in each other's arms; but Susan slept on the ground beside them.

They took the little corpse (the little, unconscious sacrifice, whose early calling-home had reclaimed her poor, wandering mother) to the hills, which in her life-time she had never seen. They dared not lay her by the stern grandfather in Milne-Row churchyard, but they bore her to a lone moorland graveyard, where long ago the Quakers used to bury their dead. They laid her there on the sunny slope, where the earliest spring-flowers blow.

Will and Susan live at the Upclose Farm. Mrs Leigh and Lizzie dwell in a cottage so secluded that, until you drop into the very hollow where it is placed, you do not see it. Tom is a school-master in Rochdale, and he and Will help to support their mother. I only know that, if the cottage be hidden in a green hollow of the hills, every sound of sorrow in the whole upland is heard there – every call of suffering or of sickness for help is listened to by a sad, gentle-looking woman, who rarely smiles (and when she does, her smile is more sad than other people's tears), but who comes out of her seclusion whenever there's a shadow in any household. Many hearts bless Lizzie Leigh, but she – she prays always and ever for forgiveness –

such forgiveness as may enable her to see her child once more. Mrs Leigh is quiet and happy. Lizzie is to her eyes something precious, – as the lost piece of silver* – found once more. Susan is the bright one who brings sunshine to all. Children grow around her and call her blessed. One is called Nanny. Her, Lizzie often takes to the sunny graveyard in the uplands, and while the little creature gathers the daisies, and makes chains, Lizzie sits by a little grave and weeps bitterly.

THE OLD NURSE'S STORY

*

You know, my dears, that your mother was an orphan, and an only child; and I dare say you have heard that your grand-father was a clergyman up in Westmoreland, where I come from. I was just a girl in the village school, when, one day, your grandmother came in to ask the mistress if there was any scholar there who would do for a nurse-maid; and mighty proud I was, I can tell ye, when the mistress called me up, and spoke to my being a good girl at my needle, and a steady, honest girl, and one whose parents were very respectable, though they might be poor. I thought I should like nothing better than to serve the pretty, young lady, who was blushing as deep as I was, as she spoke of the coming baby, and what I should have to do with it. However, I see you don't care so much for this part of my story, as for what you think is to come, so I'll tell you at once. I was engaged and settled at the parsonage before Miss Rosamond (that was the baby, who is now your mother) was born. To be sure, I had little enough to do with her when she came, for she was never out of her mother's arms, and slept by her all night long; and proud enough was I sometimes when missis trusted her to me. There never was such a baby before or since, though you've all of you been fine enough in your turns; but for sweet, winning ways, you've none of you come up to your mother. She took after her mother, who was a real lady born; a Miss Furnivall, a granddaughter of Lord Furnivall's, in Northumberland. I believe she had neither brother nor sister, and had been brought up in my lord's family till she had married your grandfather, who was just a curate, son to a shopkeeper in Carlisle – but a clever, fine gentleman as ever was – and one who was a right-down hard worker in his parish, which was very wide, and scattered all abroad over the Westmoreland Fells. When your mother, little Miss Rosamond, was about four or five years old, both her parents died in a fortnight – one after the other. Ah! that was a sad time. My pretty young mistress and me was looking for another baby, when my master came home from one of his long rides, wet, and tired, and took the fever he died of; and then she never held up her head again, but lived just to see her dead baby, and have it laid on her breast before she sighed away her life. My mistress had asked me, on her death-bed, never to leave Miss Rosamond; but if she had never spoken a word, I would have gone with the little child to the end of the world.

The next thing, and before we had well stilled our sobs, the executors and guardians came to settle the affairs. They were my poor young mistress's own cousin, Lord Furnivall, and Mr Esthwaite, my master's brother, a shopkeeper in Manchester; not so well to do then, as he was afterwards, and with a large family rising about him. Well! I don't know if it were their settling, or because of a letter my mistress wrote on her death-bed to her cousin, my lord; but somehow it was settled that Miss Rosamond and me were to go to Furnivall Manor House, in Northumberland, and my lord spoke as if it had been her mother's wish that she should live with his family, and as if he had no objections, for that one or two more or less could make no difference in so grand a household. So, though that was not the way in which I should have wished the coming of my bright and pretty pet to have been looked at – who was like a sunbeam in any family, be it never so grand – I was well pleased that all the folks in the Dale should stare and admire, when they heard I was going to be young lady's maid at my Lord Furnivall's at Furnivall Manor.

But I made a mistake in thinking we were to go and live where my lord did. It turned out that the family had left Furnivall Manor House fifty years or more. I could not hear that my poor young mistress had ever been there, though she had been brought up in the family; and I was sorry for that, for I should have liked Miss Rosamond's youth to have passed where her mother's had been.

My lord's gentleman, from whom I asked as many questions as I durst, said that the Manor House was at the foot of the Cumberland Fells, and a very grand place; that an old Miss Furnivall, a great-aunt of my lord's, lived there, with only a few servants; but that it was a very healthy place, and my lord had thought that it would suit Miss Rosamond very well for a few years, and that her being there might perhaps amuse his old aunt.

I was bidden by my lord to have Miss Rosamond's things ready by a certain day. He was a stern proud man, as they say all the Lords Furnivall were; and he never spoke a word more than was necessary. Folk did say he had loved my young mistress; but that, because she knew that his father would object, she would never listen to him, and married Mr Esthwaite; but I don't know. He never married at any rate. But he never took much notice of Miss Rosamond; which I thought he might have done if he had cared for her dead mother. He sent his gentleman with us to the Manor House, telling him to join him at Newcastle that same evening; so there was no great length of time for him to make us known to all the strangers before he, too, shook us off; and we were left, two lonely young things (I was not eighteen), in the great old Manor House. It seems like yesterday that we drove there. We had left our own dear parsonage very early, and we had both cried as if our hearts would break, though we were travelling in my lord's carriage, which I thought so much of once. And now it was long past noon on a September day, and we stopped to change horses for the last time at a little, smoky town, all full of colliers and miners. Miss Rosamond had fallen asleep, but Mr Henry told me to waken her, that she might see the park and the Manor House as we drove up. I thought it rather a pity; but I did what he bade me, for fear he should complain of me to my lord. We had left all signs of a town, or even a village, and were then inside the gates of a large, wild park – not like the parks here in the south, but with rocks, and the noise of running water, and gnarled thorn-trees, and old oaks, all white and peeled with age.

The road went up about two miles, and then we saw a great and stately house, with many trees close around it, so close that in some places their branches dragged against the walls when the wind blew; and some hung broken down; for no one seemed to take much charge of the place; – to lop the wood, or to keep the moss-covered carriage-way in order. Only in front of the house all was clear. The great oval drive was without a weed; and neither tree nor creeper was allowed to grow over the long, many-windowed front; at both sides of which a wing projected, which were each the ends of other side fronts; for the house, although it was so desolate, was even grander than I expected. Behind it rose the Fells, which seemed unenclosed and bare enough; and on the left hand of the house, as you stood facing it, was a little, old-fashioned flower-garden, as I found out afterwards. A door opened out upon it from the west front; it had been scooped out of the thick dark wood for some old Lady Furnivall; but the branches of the great forest trees had grown and overshadowed it again, and there were very few flowers that would live there at that time.

When we drove up to the great front entrance, and went into the hall I thought we should be lost – it was so large, and vast, and grand. There was a chandelier all of bronze, hung down from the middle of the ceiling; and I had never seen one before, and looked at it all in amaze. Then, at one end of the hall, was a great fire-place, as large as the sides of the houses in my country, with massy andirons and dogs to hold the wood; and by it were heavy, old-fashioned sofas. At the opposite end of the hall, to the left as you went in – on the western side – was an organ built into the wall, and so large that it filled up the best part of that end. Beyond it, on the same side, was a door; and opposite, on each side of the fire-place, were also doors leading to the east front; but those I never went through as long as I stayed in the house, so I can't tell you what lay beyond.

The afternoon was closing in and the hall, which had no fire lighted in it, looked dark and gloomy, but we did not stay there a moment. The old servant, who had opened the door for us bowed to Mr Henry, and took us in through the door at the further side of the great organ, and led us through several smaller halls and passages into the west drawing-room, where he said that Miss Furnivall was sitting. Poor little Miss Rosamond held very tight to me, as if she were scared and lost in that great place, and as for myself, I was not much better. The west drawing-room was very cheerful-looking, with a warm fire in it, and plenty of good, comfortable furniture about. Miss Furnivall was an old lady not far from eighty, I should think, but I do not know. She was thin and tall, and had a face as full of fine wrinkles as if they had been drawn all over it with a needle's point. Her eyes were very watchful to make up, I suppose, for her being so deaf as to be obliged to use a trumpet. Sitting with her, working at the same great piece of tapestry, was Mrs Stark, her maid and companion, and almost as old as she was. She had lived with Miss Furnivall ever since they both were young, and now she seemed more like a friend than a servant; she looked so cold, and grey, and stony, as if she had never loved or cared for any one; and I don't suppose she did care for any one, except her mistress; and, owing to the great deafness of the latter, Mrs Stark treated her very much as if she were a child. Mr Henry gave some message from my lord, and then he bowed good-bye to us all, – taking no notice of my sweet little Miss Rosamond's out-stretched hand – and left us standing there, being looked at by the two old ladies through their spectacles.

I was right glad when they rung for the old footman who had shown us in at first, and told him to take us to our rooms. So we went out of that great drawing-room, and into another sitting-room, and out of that, and then up a great flight of stairs, and along a broad gallery – which was something like a library, having books all down one side, and windows and writing-tables all down the other – till we came to our rooms, which I was not sorry to hear were just over the kitchens; for I began to think I should be lost in that wilderness of a house. There was an old nursery, that had been used for all the little lords and ladies long ago, with a pleasant fire burning in the grate, and the kettle boiling on the hob, and tea things spread out on the table; and out of that room was the night-nursery, with a little crib for Miss Rosamond close to my bed. And old James called up Dorothy, his wife, to bid us welcome; and both he and she were so hospitable and kind, that by and by Miss Rosamond and me felt quite at home; and by the time tea was over, she was sitting on Dorothy's knee, and chattering away as fast as her little tongue could go. I soon found out that Dorothy was from Westmoreland, and that bound her and me together, as it were; and I would never wish to meet with kinder people than were old James and his wife. James had lived pretty nearly all his life in my lord's family, and thought there was no one so grand as they. He even looked down a little on his wife; because, till he had married her, she had never lived in any but a farmer's household. But he was very fond of her, as well he might be. They had one servant under them, to do all the rough work. Agnes they called her; and she and me, and James and Dorothy, with Miss Furnivall and Mrs Stark, made up the family; always remembering my sweet little Miss Rosamond! I used to wonder what they had done before she came, they thought so much of her now. Kitchen and drawing-room, it was all the same. The hard, sad Miss Furnivall, and the cold Mrs Stark, looked pleased when she came fluttering in like a bird, playing and pranking hither and thither, with a continual murmur, and pretty prattle of gladness. I am sure, they were sorry many a time when she flitted away into the kitchen, though they were too proud to ask her to stay with them, and were a little surprised at her taste; though to be sure, as Mrs Stark said, it was not to be wondered at, remembering what stock her father had come of. The great, old rambling house was a famous place for little Miss Rosamond. She made expeditions all over it, with me at her heels; all, except the east wing, which was never opened, and whither we never thought of going. But in the western and northern part was many a pleasant room; full of things that were curiosities to us, though they might not have been to people who had seen more. The windows were darkened by the sweeping boughs of the trees, and the ivy which had overgrown them: but, in the green gloom, we could manage to see old China jars and carved ivory boxes, and great, heavy books, and, above all, the old pictures!

Once, I remember, my darling would have Dorothy go with us to tell us who they all were; for they were all portraits of some of my lord's family, though Dorothy could not tell us the names of every one. We had gone through most of the rooms, when we came to the old state drawing-room over the hall, and there was a picture of Miss Furnivall; or, as she was called in those days, Miss Grace, for she was the younger sister.* Such a beauty she must have been! but with such a set, proud look, and such scorn looking out of her handsome eyes, with her eyebrows just a little raised, as if she wondered how any one could have the impertinence to look at her; and her lip curled at us, as we stood there gazing. She had a dress on, the like of which I had never seen before, but it was all the fashion when she was young: a hat of some soft, white stuff like beaver, pulled a little over her brows, and a beautiful plume of feathers sweeping round it on one side; and her gown of blue satin was open in front to a quilted, white stomacher.

'Well, to be sure!' said I, when I had gazed my fill. 'Flesh is grass, they do say; but who would have thought that Miss Furnivall had been such an out-and-out beauty, to see her now?'

'Yes,' said Dorothy. 'Folks change sadly. But if what my master's father used to say was true, Miss Furnivall, the elder sister, was handsomer than Miss Grace. Her picture is here somewhere; but, if I show it you, you must never let on, even to James, that you have seen it. Can the little lady hold her tongue, think you?' asked she.

I was not so sure, for she was such a little, sweet, bold, open-spoken child, so I set her to hide herself; and then I helped Dorothy to turn a great picture, that leaned with its face towards the wall, and was not hung up as the others were. To be sure, it beat Miss Grace for beauty; and, I think, for scornful pride, too, though in that matter it might be hard to choose. I could have looked at it an hour, but Dorothy seemed half frightened at having shown it to me, and hurried it back again, and bade me run and find Miss Rosamond, for that there were some ugly places about the house, where she should like ill for the child to go. I was a brave, high-spirited girl, and thought little of what the old woman said, for I liked hide-and-seek as well as any child in the parish; so off I ran to find my little one.

As winter drew on, and the days grew shorter, I was some-times almost certain that I heard a noise as if some one was playing on the great organ in the hall. I did not hear it every evening; but, certainly, I did very often; usually when I was sitting with Miss Rosamond, after I had put her to bed, and keeping quite still and silent in the bed-room. Then I used to hear it booming and swelling away in the distance. The first night, when I went down to my supper, I asked Dorothy who had been playing music, and James said very shortly that I was a gowk to take the wind soughing among the trees for music: but I saw Dorothy look at him very fearfully, and Agnes, the kitchen-maid, said something beneath her breath, and went quite white. I saw they did not like my question, so I held my peace till I was with Dorothy alone, when I knew I could get a good deal out of her. So, the next day, I watched my time, and I coaxed and asked her who it was that played the organ; for I knew that it was the organ and not the wind well enough, for all I had kept silence before James. But Dorothy had had her lesson I'll warrant, and never a word could I get from her. So then I tried Agnes, though I had always held my head rather above her, as I was evened to James and Dorothy, and she was little better than their servant. So she said I must never, never tell; and if I ever told, I was never to say *she* had told me; but it was a very strange noise, and she had heard it many a time, but most of all on winter nights, and before storms; and folks did say, it was the old lord playing on the great organ in the hall, just as he used to do when he was alive; but who the old lord was, or why he played, and why he played on stormy winter evenings in particular, she either could not or would not tell me. Well! I told you I had a brave heart; and I thought it was rather pleasant to have that grand music rolling about the house, let who would be the player; for now it rose above the great gusts of wind, and wailed and triumph-ed just like a living creature, and then it fell to a softness most complete; only it was always music, and tunes, so it was non-sense to call it the wind. I thought at first, that it might be Miss Furnivall who played, unknown to Agnes; but, one day when I was in the hall by myself, I opened the organ and peeped all about it and around it, as I had done to the organ in Crosthwaite Church* once before, and I saw it was all broken and destroyed inside, though it looked so brave and fine; and then, though it was noon-day, my flesh began to creep a little, and I shut it up, and run away pretty quickly to my own bright nursery; and I did not like hearing the music for some time after that, any more than James and Dorothy did. All this time Miss Rosamond was making herself more and more beloved. The old ladies liked her to dine with them at their early dinner; James stood behind Miss Furnivall's chair, and I behind Miss Rosamond's all in state; and, after dinner, she would play about in a corner of the great drawing-room, as still as any mouse, while Miss Furnivall slept, and I had my dinner in the kitchen. But she was glad enough to come to me in the nursery afterwards; for, as she said, Miss Furnivall was so sad, and Mrs Stark so dull; but she and I were merry enough; and, by-and-by, I got not to care for that weird rolling music, which did one no harm, if we did not know where it came from.

That winter was very cold. In the middle of October the frosts began, and lasted many, many weeks. I remember, one day at dinner, Miss Furnivall lifted up her sad, heavy eyes, and said to Mrs Stark, 'I am afraid we shall have a terrible winter,' in a strange kind of meaning way. But Mrs Stark pretended not to hear, and talked very loud of something else. My little lady and I did not care for the frost; not we! As long as it was dry we climbed up the steep brows, behind the house, and went up on the Fells, which were bleak, and bare enough, and there we ran races in the fresh, sharp air; and once we came down by a new path that took us past the two old, gnarled holly-trees, which grew about half-way down by the east side of the house. But the days grew shorter, and shorter; and the old lord, if it was he, played away more, and more stormily and sadly on the great organ. One Sunday afternoon, – it must have been towards the end of November – I asked Dorothy to take charge of little Missey when she came out of the drawing-room, after Miss Furnivall had had her nap; for it was too cold to take her with me to church, and yet I wanted to go. And Dorothy was glad enough to promise, and was so fond of the child that all seemed well; and Agnes and I set off very briskly, though the sky hung heavy and black over the white earth, as if the night had never fully gone away; and the air, though still, was very biting and keen.

'We shall have a fall of snow,' said Agnes to me. And sure enough, even while we were in church, it came down thick, in great, large flakes, so thick it almost darkened the windows. It had stopped snowing before we came out, but it lay soft, thick and deep beneath our feet, as we tramped home. Before we got to the hall the moon rose, and I think it was lighter then, – what with the moon, and what with the white dazzling snow – than it had been when we went to church, between two and three o'clock. I have not told you that Miss Furnivall and Mrs Stark never went to church: they used to read the prayers together, in their quiet, gloomy way; they seemed to

feel the Sunday very long without their tapestry-work to be
busy at. So when I went to Dorothy in the kitchen, to fetch
Miss Rosamond and take her up-stairs with me, I did not
much wonder when the old woman told me that the ladies had
kept the child with them, and that she had never come to the
kitchen, as I had bidden her, when she was tired of behaving
pretty in the drawing-room. So I took off my things and went
to find her, and bring her to her supper in the nursery. But
when I went into the best drawing-room, there sate the two
old ladies, very still and quiet, dropping out a word now and
then, but looking as if nothing so bright and merry as Miss
Rosamond had ever been near them. Still I thought she might
be hiding from me; it was one of her pretty ways; and that she
had persuaded them to look as if they knew nothing about
her; so I went softly peeping under this sofa, and behind that
chair, making believe I was sadly frightened at not finding her.

'What's the matter, Hester?' said Mrs Stark sharply. I don't
know if Miss Furnivall had seen me, for, as I told you, she was
very deaf, and she sate quite still, idly staring into the fire, with
her hopeless face. 'I'm only looking for my little Rosy-Posy,'
replied I, still thinking that the child was there, and near me,
though I could not see her.

'Miss Rosamond is not here,' said Mrs Stark. 'She went
away more than an hour ago to find Dorothy.' And she too
turned and went on looking into the fire.

My heart sank at this, and I began to wish I had never left
my darling. I went back to Dorothy and told her. James was
gone out for the day, but she and me and Agnes took lights
and went up into the nursery first, and then we roamed over
the great large house, calling and entreating Miss Rosamond
to come out of her hiding place, and not frighten us to death
in that way. But there was no answer; no sound.

'Oh!' said I at last. 'Can she have got into the east wing and
hidden there?'

But Dorothy said it was not possible, for that she herself had
never been in there; that the doors were always locked, and
my lord's steward had the keys, she believed; at any rate,
neither she nor James had ever seen them: so, I said I would
go back, and see if, after all, she was not hidden in the drawing-room, unknown to the old ladies; and if I found her

there, I said, I would whip her well for the fright she had given me; but I never meant to do it. Well, I went back to the west drawing-room, and I told Mrs Stark we could not find her anywhere, and asked for leave to look all about the furniture there, for I thought now, that she might have fallen asleep in some warm, hidden corner; but no! we looked, Miss Furnivall got up and looked, trembling all over, and she was no where there; then we set off again, every one in the house, and looked in all the places we had searched before, but we could not find her. Miss Furnivall shivered and shook so much, that Mrs Stark took her back into the warm drawing-room; but not before they had made me promise to bring her to them when she was found. Well-a-day! I began to think she never would be found, when I bethought me to look out into the great front court, all covered with snow. I was up-stairs when I looked out; but, it was such clear moonlight, I could see quite plain two little footprints, which might be traced from the hall door, and round the corner of the east wing. I don't know how I got down, but I tugged open the great, stiff hall door; and, throwing the skirt of my gown over my head for a cloak, I ran out. I turned the east corner, and there a black shadow fell on the snow; but when I came again into the moonlight, there were the little footmarks going up – up to the Fells. It was bitter cold; so cold that the air almost took the skin off my face as I ran, but I ran on, crying to think how my poor little darling must be perished,* and frightened. I was within sight of the holly-trees, when I saw a shepherd coming down the hill, bearing something in his arms wrapped in his maud.* He shouted to me, and asked me if I had lost a bairn; and, when I could not speak for crying, he bore towards me, and I saw my wee bairnie lying still, and white, and stiff, in his arms, as if she had been dead. He told me he had been up the Fells to gather in his sheep, before the deep cold of night came on, and that under the holly-trees (black marks on the hill-side, where no other bush was for miles around) he had found my little lady – my lamb – my queen – my darling – stiff, and cold, in the terrible sleep which is frost-begotten. Oh! the joy, and the tears, of having her in my arms once again! for I would not let him carry her; but took her, maud and all, into my own arms, and held her near my own warm neck, and heart, and felt the life stealing slowly back again into her little, gentle limbs. But she was still insensible when we reached the hall, and I had no breath for speech. We went in by the kitchen door.

'Bring the warming-pan,' said I; and I carried her up-stairs and began undressing her by the nursery fire, which Agnes had kept up. I called my little lammie all the sweet and playful names I could think of, – even while my eyes were blinded by my tears; and at last, oh! at length she opened her large, blue eyes. Then I put her into her warm bed, and sent Dorothy down to tell Miss Furnivall that all was well; and I made up my mind to sit by my darling's bedside the live-long night. She fell away into a soft sleep as soon as her pretty head had touched the pillow, and I watched by her till morning light; when she wakened up bright and clear – or so I thought at first – and, my dears, so I think now.

She said, that she had fancied that she should like to go to Dorothy, for that both the old ladies were asleep, and it was very dull in the drawing-room; and that, as she was going through the west lobby, she saw the snow through the high window falling – falling – soft and steady; but she wanted to see it lying pretty and white on the ground; so she made her way into the great hall; and then, going to the window, she saw it bright and soft upon the drive; but while she stood there, she saw a little girl, not as old as she was, 'but so pretty,' said my darling, 'and this little girl beckoned to me to come out; and oh, she was so pretty and so sweet, I could not choose but go.' And then this other little girl had taken her by the hand, and side by side the two had gone round the east corner.

'Now you are a naughty little girl, and telling stories,' said I. 'What would your good mamma, that is in heaven, and never told a story in her life, say to her little Rosamond, if she heard her – and I dare say she does – telling stories!'

'Indeed, Hester,' sobbed out my child, 'I'm telling you true. Indeed I am.'

'Don't tell me!' said I, very stern. 'I tracked you by your foot-marks through the snow; there were only yours to be seen: and if you had had a little girl to go hand-in-hand with you up the hill, don't you think the foot-prints would have gone along with yours?'

'I can't help it, dear, dear Hester,' said she, crying, 'if they did not; I never looked at her feet, but she held my hand fast and tight in her little one, and it was very, very cold. She took me up the Fell-path, up to the holly trees; and there I saw a lady weeping and crying; but when she saw me, she hushed her weeping, and smiled very proud and grand, and took me on her knee, and began to lull me to sleep; and that's all, Hester – but that is true; and my dear mamma knows it is,' said she, crying. So I thought the child was in a fever, and pretended to believe her, as she went over her story – over and over again, and always the same. At last Dorothy knocked at the door with Miss Rosamond's breakfast; and she told me the old ladies were down in the eating parlour, and that they wanted to speak to me. They had both been into the night-nursery the evening before, but it was after Miss Rosamond was asleep; so they had only looked at her – not asked me any questions.

'I shall catch it,' thought I to myself, as I went along the north gallery. 'And yet,' I thought, taking courage, 'it was in their charge I left her; and it's they that's to blame for letting her steal away unknown and unwatched.' So I went in boldly, and told my story. I told it all to Miss Furnivall, shouting it close to her ear; but when I came to the mention of the other little girl out in the snow, coaxing and tempting her out, and wiling her up to the grand and beautiful lady by the holly-tree, she threw her arms up – her old and withered arms – and cried aloud, 'Oh! Heaven, forgive! Have mercy!'

Mrs Stark took hold of her; roughly enough, I thought; but she was past Mrs Stark's management, and spoke to me, in a kind of wild warning and authority.

'Hester! keep her from that child! It will lure her to her death! That evil child! Tell her it is a wicked, naughty child.' Then, Mrs Stark hurried me out of the room; where, indeed, I was glad enough to go; but Miss Furnivall kept shrieking out, 'Oh! have mercy! Wilt Thou never forgive! It is many a long year ago –'

I was very uneasy in my mind after that. I durst never leave Miss Rosamond, night or day, for fear lest she might slip off again, after some fancy or other; and all the more, because I thought I could make out that Miss Furnivall was crazy, from their odd ways about her; and I was afraid lest something of the same kind (which might be in the family, you know) hung over my darling. And the great frost never ceased all this time; and, whenever it was a more stormy night than usual, between the gusts, and through the wind, we heard the old lord playing on the great organ. But, old lord, or not, wherever Miss Rosamond went, there I followed; for my love for her, pretty, helpless orphan, was stronger than my fear for the grand and terrible sound. Besides, it rested with me to keep her cheerful and merry, as beseemed her age. So we played together, and wandered together, here and there, and everywhere; for I never dared to lose sight of her again in that large and rambling house. And so it happened, that one afternoon, not long before Christmas day, we were playing together on the billiard-table in the great hall (not that we knew the right way of playing, but she liked to roll the smooth ivory balls with her pretty hands, and I liked to do whatever she did); and, by-and-by, without our noticing it, it grew dusk indoors, though it was still light in the open air, and I was thinking of taking her back into the nursery, when, all of a sudden, she cried out, –

'Look, Hester! look! there is my poor little girl out in the snow!'

I turned towards the long, narrow windows, and there, sure enough, I saw a little girl, less than my Miss Rosamond – dressed all unfit to be out-of-doors such a bitter night – crying, and beating against the window-panes, as if she wanted to be let in. She seemed to sob and wail, till Miss Rosamond could bear it no longer, and was flying to the door to open it, when, all of a sudden, and close upon us, the great organ pealed out so loud and thundering, it fairly made me tremble; and all the more, when I remembered me that, even in the stillness of that dead-cold weather, I had heard no sound of little battering hands upon the window-glass, although the Phantom Child had seemed to put forth all its force; and, although I had seen it wail and cry, no faintest touch of sound had fallen upon my ears. Whether I remembered all this at the very moment, I do not know; the great organ sound had so stunned me into terror; but this I know, I caught up Miss Rosamond before she got the hall-door opened, and clutched her, and carried her away, kicking and screaming, into the large, bright kitchen, where Dorothy and Agnes were busy with their mince-pies.

'What is the matter with my sweet one?' cried Dorothy, as I bore in Miss Rosamond, who was sobbing as if her heart would break.

'She won't let me open the door for my little girl to come in; and she'll die if she is out on the Fells all night. Cruel, naughty Hester,' she said, slapping me; but she might have struck harder, for I had seen a look of ghastly terror on Dorothy's face, which made my very blood run cold.

'Shut the back kitchen door fast, and bolt it well,' said she to Agnes. She said no more; she gave me raisins and almonds to quiet Miss Rosamond: but she sobbed about the little girl in the snow, and would not touch any of the good things. I was thankful when she cried herself to sleep in bed. Then I stole down to the kitchen, and told Dorothy I had made up my mind. I would carry my darling back to my father's house in Applethwaite; where, if we lived humbly, we lived at peace. I said I had been frightened enough with the old lord's organ-playing; but now that I had seen for myself this little, moaning child, all decked out as no child in the neighbourhood could be, beating and battering to get in, yet always without any sound or noise – with the dark wound on its right shoulder; and that Miss Rosamond had known it again for the phantom that had nearly lured her to her death (which Dorothy knew was true); I would stand it no longer.

I saw Dorothy change colour once or twice. When I had done, she told me she did not think I could take Miss Rosamond with me, for that she was my lord's ward, and I had no right over her; and she asked me, would I leave the child that I was so fond of, just for sounds and sights that could do me no harm; and that they had all had to get used to in their turns? I was all in a hot, trembling passion; and I said it was very well for her to talk, that knew what these sights and noises betokened, and that had, perhaps, had something to do with the Spectre-Child while it was alive. And I taunted her so, that she told me all she knew, at last; and then I wished I had never been told, for it only made me more afraid than ever.

She said she had heard the tale from old neighbours, that

were alive when she was first married; when folks used to come to the hall sometimes, before it had got such a bad name on the country side: it might not be true, or it might, what she had been told.

The old lord was Miss Furnivall's father – Miss Grace, as Dorothy called her, for Miss Maude was the elder, and Miss Furnivall by rights. The old lord was eaten up with pride. Such a proud man was never seen or heard of; and his daughters were like him. No one was good enough to wed them, although they had choice enough; for they were the great beauties of their day, as I had seen by their portraits, where they hung in the state drawing-room. But, as the old saying is, 'Pride will have a fall'; and these two haughty beauties fell in love with the same man, and he no better than a foreign musician, whom their father had down from London to play music with him at the Manor House. For, above all things, next to his pride, the old lord loved music. He could play on nearly every instrument that ever was heard of: and it was a strange thing it did not soften him; but he was a fierce, dour, old man, and had broken his poor wife's heart with his cruelty, they said. He was mad after music, and would pay any money for it. So he got this foreigner to come; who made such beautiful music, that they said the very birds on the trees stopped their singing to listen. And, by degrees, this foreign gentleman got such a hold over the old lord, that nothing would serve him but that he must come every year; and it was he that had the great organ brought from Holland, and built up in the hall, where it stood now. He taught the old lord to play on it; but many and many a time, when Lord Furnivall was thinking of nothing but his fine organ, and his finer music, the dark foreigner was walking abroad in the woods with one of the young ladies; now Miss Maude, and then Miss Grace.

Miss Maude won the day and carried off the prize, such as it was; and he and she were married, all unknown to any one; and before he made his next yearly visit, she had been confined of a little girl at a farm-house on the Moors, while her father and Miss Grace thought she was away at Doncaster Races. But though she was a wife and a mother, she was not a bit softened, but as haughty and as passionate as ever; and perhaps more so, for she was jealous of Miss Grace, to whom her foreign husband paid a deal of court – by way of blinding her – as he told his wife. But Miss Grace triumphed over Miss Maude, and Miss Maude grew fiercer and fiercer, both with her husband and with her sister; and the former – who could easily shake off what was disagreeable, and hide himself in foreign countries – went away a month before his usual time that summer, and half-threatened that he would never come back again. Meanwhile, the little girl was left at the farm-house, and her mother used to have her horse saddled and gallop wildly over the hills to see her once every week, at the very least – for where she loved, she loved; and where she hated, she hated. And the old lord went on playing – playing on his organ; and the servants thought the sweet music he made had soothed down his awful temper, of which (Dorothy said) some terrible tales could be told. He grew infirm too, and had to walk with a crutch; and his son – that was the present Lord Furnivall's father – was with the army in America,* and the other son at sea; so Miss Maude had it pretty much her own way, and she and Miss Grace grew colder and bitterer to each other every day; till at last they hardly ever spoke, except when the old lord was by. The foreign musician came again the next summer, but it was for the last time; for they led him such a life with their jealousy and their passions, that he grew weary, and went away, and never was heard of again. And Miss Maude, who had always meant to have her marriage acknowledged when her father should be dead, was left now a deserted wife – whom nobody knew to have been married – with a child that she dared not own, although she loved it to distraction; living with a father whom she feared, and a sister whom she hated. When the next summer passed over and the dark foreigner never came, both Miss Maude and Miss Grace grew gloomy and sad; they had a haggard look about them, though they looked handsome as ever. But by-and-by Miss Maude brightened; for her father grew more and more infirm, and more than ever carried away by his music; and she and Miss Grace lived almost entirely apart, having separate rooms, the one on the west side, Miss Maude on the east – those very rooms which were now shut up. So she thought she might have her little girl with her, and no one need ever know except those who dared not speak about it, and were bound to believe that it was, as she said, a cottager's child she had taken a fancy to. All this Dorothy said, was pretty well known; but what came afterwards no one knew, except Miss Grace, and Mrs Stark, who was even then her maid, and much more of a friend to her than ever her sister had been. But the servants supposed, from words that were dropped, that Miss Maude had triumphed over Miss Grace, and told her that all the time the dark foreigner had been mocking her with pretended love – he was her own husband; the colour left Miss Grace's cheek and lips that very day for ever, and she was heard to say many a time that sooner or later she would have her revenge; and Mrs Stark was for ever spying about the east rooms.

One fearful night, just after the New Year had come in, when the snow was lying thick and deep, and the flakes were still falling – fast enough to blind any one who might be out and abroad – there was a great and violent noise heard, and the old lord's voice above all, cursing and swearing awfully, – and the cries of a little child, – and the proud defiance of a fierce woman, – and the sound of a blow, – and a dead stillness, – and moans and wailings dying away on the hill-side! Then the old lord summoned all his servants, and told them, with terrible oaths, and words more terrible, that his daughter had disgraced herself, and that he had turned her out of doors, – her, and her child, – and that if ever they gave her help, – or food, – or shelter, – he prayed that they might never enter Heaven. And, all the while, Miss Grace stood by him, white and still as any stone; and when he had ended she heaved a great sigh, as much as to say her work was done, and her end was accomplished. But the old lord never touched his organ again, and died within the year; and no wonder! for, on the morrow of that wild and fearful night, the shepherds, coming down the Fell-side, found Miss Maude sitting, all crazy and smiling, under the holly-trees, nursing a dead child, – with a terrible mark on its right shoulder. 'But that was not what killed it,' said Dorothy; 'it was the frost and the cold; – every wild creature was in its hole, and every beast in its fold, – while the child and its mother were turned out to wander on the Fells! And now you know all! and I wonder if you are less frightened now?'

I was more frightened than ever; but I said I was not. I wished Miss Rosamond and myself well out of that dreadful house for ever; but I would not leave her, and I dared not take her away. But oh! how I watched her, and guarded her! We bolted the doors, and shut the window-shutters fast, an hour or more before dark, rather than leave them open five minutes too late. But my little lady still heard the weird child crying and mourning; and not all we could do or say, could keep her from wanting to go to her, and let her in from the cruel wind and the snow. All this time, I kept away from Miss Furnivall and Mrs Stark, as much as ever I could; for I feared them – I knew no good could be about them, with their grey hard faces, and their dreamy eyes, looking back into the ghastly years that were gone. But, even in my fear, I had a kind of pity – for Miss Furnivall, at least. Those gone down to the pit can hardly have a more hopeless look than that which was ever on her face. At last I even got so sorry for her – who never said a word but what was quite forced from her – that I prayed for her; and I taught Miss Rosamond to pray for one who had done a deadly sin; but often when she came to those words, she would listen, and start up from her knees, and say, 'I hear my little girl plaining and crying very sad – Oh! let her in, or she will die!'

One night – just after New Year's Day had come at last, and the long winter had taken a turn, as I hoped – I heard the west drawing-room bell ring three times, which was the signal for me. I would not leave Miss Rosamond alone, for all she was asleep – for the old lord had been playing wilder than ever – and I feared lest my darling should waken to hear the spectre child; see her I knew she could not. I had fastened the windows too well for that. So, I took her out of her bed and wrapped her up in such outer clothes as were most handy, and carried her down to the drawing-room, where the old ladies sate at their tapestry work as usual. They looked up when I came in, and Mrs Stark asked, quite astounded, 'Why did I bring Miss Rosamond there, out of her warm bed?' I had begun to whisper, 'Because I was afraid of her being tempted out while I was away, by the wild child in the snow,' when she stopped me short (with a glance at Miss Furnivall), and said Miss Furnivall wanted me to undo some work she had done wrong, and which neither of them could see to unpick. So, I laid my pretty dear on the sofa, and sate down on a stool by them, and hardened my heart against them, as I heard the wind rising and howling.

Miss Rosamond slept on sound, for all the wind blew so; and Miss Furnivall said never a word, nor looked round when the gusts shook the windows. All at once she started up to her full height, and put up one hand, as if to bid us listen.

'I hear voices!' said she. 'I hear terrible screams – I hear my father's voice!'

Just at that moment, my darling wakened with a sudden start: 'My little girl is crying, oh, how she is crying!' and she tried to get up and go to her, but she got her feet entangled in the blanket, and I caught her up; for my flesh had begun to creep at these noises, which they heard while we could catch no sound. In a minute or two the noises came, and gathered fast, and filled our ears; we, too, heard voices and screams, and no longer heard the winter's wind that raged abroad. Mrs Stark looked at me, and I at her, but we dared not speak. Suddenly Miss Furnivall went towards the door, out into the ante-room, through the west lobby, and opened the door into the great hall. Mrs Stark followed, and I durst not be left, though my heart almost stopped beating for fear. I wrapped my darling tight in my arms, and went out with them. In the hall the screams were louder than ever; they sounded to come from the east wing – nearer and nearer – close on the other side of the locked-up doors – close behind them. Then I noticed that the great bronze chandelier seemed all alight, though the hall was dim, and that a fire was blazing in the vast hearth-place, though it gave no heat; and I shuddered up with terror, and folded my darling closer to me. But as I did so, the east door shook, and she, suddenly struggling to get free from me, cried, 'Hester! I must go! My little girl is there; I hear her; she is coming! Hester, I must go!'

I held her tight with all my strength; with a set will, I held her. If I had died, my hands would have grasped her still, I was so resolved in my mind. Miss Furnivall stood listening, and paid no regard to my darling, who had got down to the ground, and whom I, upon my knees now, was holding with both my arms clasped round her neck; she still striving and crying to get free.

All at once, the east door gave way with a thundering crash, as if torn open in a violent passion, and there came into that broad and mysterious light, the figure of a tall, old man, with grey hair and gleaming eyes. He drove before him, with many a relentless gesture of abhorrence, a stern and beautiful woman, with a little child clinging to her dress.

'Oh Hester! Hester!' cried Miss Rosamond. 'It's the lady! the lady below the holly-trees; and my little girl is with her. Hester! Hester! let me go to her; they are drawing me to them. I feel them – I feel them. I must go!'

Again she was almost convulsed by her efforts to get away; but I held her tighter and tighter, till I feared I should do her a hurt; but rather that than let her go towards those terrible phantoms. They passed along towards the great hall-door, where the winds howled and ravened for their prey; but before they reached that, the lady turned; and I could see that she defied the old man with a fierce and proud defiance; but then she quailed – and then she threw her arms wildly and piteously to save her child – her little child – from a blow from his up-lifted crutch.

And Miss Rosamond was torn as by a power stronger than mine, and writhed in my arms, and sobbed (for by this time the poor darling was growing faint).

'They want me to go with them on to the Fells – they are drawing me to them. Oh, my little girl! I would come, but cruel, wicked Hester holds me very tight.' But when she saw the uplifted crutch she swooned away, and I thanked God for it. Just at this moment – when the tall, old man, his hair streaming as in the blast of a furnace, was going to strike the little, shrinking child – Miss Furnivall, the old woman by my side, cried out, 'Oh, father! father! spare the little, innocent child!' But just then I saw – we all saw – another phantom shape itself, and grow clear out of the blue and misty light that filled the hall; we had not seen her till now, for it was another lady who stood by the old man, with a look of re-lentless hate and triumphant scorn. That figure was very beautiful to look upon, with a soft, white hat drawn down over the proud brows, and a red and curling lip. It was dressed in an open robe of blue satin. I had seen that figure before. It was the likeness of Miss Furnivall in her youth; and the terrible phantoms moved on, regardless of old Miss Furnivall's wild entreaty, – and the uplifted crutch fell on the right shoulder of the little child, and the younger sister looked on, stony and deadly serene. But at that moment, the dim lights, and the fire that gave no heat, went out of themselves, and Miss Furnivall lay at our feet stricken down by the palsy – death-stricken.

Yes! she was carried to her bed that night never to rise again. She lay with her face to the wall, muttering low, but muttering alway: 'Alas! alas! what is done in youth can never be undone in age! What is done in youth can never be undone in age!'

HALF A LIFE-TIME AGO

*

CHAPTER I

HALF a life-time ago, there lived in one of the Westmoreland dales a single woman, of the name of Susan Dixon. She was owner of the small farm-house where she resided, and of some thirty or forty acres of land by which it was surrounded. She had also an hereditary right to a sheep-walk, extending to the wild fells that overhang Blea Tarn. In the language of the country, she was a Stateswoman. Her house is yet to be seen on the Oxenfell road, between Skelwith and Coniston. You go along a moorland track, made by the carts that occasionally came for turf from the Oxenfell. A brook babbles and brattles by the wayside, giving you a sense of companionship, which relieves the deep solitude in which this way is usually traversed. Some miles on this side of Coniston there is a farmstead – a grey stone house, and a square of farm-buildings surrounding a green space of rough turf, in the midst of which stands a mighty, funereal umbrageous yew, making a solemn shadow, as of death, in the very heart and centre of the light and heat of the brightest summer day. On the side away from the house, this yard slopes down to a dark-brown pool, which is supplied with fresh water from the overflowings of a stone cistern, into which some rivulet of the brook before mentioned continually and melodiously falls bubbling. The cattle drink out of this cistern. The household bring their pitchers and fill them with drinking-water by a dilatory, yet pretty, process. The water-carrier brings with her a leaf of the hound's-tongue fern, and, inserting it in the crevice of the grey rock, makes a cool, green spout for the sparkling stream.

The house is no specimen, at the present day, of what it was in the lifetime of Susan Dixon. Then, every small diamond-pane in the windows glittered with cleanliness. You might have eaten off the floor; you could see yourself in the pewter plates and the polished oaken awmry, or dresser, of the state kitchen into which you entered. Few strangers penetrated further than this room. Once or twice, wandering tourists, attracted by the lonely picturesqueness of the situation, and the exquisite cleanliness of the house itself, made their way into this house-place, and offered money enough (as they thought) to tempt the hostess to receive them as lodgers. They would give no trouble, they said; they would be out rambling or sketching all day long; would be perfectly content with a share of the food which she provided for herself; or would procure what they required from the Waterhead Inn at Coniston. But no liberal sum – no fair words – moved her from her stony manner, or her monotonous tone of indifferent refusal. No persuasion could induce her to show any more of the house than that first room; no appearance of fatigue procured for the weary an invitation to sit down and rest; and if one more bold and less delicate did so without being asked, Susan stood by, cold and apparently deaf, or only replying by the briefest monosyllables, till the unwelcome visitor had departed. Yet those with whom she had dealings, in the way of selling her cattle or her farm produce, spoke of her as keen after a bargain – a hard one to have to do with; and she never spared herself exertion or fatigue, at market or in the field, to make the most of her produce. She led the haymakers with her swift, steady rake, and her noiseless evenness of motion. She was about among the earliest in the market, examining samples of oats, pricing them, and then turning with grim satisfaction to her own cleaner corn.

She was served faithfully and long by those who were rather her fellow-labourers than her servants. She was even and just in her dealings with them. If she was peculiar and silent, they knew her, and knew that she might be relied on. Some of them had known her from her childhood; and deep in their hearts was an unspoken – almost unconscious – pity for her; for they knew her story, though they never spoke of it.

Yes; the time had been when that tall, gaunt, hard-featured, angular woman – who never smiled, and hardly ever spoke an unnecessary word – had been a fine-looking girl, bright-spirited and rosy; and when the hearth at the Yew Nook had been as bright as she, with family love and youthful hope and mirth. Fifty or fifty-one years ago, William Dixon and his wife

Margaret were alive; and Susan, their daughter, was about eighteen years old – ten years older than the only other child, a boy named after his father. William and Margaret Dixon were rather superior people, of a character belonging – as far as I have seen – exclusively to the class of Westmoreland and Cumberland statesmen – just, independent, upright; not given to much speaking; kind-hearted, but not demonstrative; disliking change, and new ways, and new people; sensible and shrewd; each household self-contained, and its members having little curiosity as to their neighbours, with whom they rarely met for any social intercourse, save at the stated times of sheep-shearing and Christmas; having a certain kind of sober pleasure in amassing money, which occasionally made them miserable (as they call miserly people up in the north) in their old age; reading no light or ephemeral literature; but the grave, solid books brought round by the pedlars (such as the 'Paradise Lost' and 'Regained,' 'The Death of Abel,' 'The Spiritual Quixote,' and 'The Pilgrim's Progress')* were to be found in nearly every house: the men occasionally going off laking, *i.e.* playing, *i.e.* drinking for days together, and having to be hunted up by anxious wives, who dared not leave their husbands to the chances of the wild precipitous roads, but walked miles and miles, lantern in hand, in the dead of night, to discover and guide the solemnly-drunken husband home; who had a dreadful headache the next day, and the day after that came forth as grave, and sober, and virtuous-looking as if there were no such things as malt and spirituous liquors in the world; and who were seldom reminded of their misdoings by their wives, to whom such occasional outbreaks were as things of course, when once the immediate anxiety produced by them was over. Such were – such are – the characteristics of a class now passing away from the face of the land, as their compeers, the yeomen, have done before them. Of such was William Dixon. He was a shrewd, clever farmer, in his day and generation, when shrewdness was rather shown in the breeding and rearing of sheep and cattle than in the cultivation of land. Owing to this character of his, statesmen from a distance, from beyond Kendal, or from Borrowdale, of greater wealth than he, would send their sons to be farm-servants for a year or two with him, in order to learn some of

his methods before setting up on land of their own. When
Susan, his daughter, was about seventeen, one Michael Hurst
was farm-servant at Yew Nook. He worked with the master,
and lived with the family, and was in all respects treated as an
equal, except in the field. His father was a wealthy statesman
at Wythburne, up beyond Grasmere; and through Michael's
servitude the families had become acquainted, and the Dixons
went over to the High Beck sheep-shearing, and the Hursts
came down by Red Bank and Loughrig Tarn and across the
Oxenfell when there was the Christmas-tide feasting at Yew
Nook. The fathers strolled round the fields together, examined
cattle and sheep, and looked knowing over each other's
horses. The mothers inspected the dairies and household
arrangements, each openly admiring the plans of the other,
but secretly preferring their own. Both fathers and mothers
cast a glance from time to time at Michael and Susan, who
were thinking of nothing less than farm or dairy, but whose
unspoken attachment was, in all ways, so suitable and natural
a thing that each parent rejoiced over it, although with
characteristic reserve it was never spoken about – not even
between husband and wife.

Susan had been a strong, independent, healthy girl; a clever
help to her mother, and a spirited companion to her father;
more of a man in her (as he often said) than her delicate little
brother ever would have. He was his mother's darling, although she loved Susan well. There was no positive engagement between Michael and Susan – I doubt whether even
plain words of love had been spoken; when one winter-time
Margaret Dixon was seized with inflammation consequent
upon a neglected cold. She had always been strong and notable,
and had been too busy to attend to the earliest symptoms of
illness. It would go off, she said to the woman who helped in
the kitchen; or if she did not feel better when they had got the
hams and bacon out of hand, she would take some herb-tea
and nurse up a bit. But Death could not wait till the hams and
bacon were cured: he came on with rapid strides, and shooting
arrows of portentous agony. Susan had never seen illness –
never knew how much she loved her mother till now, when
she felt a dreadful, instinctive certainty that she was losing her.
Her mind was thronged with recollections of the many times

she had slighted her mother's wishes; her heart was full of the echoes of careless and angry replies that she had spoken. What would she not now give to have opportunities of service and obedience, and trials of her patience and love, for that dear mother who lay gasping in torture! And yet Susan had been a good girl and an affectionate daughter.

The sharp pain went off, and delicious ease came on; yet still her mother sunk. In the midst of this languid peace she was dying. She motioned Susan to her bedside, for she could only whisper; and then, while the father was out of the room, she spoke as much to the eager, hungering eyes of her daughter by the motion of her lips, as by the slow, feeble sounds of her voice.

'Susan, lass, thou must not fret. It is God's will, and thou wilt have a deal to do. Keep father straight if thou canst; and if he goes out Ulverstone ways, see that thou meet him before he gets to the Old Quarry. It's a dree bit* for a man who has had a drop. As for lile Will' – here the poor woman's face began to work and her fingers to move nervously as they lay on the bed-quilt – 'lile Will will miss me most of all. Father's often vexed with him because he's not a quick, strong lad; he is not, my poor lile chap. And father thinks he's saucy, because he cannot always stomach oat-cake and porridge. There's better than three pound in th' old black teapot on the top shelf of the cupboard. Just keep a piece of loaf-bread by you, Susan dear, for Will to come to when he's not taken his breakfast. I have, may be, spoilt him; but there'll be no one to spoil him now.'

She began to cry a low, feeble cry, and covered up her face that Susan might not see her. That dear face! those precious moments while yet the eyes could look out with love and intelligence. Susan laid her head down close by her mother's ear.

'Mother, I'll take tent* of Will. Mother, do you hear? He shall not want ought I can give or get for him, least of all the kind words which you had ever ready for us both. Bless you! bless you! my own mother.'

'Thou'lt promise me that, Susan, wilt thou? I can die easy if thou'lt take charge of him. But he's hardly like other folk; he tries father at times, though I think father'll be tender of him when I'm gone, for my sake. And, Susan, there's one thing more. I never spoke on it for fear of the bairn being called a tell-tale, but I just comforted him up. He vexes Michael at times, and Michael has struck him before now. I did not want to make a stir; but he's not strong, and a word from thee, Susan, will go a long way with Michael.'

Susan was as red now as she had been pale before; it was the first time that her influence over Michael had been openly acknowledged by a third person, and a flash of joy came athwart the solemn sadness of the moment. Her mother had spoken too much, and now came on the miserable faintness. She never spoke again coherently; but when her children and her husband stood by her bedside, she took lile Will's hand and put it into Susan's, and looked at her with imploring eyes. Susan clasped her arms round Will, and leaned her head upon his curly little one, and vowed within herself to be as a mother to him.

Henceforward she was all in all to her brother. She was a more spirited and amusing companion to him than his mother had been, from her greater activity, and perhaps, also, from her originality of character, which often prompted her to perform her habitual actions in some new and racy manner. She was tender to lile Will when she was prompt and sharp with everybody else – with Michael most of all; for somehow the girl felt that, unprotected by her mother, she must keep up her own dignity, and not allow her lover to see how strong a hold he had upon her heart. He called her hard and cruel, and left her so; and she smiled softly to herself, when his back was turned, to think how little he guessed how deeply he was loved. For Susan was merely comely and fine-looking; Michael was strikingly handsome, admired by all the girls for miles round, and quite enough of a country coxcomb to know it and plume himself accordingly. He was the second son of his father; the eldest would have High Beck farm, of course, but there was a good penny in the Kendal bank in store for Michael. When harvest was over, he went to Chapel Langdale to learn to dance; and at night, in his merry moods, he would do his steps on the flag-floor of the Yew Nook kitchen, to the secret admiration of Susan, who had never learned dancing, but who flouted him perpetually, even while she admired, in accordance with the rule she seemed to have made for herself about keeping him at a distance so long as he lived under the same roof with her. One evening he sulked at some saucy remark of hers; he sitting in the chimney-corner with his arms on his knees, and his head bent forwards, lazily gazing into the wood-fire on the hearth, and luxuriating in rest after a hard day's labour; she sitting among the geraniums on the long, low window-seat, trying to catch the last slanting rays of the autumnal light to enable her to finish stitching a shirt-collar for Will, who lounged full length on the flags at the other side of the hearth to Michael, poking the burning wood from time to time with a long hazel-stick to bring out the leap of glittering sparks.

'And if you can dance a threesome reel, what good does it do ye?' asked Susan, looking askance at Michael, who had just been vaunting his proficiency. 'Does it help you plough, or reap, or even climb the rocks to take a raven's nest? If I were a man, I'd be ashamed to give in to such softness.'

'If you were a man, you'd be glad to do anything which made the pretty girls stand round and admire.'

'As they do to you, eh! Ho, Michael, that would not be my way o' being a man!'

'What would then?' asked he, after a pause, during which he had expected in vain that she would go on with her sentence. No answer.

'I should not like you as a man, Susy; you'd be too hard and headstrong.'

'Am I hard and headstrong?' asked she, with as indifferent a tone as she could assume, but which yet had a touch of pique in it. His quick ear detected the inflexion.

'No, Susy! You're wilful at times, and that's right enough. I don't like a girl without spirit. There's a mighty pretty girl comes to the dancing-class; but she is all milk and water. Her eyes never flash like yours when you're put out; why, I can see them flame across the kitchen like a cat's in the dark. Now, if you were a man, I should feel queer before those looks of yours; as it is, I rather like them, because – '

'Because what?' asked she, looking up and perceiving that he had stolen close up to her.

'Because I can make all right in this way,' said he, kissing her suddenly.

'Can you?' said she, wrenching herself out of his grasp and panting, half with rage. 'Take that, by way of proof that making right is none so easy.' And she boxed his ears pretty sharply. He went back to his seat discomfited and out of temper. She could no longer see to look, even if her face had not burnt and her eyes dazzled, but she did not choose to move her seat, so she still preserved her stooping attitude and pretended to go on sewing.

'Eleanor Hebthwaite may be milk-and-water,' muttered he, 'but – Confound thee, lad! what art doing?' exclaimed Michael, as a great piece of burning wood was cast into his face by an unlucky poke of Will's. 'Thou great lounging, clumsy chap, I'll teach thee better!' and with one or two good, round kicks he sent the lad whimpering away into the back-kitchen. When he had a little recovered himself from his passion, he saw Susan standing before him, her face looking strange and almost ghastly by the reversed position of the shadows, arising from the fire-light shining upwards right under it.

'I tell thee what, Michael,' said she, 'that lad's motherless, but not friendless.'

'His own father leathers him, and why should not I, when he's given me such a burn on my face?' said Michael, putting up his hand to his cheek as if in pain.

'His father's his father, and there is nought more to be said. But if he did burn thee, it was by accident, and not o' purpose, as thou kicked him; it's a mercy if his ribs are not broken.'

'He howls loud enough, I'm sure. I might ha' kicked many a lad twice as hard and they'd ne'er ha' said ought but "damn ye;" but yon lad must needs cry out like a stuck pig if one touches him,' replied Michael, sullenly.

Susan went back to the window-seat, and looked absently out of the window at the drifting clouds for a minute or two, while her eyes filled with tears. Then she got up and made for the outer door which led into the back-kitchen. Before she reached it, however, she heard a low voice, whose music made her thrill, say, –

'Susan, Susan!'

Her heart melted within her, but it seemed like treachery to her poor boy, like faithlessness to her dead mother, to turn to her lover while the tears which he had caused to flow were yet unwiped on Will's cheeks. So she seemed to take no heed, but passed into the darkness, and, guided by the sobs, she found her way to where Willie sat crouched among disused tubs and churns.

'Come out wi' me, lad;' and they went into the orchard, where the fruit-trees were bare of leaves, but ghastly in their tattered covering of grey moss: and the soughing November wind came with long sweeps over the fells till it rattled among the crackling boughs, underneath which the brother and sister sate in the dark; he in her lap, and she hushing his head against her shoulder.

'Thou should'st na' play wi' fire. It's a naughty trick. Thou'lt suffer for it in worse ways nor this before thou'st done, I'm afeared. I should ha' hit thee twice as lungeous* kicks as Mike, if I'd been in his place. He did na' hurt thee, I am sure,' she assumed, half as a question.

'Yes! but he did. He turned me quite sick.' And he let his head fall languidly down on his sister's breast.

'Come lad! come lad!' said she, anxiously. 'Be a man. It was not much that I saw. Why, when first the red cow came, she kicked me far harder for offering to milk her before her legs were tied. See thee! here's a peppermint-drop, and I'll make thee a pasty to-night; only don't give way so, for it hurts me sore to think that Michael has done thee any harm, my pretty.'

Willie roused himself up, and put back the wet and ruffled hair from his heated face; and he and Susan rose up, and hand-in-hand went towards the house, walking slowly and quietly except for a kind of sob which Willie could not repress. Susan took him to the pump and washed his tear-stained face, till she thought she had obliterated all traces of the recent disturbance, arranging his curls for him, and then she kissed him tenderly, and led him in, hoping to find Michael in the kitchen, and make all straight between them. But the blaze had dropped down into darkness; the wood was a heap of grey ashes in which the sparks ran hither and thither; but, even in the groping darkness, Susan knew by the sinking at her heart that Michael was not there. She threw another brand on the hearth and lighted the candle, and sate down to her work in silence. Willie cowered on his stool by the side of the fire, eyeing his sister from time to time, and sorry and oppressed, he knew not why, by the sight of her grave, almost stern face. No one came. They two were in the house alone. The old woman who helped Susan with the household work had gone out for the night to some friend's dwelling. William Dixon, the father, was up on the fells seeing after his sheep. Susan had no heart to prepare the evening meal.

'Susy, darling, are you angry with me?' said Willie, in his little piping, gentle voice. He had stolen up to his sister's side. 'I won't never play with fire again; and I'll not cry if Michael does kick me. Only don't look so like dead mother – don't – don't – please don't!' he exclaimed, hiding his face on her shoulder.

'I'm not angry, Willie,' said she. 'Don't be feared on me. You want your supper, and you shall have it; and don't you be feared on Michael. He shall give reason for every hair of your head that he touches – he shall.'

When William Dixon came home, he found Susan and Willie sitting together, hand-in-hand, and apparently pretty cheerful. He bade them go to bed, for that he would sit up for Michael; and the next morning, when Susan came down, she found that Michael had started an hour before with the cart for lime. It was a long day's work; Susan knew it would be late, perhaps later than on the preceding night, before he returned – at any rate, past her usual bed-time; and on no account would she stop up a minute beyond that hour in the kitchen, whatever she might do in her bed-room. Here she sate and watched till past midnight; and when she saw him coming up the brow with the carts, she knew full well, even in that faint moonlight, that his gait was the gait of a man in liquor. But though she was annoyed and mortified to find in what way he had chosen to forget her, the fact did not disgust or shock her as it would have done many a girl, even at that day, who had not been brought up as Susan had, among a class who considered it no crime, but rather a mark of spirit, in a man to get drunk occasionally. Nevertheless, she chose to hold herself very high all the next day when Michael was, perforce, obliged to give up any attempt to do heavy work, and hung about the out-buildings and farm in a very disconsolate and sickly state. Willie had far more pity on him than Susan.

Before evening, Willie and he were fast, and on his side, ostentatious friends. Willie rode the horses down to water; Willie helped him to chop wood. Susan sate gloomily at her work, hearing an indistinct but cheerful conversation going on in the shippon, while the cows were being milked. She almost felt irritated with her little brother, as if he were a traitor, and had gone over to the enemy in the very battle that she was fighting in his cause. She was alone with no one to speak to, while they prattled on, regardless if she were glad or sorry.

Soon Willie burst in. 'Susan! Susan! come with me; I've something so pretty to show you. Round the corner of the barn – run! run!' (He was dragging her along, half reluctant, half desirous of some change in that weary day.) Round the corner of the barn; and caught hold of by Michael, who stood there awaiting her.

'O Willie!' cried she, 'you naughty boy. There is nothing pretty – what have you brought me here for? Let me go; I won't be held.'

'Only one word. Nay, if you wish it so much, you may go,' said Michael, suddenly loosing his hold as she struggled. But now she was free, she only drew off a step or two, murmuring something about Willie.

'You are going, then?' said Michael, with seeming sadness. 'You won't hear me say a word of what is in my heart.'

'How can I tell whether it is what I should like to hear?' replied she, still drawing back.

'That is just what I want you to tell me; I want you to hear it, and then to tell me whether you like it or not.'

'Well, you may speak,' replied she, turning her back, and beginning to plait the hem of her apron.

He came close to her ear.

'I'm sorry I hurt Willie the other night. He has forgiven me. Can you?'

'You hurt him very badly,' she replied. 'But you are right to be sorry. I forgive you.'

'Stop, stop!' said he, laying his hand upon her arm. 'There is something more I've got to say. I want you to be my – what is it they call it, Susan?'

'I don't know,' said she, half-laughing, but trying to get

away with all her might now; and she was a strong girl, but she could not manage it.

'You do. My – what is it I want you to be?'

'I tell you I don't know, and you had best be quiet, and just let me go in, or I shall think you're as bad now as you were last night.'

'And how did you know what I was last night? It was past twelve when I came home. Were you watching? Ah, Susan! be my wife, and you shall never have to watch for a drunken husband. If I were your husband, I would come straight home, and count every minute an hour till I saw your bonny face. Now you know what I want you to be. I ask you to be my wife. Will you, my own dear Susan?'

She did not speak for some time. Then she only said, 'Ask father.' And now she was really off like a lapwing round the corner of the barn, and up in her own little room, crying with all her might, before the triumphant smile had left Michael's face where he stood.

The 'Ask father' was a mere form to be gone through. Old Daniel Hurst and William Dixon had talked over what they could respectively give their children long before this; and that was the parental way of arranging such matters. When the probable amount of worldly gear that he could give his child had been named by each father, the young folk, as they said, might take their own time in coming to the point which the old men, with the prescience of experience, saw that they were drifting to; no need to hurry them, for they were both young, and Michael, though active enough, was too thoughtless, old Daniel said, to be trusted with the entire management of a farm. Meanwhile, his father would look about him, and see after all the farms that were to be let.

Michael had a shrewd notion of this preliminary understanding between the fathers, and so felt less daunted than he might otherwise have done at making the application for Susan's hand. It was all right, there was not an obstacle; only a deal of good advice, which the lover thought might have as well been spared, and which it must be confessed he did not much attend to, although he assented to every part of it. Then Susan was called down stairs, and slowly came dropping into view down the steps which led from the two family apartments into the house-place. She tried to look composed and quiet, but it could not be done. She stood side by side with her lover, with her head drooping, her cheeks burning, not daring to look up or move, while her father made the newly-betrothed a somewhat formal address in which he gave his consent, and many a piece of worldly wisdom beside. Susan listened as well as she could for the beating of her heart; but when her father solemnly and sadly referred to his own lost wife, she could keep from sobbing no longer; but throwing her apron over her face, she sate down on the bench by the dresser, and fairly gave way to pent-up tears. Oh, how strangely sweet to be comforted as she was comforted, by tender caress, and many a low-whispered promise of love! Her father sate by the fire, thinking of the days that were gone; Willie was still out of doors; but Susan and Michael felt no one's presence or absence – they only knew they were together as betrothed husband and wife.

In a week, or two, they were formally told of the arrangements to be made in their favour. A small farm in the neighbourhood happened to fall vacant; and Michael's father offered to take it for him, and be responsible for the rent for the first year, while William Dixon was to contribute a certain amount of stock, and both fathers were to help towards the furnishing of the house. Susan received all this information in a quiet, indifferent way; she did not care much for any of these preparations, which were to hurry her through the happy hours; she cared least of all for the money amount of dowry and of substance. It jarred on her to be made the confidant of occasional slight repinings of Michael's, as one by one his future father-in-law set aside a beast or a pig for Susan's portion, which were not always the best animals of their kind upon the farm. But he also complained of his own father's stinginess, which somewhat, though not much, alleviated Susan's dislike to being awakened out of her pure dream of love to the consideration of worldly wealth.

But in the midst of all this bustle, Willie moped and pined. He had the same chord of delicacy running through his mind that made his body feeble and weak. He kept out of the way, and was apparently occupied in whittling and carving uncouth heads on hazel-sticks in an out-house. But he positively avoided Michael, and shrunk away even from Susan. She was too much occupied to notice this at first. Michael pointed it out to her, saying, with a laugh, –

'Look at Willie! he might be a cast-off lover and jealous of me, he looks so dark and downcast at me.' Michael spoke this jest out loud, and Willie burst into tears, and ran out of the house.

'Let me go. Let me go!' said Susan (for her lover's arm was round her waist). 'I must go to him if he's fretting. I promised mother I would!' She pulled herself away, and went in search of the boy. She sought in byre and barn, through the orchard, where indeed in this leafless winter-time there was no great concealment, up into the room where the wool was usually stored in the later summer, and at last she found him, sitting at bay, like some hunted creature, up behind the wood-stack.

'What are ye gone for, lad, and me seeking you everywhere?' asked she, breathless.

'I did not know you would seek me. I've been away many a time, and no one has cared to seek me,' said he, crying afresh.

'Nonsense,' replied Susan, 'don't be so foolish, ye little good-for-nought.' But she crept up to him in the hole he had made underneath the great, brown sheafs of wood, and squeezed herself down by him. 'What for should folk seek after you, when you get away from them whenever you can?' asked she.

'They don't want me to stay. Nobody wants me. If I go with father, he says I hinder more than I help. You used to like to have me with you. But now, you've taken up with Michael, and you'd rather I was away; and I can just bide away; but I cannot stand Michael jeering at me. He's got you to love him and that might serve him.'

'But I love you, too, dearly, lad!' said she, putting her arm round his neck.

'Which on us do you like best?' said he, wistfully, after a little pause, putting her arm away, so that he might look in her face, and see if she spoke truth.

She went very red.

'You should not ask such questions. They are not fit for you to ask, nor for me to answer.'

'But mother bade you love me!' said he, plaintively.

'And so I do. And so I ever will do. Lover nor husband shall come betwixt thee and me, lad – ne'er a one of them. That I promise thee (as I promised mother before), in the sight of God and with her hearkening now, if ever she can hearken to earthly word again. Only I cannot abide to have thee fretting, just because my heart is large enough for two.'

'And thou'lt love me always?'

'Always, and ever. And the more – the more thou'lt love Michael,' said she, dropping her voice.

'I'll try,' said the boy, sighing, for he remembered many a harsh word and blow of which his sister knew nothing. She would have risen up to go away, but he held her tight, for here and now she was all his own, and he did not know when such a time might come again. So the two sate crouched up and silent, till they heard the horn blowing at the field-gate, which was the summons home to any wanderers belonging to the farm, and at this hour of the evening, signified that supper was ready. Then the two went in.

CHAPTER II

SUSAN and Michael were to be married in April. He had already gone to take possession of his new farm, three or four miles away from Yew Nook – but that is neighbouring, according to the acceptation of the word in that thinly-populated district, – when William Dixon fell ill. He came home one evening, complaining of head-ache and pains in his limbs, but seemed to loathe the posset which Susan prepared for him; the treacle-posset which was the homely country remedy against an incipient cold. He took to his bed with a sensation of exceeding weariness, and an odd, unusual looking-back to the days of his youth, when he was a lad living with his parents, in this very house.

The next morning he had forgotten all his life since then, and did not know his own children; crying, like a newly-weaned baby, for his mother to come and soothe away his terrible pain. The doctor from Coniston said it was the typhus-fever, and warned Susan of its infectious character, and shook his head over his patient. There were no friends near to come and share her anxiety; only good, kind old Peggy, who was faithfulness itself, and one or two labourers' wives, who would fain have helped her, had not their hands been tied by their responsibility to their own families. But, somehow, Susan neither feared nor flagged. As for fear, indeed, she had no time to give way to it, for every energy of both body and mind was required. Besides, the young have had too little experience of the danger of infection to dread it much. She did indeed wish, from time to time, that Michael had been at home to have taken Willie over to his father's at High Beck; but then, again, the lad was docile and useful to her, and his fecklessness in many things might make him be harshly treated by strangers; so, perhaps, it was as well that Michael was away at Appleby fair, or even beyond that – gone into Yorkshire after horses.

Her father grew worse; and the doctor insisted on sending over a nurse from Coniston. Not a professed nurse – Coniston could not have supported such a one; but a widow who was ready to go where the doctor sent her for the sake of the payment. When she came, Susan suddenly gave way; she was felled by the fever herself, and lay unconscious for long weeks. Her consciousness returned to her one spring afternoon; early spring; April, – her wedding-month. There was a little fire burning in the small corner-grate, and the flickering of the blaze was enough for her to notice in her weak state. She felt that there was some one sitting on the window-side of her bed, behind the curtain, but she did not care to know who it was; it was even too great a trouble for her languid mind to consider who it was likely to be. She would rather shut her eyes, and melt off again into the gentle luxury of sleep. The next time she wakened, the Coniston nurse perceived her movement, and made her a cup of tea, which she drank with eager relish; but still they did not speak, and once more Susan lay motionless – not asleep, but strangely, pleasantly conscious of all the small chamber and household sounds; the fall of a cinder on the hearth, the fitful singing of the half-empty kettle, the cattle tramping out to field again after they had been milked, the aged step on the creaking stair – old Peggy's, as she knew. It came to her door; it stopped; the person outside listened for a moment, and then lifted the wooden latch, and looked in. The watcher by the bedside arose, and went to her. Susan would have been glad to see Peggy's face once more, but was far too weak to turn, so she lay and listened.

'How is she?' whispered one trembling, aged voice.

'Better,' replied the other. 'She's been awake, and had a cup of tea. She'll do now.'

'Has she asked after him?'

'Hush! No; she has not spoken a word.'

'Poor lass! poor lass!'

The door was shut. A weak feeling of sorrow and self-pity came over Susan. What was wrong? Whom had she loved? And dawning, dawning, slowly rose the sun of her former life, and all particulars were made distinct to her. She felt that some sorrow was coming to her, and cried over it before she knew what it was, or had strength enough to ask. In the dead of night, – and she had never slept again, – she softly called to the watcher, and asked, –

'Who?'

'Who what?' replied the woman, with a conscious affright, ill-veiled by a poor assumption of ease. 'Lie still, there's a darling, and go to sleep. Sleep's better for you than all the doctor's stuff.'

'Who?' repeated Susan. 'Something is wrong. Who?'

'Oh, dear!' said the woman. 'There's nothing wrong. Willie has taken the turn, and is doing nicely.'

'Father?'

'Well! he's all right now,' she answered, looking another way, as if seeking for something.

'Then it's Michael! Oh, me! oh, me!' She set up a succession of weak, plaintive, hysterical cries before the nurse could pacify her, by declaring that Michael had been at the house not three hours before to ask after her, and looked as well and as hearty as ever man did.

'And you heard of no harm to him since?' inquired Susan.

'Bless the lass, no, for sure! I've ne'er heard his name named since I saw him go out of the yard as stout a man as ever trod shoe-leather.'

It was well, as the nurse said afterwards to Peggy, that Susan had been so easily pacified by the equivocating answer in respect to her father. If she had pressed the questions home in his case as she did in Michael's, she would have learnt that he was dead and buried more than a month before. It was well, too, that in her weak state of convalescence (which lasted long after this first day of consciousness) her perceptions were not sharp enough to observe the sad change that had taken place in Willie. His bodily strength returned, his appetite was something enormous, but his eyes wandered continually; his regard could not be arrested; his speech became slow, impeded, and incoherent. People began to say, that the fever had taken away the little wit Willie Dixon had ever possessed, and that they feared that he would end in being a 'natural', as they call an idiot in the Dales.

The habitual affection and obedience to Susan lasted longer than any other feeling that the boy had had previous to his illness; and, perhaps, this made her be the last to perceive what every one else had long anticipated. She felt the awakening rude when it did come. It was in this wise: –

One June evening, she sate out of doors under the yew-tree, knitting. She was pale still from her recent illness; and her languor, joined to the fact of her black dress, made her look more than usually interesting. She was no longer the buoyant self-sufficient Susan, equal to every occasion. The men were bringing in the cows to be milked, and Michael was about in the yard giving orders and directions with somewhat the air of a master, for the farm belonged of right to Willie, and Susan had succeeded to the guardianship of her brother. Michael and she were to be married as soon as she was strong enough – so, perhaps, his authoritative manner was justified; but the labourers did not like it, although they said little. They remembered him a stripling on the farm, knowing far less than they did, and often glad to shelter his ignorance of all agricultural matters behind their superior knowledge. They would have taken orders from Susan with far more willingness; nay! Willie himself might have commanded them; and from the old hereditary feeling toward the owners of land, they would have obeyed him with far greater cordiality than they now showed to Michael. But Susan was tired with even three rounds of knitting, and seemed not to notice, or to care, how things went on around her; and Willie – poor Willie! – there he stood lounging against the door-sill, enormously grown and developed, to be sure, but with restless eyes and ever-open mouth, and every now and then setting up a strange kind of howling cry, and then smiling vacantly to himself at the sound he had made. As the two old labourers passed him, they looked at each other ominously, and shook their heads.

'Willie, darling,' said Susan, 'don't make that noise – it makes my head ache.'

She spoke feebly, and Willie did not seem to hear; at any rate, he continued his howl from time to time.

'Hold thy noise, wilt 'a?' said Michael, roughly, as he passed near him, and threatening him with his fist. Susan's back was turned to the pair. The expression of Willie's face changed from vacancy to fear, and he came shambling up to Susan, and put her arm round him, and, as if protected by that shelter, he began making faces at Michael. Susan saw what was going on, and, as if now first struck by the strangeness of her brother's manner, she looked anxiously at Michael for an explanation. Michael was irritated at Willie's defiance of him, and did not mince the matter.

'It's just that the fever has left him silly – he never was as wise as other folk, and now I doubt if he will ever get right.'

Susan did not speak, but she went very pale, and her lip quivered. She looked long and wistfully at Willie's face, as he watched the motion of the ducks in the great stable-pool. He laughed softly to himself every now and then.

'Willie likes to see the ducks go overhead,' said Susan, instinctively adopting the form of speech she would have used to a young child.

'Willie, boo! Willie, boo!' he replied, clapping his hands, and avoiding her eye.

'Speak properly, Willie,' said Susan, making a strong effort at self-control, and trying to arrest his attention.

'You know who I am – tell me my name!' She grasped his arm almost painfully tight to make him attend. Now he looked at her, and, for an instant, a gleam of recognition quivered over his face; but the exertion was evidently painful, and he began to cry at the vainness of the effort to recall her name. He hid his face upon her shoulder with the old affectionate trick of manner. She put him gently away, and went into the house into her own little bedroom. She locked the door, and did not reply at all to Michael's calls for her, hardly spoke to old Peggy, who tried to tempt her out to receive some homely sympathy, and through the open casement there still came the idiotic sound of 'Willie, boo! Willie, boo!'

CHAPTER III

AFTER the stun of the blow came the realisation of the consequences. Susan would sit for hours trying patiently to recall and piece together fragments of recollection and consciousness in her brother's mind. She would let him go and pursue some senseless bit of play, and wait until she could catch his eye or his attention again, when she would resume her self-imposed task. Michael complained that she never had a word for him, or a minute of time to spend with him now; but she only said she must try, while there was yet a chance, to bring back her brother's lost wits. As for marriage in this state of uncertainty, she had no heart to think of it. Then Michael stormed, and absented himself for two or three days; but it was of no use. When he came back, he saw that she had been crying till her eyes were all swollen up, and he gathered from Peggy's scoldings (which she did not spare him) that Susan had eaten nothing since he went away. But she was as inflexible as ever.

'Not just yet. Only not just yet. And don't say again that I do not love you,' said she, suddenly hiding herself in his arms.

And so matters went on through August. The crop of oats was gathered in; the wheat-field was not ready as yet, when one fine day Michael drove up in a borrowed shandry,* and offered to take Willie a ride. His manner, when Susan asked him where he was going to, was rather confused; but the answer was straight and clear enough.

'He had business in Ambleside. He would never lose sight of the lad, and have him back safe and sound before dark.' So Susan let him go.

Before night they were at home again: Willie in high delight at a little rattling, paper windmill that Michael had bought for him in the street, and striving to imitate this new sound with perpetual buzzings. Michael, too, looked pleased.

Susan knew the look, although afterwards she remembered that he had tried to veil it from her, and had assumed a grave appearance of sorrow whenever he caught her eye. He put up his horse; for, although he had three miles further to go, the moon was up – the bonny harvest-moon – and he did not care how late he had to drive on such a road by such a light. After the supper which Susan had prepared for the travellers was over, Peggy went up-stairs to see Willie safe in bed; for he had to have the same care taken of him that a little child of four years old requires.

Michael drew near to Susan.

'Susan,' said he, 'I took Will to see Dr Preston, at Kendal. He's the first doctor in the county. I thought it were better for us – for you – to know at once what chance there were for him.'

'Well!' said Susan, looking eagerly up. She saw the same strange glance of satisfaction, the same instant change to apparent regret and pain. 'What did he say?' said she. 'Speak! can't you?'

'He said he would never get better of his weakness.'

'Never!'

'No; never. It's a long word, and hard to bear. And there's worse to come, dearest. The doctor thinks he will get badder from year to year. And he said, if he was us – you – he would send him off in time to Lancaster Asylum. They've ways there both of keeping such people in order and making them happy. I only tell you what he said,' continued he, seeing the gathering storm in her face.

'There was no harm in his saying it,' she replied, with great self-constraint, forcing herself to speak coldly instead of angrily. 'Folk is welcome to their opinions.'

They sate silent for a minute or two, her breast heaving with suppressed feeling.

'He's counted a very clever man,' said Michael, at length.

'He may be. He's none of my clever men, nor am I going to be guided by him, whatever he may think. And I don't thank them that went and took my poor lad to have such harsh notions formed about him. If I'd been there, I could have called out the sense that is in him.'

'Well! I'll not say more to-night, Susan. You're not taking

it rightly, and I'd best be gone, and leave you to think it over. I'll not deny they are hard words to hear, but there's sense in them, as I take it; and I reckon you'll have to come to 'em. Anyhow, it's a bad way of thanking me for my pains, and I don't take it well in you, Susan,' said he, getting up, as if offended.

'Michael, I'm beside myself with sorrow. Don't blame me, if I speak sharp. He and me is the only ones, you see. And mother did so charge me to have a care of him! And this is what he's come to, poor lile chap!' She began to cry, and Michael to comfort her with caresses.

'Don't,' said she. 'It's no use trying to make me forget poor Willie is a natural. I could hate myself for being happy with you, even for just a little minute. Go away, and leave me to face it out.'

'And you'll think it over, Susan, and remember what the doctor says?'

'I can't forget it,' said she. She meant she could not forget what the doctor had said about the hopelessness of her brother's case; Michael had referred to the plan of sending Willie away to an asylum, or madhouse, as they were called in that day and place. The idea had been gathering force in Michael's mind for some time; he had talked it over with his father, and secretly rejoiced over the possession of the farm and land which would then be his in fact, if not in law, by right of his wife. He had always considered the good penny* her father could give her in his catalogue of Susan's charms and attractions. But of late he had grown to esteem her as the heiress of Yew Nook. He, too, should have land like his brother – land to possess, to cultivate, to make profit from, to bequeath. For some time he had wondered that Susan had been so much absorbed in Willie's present, that she had never seemed to look forward to his future, state. Michael had long felt the boy to be a trouble; but of late he had absolutely loathed him. His gibbering, his uncouth gestures, his loose, shambling gait, all irritated Michael inexpressibly. He did not come near the Yew Nook for a couple of days. He thought that he would leave her time to become anxious to see him and reconciled to his plan. They were strange, lonely days to Susan. They were the first she had spent face to face with the sorrows that had turned her from a girl into a woman; for hitherto Michael had never let twenty-four hours pass by without coming to see her since she had had the fever. Now that he was absent, it seemed as though some cause of irritation was removed from Will, who was much more gentle and tractable than he had been for many weeks. Susan thought that she observed him making efforts at her bidding, and there was something piteous in the way in which he crept up to her, and looked wistfully in her face, as if asking her to restore him the faculties that he felt to be wanting.

'I never will let thee go, lad. Never! There's no knowing where they would take thee to, or what they would do with thee. As it says in the Bible, "Nought but death shall part thee and me!" '*

The country-side was full, in those days, of stories of the brutal treatment offered to the insane; stories that were, in fact, but too well founded, and the truth of one of which only would have been a sufficient reason for the strong prejudice existing against all such places. Each succeeding hour that Susan passed, alone, or with the poor affectionate lad for her sole companion, served to deepen her solemn resolution never to part with him. So, when Michael came, he was annoyed and surprised by the calm way in which she spoke, as if following Dr Preston's advice was utterly and entirely out of the question. He had expected nothing less than a consent, reluctant it might be, but still a consent; and he was extremely irritated. He could have repressed his anger, but he chose rather to give way to it; thinking that he could thus best work upon Susan's affection, so as to gain his point. But, somehow, he over-reached himself; and now he was astonished in his turn at the passion of indignation that she burst into.

'Thou wilt not bide in the same house with him, say'st thou? There's no need for thy biding, as far as I can tell. There's solemn reason why I should bide with my own flesh and blood, and keep to the word I pledged my mother on her death-bed; but, as for thee, there's no tie that I know on to keep thee fro' going to America or Botany Bay this very night, if that were thy inclination. I will have no more of your threats to make me send my bairn away. If thou marry me, thou'lt help me to take charge of Willie. If thou doesn't choose to marry me on those terms – why! I can snap my fingers at thee, never fear. I'm not so far gone in love as that. But I will not have thee, if thou say'st in such a hectoring way that Willie must go out of the house – and the house his own too – before thou'lt set foot in it. Willie bides here, and I bide with him.'

'Thou hast maybe spoken a word too much,' said Michael, pale with rage. 'If I am free, as thou say'st, to go to Canada or Botany Bay, I reckon I'm free to live where I like, and that will not be with a natural who may turn into a madman some day, for aught I know. Choose between him and me, Susy, for I swear to thee, thou shan't have both.'

'I have chosen,' said Susan, now perfectly composed and still. 'Whatever comes of it, I bide with Willie.'

'Very well,' replied Michael, trying to assume an equal composure of manner. 'Then I'll wish you a very good night.' He went out of the house-door, half-expecting to be called back again; but, instead, he heard a hasty step inside, and a bolt drawn.

'Whew!' said he to himself, 'I think I must leave my lady alone for a week or two, and give her time to come to her senses. She'll not find it so easy as she thinks to let me go.'

So he went past the kitchen-window in nonchalant style, and was not seen again at Yew Nook for some weeks. How did he pass the time? For the first day or two, he was unusually cross with all things and people that came athwart him. Then wheat-harvest began, and he was busy, and exultant about his heavy crop. Then a man came from a distance to bid for the lease of his farm, which, by his father's advice, had been offered for sale, as he himself was so soon likely to remove to the Yew Nook. He had so little idea that Susan really would remain firm to her determination, that he at once began to haggle with the man who came after his farm, showed him the crop just got in, and managed skilfully enough to make a good bargain for himself. Of course, the bargain had to be sealed at the public-house; and the companions he met with there soon became friends enough to tempt him into Langdale, where again he met with Eleanor Hebthwaite.

How did Susan pass the time? For the first day or so, she was too angry and offended to cry. She went about her household duties in a quick, sharp, jerking, yet absent way; shrinking one moment from Will, overwhelming him with remorseful caresses the next. The third day of Michael's absence, she had the relief of a good fit of crying; and after that, she grew softer and more tender; she felt how harshly she had spoken to him, and remembered how angry she had been. She made excuses for him. 'It was no wonder,' she said to herself, 'that he had been vexed with her; and no wonder he would not give in, when she had never tried to speak gently or to reason with him. She was to blame, and she would tell him so, and tell him once again all that her mother had bade her be to Willie, and all the horrible stories she had heard about madhouses, and he would be on her side at once.'

And so she watched for his coming, intending to apologise as soon as ever she saw him. She hurried over her household work, in order to sit quietly at her sewing, and hear the first distant sound of his well-known step or whistle. But even the sound of her flying needle seemed too loud – perhaps she was losing an exquisite instant of anticipation; so she stopped sewing, and looked longingly out through the geranium leaves, in order that her eye might catch the first stir of the branches in the wood-path by which he generally came. Now and then a bird might spring out of the covert; otherwise the leaves were heavily still in the sultry weather of early autumn. Then she would take up her sewing, and, with a spasm of resolution, she would determine that a certain task should be fulfilled before she would again allow herself the poignant luxury of expectation. Sick at heart was she when the evening closed in, and the chances of that day diminished. Yet she stayed up longer than usual, thinking that if he were coming – if he were only passing along the distant road – the sight of a light in the window might encourage him to make his appearance even at that late hour, while seeing the house all darkened and shut up might quench any such intention.

Very sick and weary at heart, she went to bed; too desolate and despairing to cry, or make any moan. But in the morning hope came afresh. Another day – another chance! And so it went on for weeks. Peggy understood her young mistress's sorrow full well, and respected it by her silence on the subject. Willie seemed happier now that the irritation of Michael's presence was removed; for the poor idiot had a sort of antipathy to Michael, which was a kind of heart's echo to the repugnance in which the latter held him. Altogether, just at this time, Willie was the happiest of the three.

As Susan went into Coniston, to sell her butter, one Saturday, some inconsiderate person told her that she had seen Michael Hurst the night before. I said inconsiderate, but I might rather have said unobservant; for any one who had spent half-an-hour in Susan Dixon's company might have seen that she disliked having any reference made to the subjects nearest her heart, were they joyous or grievous. Now she went a little paler than usual (and she had never recovered her colour since she had had the fever), and tried to keep silence. But an irrepressible pang forced out the question, –

'Where?'

'At Thomas Applethwaite's, in Langdale. They had a kind of harvest-home, and he were there among the young folk, very thick wi' Nelly Hebthwaite, old Thomas's niece. Thou'lt have to look after him a bit, Susan!'

She neither smiled nor sighed. The neighbour who had been speaking to her was struck with the grey stillness of her face. Susan herself felt how well her self-command was obeyed by every little muscle, and said to herself in her Spartan manner, 'I can bear it without either wincing or blenching.' She went home early, at a tearing, passionate pace, trampling and breaking through all obstacles of briar or bush. Willie was moping in her absence – hanging listlessly on the farm-yard gate to watch for her. When he saw her, he set up one of his strange, inarticulate cries, of which she was now learning the meaning, and came towards her with his loose, galloping run, head and limbs all shaking and wagging with pleasant excitement. Suddenly she turned from him, and burst into tears. She sate down on a stone by the wayside, not a hundred yards from home, and buried her face in her hands, and gave way to a passion of pent-up sorrow; so terrible and full of agony were her low cries, that the idiot stood by her, aghast and silent. All his joy gone for the time, but not, like her joy, turned into ashes. Some thought struck him. Yes! the sight of her woe made him think, great as the exertion was. He ran, and stumbled, and shambled home, buzzing with his lips all the time. She never missed him. He came back in a trice, bringing with him his cherished paper windmill, bought on that fatal day when Michael had taken him into Kendal to have his doom of perpetual idiotcy pronounced. He thrust it into Susan's face, her hands, her lap, regardless of the injury his frail plaything thereby received. He leapt before her to think how he had cured all heart-sorrow, buzzing louder than ever. Susan looked up at him, and that glance of her sad eyes sobered him. He began to whimper, he knew not why: and she now, comforter in her turn, tried to soothe him by twirling his windmill. But it was broken; it made no noise; it would not go round. This seemed to afflict Susan more than him. She tried to make it right, although she saw the task was hopeless; and while she did so, the tears rained down unheeded from her bent head on the paper toy.

'It won't do,' said she, at last. 'It will never do again.' And, somehow, she took the accident and her words as omens of the love that was broken, and that she feared could never be pieced together more. She rose up and took Willie's hand, and the two went slowly in to the house.

To her surprise, Michael Hurst sate in the house-place. House-place is a sort of better kitchen, where no cookery is done, but which is reserved for state occasions. Michael had gone in there because he was accompanied by his only sister, a woman older than himself, who was well married beyond Keswick, and who now came for the first time to make acquaintance with Susan. Michael had primed his sister with his wishes regarding Will, and the position in which he stood with Susan; and arriving at Yew Nook in the absence of the latter, he had not scrupled to conduct his sister into the guest-room, as he held Mrs Gale's worldly position in respect and admiration, and therefore wished her to be favourably impressed with all the signs of property which he was beginning to consider as Susan's greatest charms. He had secretly said to himself, that if Eleanor Hebthwaite and Susan Dixon were equal in point of riches, he would sooner have Eleanor by far. He had begun to consider Susan as a termagant; and when he thought of his intercourse with her, recollections of her somewhat warm and hasty temper came far more readily to his mind than any remembrance of her generous, loving nature.

And now she stood face to face with him; her eyes tear-swollen, her garments dusty, and here and there torn in consequence of her rapid progress through the bushy by-paths. She did not make a favourable impression on the well-clad Mrs Gale, dressed in her best silk gown, and therefore unusually susceptible to the appearance of another. Nor were Susan's manners gracious or cordial. How could they be, when she remembered what had passed between Michael and herself the last time they met? For her penitence had faded away under the daily disappointment of these last weary weeks.

But she was hospitable in substance. She bade Peggy hurry on the kettle, and busied herself among the tea-cups, thankful that the presence of Mrs Gale, as a stranger, would prevent the immediate recurrence to the one subject which she felt must be present in Michael's mind as well as in her own. But Mrs Gale was withheld by no such feelings of delicacy. She had come ready-primed with the case, and had undertaken to bring the girl to reason. There was no time to be lost. It had been prearranged between the brother and sister that he was to stroll out into the farm-yard before his sister introduced the subject; but she was so confident in the success of her arguments, that she must needs have the triumph of a victory as soon as possible; and, accordingly, she brought a hail-storm of good reasons to bear upon Susan. Susan did not reply for a long time; she was so indignant at this intermeddling of a stranger in the deep family sorrow and shame. Mrs Gale thought she was gaining the day, and urged her arguments more pitilessly. Even Michael winced for Susan, and wondered at her silence. He shrunk out of sight, and into the shadow, hoping that his sister might prevail, but annoyed at the hard way in which she kept putting the case.

Suddenly Susan turned round from the occupation she had pretended to be engaged in, and said to him in a low voice, which yet not only vibrated itself, but made its hearers thrill through all their obtuseness, –

'Michael Hurst! does your sister speak truth, think you?'

Both women looked at him for his answer; Mrs Gale without anxiety, for had she not said the very words they had spoken together before; had she not used the very arguments that he himself had suggested? Susan, on the contrary, looked to his answer as settling her doom for life; and in the gloom of her eyes you might have read more despair than hope.

He shuffled his position. He shuffled in his words.

'What is it you ask? My sister has said many things.'

'I ask you,' said Susan, trying to give a crystal clearness both to her expressions and her pronunciation, 'if, knowing as you do how Will is afflicted, you will help me to take that charge of him which I promised my mother on her death-bed that I would do; and which means, that I shall keep him always with me, and do all in my power to make his life happy. If you will do this, I will be your wife; if not, I remain unwed.'

'But he may get dangerous; he can be but a trouble; his being here is a pain to you, Susan, not a pleasure.'

'I ask you for either yes or no,' said she, a little contempt at his evading her question mingling with her tone. He perceived it, and it nettled him.

'And I have told you. I answered your question the last time I was here. I said I would ne'er keep house with an idiot; no more I will. So now you've gotten your answer.'

'I have,' said Susan. And she sighed deeply.

'Come, now,' said Mrs Gale, encouraged by the sigh; 'one would think you don't love Michael, Susan, to be so stubborn in yielding to what I'm sure would be best for the lad.'

'Oh! she does not care for me,' said Michael. 'I don't believe she ever did.'

'Don't I? Haven't I?' asked Susan, her eyes blazing out fire. She left the room directly, and sent Peggy in to make the tea; and catching at Will, who was lounging about in the kitchen, she went up-stairs with him and bolted herself in, straining the boy to her heart, and keeping almost breathless, lest any noise she made might cause him to break out into the howls and sounds which she could not bear that those below should hear.

A knock at the door. It was Peggy.

'He wants for to see you, to wish you good-bye.'

'I cannot come. Oh, Peggy, send them away.'

It was her only cry for sympathy; and the old servant understood it. She sent them away, somehow; not politely, as I have been given to understand.

'Good go with them,' said Peggy, as she grimly watched

their retreating figures. 'We're rid of bad rubbish, anyhow.' And she turned into the house, with the intention of making ready some refreshment for Susan, after her hard day at the market, and her harder evening. But in the kitchen, to which she passed through the empty house-place, making a face of contemptuous dislike at the used tea-cups and fragments of a meal yet standing there, she found Susan, with her sleeves tucked up and her working apron on, busied in preparing to make clap-bread, one of the hardest and hottest domestic tasks of a Daleswoman. She looked up, and first met and then avoided Peggy's eye; it was too full of sympathy. Her own cheeks were flushed, and her own eyes were dry and burning.

'Where's the board, Peggy? We need clap-bread; and, I reckon, I've time to get through with it to-night.' Her voice had a sharp, dry tone in it, and her motions a jerking angularity about them.

Peggy said nothing, but fetched her all that she needed. Susan beat her cakes thin with vehement force. As she stooped over them, regardless even of the task in which she seemed so much occupied, she was surprised by a touch on her mouth of something – what she did not see at first. It was a cup of tea, delicately sweetened and cooled, and held to her lips, when exactly ready, by the faithful old woman. Susan held it off a hand's breadth, and looked into Peggy's eyes, while her own filled with the strange relief of tears.

'Lass!' said Peggy, solemnly, 'thou hast done well. It is not long to bide, and then the end will come.'

'But you are very old, Peggy,' said Susan, quivering.

'It is but a day sin' I were young,' replied Peggy; but she stopped the conversation by again pushing the cup with gentle force to Susan's dry and thirsty lips. When she had drunken she fell again to her labour, Peggy heating the hearth, and doing all that she knew would be required, but never speaking another word. Willie basked close to the fire, enjoying the animal luxury of warmth, for the autumn evenings were beginning to be chilly. It was one o'clock before they thought of going to bed on that memorable night.

CHAPTER IV

THE vehemence with which Susan Dixon threw herself into occupation could not last for ever. Times of languor and remembrance would come – times when she recurred with a passionate yearning to bygone days, the recollection of which was so vivid and delicious, that it seemed as though it were the reality, and the present bleak bareness the dream. She smiled anew at the magical sweetness of some touch or tone which in memory she felt and heard, and drank the delicious cup of poison, although at the very time she knew what the consequences of racking pain would be.

'This time, last year,' thought she, 'we went nutting together – this very day last year; just such a day as to-day. Purple and gold were the lights on the hills; the leaves were just turning brown; here and there on the sunny slopes the stubble-fields looked tawny; down in a cleft of yon purple slate-rock the beck fell like a silver glancing thread; all just as it is to-day. And he climbed the slender, swaying nut-trees, and bent the branches for me to gather; or made a passage through the hazel copses, from time to time claiming a toll. Who could have thought he loved me so little? – who? – who?'

Or, as the evening closed in, she would allow herself to imagine that she heard his coming step, just that she might recall the feeling of exquisite delight which had passed by without the due and passionate relish at the time. Then she would wonder how she could have had strength, the cruel, self-piercing strength, to say what she had done; to stab herself with that stern resolution, of which the scar would remain till her dying day. It might have been right; but, as she sickened, she wished she had not instinctively chosen the right. How luxurious a life haunted by no stern sense of duty must be! And many led this kind of life; why could not she? O, for one hour again of his sweet company! If he came now, she would agree to whatever he proposed.

It was a fever of the mind. She passed through it, and came out healthy, if weak. She was capable once more of taking pleasure in following an unseen guide through briar and brake.

She returned with tenfold affection to her protecting care of Willie. She acknowledged to herself that he was to be her all-in-all in life. She made him her constant companion. For his sake, as the real owner of Yew Nook, and she as his steward and guardian, she began that course of careful saving, and that love of acquisition, which afterwards gained for her the reputation of being miserly. She still thought that he might regain a scanty portion of sense – enough to require some simple pleasures and excitement, which would cost money. And money should not be wanting. Peggy rather assisted her in the formation of her parsimonious habits than otherwise; economy was the order of the district, and a certain degree of respectable avarice the characteristic of her age. Only Willie was never stinted nor hindered of anything that the two women thought could give him pleasure, for want of money.

There was one gratification which Susan felt was needed for the restoration of her mind to its more healthy state, after she had passed through the whirling fever, when duty was as nothing, and anarchy reigned; a gratification – that, somehow, was to be her last burst of unreasonableness; of which she knew and recognised pain as the sure consequence. She must see him once more, – herself unseen.

The week before the Christmas of this memorable year, she went out in the dusk of the early winter evening, wrapped close in shawl and cloak. She wore her dark shawl under her cloak, putting it over her head in lieu of a bonnet; for she knew that she might have to wait long in concealment. Then she tramped over the wet fell-path, shut in by misty rain for miles and miles, till she came to the place where he was lodging; a farm-house in Langdale, with a steep, stony lane leading up to it: this lane was entered by a gate out of the main road, and by the gate were a few bushes – thorns; but of them the leaves had fallen, and they offered no concealment: an old wreck of a yew-tree grew among them, however, and underneath that Susan cowered down, shrouding her face, of which the colour might betray her, with a corner of her shawl. Long did she wait; cold and cramped she became, too damp and stiff to change her posture readily. And after all, he might never come! But, she would wait till daylight, if need were; and she pulled out a crust, with which she had providently supplied herself. The rain had ceased, – a dull, still, brooding weather had succeeded; it was a night to hear distant sounds. She heard horses' hoofs striking and plashing in the stones, and in the pools of the road at her back. Two horses; not well-ridden, or evenly guided, as she could tell.

Michael Hurst and a companion drew near; not tipsy, but not sober. They stopped at the gate to bid each other a maudlin farewell. Michael stooped forward to catch the latch with the hook of the stick which he carried; he dropped the stick, and it fell with one end close to Susan, – indeed, with the slightest change of posture she could have opened the gate for him. He swore a great oath, and struck his horse with his closed fist, as if that animal had been to blame; then he dismounted, opened the gate, and fumbled about for his stick. When he had found it (Susan had touched the other end) his first use of it was to flog his horse well, and she had much ado to avoid its kicks and plunges. Then, still swearing, he staggered up the lane, for it was evident he was not sober enough to remount.

By daylight Susan was back and at her daily labours at Yew Nook. When the spring came, Michael Hurst was married to Eleanor Hebthwaite. Others, too, were married, and christenings made their firesides merry and glad; or they travelled, and came back after long years with many wondrous tales. More rarely, perhaps, a Dalesman changed his dwelling. But to all households more change came than to Yew Nook. There the seasons came round with monotonous sameness; or, if they brought mutation, it was of a slow, and decaying, and depressing kind. Old Peggy died. Her silent sympathy, concealed under much roughness, was a loss to Susan Dixon. Susan was not yet thirty when this happened, but she looked a middle-aged, not to say an elderly woman. People affirmed that she had never recovered her complexion since that fever, a dozen years ago, which killed her father, and left Will Dixon an idiot. But besides her grey sallowness, the lines in her face were strong, and deep, and hard. The movements of her eyeballs were slow and heavy; the wrinkles at the corners of her mouth and eyes were planted firm and sure; not an ounce of unnecessary flesh was there on her bones – every muscle started strong and ready for use. She needed all this bodily strength, to a degree that no human creature, now Peggy was dead, knew of: for Willie had grown up large and strong in body, and, in general, docile enough in mind; but, every now and then, he became first moody, and then violent. These paroxysms lasted but a day or two; and it was Susan's anxious care to keep their very existence hidden and unknown. It is true, that occasional passers-by on that lonely road heard sounds at night of knocking about of furniture, blows, and cries, as of some tearing demon within the solitary farm-house; but these fits of violence usually occurred in the night: and whatever had been their consequence, Susan had tidied and redded up* all signs of aught unusual before the morning. For, above all, she dreaded lest some one might find out in what danger and peril she occasionally was, and might assume a right to take away her brother from her care. The one idea of taking charge of him had deepened and deepened with years. It was graven into her mind as the object for which she lived. The sacrifice she had made for this object only made it more precious to her. Besides, she separated the idea of the docile, affectionate, loutish, indolent Will, and kept it distinct from the terror which the demon that occasionally possessed him inspired her with. The one was her flesh and her blood, – the child of her dead mother; the other was some fiend who came to torture and convulse the creature she so loved. She believed that she fought her brother's battle in holding down those tearing hands, in binding whenever she could those uplifted restless arms prompt and prone to do mischief. All the time she sub-dued him with her cunning or her strength, she spoke to him in pitying murmurs, or abused the third person, the fiendish enemy, in no unmeasured tones. Towards morning the paroxysm was exhausted, and he would fall asleep, perhaps only to waken with evil and renewed vigour. But when he was laid down, she would sally out to taste the fresh air, and to work off her wild sorrow in cries and mutterings to herself. The early labourers saw her gestures at a distance, and thought her as crazed as the idiot-brother who made the neighbourhood a haunted place. But did any chance person call at Yew Nook later on in the day, he would find Susan Dixon cold, calm, collected; her manner curt, her wits keen.

Once this fit of violence lasted longer than usual. Susan's

strength both of mind and body was nearly worn out; she wrestled in prayer that somehow it might end before she, too, was driven mad; or, worse, might be obliged to give up life's aim, and consign Willie to a madhouse. From that moment of prayer (as she afterwards superstitiously thought) Willie calmed – and then he drooped – and then he sank – and, last of all, he died in reality from physical exhaustion.

But he was so gentle and tender as he lay on his dying bed; such strange, child-like gleams of returning intelligence came over his face, long after the power to make his dull, inarticulate sounds had departed, that Susan was attracted to him by a stronger tie than she had ever felt before. It was something to have even an idiot loving her with dumb, wistful, animal affection; something to have any creature looking at her with such beseeching eyes, imploring protection from the insidious enemy stealing on. And yet she knew that to him death was no enemy, but a true friend, restoring light and health to his poor clouded mind. It was to her that death was an enemy; to her, the survivor, when Willie died; there was no one to love her. Worse doom still, there was no one left on earth for her to love.

You now know why no wandering tourist could persuade her to receive him as a lodger; why no tired traveller could melt her heart to afford him rest and refreshment; why long habits of seclusion had given her a moroseness of manner, and how care for the interests of another had rendered her keen and miserly.

But there was a third act in the drama of her life.

CHAPTER V

IN spite of Peggy's prophecy that Susan's life should not seem long, it did seem wearisome and endless, as the years slowly uncoiled their monotonous circles. To be sure, she might have made change for herself, but she did not care to do it. It was, indeed, more than 'not caring', which merely implies a certain degree of *vis inertiae** to be subdued before an object can be attained, and that the object itself does not seem to be of sufficient importance to call out the requisite energy. On the contrary, Susan exerted herself to avoid change and variety. She had a morbid dread of new faces, which originated in her desire to keep poor dead Willie's state a profound secret. She had a contempt for new customs; and, indeed, her old ways prospered so well under her active hand and vigilant eye, that it was difficult to know how they could be improved upon. She was regularly present in Coniston market with the best butter and the earliest chickens of the season. Those were the common farm produce that every farmer's wife about had to sell; but Susan, after she had disposed of the more feminine articles, turned to on the man's side. A better judge of a horse or cow there was not in all the country round. Yorkshire itself might have attempted to jockey* her, and would have failed. Her corn was sound and clean; her potatoes well preserved to the latest spring. People began to talk of the hoards of money Susan Dixon must have laid up somewhere; and one young ne'er-do-weel of a farmer's son undertook to make love to the woman of forty, who looked fifty-five, if a day. He made up to her by opening a gate on the road-path home, as she was riding on a bare-backed horse, her purchase not an hour ago. She was off before him, refusing his civility; but the remounting was not so easy, and rather than fail she did not choose to attempt it. She walked, and he walked alongside, improving his opportunity, which, as he vainly thought, had been consciously granted to him. As they drew near Yew Nook, he ventured on some expression of a wish to keep company with her. His words were vague and clumsily arranged. Susan turned round and coolly asked him to explain himself. He took courage, as he thought of her reputed wealth, and expressed his wishes this second time pretty plainly. To his surprise, the reply she made was in a series of smart strokes across his shoulders, administered through the medium of a supple hazel-switch.

'Take that!' said she, almost breathless, 'to teach thee how thou darest make a fool of an honest woman old enough to be thy mother. If thou com'st a step nearer the house, there's a good horse-pool, and there's two stout fellows who'll like no better fun than ducking thee. Be off wi' thee.'

And she strode into her own premises, never looking round to see whether he obeyed her injunction or not.

Sometimes three or four years would pass over without her hearing Michael Hurst's name mentioned. She used to wonder at such times whether he were dead or alive. She would sit for hours by the dying embers of her fire on a winter's evening, trying to recall the scenes of her youth; trying to bring up living pictures of the faces she had then known – Michael's most especially. She thought it was possible, so long had been the lapse of years, that she might now pass by him in the street unknowing and unknown. His outward form she might not recognise, but himself she should feel in the thrill of her whole being. He could not pass her unawares.

What little she did hear about him, all testified a downward tendency. He drank – not at stated times when there was no other work to be done, but continually, whether it was seed-time or harvest. His children were all ill at the same time; then one died, while the others recovered, but were poor sickly things. No one dared to give Susan any direct intelligence of her former lover; many avoided all mention of his name in her presence; but a few spoke out either in indifference to, or ignorance of, those bygone days. Susan heard every word, every whisper, every sound that related to him. But her eye never changed, nor did a muscle of her face move.

Late one November night she sate over her fire; not a human being besides herself in the house; none but she had ever slept there since Willie's death. The farm-labourers had foddered the cattle and gone home hours before. There were crickets chirping all round the warm hearth-stones; there was the clock ticking with the peculiar beat Susan had known from her childhood, and which then and ever since she had oddly associated with the idea of a mother and child talking together, one loud tick, and quick – a feeble, sharp one following.

The day had been keen, and piercingly cold. The whole lift* of heaven seemed a dome of iron. Black and frost-bound was the earth under the cruel east wind. Now the wind had dropped, and as the darkness had gathered in, the weather-wise old labourers prophesied snow. The sounds in the air arose again, as Susan sate still and silent. They were of a different character to what they had been during the prevalence of the east wind. Then they had been shrill and piping; now they were like low distant growling; not unmusical, but strangely threatening. Susan went to the window, and drew aside the little curtain. The whole world was white – the air was blinded with the swift and heavy fall of snow. At present it came down straight, but Susan knew those distant sounds in the hollows and gulleys of the hills portended a driving wind and a more cruel storm. She thought of her sheep; were they all folded? the new-born calf, was it bedded well? Before the drifts were formed too deep for her to pass in and out – and by the morning she judged that they would be six or seven feet deep – she would go out and see after the comfort of her beasts. She took a lantern, and tied a shawl over her head, and went out into the open air. She had tenderly provided for all her animals, and was returning, when, borne on the blast as if some spirit-cry – for it seemed to come rather down from the skies than from any creature standing on earth's level – she heard a voice of agony; she could not distinguish words; it seemed rather as if some bird of prey was being caught in the whirl of the icy wind, and torn and tortured by its violence. Again! up high above! Susan put down her lantern, and shouted loud in return; it was an instinct, for if the creature were not human, which she had doubted but a moment before, what good could her responding cry do? And her cry was seized on by the tyrannous wind, and borne farther away in the opposite direction to that from which the call of agony had proceeded. Again she listened; no sound: then again it rang through space; and this time she was sure it was human. She turned into the house, and heaped turf and wood on the fire, which, careless of her own sensations, she had allowed to fade and almost die out. She put a new candle in her lantern; she changed her shawl for a maud, and leaving the door on latch, she sallied out. Just at the moment when her ear first encountered the weird noises of the storm, on issuing forth into the open air, she thought she heard the words, 'O God! O help!' They were a guide to her, if words they were, for they came straight from a rock not a quarter of a mile from Yew Nook, but only to be reached, on account of its pre-cipitous character, by a round-about path. Thither she steered, defying wind and snow; guided by here a thorn-tree, there an old, doddered* oak, which had not quite lost their identity

under the whelming mask of snow. Now and then she stopped
to listen; but never a word or sound heard she, till right from
where the copse-wood grew thick and tangled at the base of
the rock, round which she was winding, she heard a moan.
Into the brake – all snow in appearance – almost a plain of
snow looked on from the little eminence where she stood –
she plunged, breaking down the bush, stumbling, bruising
herself, fighting her way; her lantern held between her teeth,
and she herself using head as well as hands to butt away a
passage, at whatever cost of bodily injury. As she climbed or
staggered, owing to the unevenness of the snow-covered
ground, where the briars and weeds of years were tangled and
matted together, her foot felt something strangely soft and
yielding. She lowered her lantern; there lay a man, prone on
his face, nearly covered by the fast-falling flakes; he must have
fallen from the rock above, as, not knowing of the circuitous
path, he had tried to descend its steep, slippery face. Who
could tell? it was no time for thinking. Susan lifted him up
with her wiry strength; he gave no help – no sign of life; but
for all that he might be alive: he was still warm; she tied her
maud round him; she fastened the lantern to her apron-string;
she held him tight: half-carrying, half-dragging – what did a
few bruises signify to him, compared to dear life, to precious
life! She got him through the brake, and down the path.
There, for an instant, she stopped to take breath; but, as if
stung by the Furies, she pushed on again with almost superhuman strength. Clasping him round the waist, and leaning
his dead weight against the lintel of the door, she tried to
undo the latch; but now, just at this moment, a trembling
faintness came over her, and a fearful dread took possession of
her – that here, on the very threshold of her home, she might
be found dead, and buried under the snow, when the farm-
servants came in the morning. This terror stirred her up to one
more effort. Then she and her companion were in the warmth
of the quiet haven of that kitchen; she laid him on the settle,
and sank on the floor by his side. How long she remained in
this swoon she could not tell; not very long she judged by the
fire, which was still red and sullenly glowing when she came
to herself. She lighted the candle, and bent over her late
burden to ascertain if indeed he were dead. She stood long

gazing. The man lay dead. There could be no doubt about it. His filmy eyes glared at her, unshut. But Susan was not one to be affrighted by the stony aspect of death. It was not that; it was the bitter, woeful recognition of Michael Hurst!

She was convinced he was dead; but after a while she refused to believe in her conviction. She stripped off his wet outer-garments with trembling, hurried hands. She brought a blanket down from her own bed; she made up the fire. She swathed him in fresh, warm wrappings, and laid him on the flags before the fire, sitting herself at his head, and holding it in her lap, while she tenderly wiped his loose, wet hair, curly still, although its colour had changed from nut-brown to iron-grey since she had seen it last. From time to time she bent over the face afresh, sick, and fain to believe that the flicker of the fire-light was some slight convulsive motion. But the dim, staring eyes struck chill to her heart. At last she ceased her delicate, busy cares; but she still held the head softly, as if caressing it. She thought over all the possibilities and chances in the mingled yarn of their lives that might, by so slight a turn, have ended far otherwise. If her mother's cold had been early tended, so that the responsibility as to her brother's weal or woe had not fallen upon her; if the fever had not taken such rough, cruel hold on Will; nay, if Mrs Gale, that hard, worldly sister, had not accompanied him on his last visit to Yew Nook – his very last before this fatal, stormy night; if she had heard his cry, – cry uttered by those pale, dead lips with such wild, despairing agony, not yet three hours ago! – O! if she had but heard it sooner, he might have been saved before that blind, false step had precipitated him down the rock! In going over this weary chain of unrealised possibilities, Susan learnt the force of Peggy's words. Life was short, looking back upon it. It seemed but yesterday since all the love of her being had been poured out, and run to waste. The intervening years – the long monotonous years that had turned her into an old woman before her time – were but a dream.

The labourers coming in the dawn of the winter's day were surprised to see the fire-light through the low kitchen-window. They knocked, and hearing a moaning answer, they entered, fearing that something had befallen their mistress. For all explanation they got these words, –

'It is Michael Hurst. He was belated, and fell down the Raven's Crag. Where does Eleanor, his wife, live?'

How Michael Hurst got to Yew Nook no one but Susan ever knew. They thought he had dragged himself there, with some sore, internal bruise sapping away his minuted life. They could not have believed the superhuman exertion which had first sought him out, and then dragged him hither. Only Susan knew of that.

She gave him into the charge of her servants, and went out and saddled her horse. Where the wind had drifted the snow on one side, and the road was clear and bare, she rode, and rode fast; where the soft, deceitful heaps were massed up, she dismounted and led her steed, plunging in deep, with fierce energy, the pain at her heart urging her onwards with a sharp, digging spur.

The grey, solemn, winter's noon was more night-like than the depth of summer's night; dim-purple brooded the low skies over the white earth, as Susan rode up to what had been Michael Hurst's abode while living. It was a small farm-house, carelessly kept outside, slatternly tended within. The pretty Nelly Hebthwaite was pretty still; her delicate face had never suffered from any long-enduring feeling. If anything, its expression was that of plaintive sorrow; but the soft, light hair had scarcely a tinge of grey; the wood-rose tint of complexion yet remained, if not so brilliant as in youth; the straight nose, the small mouth were untouched by time. Susan felt the contrast even at that moment. She knew that her own skin was weather-beaten, furrowed, brown, – that her teeth were gone, and her hair grey and ragged. And yet she was not two years older than Nelly, – she had not been, in youth, when she took account of these things. Nelly stood wondering at the strange-enough horse-woman, who stopped and panted at the door, holding her horse's bridle, and refusing to enter.

'Where is Michael Hurst?' asked Susan, at last.

'Well, I can't rightly say. He should have been at home last night, but he was off, seeing after a public-house to be let at Ulverstone, for our farm does not answer, and we were thinking — '

'He did not come home last night?' said Susan, cutting short the story, and half-affirming, half-questioning, by way of letting in a ray of the awful light before she let it full in, in its consuming wrath.

'No! he'll be stopping somewhere out Ulverstone ways. I'm sure we've need of him at home, for I've no one but lile Tommy to help me tend the beasts. Things have not gone well with us, and we don't keep a servant now. But you're trembling all over, ma'am. You'd better come in, and take something warm, while your horse rests. That's the stable-door, to your left.'

Susan took her horse there; loosened his girths, and rubbed him down with a wisp of straw. Then she looked about her for hay; but the place was bare of food, and smelt damp and unused. She went to the house, thankful for the respite, and got some clap-bread, which she mashed up in a pailful of luke-warm water. Every moment was a respite, and yet every moment made her dread the more the task that lay before her. It would be longer than she thought at first. She took the saddle off, and hung about her horse, which seemed, somehow, more like a friend than anything else in the world. She laid her cheek against its neck, and rested there, before returning to the house for the last time.

Eleanor had brought down one of her own gowns, which hung on a chair against the fire, and had made her unknown visitor a cup of hot tea. Susan could hardly bear all these little attentions: they choked her, and yet she was so wet, so weak with fatigue and excitement, that she could neither resist by voice or by action. Two children stood awkwardly about, puzzled at the scene, and even Eleanor began to wish for some explanation of who her strange visitor was.

'You've, may-be, heard him speaking of me? I'm called Susan Dixon.'

Nelly coloured, and avoided meeting Susan's eye.

'I've heard other folk speak of you. He never named your name.'

This respect of silence came like balm to Susan: balm not felt or heeded at the time it was applied, but very grateful in its effects for all that.

'He is at my house,' continued Susan, determined not to stop or quaver in the operation – the pain which must be inflicted.

'At your house? Yew Nook?' questioned Eleanor, surprised. 'How came he there?' – half jealously. 'Did he take
shelter from the coming storm? Tell me, – there is something
– tell me, woman!'

'He took no shelter. Would to God he had!'

'O! would to God! would to God!' shrieked out Eleanor,
learning all from the woeful import of those dreary eyes. Her
cries thrilled through the house; the children's piping wailings
and passionate cries on 'Daddy! Daddy!' pierced into Susan's
very marrow. But she remained as still and tearless as the great
round face upon the clock.

At last, in a lull of crying, she said, – not exactly questioning – but as if partly to herself, –

'You loved him, then?'

'Loved him! he was my husband! He was the father of
three bonny bairns that lie dead in Grasmere Churchyard. I
wish you'd go, Susan Dixon, and let me weep without your
watching me! I wish you'd never come near the place.'

'Alas! alas! it would not have brought him to life. I would
have laid down my own to save his. My life has been so very
sad! No one would have cared if I had died. Alas! alas!'

The tone in which she said this was so utterly mournful and
despairing that it awed Nelly into quiet for a time. But by-
and-by she said, 'I would not turn a dog out to do it harm;
but the night is clear, and Tommy shall guide you to the Red
Cow. But, O! I want to be alone. If you'll come back to-
morrow, I'll be better, and I'll hear all, and thank you for
every kindness you have shown him, – and I do believe you've
showed him kindness, – though I don't know why.'

Susan moved heavily and strangely.

She said something – her words came thick and unintelligible. She had had a paralytic stroke since she had last
spoken. She could not go, even if she would. Nor did Eleanor,
when she became aware of the state of the case, wish her to
leave. She had her laid on her own bed, and weeping silently
all the while for her lost husband, she nursed Susan like a
sister. She did not know what her guest's worldly position
might be; and she might never be repaid. But she sold many a
little trifle to purchase such small comforts as Susan needed.
Susan, lying still and motionless, learnt much. It was not a

severe stroke; it might be the forerunner of others yet to
come, but at some distance of time. But for the present she
recovered, and regained much of her former health. On her
sick-bed she matured her plans. When she returned to Yew
Nook, she took Michael Hurst's widow and children with her
to live there, and fill up the haunted hearth with living forms
that should banish the ghosts.

And so it fell out that the latter days of Susan Dixon's life
were better than the former.

LOIS THE WITCH

*

In the year 1691, Lois Barclay stood on a little wooden pier steadying herself on the stable land, in much the same manner as, eight or nine weeks ago, she had tried to steady herself on the deck of the rocking ship which had carried her across from Old to New England. It seemed as strange now to be on solid earth as it had been, not long ago, to be rocked by the sea, both by day and by night; and the aspect of the land was equally strange. The forests which showed in the distance all round, and which, in truth, were not very far from the wooden houses forming the town of Boston, were of different shades of green, and different, too, in shape of outline to those which Lois Barclay knew well in her old home in Warwickshire. Her heart sank a little as she stood alone, waiting for the captain of the good ship Redemption, the kind, rough old sailor, who was her only known friend in this unknown continent. Captain Holdernesse was busy, however, as she saw, and it would probably be some time before he would be ready to attend to her; so Loise sate down on one of the casks that lay about, and wrapped her grey duffle cloak tight around her, and sheltered herself under her hood, as well as might be, from the piercing wind, which seemed to follow those whom it had tyrannized over at sea with a dogged wish of still tormenting them on land. Very patiently did Lois sit there, although she was weary, and shivering with cold; for the day was severe for May, and the Redemption, with store of necessaries and comforts for the Puritan colonists of New England, was the earliest ship that had ventured across the seas.

How could Lois help thinking of the past, and speculating on the future, as she sate on Boston pier, at this breathing-time of her life? In the dim sea-mist which she gazed upon with aching eyes (filled, against her will, with tears, from time to time), there rose the little village church of Barford (not three miles from Warwick – you may see it yet), where her father had preached ever since 1661, long before she was born. He and her mother both lay dead in Barford churchyard; and the old low grey church could hardly come before her vision without her seeing the old parsonage too, the cottage covered with Austrian roses, and yellow jessamine, where she had been born, sole child of parents already long past the prime of youth. She saw the path, not a hundred yards long, from the parsonage to the vestry door: that path which her father trod daily; for the vestry was his study, and the sanctum, where he pored over the ponderous tomes of the Fathers, and compared their precepts with those of the authorities of the Anglican Church of that day – the day of the later Stuarts; for Barford Parsonage at that time scarcely exceeded in size and dignity the cottages by which it was surrounded: it only contained three rooms on a floor, and was but two stories high. On the first, or ground floor, were the parlour, kitchen, and back or working kitchen; up-stairs, Mr and Mrs Barclay's room, that belonging to Lois, and the maid-servant's room. If a guest came, Lois left her own chamber, and shared old Clemence's bed. But those days were over. Never more should Lois see father or mother on earth; they slept, calm and still, in Barford churchyard, careless of what became of their orphan child, as far as earthly manifestations of care or love went. And Clemence lay there too, bound down in her grassy bed by withes of the briar-rose, which Lois had trained over those three precious graves before leaving England for ever.

There were some who would fain have kept her there; one who swore in his heart a great oath unto the Lord that he would seek her sooner or later, if she was still upon the earth. But he was the rich heir and only son of the Miller Lucy, whose mill stood by the Avon-side in the grassy Barford meadows, and his father looked higher for him than the penniless daughter of Parson Barclay (so low were clergymen esteemed in those days!); and the very suspicion of Hugh Lucy's attachment to Lois Barclay made his parents think it more prudent not to offer the orphan a home, although none other of the parishioners had the means, even if they had the will, to do so.

So Lois swallowed her tears down till the time came for crying, and acted upon her mother's words, –

'Lois, thy father is dead of this terrible fever, and I am dying. Nay, it is so, though I am easier from pain for these few hours, the Lord be praised! The cruel men of the Commonwealth have left thee very friendless. Thy father's only brother was shot down at Edgehill.* I, too, have a brother, though thou hast never heard me speak of him, for he was a schismatic;* and thy father and he had words, and he left for that new country beyond the seas, without ever saying farewell to us. But Ralph was a kind lad until he took up these new-fangled notions, and for the old days' sake he will take thee in, and love thee as a child, and place thee among his children. Blood is thicker than water. Write to him as soon as I am gone – for Lois, I am going – and I bless the Lord that has letten me join my husband again so soon.' Such was the selfishness of conjugal love; she thought little of Lois's desolation in comparison with her rejoicing over her speedy reunion with her dead husband! 'Write to thine uncle, Ralph Hickson, Salem, New England (put it down, child, on thy tablets), and say that I, Henrietta Barclay, charge him, for the sake of all he holds dear in heaven or on earth, – for his salvation's sake, as well as for the sake of the old home at Lester-bridge, – for the sake of the father and mother that gave us birth, as well as for the sake of the six little children who lie dead between him and me, – that he take thee into his home as if thou wert his own flesh and blood, as indeed thou art. He has a wife and children of his own, and no one need fear having thee, my Lois, my darling, my baby, among his household. Oh, Lois, would that thou wert dying with me! The thought of thee makes death sore!' Lois comforted her mother more than herself, poor child, by promises to obey her dying wishes to the letter, and by expressing hopes she dared not feel of her uncle's kindness.

'Promise me' – the dying woman's breath came harder and harder – 'that thou wilt go at once. The money our goods will bring – the letter thy father wrote to Captain Holdernesse, his old schoolfellow – thou knowest all I would say – my Lois, God bless thee!'

Solemnly did Lois promise; strictly she kept her word. It

was all the more easy, for Hugh Lucy met her, and told her, in one great burst of love, of his passionate attachment, his vehement struggles with his father, his impotence at present, his hopes and resolves for the future. And, intermingled with all this, came such outrageous threats and expressions of uncontrolled vehemence, that Lois felt that in Barford she must not linger to be a cause of desperate quarrel between father and son, while her absence might soften down matters, so that either the rich old miller might relent, or – and her heart ached to think of the other possibility – Hugh's love might cool, and the dear play-fellow of her childhood learn to forget. If not – if Hugh were to be trusted in one tithe of what he said – God might permit him to fulfil his resolve of coming to seek her out before many years were over. It was all in God's hands, and that was best, thought Lois Barclay.

She was roused out of her trance of recollections by Captain Holdernesse, who, having done all that was necessary in the way of orders and directions to his mate, now came up to her, and, praising her for her quiet patience, told her that he would now take her to the Widow Smith's, a decent kind of house, where he and many other sailors of the better order were in the habit of lodging, during their stay on the New England shores. Widow Smith, he said, had a parlour for herself and her daughters, in which Lois might sit, while he went about the business that, as he had told her, would detain him in Boston for a day or two, before he could accompany her to her uncle's at Salem. All this had been to a certain degree arranged on ship-board; but Captain Holdernesse, for want of anything else that he could think of to talk about, recapitulated it as he and Lois walked along. It was his way of showing sympathy with the emotion that made her grey eyes full of tears, as she started up from the pier at the sound of his voice. In his heart he said, 'Poor wench! poor wench! it's a strange land to her, and they are all strange folks, and, I reckon, she will be feeling desolate. I'll try and cheer her up.' So he talked on about hard facts, connected with the life that lay before her, until they reached Widow Smith's; and perhaps Lois was more brightened by this style of conversation, and the new ideas it presented to her, than she would have been by the tenderest woman's sympathy.

'They are a queer set, these New Englanders,' said Captain Holdernesse. 'They are rare chaps for praying; down on their knees at every turn of their life. Folk are none so busy in a new country, else they would have to pray like me, with a "Yo-hoy!" on each side of my prayer, and a rope cutting like fire through my hand. Yon pilot was for calling us all to thanksgiving for a good voyage, and lucky escape from the pirates; but I said I always put up my thanks on dry land, after I had got my ship into harbour. The French colonists, too, are vowing vengeance for the expedition against Canada, and the people here are raging like heathens – at least, as like as godly folk can be – for the loss of their charter. All that is the news the pilot told me; for, for all he wanted us to be thanksgiving instead of casting the lead, he was as down in the mouth as could be about the state of the country. But here we are at Widow Smith's! Now cheer up, and show the godly a pretty smiling Warwickshire lass!'

Anybody would have smiled at Widow Smith's greeting. She was a comely, motherly woman, dressed in the primmest fashion in vogue twenty years before, in England, among the class to which she belonged. But, somehow, her pleasant face gave the lie to her dress; were it as brown and sober-coloured as could be, folk remembered it bright and cheerful, because it was a part of Widow Smith herself.

She kissed Lois on both cheeks, before she rightly understood who the stranger maiden was, only because she was a stranger, and looked sad and forlorn; and then she kissed her again, because Captain Holdernesse commended her to the widow's good offices. And so she led Lois by the hand into her rough, substantial log-house, over the door of which hung a great bough of a tree,* by way of sign of entertainment for man and horse. Yet not all men were received by Widow Smith. To some she could be as cold and reserved as need be, deaf to all inquiries save one – where else they could find accommodation? To this question she would give a ready answer, and speed the unwelcome guest on his way. Widow Smith was guided in these matters by instinct: one glance at a man's face told her whether or not she chose to have him as an inmate of the same house as her daughters; and her promptness of decision in these matters gave her manner a kind of authority which no one liked to disobey, especially as she had stalwart neighbours within call to back her, if her assumed deafness in the first instance, and her voice and gesture in the second, were not enough to give the would-be guest his dismissal. Widow Smith chose her customers merely by their physical aspect; not one whit with regard to their apparent worldly circumstances. Those who had been staying at her house once, always came again, for she had the knack of making every one beneath her roof comfortable and at his ease. Her daughters, Prudence and Hester, had somewhat of their mother's gifts, but not in such perfection. They reasoned a little upon a stranger's appearance, instead of knowing at the first moment whether they liked him or no; they noticed the indications of his clothes, the quality and cut thereof, as telling somewhat of his station in society; they were more reserved, they hesitated more than their mother; they had not her prompt authority, her happy power. Their bread was not so light, their cream went sometimes to sleep when it should have been turning into butter, their hams were not always 'just like the hams of the old country', as their mother's were invariably pronounced to be; yet they were good, orderly, kindly girls, and rose and greeted Lois with a friendly shake of the hand, as their mother, with her arm round the stranger's waist, led her into the private room which she called her parlour. The aspect of this room was strange in the English girl's eyes. The logs of which the house was built, showed here and there through the mud plaster, although before both plaster and logs were hung the skins of many curious animals, – skins presented to the widow by many a trader of her acquaintance, just as her sailor guests brought her another description of gift – shells, strings of wampum-beads,* seabirds' eggs, and presents from the old country. The room was more like a small museum of natural history of these days than a parlour; and it had a strange, peculiar, but not unpleasant smell about it, neutralized in some degree by the smoke from the enormous trunk of pinewood which smouldered on the hearth.

The instant their mother told them that Captain Holdernesse was in the outer room, the girls began putting away their spinning-wheel and knitting-needles, and preparing for a meal of some kind; what meal, Lois, sitting there and unconsciously watching, could hardly tell. First, dough was set to rise for cakes; then came out of a corner cupboard – a present from England – an enormous square bottle of a cordial called Golden Wasser; next, a mill for grinding chocolate – a rare unusual treat anywhere at that time; then a great Cheshire cheese. Three venison steaks were cut ready for broiling, fat cold pork sliced up and treacle poured over it, a great pie something like a mince-pie, but which the daughters spoke of with honour as the 'punken-pie',* fresh and salt fish brandered,* oysters cooked in various ways. Lois wondered where would be the end of the provisions for hospitably receiving the strangers from the old country. At length everything was placed on the table, the hot food smoking; but all was cool, not to say cold, before Elder Hawkins (an old neighbour of much repute and standing, who had been invited in by Widow Smith to hear the news) had finished his grace, into which was embodied thanksgivings for the past and prayers for the future lives of every individual present, adapted to their several cases, as far as the elder could guess at them from appearances. This grace might not have ended so soon as it did, had it not been for the somewhat impatient drumming of his knife-handle on the table with which Captain Holdernesse accompanied the latter half of the elder's words.

When they first sate down to their meal, all were too hungry for much talking; but as their appetites diminished their curiosity increased, and there was much to be told and heard on both sides. With all the English intelligence Lois was, of course, well acquainted; but she listened with natural attention to all that was said about the new country, and the new people among whom she had come to live. Her father had been a Jacobite,* as the adherents of the Stuarts were beginning at this time to be called. His father, again, had been a follower of Archbishop Laud;* so Lois had hitherto heard little of the conversation, and seen little of the ways of the Puritans. Elder Hawkins was one of the strictest of the strict, and evidently his presence kept the two daughters of the house considerably in awe. But the widow herself was a privileged person; her known goodness of heart (the effects of which had been experienced by many) gave her the liberty of speech which was

tacitly denied to many, under penalty of being esteemed ungodly if they infringed certain conventional limits. And Captain
Holdernesse and his mate spoke out their minds, let who
would be present. So that on this first landing in New England,
Lois was, as it were, gently let down into the midst of the
Puritan peculiarities, and yet they were sufficient to make her
feel very lonely and strange.

The first subject of conversation was the present state of the
colony – Lois soon found out that, although at the beginning
she was not a little perplexed by the frequent reference to
names of places which she naturally associated with the old
country. Widow Smith was speaking: 'In county of Essex
the folk are ordered to keep four scouts, or companies of
minute-men; six persons in each company; to be on the look-
out for the wild Indians, who are for ever stirring about in the
woods, stealthy brutes as they are! I am sure, I got such a
fright the first harvest-time after I came over to New England,
I go on dreaming, now near twenty years after Lothrop's
business, of painted Indians, with their shaven scalps and their
war-streaks, lurking behind the trees, and coming nearer and
nearer with their noiseless steps.'

'Yes,' broke in one of her daughters; 'and, mother, don't
you remember how Hannah Benson told us how her husband
had cut down every tree near his house at Deerbrook, in order
that no one might come near him, under cover; and how one
evening she was a-sitting in the twilight, when all her family
were gone to bed, and her husband gone off to Plymouth on
business, and she saw a log of wood, just like a trunk of a
felled tree, lying in the shadow, and thought nothing of it, till,
on looking again a while after, she fancied it was come a bit
nearer to the house, and how her heart turned sick with fright,
and how she dared not stir at first, but shut her eyes while she
counted a hundred, and looked again, and the shadow was
deeper, but she could see that the log was nearer; so she ran
in and bolted the door, and went up to where her eldest lad
lay. It was Elijah, and he was but sixteen then; but he rose up
at his mother's words, and took his father's long duck-gun
down, and he tried the loading, and spoke for the first time to
put up a prayer that God would give his aim good guidance,
and went to a window that gave a view upon the side where

the log lay, and fired, and no one dared to look what came of it, but all the household read the Scriptures, and prayed the whole night long, till morning came and showed a long stream of blood lying on the grass close by the log, which the full sun-light showed to be no log at all, but just a Red Indian covered with bark, and painted most skilfully, with his war-knife by his side.'

All were breathless with listening, though to most the story, or such like it, were familiar. Then another took up the tale of horror, –

'And the pirates have been down at Marblehead since you were here, Captain Holdernesse. 'Twas only the last winter they landed, – French Papist pirates; and the people kept close within their houses, for they knew not what would come of it; and they dragged folk ashore. There was one woman among those folk – prisoners from some vessel, doubtless – and the pirates took them by force to the inland marsh; and the Marblehead folk kept still and quiet, every gun loaded, and every ear on the watch, for who knew but what the wild sea-robbers might take a turn on land next; and, in the dead of the night, they heard a woman's loud and pitiful outcry from the marsh, "Lord Jesu! have mercy on me! Save me from the power of man, O Lord Jesu!" And the blood of all who heard the cry ran cold with terror, till old Nance Hickson, who had been stone-deaf and bedridden for years, stood up in the midst of the folk all gathered together in her grandson's house, and said, that as they, the dwellers in Marblehead, had not had brave hearts or faith enough to go and succour the helpless, that cry of a dying woman should be in their ears, and in their children's ears, till the end of the world. And Nance dropped down dead as soon as she had made an end of speaking, and the pirates set sail from Marblehead at morning dawn; but the folk there hear the cry still, shrill and pitiful, from the waste marshes, "Lord Jesu! have mercy on me! Save me from the power of man, O Lord Jesu!"'

'And by token,' said Elder Hawkins's deep bass voice, speaking with the strong nasal twang of the Puritans (who, says Butler,

'Blasphemed custard through the nose'),*

'godly Mr Noyes ordained a fast at Marblehead, and preached a soul-stirring discourse on the words, "Inasmuch as ye did it not unto one of the least of these, my brethren, ye did it not unto me." But it has been borne in upon me at times, whether the whole vision of the pirates and the cry of the woman was not a device of Satan's to sift the Marblehead folk, and see what fruit their doctrine bore, and so to condemn them in the sight of the Lord. If it were so, the enemy had a great triumph, for assuredly it was no part of Christian men to leave a helpless woman unaided in her sore distress.'

'But, Elder,' said Widow Smith, 'it was no vision; they were real living men who went ashore, men who broke down branches and left their footmarks on the ground.'

'As for that matter, Satan hath many powers, and if it be the day when he is permitted to go about like a roaring lion,* he will not stick at trifles, but make his work complete. I tell you, many men are spiritual enemies in visible forms, permitted to roam about the waste places of the earth. I myself believe that these Red Indians are indeed the evil creatures of whom we read in Holy Scripture; and there is no doubt that they are in league with those abominable Papists, the French people in Canada. I have heard tell, that the French pay the Indians so much gold for every dozen scalps off Englishmen's heads.'

'Pretty cheerful talk this,' said Captain Holdernesse to Lois, perceiving her blanched cheek and terror-stricken mien. 'Thou art thinking that thou hadst better have stayed at Barford, I'll answer for it, wench. But the devil is not so black as he is painted.'

'Ho! there again!' said Elder Hawkins. 'The devil is painted, it hath been said so from old times; and are not these Indians painted, even like unto their father?'

'But is it all true?' asked Lois, aside, of Captain Holdernesse, letting the elder hold forth unheeded by her, though listened to, however, with the utmost reverence by the two daughters of the house.

'My wench,' said the old sailor, 'thou hast come to a country where there are many perils, both from land and from sea. The Indians hate the white men. Whether other white men' (meaning the French away to the north) 'have hounded on the savages, or whether the English have taken their lands and hunting-grounds without due recompense, and so raised the cruel vengeance of the wild creatures – who knows? But it is true that it is not safe to go far into the woods, for fear of the lurking painted savages; nor has it been safe to build a dwelling far from a settlement; and it takes a brave heart to make a journey from one town to another, and folk do say the Indian creatures rise up out of the very ground to waylay the English; and then others affirm they are all in league with Satan to affright the Christians out of the heathen country over which he has reigned so long. Then, again, the seashore is infested by pirates, the scum of all nations: they land, and plunder, and ravage, and burn, and destroy. Folk get affrighted of the real dangers, and in their fright imagine, perchance, dangers that are not. But who knows? Holy Scripture speaks of witches and wizards, and of the power of the Evil One in desert places; and even in the old country we have heard tell of those who have sold their souls for ever for the little power they get for a few years on earth.'

By this time the whole table was silent, listening to the captain; it was just one of those chance silences that sometimes occur, without any apparent reason, and often without any apparent consequence. But all present had reason, before many months had passed over, to remember the words which Lois spoke in answer, although her voice was low, and she only thought, in the interest of the moment, of being heard by her old friend the captain.

'They are fearful creatures, the witches! and yet I am sorry for the poor old women, whilst I dread them. We had one in Barford, when I was a little child. No one knew whence she came, but she settled herself down in a mud hut by the common side; and there she lived, she and her cat.' (At the mention of the cat, Elder Hawkins shook his head long and gloomily.) 'No one knew how she lived, if it were not on nettles and scraps of oatmeal and such-like food given her more for fear than for pity. She went double, always talking and muttering to herself. Folk said she snared birds and rabbits, in the thicket that came down to her hovel. How it came to pass I cannot say, but many a one fell sick in the village, and much cattle died one spring, when I was near four years old. I never heard much about it, for my father said it was ill talking about such things; I only know I got a sick fright one afternoon, when the maid had gone out for milk and had taken me with her, and we were passing a meadow where the Avon, circling, makes a deep round pool, and there was a crowd of folk, all still – and a still, breathless crowd makes the heart beat worse than a shouting, noisy one. They were all gazing towards the water, and the maid held me up in her arms to see the sight above the shoulders of the people; and I saw old Hannah in the water, her grey hair all streaming down her shoulders, and her face bloody and black with the stones and the mud they had been throwing at her, and her cat tied round her neck. I hid my face, I know, as soon as I saw the fearsome sight, for her eyes met mine as they were glaring with fury – poor, helpless, baited creature! – and she caught the sight of me, and cried out, "Parson's wench, parson's wench, yonder, in thy nurse's arms, thy dad hath never tried fr too save me, and none shall save thee when thou art brought up for a witch." Oh! the words rang in my ears, when I was dropping asleep, for years after. I used to dream that I was in that pond, all men hating me with their eyes because I was a witch; and, at times, her black cat used to seem living again, and say over those dreadful words.'

Lois stopped: the two daughters looked at her excitement with a kind of shrinking surprise, for the tears were in her eyes. Elder Hawkins shook his head, and muttered texts from Scripture; but cheerful Widow Smith, not liking the gloomy turn of the conversation, tried to give it a lighter cast by saying, 'And I don't doubt but what the parson's bonny lass has bewitched many a one since, with her dimples and her pleasant ways – eh, Captain Holdernesse? It's you must tell us tales of this young lass's doings in England.'

'Aye, aye,' said the captain, 'there's one under her charms in Warwickshire who will never get the better of it, I'm thinking.'

Elder Hawkins rose to speak; he stood leaning on his hands, which were placed on the table: 'Brethren,' said he, 'I must upbraid you if ye speak lightly; charms and witchcraft are evil things. I trust this maiden hath had nothing to do with them, even in thought. But my mind misgives me at her story. The hellish witch might have power from Satan to infect her mind, she being yet a child, with the deadly sin. Instead of vain talking, I call upon you all to join with me in prayer for this stranger in our land, that her heart may be purged from all iniquity. Let us pray.'

'Come, there's no harm in that,' said the captain; 'but, Elder Hawkins, when you are at work, just pray for us all, for I am afeard there be some of us need purging from iniquity a good deal more than Lois Barclay, and a prayer for a man never does mischief.'

Captain Holdernesse had business in Boston which detained him there for a couple of days, and during that time Lois remained with the Widow Smith, seeing what was to be seen of the new land that contained her future home. The letter of her dying mother was sent off to Salem, meanwhile, by a lad going thither, in order to prepare her Uncle Ralph Hickson for his niece's coming, as soon as Captain Holdernesse could find leisure to take her; for he considered her given into his own personal charge, until he could consign her to her uncle's care. When the time came for going to Salem, Lois felt very sad at leaving the kindly woman under whose roof she had been staying, and looked back as long as she could see anything of Widow Smith's dwelling. She was packed into a rough kind of country cart, which just held her and Captain Holdernesse, beside the driver. There was a basket of provisions under their feet, and behind them hung a bag of provender for the horse; for it was a good day's journey to Salem, and the road was reputed so dangerous that it was ill tarrying a minute longer than necessary for refreshment. English roads were bad enough at that period and for long after, but in America the way was simply the cleared ground of the forest; the stumps of the felled trees still remaining in the direct line, forming obstacles, which it required the most careful driving to avoid; and in the hollows, where the ground was swampy, the pulpy nature of it was obviated by logs of wood laid across the boggy part. The deep green forest, tangled into heavy darkness even thus early in the year, came within a few yards of the road all the way, though efforts were regularly made by the inhabitants of the neighbouring settlements to keep a certain space clear on each side, for fear of the lurking Indians, who might otherwise come upon them unawares. The cries of

strange birds, the unwonted colour of some of them, all
suggested to the imaginative or unaccustomed traveller the
idea of war-whoops and painted deadly enemies. But at last
they drew near to Salem, which rivalled Boston in size in
those days, and boasted the name of one or two streets,
although to an English eye they looked rather more like
irregularly built houses, clustered round the meeting-house,
or rather one of the meeting-houses, for a second was in process of building. The whole place was surrounded with two
circles of stockades; between the two were the gardens and
grazing ground for those who dreaded their cattle straying
into the woods, and the consequent danger of reclaiming
them.

The lad who drove them flogged his spent horse into a trot,
as they went through Salem to Ralph Hickson's house. It was
evening, the leisure time for the inhabitants, and their children
were at play before the houses. Lois was struck by the beauty
of one wee toddling child, and turned to look after it; it caught
its little foot in a stump of wood, and fell with a cry that
brought the mother out in affright. As she ran out her eye
caught Lois's anxious gaze, although the noise of the heavy
wheels drowned the sound of her words of inquiry as to the
nature of the hurt the child had received. Nor had Lois time
to think long upon the matter, for the instant after, the horse
was pulled up at the door of a good, square, substantial wooden
house, plastered over into a creamy white, perhaps as handsome a house as any in Salem; and there she was told by the
driver that her uncle, Ralph Hickson, lived. In the flurry of the
moment she did not notice, but Captain Holdernesse did, that
no one came out at the unwonted sound of wheels, to receive
and welcome her. She was lifted down by the old sailor, and
led into a large room, almost like the hall of some English
manor-house as to size. A tall, gaunt young man of three- or
four-and-twenty, sat on a bench by one of the windows,
reading a great folio by the fading light of day. He did not rise
when they came in, but looked at them with surprise, no gleam
of intelligence coming into his stern, dark face. There was no
woman in the house-place. Captain Holdernesse paused a
moment, and then said, –

'Is this house Ralph Hickson's?'

'It is,' said the young man, in a slow, deep voice. But he added no word further.

'This is his niece, Lois Barclay,' said the captain, taking the girl's arm, and pushing her forwards. The young man looked at her steadily and gravely for a minute; then rose, and carefully marking the page in the folio which hitherto had lain upon his knee, said, still in the same heavy, indifferent manner, 'I will call my mother, she will know.'

He opened a door which looked into a warm bright kitchen, ruddy with the light of the fire over which three women were apparently engaged in cooking something, while a fourth, an old Indian woman, of a greenish-brown colour, shrivelled up and bent with apparent age, moved backwards and forwards, evidently fetching the others the articles they required.

'Mother,' said the young man; and having arrested her attention, he pointed over his shoulder to the newly-arrived strangers, and returned to the study of his book, from time to time, however, furtively examining Lois from beneath his dark shaggy eyebrows.

A tall, largely made woman, past middle life, came in from the kitchen, and stood reconnoitring the strangers.

Captain Holdernesse spoke.

'This is Lois Barclay, Master Ralph Hickson's niece.'

'I know nothing of her,' said the mistress of the house, in a deep voice, almost as masculine as her son's.

'Master Hickson received his sister's letter, did he not? I sent it off myself by a lad named Elias Wellcome, who left Boston for this place yester morning.'

'Ralph Hickson has received no such letter. He lies bedridden in the chamber beyond. Any letters for him must come through my hands; wherefore I can affirm with certainty that no such letter has been delivered here. His sister Barclay, she that was Henrietta Hickson, and whose husband took the oaths to Charles Stuart,* and stuck by his living when all godly men left theirs – '

Lois, who had thought her heart was dead and cold a minute before at the ungracious reception she had met with, felt words come up into her mouth at the implied insult to her father, and spoke out, to her own and the captain's astonishment, –

'They might be godly men who left their churches on that day of which you speak, madam; but they alone were not the godly men, and no one has a right to limit true godliness for mere opinion's sake.'

'Well said, lass,' spoke out the captain, looking round upon her with a kind of admiring wonder, and patting her on the back.

Lois and her aunt gazed into each other's eyes unflinchingly, for a minute or two of silence; but the girl felt her colour coming and going, while the elder woman's never varied; and the eyes of the young maiden were filling fast with tears, while those of Grace Hickson kept on their stare, dry and un-wavering.

'Mother!' said the young man, rising up with a quicker motion than any one had yet used in this house, 'it is ill speaking of such matters when my cousin comes first among us. The Lord may give her grace hereafter, but she has travelled from Boston city to-day, and she and this seafaring man must need rest and food.'

He did not attend to see the effect of his words, but sate down again, and seemed to be absorbed in his book in an in-stant. Perhaps he knew that his word was law with his grim mother, for he had hardly ceased speaking before she had pointed to a wooden settle; and smoothing the lines on her countenance, she said, 'What Manasseh says is true. Sit down here, while I bid Faith and Nattee get food ready; and mean-while I will go tell my husband, that one who calls herself his sister's child is come over to pay him a visit.'

She went to the door leading into the kitchen, and gave some directions to the elder girl, whom Lois now knew to be the daughter of the house. Faith stood impassive, while her mother spoke, scarcely caring to look at the newly-arrived strangers. She was like her brother Manasseh in complexion, but had handsomer features, and large, mysterious-looking eyes, as Lois saw, when once she lifted them up, and took in, as it were, the aspect of the sea-captain and her cousin with one swift searching look. About the stiff, tall, angular mother, and the scarce more pliant figure of the daughter, a girl of twelve years old, or thereabouts, played all manner of impish antics, unheeded by them, as if it were her accustomed habit to peep about, now under their arms, now at this side, now at that, making grimaces all the while at Lois and Captain Holdernesse, who sate facing the door, weary, and somewhat disheartened by their reception. The captain pulled out tobacco, and began to chew it by way of consolation; but in a moment or two, his usual elasticity of spirit came to his rescue, and he said in a low voice to Lois, –

'That scoundrel Elias, I will give it him! If the letter had but been delivered, thou wouldst have had a different kind of welcome; but as soon as I have had some victuals, I will go out and find the lad, and bring back the letter, and that will make all right, my wench. Nay, don't be downhearted, for I cannot stand women's tears. Thou'rt just worn out with the shaking and the want of food.'

Lois brushed away her tears, and looking round to try and divert her thoughts by fixing them on present objects, she caught her cousin Manasseh's deep-set eyes furtively watching her. It was with no unfriendly gaze, yet it made Lois uncomfortable, particularly as he did not withdraw his looks after he must have seen that she observed him. She was glad when her aunt called her into an inner room to see her uncle, and she escaped from the steady observance of her gloomy, silent cousin.

Ralph Hickson was much older than his wife, and his illness made him look older still. He had never had the force of character that Grace, his spouse, possessed, and age and sickness had now rendered him almost childish at times. But his nature was affectionate, and stretching out his trembling arms from where he lay bedridden, he gave Lois an unhesitating welcome, never waiting for the confirmation of the missing letter before he acknowledged her to be his niece.

'Oh! 'tis kind in thee to come all across the sea to make acquaintance with thine uncle; kind in Sister Barclay to spare thee!'

Lois had to tell him that there was no one living to miss her at home in England; that in fact she had no home in England, no father nor mother left upon earth; and that she had been bidden by her mother's last words to seek him out, and ask him for a home. Her words came up, half choked from a heavy heart, and his dulled wits could not take their meaning in

without several repetitions; and then he cried like a child,
rather at his own loss of a sister, whom he had not seen for
more than twenty years, than at that of the orphan's standing
before him, trying hard not to cry, but to start bravely in this
new strange home. What most of all helped Lois in her self-
restraint was her aunt's unsympathetic look. Born and bred in
New England, Grace Hickson had a kind of jealous dislike to
her husband's English relations, which had increased since of
late years his weakened mind yearned after them, and he forgot the good reason he had had for his self-exile, and moaned
over the decision which had led to it as the great mistake of
his life. 'Come,' said she, 'it strikes me that, in all this sorrow
for the loss of one who died full of years, ye are forgetting in
Whose hands life and death are!'

True words, but ill-spoken at that time. Lois looked up at
her with a scarcely disguised indignation; which increased as
she heard the contemptuous tone in which her aunt went on
talking to Ralph Hickson, even while she was arranging his
bed with a regard to his greater comfort.

'One would think thou wert a godless man, by the moan
thou art always making over spilt milk; and truth is, thou art
but childish in thine old age. When we were wed, thou left all
things to the Lord; I would never have married thee else. Nay,
lass,' said she, catching the expression on Lois's face, 'thou
art never going to browbeat me with thine angry looks. I do
my duty as I read it, and there is never a man in Salem that dare
speak a word to Grace Hickson about either her works or her
faith. Godly Mr Cotton Mather hath said, that even he might
learn of me; and I would advise thee rather to humble thyself,
and see if the Lord may not convert thee from thy ways, since
he has sent thee to dwell, as it were, in Zion, where the
precious dew falls daily on Aaron's beard.'*

Lois felt ashamed and sorry to find that her aunt had so
truly interpreted the momentary expression of her features;
she blamed herself a little for the feeling that had caused that
expression, trying to think how much her aunt might have
been troubled with something before the unexpected irrup-
tion of the strangers, and again hoping that the remembrance
of this little misunderstanding would soon pass away. So she
endeavoured to reassure herself, and not to give way to her

uncle's tender trembling pressure of her hand, as, at her aunt's bidding, she wished him good night, and returned into the outer, or 'keeping' -room, where all the family were now assembled, ready for the meal of flourcakes and venison-steaks which Nattee, the Indian servant, was bringing in from the kitchen. No one seemed to have been speaking to Captain Holdernesse while Lois had been away. Manasseh sate quiet and silent where he did, with the book open upon his knee, his eyes thoughtfully fixed on vacancy, as if he saw a vision, or dreamed dreams. Faith stood by the table, lazily directing Nattee in her preparations; and Prudence lolled against the door-frame, between kitchen and keeping-room, playing tricks on the old Indian woman as she passed backwards and forwards, till Nattee appeared to be in a strong state of irritation, which she tried in vain to repress, as whenever she showed any sign of it, Prudence only seemed excited to greater mischief. When all was ready, Manasseh lifted his right hand, and 'asked a blessing', as it was termed; but the grace became a long prayer for abstract spiritual blessings, for strength to combat Satan, and to quench his fiery darts, and at length assumed, so Lois thought, a purely personal character, as if the young man had forgotten the occasion, and even the people present, but was searching into the nature of the diseases that beset his own sick soul, and spreading them out before the Lord. He was brought back by a pluck at the coat from Prudence; he opened his shut eyes, cast an angry glance at the child, who made a face at him for sole reply, and then he sate down, and they all fell to. Grace Hickson would have thought her hospitality sadly at fault, if she had allowed Captain Holdernesse to go out in search of a bed. Skins were spread for him on the floor of the keeping-room; a Bible, and a square bottle of spirits were placed on the table, to supply his wants during the night; and in spite of all the cares and troubles, temptations, or sins of the members of that household, they were all asleep before the town clock struck ten.

In the morning, the captain's first care was to go out in search of the boy Elias, and the missing letter. He met him bringing it with an easy conscience, for, thought Elias, a few hours sooner or later will make no difference; to-night or

the morrow morning will be all the same. But he was startled
into a sense of wrong-doing by a sound box on the ear,
from the very man who had charged him to deliver it speedily,
and whom he believed to be at that very moment in Boston
city.

The letter delivered, all possible proof being given that
Lois had a right to claim a home from her nearest relations,
Captain Holdernesse thought it best to take leave.

'Thou'lt take to them, lass, maybe, when there is no one
here to make thee think on the old country. Nay, nay! parting
is hard work at all times, and best get hard work done out of
hand. Keep up thine heart, my wench, and I'll come back and
see thee next spring, if we are all spared till then; and who
knows what fine young miller mayn't come with me? Don't
go and get wed to a praying Puritan, meanwhile. There,
there – I'm off! God bless thee!'

And Lois was left alone in New England.

CHAPTER II

It was hard up-hill work for Lois to win herself a place in this
family. Her aunt was a woman of narrow, strong affections.
Her love for her husband, if ever she had any, was burnt out
and dead long ago. What she did for him she did from duty;
but duty was not strong enough to restrain that little member,
the tongue; and Lois's heart often bled at the continual flow
of contemptuous reproof which Grace constantly addressed to
her husband, even while she was sparing no pains or trouble
to minister to his bodily ease and comfort. It was more as a
relief to herself that she spoke in this way, than with any
desire that her speeches should affect him; and he was too
deadened by illness to feel hurt by them; or, it may be, the
constant repetition of her sarcasms had made him indifferent;
at any rate, so that he had his food and his state of bodily
warmth attended to, he very seldom seemed to care much for
anything else. Even his first flow of affection towards Lois
was soon exhausted; he cared for her because she arranged his
pillows well and skilfully, and because she could prepare new

and dainty kinds of food for his sick appetite, but no longer
for her as his dead sister's child. Still he did care for her, and
Lois was too glad of this little hoard of affection to examine
how or why it was given. To him she could give pleasure, but
apparently to no one else in that household. Her aunt looked
askance at her for many reasons: the first coming of Lois to
Salem was inopportune, the expression of disapprobation on
her face on that evening still lingered and rankled in Grace's
memory; early prejudices, and feelings, and prepossessions of
the English girl were all on the side of what would now be
called Church and State,* what was then esteemed in that
country a superstitious observance of the directions of a
Popish rubric,* and a servile regard for the family of an
oppressing and irreligious king.* Nor is it to be supposed that
Lois did not feel, and feel acutely, the want of sympathy that
all those with whom she was now living manifested towards
the old hereditary loyalty (religious as well as political loyalty)
in which she had been brought up. With her aunt and Manasseh it was more than want of sympathy; it was positive, active
antipathy to all the ideas Lois held most dear. The very
allusion, however incidentally made, to the little old grey
church at Barford, where her father had preached so long, –
the occasional reference to the troubles in which her own
country had been distracted when she left, – and the adherence,
in which she had been brought up, to the notion that the king
could do no wrong, seemed to irritate Manasseh past en-
durance. He would get up from his reading, his constant employment when at home, and walk angrily about the room
after Lois had said anything of this kind, muttering to himself; and once he had even stopped before her, and in a
passionate tone bade her not talk so like a fool. Now this was
very different to his mother's sarcastic, contemptuous way of
treating all poor Lois's little loyal speeches. Grace would lead
her on – at least she did at first, till experience made Lois
wiser – to express her thoughts on such subjects, till, just
when the girl's heart was opening, her aunt would turn round
upon her with some bitter sneer that roused all the evil feelings
in Lois's disposition by its sting. Now Manasseh seemed,
through all his anger, to be so really grieved by what he considered her error, that he went much nearer to convincing her

that there might be two sides to a question. Only this was a view, that it appeared like treachery to her dead father's memory to entertain.

Somehow, Lois felt instinctively that Manasseh was really friendly towards her. He was little in the house; there was farming, and some kind of mercantile business to be transacted by him, as real head of the house; and as the season drew on, he went shooting and hunting in the surrounding forests, with a daring which caused his mother to warn and reprove him in private, although to the neighbours she boasted largely of her son's courage and disregard of danger. Lois did not often walk out for the mere sake of walking, there was generally some household errand to be transacted when any of the women of the family went abroad; but once or twice she had caught glimpses of the dreary, dark wood, hemming in the cleared land on all sides, – the great wood with its perpetual movement of branch and bough, and its solemn wail, that came into the very streets of Salem when certain winds blew, bearing the sound of the pine-trees clear upon the ears that had leisure to listen. And from all accounts, this old forest, girdling round the settlement, was full of dreaded and mysterious beasts, and still more to be dreaded Indians, stealing in and out among the shadows, intent on bloody schemes against the Christian people; panther-streaked, shaven Indians, in league by their own confession, as well as by the popular belief, with evil powers.

Nattee, the old Indian servant, would occasionally make Lois's blood run cold as she and Faith and Prudence listened to the wild stories she told them of the wizards of her race. It was often in the kitchen, in the darkening evening, while some cooking process was going on, that the old Indian crone, sitting on her haunches by the bright red wood embers which sent up no flame, but a lurid light reversing the shadows of all the faces around, told her weird stories while they were await-ing the rising of the dough, perchance, out of which the house-hold bread had to be made. There ran through these stories always a ghastly, unexpressed suggestion of some human sacrifice being needed to complete the success of any incanta-tion to the Evil One; and the poor old creature, herself be-lieving and shuddering as she narrated her tale in broken

English, took a strange, unconscious pleasure in her power over her hearers – young girls of the oppressing race, which had brought her down into a state little differing from slavery, and reduced her people to outcasts on the hunting-grounds which had belonged to her fathers.

After such tales, it required no small effort on Lois's part to go out, at her aunt's command, into the common pasture round the town, and bring the cattle home at night. Who knew but what the double-headed snake might start up from each blackberry-bush – that wicked, cunning, accursed creature in the service of the Indian wizards, that had such power over all those white maidens who met the eyes placed at either end of his long, sinuous, creeping body, so that loathe him, loathe the Indian race as they would, off they must go into the forest to seek out some Indian man, and must beg to be taken into his wigwam, adjuring faith and race for ever? Or there were spells – so Nattee said – hidden about the ground by the wizards, which changed that person's nature who found them; so that, gentle and loving as they might have been before, thereafter they took no pleasure but in the cruel torments of others, and had a strange power given to them of causing such torments at their will. Once Nattee, speaking low to Lois, who was alone with her in the kitchen, whispered out her terrified belief that such a spell had Prudence found; and when the Indian showed her arms to Lois, all pinched black and blue by the impish child, the English girl began to be afraid of her cousin as of one possessed. But it was not Nattee alone, nor young imaginative girls alone, that believed in these stories. We can afford to smile at them now; but our English ancestors entertained superstitions of much the same character at the same period, and with less excuse, as the circumstances surrounding them were better known, and consequently more explicable by common sense than the real mysteries of the deep, untrodden forests of New England. The gravest divines not only believed stories similar to that of the double-headed serpent, and other tales of witchcraft, but they made such narrations the subjects of preaching and prayer; and as cowardice makes us all cruel, men who were blameless in many of the relations of life, and even praiseworthy in some, became, from superstition, cruel persecutors about this time, showing no mercy towards any one whom they believed to be in league with the Evil One.

Faith was the person with whom the English girl was the most intimately associated in her uncle's house. The two were about the same age, and certain household employments were shared between them. They took it in turns to call in the cows, to make up the butter which had been churned by Hosea, a stiff old out-door servant, in whom Grace Hickson placed great confidence; and each lassie had her great spinning-wheel for wool, and her lesser for flax, before a month had elapsed after Lois's coming. Faith was a grave, silent person, never merry, sometimes very sad, though Lois was a long time in even guessing why. She would try in her sweet, simple fashion to cheer her cousin up, when the latter was depressed, by telling her old stories of English ways and life. Occasionally, Faith seemed to care to listen, occasionally she did not heed one word, but dreamed on. Whether of the past or of the future, who could tell?

Stern old ministers came in to pay their pastoral visits. On such occasions, Grace Hickson would put on clean apron and clean cap, and make them more welcome than she was ever seen to do any one else, bringing out the best provisions of her store, and setting of all before them. Also, the great Bible was brought forth, and Hosea and Nattee summoned from their work to listen while the minister read a chapter, and, as he read, expounded it at considerable length. After this all knelt, while he, standing, lifted up his right hand, and prayed for all possible combinations of Christian men, for all possible cases of spiritual need; and lastly, taking the individuals before him, he would put up a very personal supplication for each, according to his notion of their wants. At first Lois wondered at the aptitude of one or two of his prayers of this description to the outward circumstances of each case; but when she perceived that her aunt had usually a pretty long confidential conversation with the minister in the early part of his visit, she became aware that he received both his impressions and his knowledge through the medium of 'that godly woman, Grace Hickson'; and I am afraid she paid less regard to the prayer 'for the maiden from another land, who hath brought the errors of that land as a seed with her, even across the great ocean, and who is letting even now the little seeds shoot up into an evil tree, in which all unclean creatures may find shelter.'

'I like the prayers of our Church better,' said Lois, one day to Faith. 'No clergyman in England can pray his own words, and therefore it is that he cannot judge of others so as to fit his prayers to what he esteems to be their case, as Mr Tappau did this morning.'

'I hate Mr Tappau!' said Faith, shortly, a passionate flash of light coming out of her dark, heavy eyes.

'Why so, cousin? It seems to me as if he were a good man, although I like not his prayers.'

Faith only repeated her words, 'I hate him.'

Lois was sorry for this strong bad feeling; instinctively sorry, for she was loving herself, delighted in being loved, and felt a jar run through her at every sign of want of love in others. But she did not know what to say, and was silent at the time. Faith, too, went on turning her wheel with vehemence, but spoke never a word until her thread snapped, and then she pushed the wheel away hastily and left the room.

Then Prudence crept softly up to Lois's side. This strange child seemed to be tossed about by varying moods: to-day she was caressing and communicative, to-morrow she might be deceitful, mocking, and so indifferent to the pain or sorrows of others that you could call her almost inhuman.

'So thou dost not like Pastor Tappau's prayers?' she whispered.

Lois was sorry to have been overheard, but she neither would nor could take back her words.

'I like them not so well as the prayers I used to hear at home.'

'Mother says thy home was with the ungodly. Nay, don't look at me so – it was not I that said it. I'm none so fond of praying myself, nor of Pastor Tappau for that matter. But Faith cannot abide him, and I know why. Shall I tell thee, Cousin Lois?'

'No! Faith did not tell me, and she was the right person to give her own reasons.'

'Ask her where young Mr Nolan is gone to, and thou wilt hear. I have seen Faith cry by the hour together about Mr Nolan.'

'Hush, child, hush!' said Lois, for she heard Faith's approaching step, and feared lest she should overhear what they were saying.

The truth was that, a year or two before, there had been a great struggle in Salem village, a great division in the religious body, and Pastor Tappau had been the leader of the more violent, and, ultimately, the successful party. In consequence of this, the less popular minister, Mr Nolan, had had to leave the place. And him Faith Hickson loved with all the strength of her passionate heart, although he never was aware of the attachment he had excited, and her own family were too regardless of manifestations of mere feeling to ever observe the signs of any emotion on her part. But the old Indian servant Nattee saw and observed them all. She knew, as well as if she had been told the reason, why Faith had lost all care about father or mother, brother and sister, about household work and daily occupation, nay, about the observances of religion as well. Nattee read the meaning of the deep smouldering of Faith's dislike to Pastor Tappau aright; the Indian woman understood why the girl (whom alone of all the white people she loved) avoided the old minister, – would hide in the wood-stack sooner than be called in to listen to his exhortations and prayers. With savage, untutored people, it is not 'Love me, love my dog', – they are often jealous of the creature beloved; but it is, 'Whom thou hatest I will hate'; and Nattee's feeling towards Pastor Tappau was even an exaggeration of the mute, unspoken hatred of Faith.

For a long time, the cause of her cousin's dislike and avoidance of the minister was a mystery to Lois; but the name of Nolan remained in her memory whether she would or no, and it was more from girlish interest in a suspected love affair, than from any indifferent and heartless curiosity, that she could not help piecing together little speeches and actions, with Faith's interest in the absent banished minister, for an explanatory clue, till not a doubt remained in her mind. And this without any further communication with Prudence, for Lois declined hearing any more on the subject from her, and so gave deep offence.

Faith grew sadder and duller as the autumn drew on. She lost her appetite, her brown complexion became sallow and colourless, her dark eyes looked hollow and wild. The first of November was near at hand. Lois, in her instinctive, well-intentioned efforts to bring some life and cheerfulness into the monotonous household, had been telling Faith of many English customs, silly enough, no doubt, and which scarcely lighted up a flicker of interest in the American girl's mind. The cousins were lying awake in their bed in the great unplastered room, which was in part store-room, in part bedroom. Lois was full of sympathy for Faith that night. For long she had listened to her cousin's heavy, irrepressible sighs, in silence. Faith sighed because her grief was of too old a date for violent emotion or crying. Lois listened without speaking in the dark, quiet night hours, for a long, long time. She kept quite still, because she thought such vent for sorrow might relieve her cousin's weary heart. But when at length, instead of lying motionless, Faith seemed to be growing restless even to convulsive motions of her limbs, Lois began to speak, to talk about England, and the dear old ways at home, without exciting much attention on Faith's part, until at length she fell upon the subject of Hallow-e'en, and told about customs then and long afterwards practised in England, and that have scarcely yet died out in Scotland. As she told of tricks she had often played, of the apple eaten facing a mirror, of the dripping sheet, of the basins of water, of the nuts burning side by side, and many other such innocent ways of divination,* by which laughing, trembling English maidens sought to see the form of their future husbands, if husbands they were to have, then Faith listened breathlessly, asking short, eager questions, as if some ray of hope had entered into her gloomy heart. Lois went on speaking, telling her of all the stories that would confirm the truth of the second sight vouchsafed to all seekers in the accustomed methods, half believing, half incredulous herself, but desiring, above all things, to cheer up poor Faith.

Suddenly, Prudence rose up from her truckle-bed in the dim corner of the room. They had not thought that she was awake, but she had been listening long.

'Cousin Lois may go out and meet Satan by the brook-side, if she will, but if thou goest, Faith, I will tell mother – aye, and

I will tell Pastor Tappau, too. Hold thy stories, Cousin Lois, I am afeared of my very life. I would rather never be wed at all, than feel the touch of the creature that would take the apple out of my hand, as I held it over my left shoulder.' The excited girl gave a loud scream of terror at the image her fancy had conjured up. Faith and Lois sprang out towards her, flying across the moonlit room in their white nightgowns. At the same instant, summoned by the same cry, Grace Hickson came to her child.

'Hush! hush!' said Faith, authoritatively.

'What is it, my wench?' asked Grace. While Lois, feeling as if she had done all the mischief, kept silence.

'Take her away, take her away!' screamed Prudence. 'Look over her shoulder – her left shoulder – the Evil One is there now, I see him stretching over for the half-bitten apple.'

'What is this she says?' said Grace, austerely.

'She is dreaming,' said Faith; 'Prudence, hold thy tongue.' And she pinched the child severely, while Lois more tenderly tried to soothe the alarms she felt that she had conjured up.

'Be quiet, Prudence,' said she, 'and go to sleep. I will stay by thee till thou hast gone off into slumber.'

'No, no! go away,' sobbed Prudence, who was really terrified at first, but was now assuming more alarm than she felt, from the pleasure she received at perceiving herself the centre of attention. 'Faith shall stay by me, not you, wicked English witch!'

So Faith sate by her sister; and Grace, displeased and perplexed, withdrew to her own bed, purposing to inquire more into the matter in the morning. Lois only hoped it might all be forgotten by that time, and resolved never to talk again of such things. But an event happened in the remaining hours of the night to change the current of affairs. While Grace had been absent from her room, her husband had had another paralytic stroke: whether he, too, had been alarmed by that eldritch scream no one could ever know. By the faint light of the rush candle burning at the bed-side, his wife perceived that a great change had taken place in his aspect on her return: the irregular breathing came almost like snorts – the end was drawing near. The family were roused, and all help given that either the doctor or experience could suggest. But before the late November morning light, all was ended for Ralph Hickson.

The whole of the ensuing day, they sat or moved in darkened rooms, and spoke a few words, and those below their breath. Manasseh kept at home, regretting his father, no doubt, but showing little emotion. Faith was the child that bewailed her loss most grievously; she had a warm heart, hidden away somewhere under her moody exterior, and her father had shown her far more passive kindness than ever her mother had done, for Grace made distinct favourites of Manasseh, her only son, and Prudence, her youngest child. Lois was about as unhappy as any of them, for she had felt strongly drawn towards her uncle as her kindest friend, and the sense of his loss renewed the old sorrow she had experienced at her own parents' death. But she had no time and no place to cry in. On her devolved many of the cares, which it would have seemed indecorous in the nearer relatives to interest themselves in enough to take an active part: the change required in their dress, the household preparations for the sad feast of the funeral – Lois had to arrange all under her aunt's stern direction.

But a day or two afterwards – the last day before the funeral – she went into the yard to fetch in some fagots for the oven; it was a solemn, beautiful, starlit evening, and some sudden sense of desolation in the midst of the vast universe thus revealed touched Lois's heart, and she sat down behind the woodstack, and cried very plentiful tears.

She was startled by Manasseh, who suddenly turned the corner of the stack, and stood before her.

'Lois crying!'

'Only a little,' she said, rising up, and gathering her bundle of fagots, for she dreaded being questioned by her grim, impassive cousin. To her surprise, he laid his hand on her arm, and said, –

'Stop one minute. Why art thou crying, cousin?'

'I don't know,' she said, just like a child questioned in like manner; and she was again on the point of weeping.

'My father was very kind to thee, Lois; I do not wonder that thou grievest after him. But the Lord who taketh away can restore tenfold. I will be as kind as my father – yea, kinder.

This is not a time to talk of marriage and giving in marriage. But after we have buried our dead, I wish to speak to thee.'

Lois did not cry now, but she shrank with affright. What did her cousin mean? She would far rather that he had been angry with her for unreasonable grieving, for folly.

She avoided him carefully – as carefully as she could, without seeming to dread him – for the next few days. Sometimes she thought it must have been a bad dream; for if there had been no English lover in the case, no other man in the whole world, she could never have thought of Manasseh as her husband; indeed, till now, there had been nothing in his words or actions to suggest such an idea. Now it had been suggested, there was no telling how much she loathed him. He might be good, and pious – he doubtless was – but his dark fixed eyes, moving so slowly and heavily, his lank black hair, his grey coarse skin, all made her dislike him now – all his personal ugliness and ungainliness struck on her senses with a jar, since those few words spoken behind the woodstack.

She knew that sooner or later the time must come for further discussion of this subject; but, like a coward, she tried to put it off, by clinging to her aunt's apron-string, for she was sure that Grace Hickson had far different views for her only son. As, indeed, she had, for she was an ambitious, as well as a religious woman; and by an early purchase of land in Salem village, the Hicksons had become wealthy people, without any great exertions of their own; partly, also, by the silent process of accumulation, for they had never cared to change their manner of living from the time when it had been suitable to a far smaller income than that which they at present enjoyed. So much for worldly circumstances. As for their worldly character, it stood as high. No one could say a word against any of their habits or actions. Their righteousness and godliness were patent to every one's eyes. So Grace Hickson thought herself entitled to pick and choose among the maidens, before she should meet with one fitted to be Manasseh's wife. None in Salem came up to her imaginary standard. She had it in her mind even at this very time – so soon after her husband's death – to go to Boston, and take counsel with the leading ministers there, with worthy Mr Cotton Mather at their head, and see if they could tell her of a well-favoured and godly young maiden in their congregations worthy of being the wife of her son. But, besides good looks and godliness, the wench must have good birth, and good wealth, or Grace Hickson would have put her contemptuously on one side. When once this paragon was found, and the ministers had approved, Grace anticipated no difficulty on her son's part. So Lois was right in feeling that her aunt would dislike any speech of marriage between Manasseh and herself.

But the girl was brought to bay one day in this wise. Manasseh had ridden forth on some business, which every one said would occupy him the whole day; but, meeting the man with whom he had to transact his affairs, he returned earlier than any one expected. He missed Lois from the keeping-room where his sisters were spinning, almost immediately. His mother sate by at her knitting – he could see Nattee in the kitchen through the open door. He was too reserved to ask where Lois was, but he quietly sought till he found her – in the great loft, already piled with winter stores of fruit and vegetables. Her aunt had sent her there to examine the apples one by one, and pick out such as were unsound, for immediate use. She was stooping down, and intent upon this work, and was hardly aware of his approach, until she lifted up her head and saw him standing close before her. She dropped the apple she was holding, went a little paler than her wont, and faced him in silence.

'Lois,' he said, 'thou rememberest the words that I spoke while we yet mourned over my father. I think that I am called to marriage now, as the head of this household. And I have seen no maiden so pleasant in my sight as thou art, Lois!' He tried to take her hand. But she put it behind her with a childish shake of her head, and, half-crying, said, –

'Please, Cousin Manasseh, do not say this to me. I dare say you ought to be married, being the head of the household now; but I don't want to be married. I would rather not.'

'That is well spoken,' replied he, frowning a little, nevertheless. 'I should not like to take to wife an over-forward maiden, ready to jump at wedlock. Besides, the congregation might talk, if we were to be married too soon after my father's death. We have, perchance, said enough, even now. But I wished thee to have thy mind set at ease as to thy future well-doing.

Thou wilt have leisure to think of it, and to bring thy mind more fully round to it.' Again he held out his hand. This time she took hold of it with a free, frank gesture.

'I owe you somewhat for your kindness to me ever since I came, Cousin Manasseh; and I have no way of paying you but by telling you truly I can love you as a dear friend, if you will let me, but never as a wife.'

He flung her hand away, but did not take his eyes off her face, though his glance was lowering and gloomy. He muttered something which she did not quite hear, and so she went on bravely although she kept trembling a little, and had much ado to keep from crying.

'Please let me tell you all. There was a young man in Barford – nay, Manasseh, I cannot speak if you are so angry; it is hard work to tell you anyhow – he said that he wanted to marry me; but I was poor, and his father would have none of it, and I do not want to marry any one; but if I did it would be –' Her voice dropped, and her blushes told the rest. Manasseh stood looking at her with sullen, hollow eyes, that had a gathering touch of wildness in them, and then he said, –

'It is borne in upon me – verily I see it as in a vision – that thou must be my spouse, and no other man's. Thou canst not escape what is foredoomed. Months ago, when I set myself to read the old godly books in which my soul used to delight until thy coming, I saw no letters of printers' ink marked on the page, but I saw a gold and ruddy type of some unknown language, the meaning whereof was whispered into my soul; it was, "Marry Lois! marry Lois!" And when my father died, I knew it was the beginning of the end. It is the Lord's will, Lois, and thou canst not escape from it.' And again he would have taken her hand and drawn her towards him. But this time she eluded him with ready movement.

'I do not acknowledge it to be the Lord's will, Manasseh,' said she. 'It is not "borne in upon me," as you Puritans call it, that I am to be your wife. I am none so set upon wedlock as to take you, even though there be no other chance for me. For I do not care for you as I ought to care for my husband. But I could have cared for you very much as a cousin – as a kind cousin.'

She stopped speaking; she could not choose the right words

with which to speak to him of her gratitude and friendliness, which yet could never be any feeling nearer and dearer, no more than two parallel lines can ever meet.

But he was so convinced, by what he considered the spirit of prophecy, that Lois was to be his wife, that he felt rather more indignant at what he considered to be her resistance to the preordained decree, than really anxious as to the result. Again he tried to convince her that neither he nor she had any choice in the matter, by saying, –

'The voice said unto me "Marry Lois," and I said, "I will, Lord." '

'But,' Lois replied, 'the voice, as you call it, has never spoken such a word to me.'

'Lois,' he answered, solemnly, 'it will speak. And then wilt thou obey, even as Samuel did?'*

'No; indeed I cannot!' she answered, briskly. 'I may take a dream to be truth, and hear my own fancies, if I think about them too long. But I cannot marry any one from obedience.'

'Lois, Lois, thou art as yet unregenerate; but I have seen thee in a vision as one of the elect, robed in white. As yet thy faith is too weak for thee to obey meekly, but it shall not always be so. I will pray that thou mayest see thy preordained course. Meanwhile, I will smooth away all worldly obstacles.'

'Cousin Manasseh! Cousin Manasseh!' cried Lois after him, as he was leaving the room, 'come back. I cannot put it in strong enough words. Manasseh, there is no power in heaven or earth that can make me love thee enough to marry thee, or to wed thee without such love. And this I say solemnly, because it is better that this should end at once.'

For a moment he was staggered; then he lifted up his hands, and said, –

'God forgive thee thy blasphemy! Remember Hazael,* who said, "Is thy servant a dog, that he should do this great thing?" and went straight and did it, because his evil courses were fixed and appointed for him from before the foundation of the world. And shall not thy paths be laid out among the godly as it hath been foretold to me?'

He went away; and for a minute or two Lois felt as if his words must come true, and that, struggle as she would, hate her doom as she would, she must become his wife; and, under the circumstances, many a girl would have succumbed to her apparent fate. Isolated from all previous connections, hearing no word from England, living in the heavy, monotonous routine of a family with one man for head, and this man esteemed a hero by most of those around him, simply because he was the only man in the family, – these facts alone would have formed strong presumptions that most girls would have yielded to the offers of such a one. But, besides this, there was much to tell upon the imagination in those days, in that place, and time. It was prevalently believed that there were manifestations of spiritual influence – of the direct influence both of good and bad spirits – constantly to be perceived in the course of men's lives. Lots were drawn, as guidance from the Lord; the Bible was opened, and the leaves allowed to fall apart, and the first text the eye fell upon was supposed to be appointed from above as a direction. Sounds were heard that could not be accounted for; they were made by the evil spirits not yet banished from the desert places of which they had so long held possession. Sights, inexplicable and mysterious, were dimly seen – Satan, in some shape, seeking whom he might devour. And at the beginning of the long winter season, such whispered tales, such old temptations and hauntings, and devilish terrors, were supposed to be peculiarly rife. Salem was, as it were, snowed up, and left to prey upon itself. The long, dark evenings, the dimly-lighted rooms, the creaking passages, where heterogeneous articles were piled away out of reach of the keen-piercing frost, and where occasionally, in the dead of night, a sound was heard, as of some heavy falling body, when, next morning, everything appeared to be in its right place – so accustomed are we to measure noises by comparison with themselves, and not with the absolute stillness of the night-season – the white mist, coming nearer and nearer to the windows every evening in strange shapes, like phantoms, – all these, and many other circumstances, such as the distant fall of mighty trees in the mysterious forests girdling them round, the faint whoop and cry of some Indian seeking his camp, and unwittingly nearer to the white men's settlement than either he or they would have liked could they have chosen, the hungry yells of the wild beasts approaching the cattle-pens, – these were the things which made that winter life in Salem, in the memorable time of 1691–2, seem strange, and haunted, and terrific to many: peculiarly weird and awful to the English girl in her first year's sojourn in America.

And now imagine Lois worked upon perpetually by Manasseh's conviction that it was decreed that she should be his wife, and you will see that she was not without courage and spirit to resist as she did, steadily, firmly, and yet sweetly. Take one instance out of many, when her nerves were subjected to a shock, slight in relation it is true, but then remember that she had been all day, and for many days, shut up within doors, in a dull light, that at mid-day was almost dark with a long-continued snow-storm. Evening was coming on, and the wood fire was more cheerful than any of the human beings surrounding it; the monotonous whirr of the smaller spinning-wheels had been going on all day, and the store of flax down stairs was nearly exhausted, when Grace Hickson bade Lois fetch down some more from the store-room, before the light so entirely waned away that it could not be found without a candle, and a candle it would be dangerous to carry into that apartment full of combustible materials, especially at this time of hard frost, when every drop of water was locked up and bound in icy hardness. So Lois went, half-shrinking from the long passage that led to the stairs leading up into the store-room, for it was in this passage that the strange night sounds were heard, which every one had begun to notice, and speak about in lowered tones. She sang, however, as she went, 'to keep her courage up' – sang, however, in a subdued voice, the evening hymn* she had so often sung in Barford church – '

'Glory to Thee, my God, this night – '

and so it was, I suppose, that she never heard the breathing or motion of any creature near her till, just as she was loading herself with flax to carry down, she heard some one – it was Manasseh – say close to her ear, –

'Has the voice spoken yet? Speak, Lois! Has the voice spoken yet to thee – that speaketh to me day and night, "Marry Lois?"'

She started and turned a little sick, but spoke almost directly in a brave, clear manner, –

'No! Cousin Manasseh. And it never will.'

'Then I must wait yet longer,' he replied, hoarsely, as if to himself. 'But all submission – all submission.'

At last a break came upon the monotony of the long, dark winter. The parishioners once more raised the discussion whether – the parish extending as it did – it was not absolutely necessary for Pastor Tappau to have help. This question had been mooted once before; and then Pastor Tappau had acquiesced in the necessity, and all had gone on smoothly for some months after the appointment of his assistant, until a feeling had sprung up on the part of the elder minister, which might have been called jealousy of the younger, if so godly a man as Pastor Tappau could have been supposed to entertain so evil a passion. However that might be, two parties were speedily formed, the younger and more ardent being in favour of Mr Nolan, the elder and more persistent – and, at the time, the more numerous – clinging to the old grey-headed, dogmatic Mr Tappau, who had married them, baptized their children, and was to them literally as a 'pillar of the church'. So Mr Nolan left Salem, carrying away with him, possibly, more hearts than that of Faith Hickson's; but certainly she had never been the same creature since.

But now – Christmas, 1691 – one or two of the older members of the congregation being dead, and some who were younger men having come to settle in Salem – Mr Tappau being also older, and, some charitably supposed, wiser – a fresh effort had been made, and Mr Nolan was returning to labour in ground apparently smoothed over. Lois had taken a keen interest in all the proceedings for Faith's sake, – far more than the latter did for herself, any spectator would have said. Faith's wheel never went faster or slower, her thread never broke, her colour never came, her eyes were never uplifted with sudden interest, all the time these discussions respecting Mr Nolan's return were going on. But Lois, after the hint given by Prudence, had found a clue to many a sigh and look of despairing sorrow, even without the help of Nattee's improvised songs, in which, under strange allegories, the helpless love of her favourite was told to ears heedless of all meaning, except those of the tender-hearted and sympathetic Lois. Occasionally, she heard a strange chant of the old Indian woman's – half in her own language, half in broken English –

droned over some simmering pipkin, from which the smell was, to say the least, unearthly. Once, on perceiving this odour in the keeping-room, Grace Hickson suddenly exclaimed, –

'Nattee is at her heathen ways again; we shall have some mischief unless she is stayed.'

But Faith, moving quicker than ordinary, said something about putting a stop to it, and so forestalled her mother's evident intention of going into the kitchen. Faith shut the door between the two rooms, and entered upon some re-monstrance with Nattee; but no one could hear the words used. Faith and Nattee seemed more bound together by love and common interest, than any other two among the self-contained individuals comprising this household. Lois some-times felt as if her presence as a third interrupted some con-fidential talk between her cousin and the old servant. And yet she was fond of Faith, and could almost think that Faith liked her more than she did either mother, brother, or sister; for the first two were indifferent as to any unspoken feelings, while Prudence delighted in discovering them only to make an amusement to herself out of them.

One day Lois was sitting by herself at her sewing table, while Faith and Nattee were holding one of the secret con-claves from which Lois felt herself to be tacitly excluded, when the outer door opened, and a tall, pale young man, in the strict professional habit of a minister, entered. Lois sprang up with a smile and a look of welcome for Faith's sake, for this must be the Mr Nolan whose name had been on the tongue of every one for days, and who was, as Lois knew, expected to arrive the day before.

He seemed half surprised at the glad alacrity with which he was received by this stranger: possibly he had not heard of the English girl, who was an inmate in the house where formerly he had seen only grave, solemn, rigid, or heavy faces, and had been received with a stiff form of welcome, very different from the blushing, smiling, dimpled looks that innocently met him with the greeting almost of an old acquaintance. Lois having placed a chair for him, hastened out to call Faith, never doubting but that the feeling which her cousin entertained for the young pastor was mutual, although it might be unrecog-nised in its full depth by either.

'Faith!' said she, bright and breathless. 'Guess – No,' checking herself to an assumed unconsciousness of any particular importance likely to be affixed to her words, 'Mr Nolan, the new pastor, is in the keeping-room. He has asked for my aunt and Manasseh. My aunt is gone to the prayer meeting at Pastor Tappau's, and Manasseh is away.' Lois went on speaking to give Faith time, for the girl had become deadly white at the intelligence, while, at the same time, her eyes met the keen, cunning eyes of the old Indian with a peculiar look of half-wondering awe, while Nattee's looks expressed triumphant satisfaction.

'Go,' said Lois, smoothing Faith's hair, and kissing the white, cold cheek, 'or he will wonder why no one comes to see him, and perhaps think he is not welcome.' Faith went without another word into the keeping-room, and shut the door of communication. Nattee and Lois were left together. Lois felt as happy as if some piece of good fortune had be-fallen herself. For the time, her growing dread of Manasseh's wild, ominous persistence in his suit, her aunt's coldness, her own loneliness, were all forgotten, and she could almost have danced with joy. Nattee laughed aloud, and talked and chuckled to herself: 'Old Indian woman great mystery. Old Indian woman sent hither and thither; go where she is told, where she hears with her ears. But old Indian woman' – and here she drew herself up, and the expression of her face quite changed – 'know how to call, and then white man must come; and old Indian have spoken never a word, and white man have heard nothing with his ears.' So the old crone muttered.

All this time, things were going on very differently in the keeping-room to what Lois imagined. Faith sate stiller even than usual; her eyes downcast, her words few. A quick ob-server might have noticed a certain tremulousness about her hands, and an occasional twitching throughout all her frame. But Pastor Nolan was not a keen observer upon this occasion; he was absorbed with his own little wonders and perplexities. His wonder was that of a carnal man – who that pretty stranger might be, who had seemed, on his first coming, so glad to see him, but had vanished instantly, apparently not to reappear. And, indeed, I am not sure if his perplexity was not that of a carnal man rather than that of a godly minister, for this was his dilemma. It was the custom of Salem (as we have already seen) for the minister, on entering a household for the visit which, among other people and in other times, would have been termed a 'morning call', to put up a prayer for the eternal welfare of the family under whose roof-tree he was. Now this prayer was expected to be adapted to the individual character, joys, sorrows, wants, and failings of every member present; and here was he, a young pastor, alone with a young woman, and he thought – vain thoughts, perhaps, but still very natural – that the implied guesses at her character, involved in the minute supplications above described, would be very awkward in a *tête-à-tête* prayer; so, whether it was his wonder or his perplexity, I do not know, but he did not contribute much to the conversation for some time, and at last, by a sudden burst of courage and impromptu hit, he cut the Gordian knot by making the usual proposal for prayer, and adding to it a request that the household might be summoned. In came Lois, quiet and decorous; in came Nattee, all one impassive, stiff piece of wood, – no look of intelligence or trace of giggling near her countenance. Solemnly recalling each wandering thought, Pastor Nolan knelt in the midst of these three to pray. He was a good and truly religious man, whose name here is the only thing disguised, and played his part bravely in the awful trial to which he was afterwards subjected; and if at the time, before he went through his fiery persecutions, the human fancies which beset all young hearts came across his, we at this day know that these fancies are no sin. But now he prays in earnest, prays so heartily for himself, with such a sense of his own spiritual need and spiritual failings, that each one of his hearers feels as if a prayer and a supplication had gone up for each of them. Even Nattee muttered the few words she knew of the Lord's Prayer; gibberish though the disjointed nouns and verbs might be, the poor creature said them because she was stirred to unwonted reverence. As for Lois, she rose up comforted and strengthened, as no special prayers of Pastor Tappau had ever made her feel. But Faith was sobbing, sobbing aloud, almost hysterically, and made no effort to rise, but lay on her outstretched arms spread out upon the settle. Lois and Pastor Nolan looked at each other for an instant. Then Lois said, –

'Sir, you must go. My cousin has not been strong for some time, and doubtless she needs more quiet than she has had to-day.'

Pastor Nolan bowed, and left the house; but in a moment he returned. Half opening the door, but without entering, he said, –

'I come back to ask, if perchance I may call this evening to inquire how young Mistress Hickson finds herself?'

But Faith did not hear this; she was sobbing louder than ever.

'Why did you send him away, Lois? I should have been better directly, and it is so long since I have seen him.'

She had her face hidden as she uttered these words, and Lois could not hear them distinctly. She bent her head down by her cousin's on the settle, meaning to ask her to repeat what she had said. But in the irritation of the moment, and prompted possibly by some incipient jealousy, Faith pushed Lois away so violently that the latter was hurt against the hard, sharp corner of the wooden settle. Tears came into her eyes; not so much because her cheek was bruised, as because of the surprised pain she felt at this repulse from the cousin towards whom she was feeling so warmly and kindly. Just for the moment, Lois was as angry as any child could have been; but some of the words of Pastor Nolan's prayer yet rang in her ears, and she thought it would be a shame if she did not let them sink into her heart. She dared not, however, stoop again to caress Faith, but stood quietly by her, sorrowfully waiting, until a step at the outer door caused Faith to rise quickly, and rush into the kitchen, leaving Lois to bear the brunt of the new-comer. It was Manasseh, returned from hunting. He had been two days away, in company with other young men belonging to Salem. It was almost the only occupation which could draw him out of his secluded habits. He stopped suddenly at the door on seeing Lois, and alone, for she had avoided him of late in every possible way.

'Where is my mother?'

'At a prayer meeting at Pastor Tappau's. She has taken Prudence. Faith has left the room this minute. I will call her.' And Lois was going towards the kitchen, when he placed himself between her and the door.

'Lois,' said he, 'the time is going by, and I cannot wait much longer. The visions come thick upon me, and my sight grows clearer and clearer. Only this last night, camping out in the woods, I saw in my soul, between sleeping and waking, the spirit come and offer thee two lots, and the colour of the one was white, like a bride's, and the other was black and red, which is, being interpreted, a violent death. And when thou didst choose the latter the spirit said unto me, "Come!" and I came, and did as I was bidden. I put it on thee with mine own hands, as it is preordained, if thou wilt not hearken unto the voice and be my wife. And when the black and red dress fell to the ground, thou wert even as a corpse three days old. Now, be advised, Lois, in time. Lois, my cousin, I have seen it in a vision, and my soul cleaveth unto thee – I would fain spare thee.'

He was really in earnest – in passionate earnest; whatever his visions, as he called them, might be, he believed in them, and this belief gave something of unselfishness to his love for Lois. This she felt at this moment, if she had never done so before, and it seemed like a contrast to the repulse she had just met with from his sister. He had drawn near her, and now he took hold of her hand, repeating in his wild, pathetic, dreamy way, –

'And the voice said unto me, "Marry Lois!" ' And Lois was more inclined to soothe and reason with him than she had ever been before, since the first time of his speaking to her on the subject, – when Grace Hickson and Prudence entered the room from the passage. They had returned from the prayer meeting by the back way, which had prevented the sound of their approach from being heard.

But Manasseh did not stir or look round; he kept his eyes fixed on Lois, as if to note the effect of his words. Grace came hastily forwards, and lifting up her strong right arm, smote their joined hands in twain, in spite of the fervour of Manasseh's grasp.

'What means this?' said she, addressing herself more to Lois than to her son, anger flashing out of her deep-set eyes.

Lois waited for Manasseh to speak. He seemed, but a few minutes before, to be more gentle and less threatening than he had been of late on this subject, and she did not wish to irritate him. But he did not speak, and her aunt stood angrily waiting for an answer.

'At any rate,' thought Lois, 'it will put an end to the thought in his mind when my aunt speaks out about it.'

'My cousin seeks me in marriage,' said Lois.

'Thee!' and Grace struck out in the direction of her niece with a gesture of supreme contempt. But now Manasseh spoke forth, –

'Yea! it is preordained. The voice has said it, and the spirit has brought her to me as my bride.'

'Spirit! an evil spirit then. A good spirit would have chosen out for thee a godly maiden of thine own people, and not a prelatist and a stranger like this girl. A pretty return, Mistress Lois, for all our kindness.'

'Indeed, Aunt Hickson, I have done all I could – Cousin Manasseh knows it – to show him I can be none of his. I have told him,' said she, blushing, but determined to say the whole out at once, 'that I am all but troth-plight to a young man of our own village at home; and, even putting all that on one side, I wish not for marriage at present.'

'Wish rather for conversion and regeneration. Marriage is an unseemly word in the mouth of a maiden. As for Manasseh, I will take reason with him in private; and, meanwhile, if thou hast spoken truly, throw not thyself in his path, as I have noticed thou hast done but too often of late.'

Lois's heart burnt within her at this unjust accusation, for she knew how much she had dreaded and avoided her cousin, and she almost looked to him to give evidence that her aunt's last words were not true. But, instead, he recurred to his one fixed idea, and said, –

'Mother, listen! If I wed not Lois, both she and I die within the year. I care not for life; before this, as you know, I have sought for death' (Grace shuddered, and was for a moment subdued by some recollection of past horror); 'but if Lois were my wife I should live, and she would be spared from what is the other lot. That whole vision grows clearer to me day by day. Yet, when I try to know whether I am one of the elect, all is dark. The mystery of Free-Will and Fore-Knowledge* is a mystery of Satan's devising, not of God's.'

'Alas, my son! Satan is abroad among the brethren even

now; but let the old vexed topics rest. Sooner than fret thyself again, thou shalt have Lois to be thy wife, though my heart was set far differently for thee.'

'No, Manasseh,' said Lois. 'I love you well as a cousin, but wife of yours I can never be. Aunt Hickson, it is not well to delude him so. I say, if ever I marry man, I am troth-plight to one in England.'

'Tush, child! I am your guardian in my dead husband's place. Thou thinkest thyself so great a prize that I would clutch at thee whether or no, I doubt not. I value thee not, save as a medicine for Manasseh, if his mind get disturbed again, as I have noted signs of late.'

This, then, was the secret explanation of much that had alarmed her in her cousin's manner: and if Lois had been a physician of modern times, she might have traced somewhat of the same temperament in his sisters as well – in Prudence's lack of natural feeling and impish delight in mischief, in Faith's vehemence of unrequited love. But as yet Lois did not know, any more than Faith, that the attachment of the latter to Mr Nolan was not merely unreturned, but even unperceived, by the young minister.

He came, it is true, – came often to the house, sat long with the family, and watched them narrowly, but took no especial notice of Faith. Lois perceived this, and grieved over it; Nattee perceived it, and was indignant at it, long before Faith slowly acknowledged it to herself, and went to Nattee the Indian woman, rather than to Lois her cousin, for sympathy and counsel.

'He cares not for me,' said Faith. 'He cares more for Lois's little finger than for my whole body,' the girl moaned out in the bitter pain of jealousy.

'Hush thee, hush thee, prairie bird! How can he build a nest, when the old bird has got all the moss and the feathers? Wait till the Indian has found means to send the old bird flying far away.' This was the mysterious comfort Nattee gave.

Grace Hickson took some kind of charge over Manasseh that relieved Lois of much of her distress at his strange behaviour. Yet at times he escaped from his mother's watchfulness, and in such opportunities he would always seek Lois, entreating her, as of old, to marry him – sometimes pleading his love for her, oftener speaking wildly of his visions and the voices which he heard foretelling a terrible futurity.

We have now to do with events which were taking place in Salem, beyond the narrow circle of the Hickson family; but as they only concern us in as far as they bore down in their consequences on the future of those who formed part of it, I shall go over the narrative very briefly. The town of Salem had lost by death, within a very short time preceding the commencement of my story, nearly all its venerable men and leading citizens – men of ripe wisdom and sound counsel. The people had hardly yet recovered from the shock of their loss, as one by one the patriarchs of the primitive little community had rapidly followed each other to the grave. They had been beloved as fathers, and looked up to as judges in the land. The first bad effect of their loss was seen in the heated dissension which sprang up between Pastor Tappau and the candidate Nolan. It had been apparently healed over; but Mr Nolan had not been many weeks in Salem, after his second coming, before the strife broke out afresh, and alienated many for life who had till then been bound together by the ties of friendship or relationship. Even in the Hickson family something of this feeling soon sprang up; Grace being a vehement partisan of the elder pastor's more gloomy doctrines, while Faith was a passionate, if a powerless, advocate of Mr Nolan. Manasseh's growing absorption in his own fancies, and imagined gift of prophecy, making him comparatively indifferent to all outward events, did not tend to either the fulfilment of his visions, or the elucidation of the dark mysterious doctrines over which he had pondered too long for the health either of his mind or body; while Prudence delighted in irritating every one by her advocacy of the views of thinking to which they were most opposed, and retailing every gossiping story to the person most likely to disbelieve, and be indignant at what she told, with an assumed unconsciousness of any such effect to be produced. There was much talk of the congregational difficulties and dissensions being carried up to the general court,* and each party naturally hoped that, if such were the course of events, the opposing pastor and that portion of the congregation which adhered to him might be worsted in the struggle.

Such was the state of things in the township when, one day

towards the end of the month of February, Grace Hickson returned from the weekly prayer meeting, which it was her custom to attend at Pastor Tappau's house, in a state of extreme excitement. On her entrance into her own house she sate down, rocking her body backwards and forwards, and praying to herself: both Faith and Lois stopped their spinning, in wonder at her agitation, before either of them ventured to address her. At length Faith rose, and spoke, –

'Mother, what is it? Hath anything happened of an evil nature?'

The brave, stern, old woman's face was blenched, and her eyes were almost set in horror, as she prayed; the great drops running down her cheeks.

It seemed almost as if she had to make a struggle to recover her sense of the present homely accustomed life, before she could find words to answer.

'Evil nature! Daughters, Satan is abroad, – is close to us. I have this very hour seen him afflict two innocent children, as of old he troubled those who were possessed by him in Judea.* Hester and Abigail Tappau have been contorted and convulsed by him and his servants into such shapes as I am afeard to think on; and when their father, godly Mr Tappau, began to exhort and to pray, their howlings were like the wild beasts of the field. Satan is of a truth let loose amongst us. The girls kept calling upon him as if he were even then present among us. Abigail screeched out that he stood at my very back in the guise of a black man; and truly, as I turned round at her words, I saw a creature like a shadow vanishing, and turned all of a cold sweat. Who knows where he is now? Faith, lay straws across on the door-sill.'

'But if he be already entered in,' asked Prudence, 'may not that make it difficult for him to depart?'

Her mother, taking no notice of her question, went on rocking herself, and praying, till again she broke out into narration.

'Reverend Mr Tappau says, that only last night he heard a sound as of a heavy body dragged all through the house by some strong power; once it was thrown against his bedroom door, and would, doubtless, have broken it in, if he had not prayed fervently and aloud at that very time; and a shriek went up at his prayer that made his hair stand on end; and this morning all the crockery in the house was found broken and piled up in the middle of the kitchen floor; and Pastor Tappau says, that as soon as he began to ask a blessing on the morning's meal, Abigail and Hester cried out, as if some one was pinching them. Lord, have mercy upon us all! Satan is of a truth let loose.'

'They sound like the old stories I used to hear in Barford,' said Lois, breathless with affright.

Faith seemed less alarmed; but then her dislike to Pastor Tappau was so great, that she could hardly sympathise with any misfortunes that befel him or his family.

Towards evening Mr Nolan came in. In general, so high did party spirit run, Grace Hickson only tolerated his visits, finding herself often engaged at such hours, and being too much abstracted in thought to show him the ready hospitality which was one of her most prominent virtues. But to-day, both as bringing the latest intelligence of the new horrors sprung up in Salem, and as being one of the Church militant (or what the Puritans considered as equivalent to the Church militant) against Satan, he was welcomed by her in an unusual manner.

He seemed oppressed with the occurrences of the day: at first it appeared to be almost a relief to him to sit still, and cogitate upon them, and his hosts were becoming almost impatient for him to say something more than mere monosyllables, when he began, –

'Such a day as this, I pray that I may never see again. It is as if the devils whom our Lord banished into the herd of swine,* had been permitted to come again upon the earth. And I would it were only the lost spirits who were tormenting us; but I much fear, that certain of those whom we have esteemed as God's people have sold their souls to Satan, for the sake of a little of his evil power, whereby they may afflict others for a time. Elder Sherringham hath lost this very day a good and valuable horse, wherewith he used to drive his family to meeting, his wife being bedridden.'

'Perchance,' said Lois, 'the horse died of some natural disease.'

'True,' said Pastor Nolan; 'but I was going on to say, that

as he entered into his house, full of dolour at the loss of his beast, a mouse ran in before him so sudden that it almost tripped him up, though an instant before there was no such thing to be seen; and he caught at it with his shoe and hit it, and it cried out like a human creature in pain, and straight ran up the chimney, caring nothing for the hot flame and smoke.'

Manasseh listened greedily to all this story, and when it was ended he smote upon his breast, and prayed aloud for deliverance from the power of the Evil One; and he continually went on praying at intervals through the evening, with every mark of abject terror on his face and in his manner – he, the bravest, most daring hunter in all the settlement. Indeed, all the family huddled together in silent fear, scarcely finding any interest in the usual household occupations. Faith and Lois sat with arms entwined, as in days before the former had become jealous of the latter; Prudence asked low, fearful questions of her mother and of the pastor as to the creatures that were abroad, and the ways in which they afflicted others; and when Grace besought the minister to pray for her and her household, he made a long and passionate supplication that none of that little flock might ever so far fall away into hopeless perdition as to be guilty of the sin without forgiveness – the Sin of Witchcraft.

CHAPTER III

'THE sin of witchcraft.' We read about it, we look on it from the outside; but we can hardly realize the terror it induced. Every impulsive or unaccustomed action, every little nervous affection, every ache or pain was noticed, not merely by those around the sufferer, but by the person himself, whoever he might be, that was acting, or being acted upon, in any but the most simple and ordinary manner. He or she (for it was most frequently a woman or girl that was the supposed subject) felt a desire for some unusual kind of food – some unusual motion or rest – her hand twitched, her foot was asleep, or her leg had the cramp; and the dreadful question immediately suggested itself, 'Is any one possessing an evil power over me, by the help of Satan?' and perhaps they went on to think, 'It is bad enough to feel that my body can be made to suffer through the power of some unknown evil-wisher to me, but what if Satan gives them still further power, and they can touch my soul, and inspire me with loathful thoughts leading me into crimes which at present I abhor?' and so on, till the very dread of what might happen, and the constant dwelling of the thoughts, even with horror, upon certain possibilities, or what were esteemed such, really brought about the corruption of imagination at last, which at first they had shuddered at. Moreover, there was a sort of uncertainty as to who might be infected – not unlike the overpowering dread of the plague, which made some shrink from their best-beloved with irrepressible fear. The brother or sister, who was the dearest friend of their childhood and youth, might now be bound in some mysterious deadly pact with evil spirits of the most horrible kind – who could tell? And in such a case it became a duty, a sacred duty, to give up the earthly body which had been once so loved, but which was now the habitation of a soul corrupt and horrible in its evil inclinations. Possibly, terror of death might bring on confession, and repentance, and purification. Or if it did not, why away with the evil creature, the witch, out of the world, down to the kingdom of the master, whose bidding was done on earth in all manner of corruption and torture of God's creatures! There were others who, to these more simple, if more ignorant, feelings of horror at witches and witchcraft, added the desire, conscious or unconscious, of revenge on those whose conduct had been in any way displeasing to them. Where evidence takes a supernatural character, there is no disproving it. This argument comes up: 'You have only the natural powers; I have supernatural. You admit the existence of the supernatural by the condemnation of this very crime of witchcraft. You hardly know the limits of the natural powers; how then can you define the supernatural? I say that in the dead of night, when my body seemed to all present to be lying in quiet sleep, I was, in the most complete and wakeful consciousness, present in my body at an assembly of witches and wizards with Satan at their head; that I was by them tortured in my body, because my soul would not acknowledge him as its king; and that I witnessed such and such deeds. What the nature of the appearance was that took the semblance of myself, sleeping quietly in my bed, I know not; but admitting, as you do, the possibility of witchcraft, you cannot disprove my evidence.' This evidence might be given truly or falsely, as the person witnessing believed it or not; but every one must see what immense and terrible power was abroad for revenge. Then, again, the accused themselves ministered to the horrible panic abroad. Some, in dread of death, confessed from cowardice to the imaginary crimes of which they were accused, and of which they were promised a pardon on confession. Some, weak and terrified, came honestly to believe in their own guilt, through the diseases of imagination which were sure to be engendered at such a time as this.

Lois sate spinning with Faith. Both were silent, pondering over the stories that were abroad. Lois spoke first.

'Oh, Faith! this country is worse than ever England was, even in the days of Master Matthew Hopkinson,* the witch-finder. I grow frightened of every one, I think. I even get afeard sometimes of Nattee!'

Faith coloured a little. Then she asked, –

'Why? What should make you distrust the Indian woman?'

'Oh! I am ashamed of my fear as soon as it arises in my mind. But, you know, her look and colour were strange to me when first I came; and she is not a christened woman; and they tell stories of Indian wizards; and I know not what the mixtures are which she is sometimes stirring over the fire, nor the meaning of the strange chants she sings to herself. And once I met her in the dusk, just close by Pastor Tappau's house, in company with Hota, his servant – it was just before we heard of the sore disturbance in his house – and I have wondered if she had aught to do with it.'

Faith sate very still, as if thinking. At last she said, –

'If Nattee has powers beyond what you and I have, she will not use them for evil; at least not evil to those whom she loves.'

'That comforts me but little,' said Lois. 'If she has powers beyond what she ought to have, I dread her, though I have done her no evil; nay, though I could almost say she bore me a kindly feeling. But such powers are only given by the Evil One; and the proof thereof is, that, as you imply, Nattee would use them on those who offend her.'

'And why should she not?' asked Faith, lifting her eyes, and flashing heavy fire out of them at the question.

'Because,' said Lois, not seeing Faith's glance, 'we are told to pray for them that despitefully use us, and to do good to them that persecute us. But poor Nattee is not a christened woman. I would that Mr Nolan would baptize her; it would, maybe, take her out of the power of Satan's temptations.'

'Are you never tempted?' asked Faith, half scornfully; 'and yet I doubt not you were well baptized!'

'True,' said Lois, sadly; 'I often do very wrong, but, perhaps, I might have done worse, if the holy form had not been observed.'

They were again silent for a time.

'Lois,' said Faith, 'I did not mean any offence. But do you never feel as if you would give up all that future life, of which the parsons talk, and which seems so vague and so distant, for a few years of real, vivid blessedness to begin to-morrow – this hour, this minute? Oh! I could think of happiness for which I would willingly give up all those misty chances of heaven – '

'Faith, Faith!' cried Lois, in terror, holding her hand before her cousin's mouth, and looking around in fright. 'Hush! you know not who may be listening; you are putting yourself in his power.'

But Faith pushed her hand away, and said, 'Lois, I believe in him no more than I believe in heaven. Both may exist, but they are so far away that I defy them. Why, all this ado about Mr Tappau's house – promise me never to tell living creature, and I will tell you a secret.'

'No!' said Lois, terrified. 'I dread all secrets. I will hear none. I will do all that I can for you, cousin Faith, in any way; but just at this time, I strive to keep my life and thoughts within the strictest bounds of godly simplicity, and I dread pledging myself to aught that is hidden and secret.'

'As you will, cowardly girl, full of terrors, which, if you had listened to me, might have been lessened, if not entirely done away with.' And Faith would not utter another word, though

Lois tried meekly to entice her into conversation on some other subject.

The rumour of witchcraft was like the echo of thunder among the hills. It had broken out in Mr Tappau's house, and his two little daughters were the first supposed to be bewitched; but round about, from every quarter of the town, came in accounts of sufferers by witchcraft. There was hardly a family without one of these supposed victims. Then arose a growl and menaces of vengeance from many a household – menaces deepened, not daunted, by the terror and mystery of the suffering that gave rise to them.

At length a day was appointed when, after solemn fasting and prayer, Mr Tappau invited the neighbouring ministers and all godly people to assemble at his house, and unite with him in devoting a day to solemn religious services, and to supplication for the deliverance of his children, and those similarly afflicted, from the power of the Evil One. All Salem poured out towards the house of the minister. There was a look of excitement on all their faces; eagerness and horror were depicted on many, while stern resolution, amounting to determined cruelty, if the occasion arose, was seen on others.

In the midst of the prayer, Hester Tappau, the younger girl, fell into convulsions; fit after fit came on, and her screams mingled with the shrieks and cries of the assembled congregation. In the first pause, when the child was partially recovered, when the people stood around exhausted and breathless, her father, the Pastor Tappau, lifted his right hand, and adjured her, in the name of the Trinity, to say who tormented her. There was a dead silence; not a creature stirred of all those hundreds. Hester turned wearily and uneasily, and moaned out the name of Hota, her father's Indian servant. Hota was present, apparently as much interested as any one; indeed, she had been busying herself much in bringing remedies to the suffering child. But now she stood aghast, transfixed, while her name was caught up and shouted out in tones of re-probation and hatred by all the crowd around her. Another moment and they would have fallen upon the trembling creature and torn her limb from limb – pale, dusky, shivering Hota, half guilty-looking from her very bewilderment. But Pastor Tappau, that gaunt, grey man, lifting himself to his utmost height, signed to them to go back, to keep still while he addressed them; and then he told them, that instant vengeance was not just, deliberate punishment; that there would be need of conviction, perchance of confession – he hoped for some redress for his suffering children from her revelations, if she were brought to confession. They must leave the culprit in his hands, and in those of his brother ministers, that they might wrestle with Satan before delivering her up to the civil power. He spoke well, for he spoke from the heart of a father seeing his children exposed to dreadful and mysterious suffering, and firmly believing that he now held the clue in his hand which should ultimately release them and their fellow-sufferers. And the congregation moaned themselves into unsatisfied submission, and listened to his long, passionate prayer, which he uplifted even while the hapless Hota stood there, guarded and bound by two men, who glared at her like bloodhounds ready to slip, even while the prayer ended in the words of the merciful Saviour.

Lois sickened and shuddered at the whole scene; and this was no intellectual shuddering at the folly and superstition of the people, but tender moral shuddering at the sight of guilt which she believed in, and at the evidence of men's hatred and abhorrence, which, when shown even to the guilty, troubled and distressed her merciful heart. She followed her aunt and cousins out into the open air, with downcast eyes and pale face. Grace Hickson was going home with a feeling of triumphant relief at the detection of the guilty one. Faith alone seemed uneasy and disturbed beyond her wont, for Manasseh received the whole transaction as the fulfilment of a prophecy, and Prudence was excited by the novel scene into a state of discordant high spirits.

'I am quite as old as Hester Tappau,' said she; 'her birthday is in September and mine in October.'

'What has that to do with it?' said Faith, sharply.

'Nothing, only she seemed such a little thing for all those grave ministers to be praying for, and so many folk come from a distance – some from Boston they said – all for her sake, as it were. Why, didst thou see, it was godly Mr Henwick that held her head when she wriggled so, and old Madam Holbrook had herself helped upon a chair to see the better. I wonder how long I might wriggle, before great and godly folk would take so much notice of me? But, I suppose, that comes of being a pastor's daughter. She'll be so set up there'll be no speaking to her now. Faith! thinkest thou that Hota really had bewitched her? She gave me corn-cakes, the last time I was at Pastor Tappau's, just like any other woman, only, perchance, a trifle more good-natured; and to think of her being a witch after all!'

But Faith seemed in a hurry to reach home, and paid no attention to Prudence's talking. Lois hastened on with Faith, for Manasseh was walking alongside of his mother, and she kept steady to her plan of avoiding him, even though she pressed her company upon Faith, who had seemed of late desirous of avoiding her.

That evening the news spread through Salem, that Hota had confessed her sin – had acknowledged that she was a witch. Nattee was the first to hear the intelligence. She broke into the room where the girls were sitting without Grace Hickson, solemnly doing nothing, because of the great prayer-meeting in the morning, and cried out, 'Mercy, mercy, mistress, everybody! take care of poor Indian Nattee, who never do wrong, but for mistress and the family! Hota one bad wicked witch, she say so herself; oh, me! oh, me!' and stooping over Faith, she said something in a low, miserable tone of voice, of which Lois only heard the word 'torture.' But Faith heard all, and turning very pale, half accompanied, half led Nattee back to her kitchen.

Presently, Grace Hickson came in. She had been out to see a neighbour; it will not do to say that so godly a woman had been gossiping; and, indeed, the subject of the conversation she had held was of too serious and momentous a nature for me to employ a light word to designate it. There was all the listening to and repeating of small details and rumours, in which the speakers have no concern, that constitutes gossiping; but in this instance, all trivial facts and speeches might be considered to bear such dreadful significance, and might have so ghastly an ending, that such whispers were occasionally raised to a tragic importance. Every fragment of intelligence that related to Mr Tappau's household was eagerly snatched at; how his dog howled all one long night through, and could not be stilled; how his cow suddenly failed in her milk only two months after she had calved; how his memory had forsaken him one morning, for a minute or two, in repeating the Lord's Prayer, and he had even omitted a clause thereof in his sudden perturbation; and how all these forerunners of his children's strange illness might now be interpreted and understood – this had formed the staple of the conversation between Grace Hickson and her friends. There had arisen a dispute among them at last, as to how far these subjections to the power of the Evil One were to be considered as a judgment upon Pastor Tappau for some sin on his part; and if so, what? It was not an unpleasant discussion, although there was considerable difference of opinion; for as none of the speakers had had their families so troubled, it was rather a proof that they had none of them committed any sin. In the midst of this talk, one, entering in from the street, brought the news that Hota had confessed all – had owned to signing a certain little red book which Satan had presented to her – had been present at impious sacraments – had ridden through the air to Newbury Falls – and, in fact, had assented to all the questions which the elders and magistrates, carefully reading over the confessions of the witches who had formerly been tried in England, in order that they might not omit a single inquiry, had asked of her. More she had owned to, but things of inferior importance, and partaking more of the nature of earthly tricks than of spiritual power. She had spoken of carefully adjusted strings, by which all the crockery in Pastor Tappau's house could be pulled down or disturbed; but of such intelligible malpractices the gossips of Salem took little heed. One of them said that such an action showed Satan's prompting, but they all preferred to listen to the grander guilt of the blasphemous sacraments and supernatural rides. The narrator ended with saying that Hota was to be hung the next morning, in spite of her confession, even although her life had been promised to her if she acknowledged her sin; for it was well to make an example of the first-discovered witch, and it was also well that she was an Indian, a heathen, whose life would be no great loss to the community. Grace Hickson on this spoke out. It was well that witches should perish off the face of the earth, Indian or English, heathen or, worse, a baptized Christian who had betrayed the Lord, even as Judas did, and had gone over to Satan. For her part, she wished that the first-discovered witch had been a member of a godly English household, that it might be seen of all men that religious folk were willing to cut off the right hand, and pluck out the right eye,* if tainted with this devilish sin. She spoke sternly and well. The last comer said, that her words might be brought to the proof, for it had been whispered that Hota had named others, and some from the most religious families of Salem, whom she had seen among the unholy communicants at the sacrament of the Evil One. And Grace replied that she would answer for it, all godly folk would stand the proof, and quench all natural affection rather than that such a sin should grow and spread among them. She herself had a weak bodily dread of witnessing the violent death even of an animal; but she would not let that deter her from standing amidst those who cast the accursed creature out from among them on the morrow morning.

Contrary to her wont, Grace Hickson told her family much of this conversation. It was a sign of her excitement on the subject that she thus spoke, and the excitement spread in different forms through her family. Faith was flushed and restless, wandering between the keeping-room and the kitchen, and questioning her mother particularly as to the more extraordinary parts of Hota's confession, as if she wished to satisfy herself that the Indian witch had really done those horrible and mysterious deeds.

Lois shivered and trembled with affright at the narration, and the idea that such things were possible. Occasionally she found herself wandering off into sympathetic thought for the woman who was to die, abhorred of all men, and unpardoned by God, to whom she had been so fearful a traitor, and who was now, at this very time – when Lois sate among her kindred by the warm and cheerful firelight, anticipating many peaceful, perchance happy, morrows – solitary, shivering, panic-stricken, guilty, with none to stand by her and exhort her, shut up in darkness between the cold walls of the town prison. But Lois almost shrank from sympathising with so loathsome an accomplice of Satan, and prayed for forgiveness for her charitable thought; and yet, again, she remembered the tender spirit of the Saviour, and allowed herself to fall into pity, till at last her sense of right and wrong became so bewildered that she could only leave all to God's disposal, and just ask that He would take all creatures and all events into His hands.

Prudence was as bright as if she were listening to some merry story – curious as to more than her mother would tell her – seeming to have no particular terror of witches or witchcraft, and yet to be especially desirous to accompany her mother the next morning to the hanging. Lois shrank from the cruel, eager face of the young girl as she begged her mother to allow her to go. Even Grace was disturbed and perplexed by her daughter's pertinacity.

'No!' said she. 'Ask me no more. Thou shalt not go. Such sights are not for the young. I go, and I sicken at the thought of it. But I go to show that I, a Christian woman, take God's part against the devil's. Thou shalt not go, I tell thee. I could whip thee for thinking of it.'

'Manasseh says Hota was well whipped by Pastor Tappau ere she was brought to confession,' said Prudence, as if anxious to change the subject of discussion.

Manasseh lifted up his head from the great folio Bible, brought by his father from England, which he was studying. He had not heard what Prudence said, but he looked up at the sound of his name. All present were startled at his wild eyes, his bloodless face. But he was evidently annoyed at the expression of their countenances.

'Why look ye at me in that manner?' asked he. And his manner was anxious and agitated. His mother made haste to speak.

'It was but that Prudence said something that thou hast told her – that Pastor Tappau defiled his hands by whipping the witch Hota. What evil thought has got hold of thee? Talk to us, and crack not thy skull against the learning of man.'

'It is not the learning of man that I study: it is the word of God. I would fain know more of the nature of this sin of witchcraft, and whether it be, indeed, the unpardonable sin against the Holy Ghost.* At times I feel a creeping influence coming over me, prompting all evil thoughts and unheard-of deeds, and I question within myself, "Is not this the power of witchcraft?" and I sicken, and loathe all that I do or say, and yet some evil creature hath the mastery over me, and I must needs do and say what I loathe and dread. Why wonder you, mother, that I, of all men, strive to learn the exact nature of witchcraft, and for that end study the word of God? Have you not seen me when I was, as it were, possessed with a devil?'

He spoke calmly, sadly, but as under deep conviction. His mother rose to comfort him.

'My son,' she said, 'no one ever saw thee do deeds, or heard thee utter words, which any one could say were prompted by devils. We have seen thee, poor lad, with thy wits gone astray for a time, but all thy thoughts sought rather God's will in forbidden places, than lost the clue to them for one moment in hankering after the powers of darkness. Those days are long past; a future lies before thee. Think not of witches or of being subject to the power of witchcraft. I did evil to speak of it before thee. Let Lois come and sit by thee, and talk to thee.'

Lois went to her cousin, grieved at heart for his depressed state of mind, anxious to soothe and comfort him, and yet recoiling more than ever from the idea of ultimately becoming his wife – an idea to which she saw her aunt reconciling herself unconsciously day by day, as she perceived the English girl's power of soothing and comforting her cousin, even by the very tones of her sweet cooing voice.

He took Lois's hand.

'Let me hold it. It does me good,' said he. 'Ah, Lois, when I am by you I forget all my troubles – will the day never come when you will listen to the voice that speaks to me continually?'

'I never hear it, Cousin Manasseh,' she said, softly; 'but do not think of the voices. Tell me of the land you hope to enclose from the forest – what manner of trees grow on it?'

Thus, by simple questions on practical affairs, she led him back, in her unconscious wisdom, to the subjects on which he had always shown strong practical sense. He talked on these with all due discretion till the hour for family prayer came round, which was early in those days. It was Manasseh's place to conduct it, as head of the family; a post which his mother had always been anxious to assign to him since her husband's death. He prayed extempore; and to-night his supplications wandered off into wild, unconnected fragments of prayer, which all those kneeling around began, each according to her anxiety for the speaker, to think would never end. Minutes elapsed, and grew to quarters of an hour, and his words only became more emphatic and wilder, praying for himself alone, and laying bare the recesses of his heart. At length his mother rose, and took Lois by the hand, for she had faith in Lois's power over her son, as being akin to that which the shepherd David, playing on his harp, had over king Saul* sitting on his throne. She drew her towards him, where he knelt facing into the circle, with his eyes upturned, and the tranced agony of his face depicting the struggle of the troubled soul within.

'Here is Lois,' said Grace, almost tenderly; 'she would fain go to her chamber.' (Down the girl's face the tears were streaming.) 'Rise, and finish thy prayer in thy closet.'

But at Lois's approach he sprang to his feet, – sprang aside.

'Take her away, mother! Lead me not into temptation. She brings me evil and sinful thoughts. She overshadows me, even in the presence of my God. She is no angel of light, or she would not do this. She troubles me with the sound of a voice bidding me marry her, even when I am at my prayers. Avaunt! Take her away!'

He would have struck at Lois if she had not shrunk back, dismayed and affrighted. His mother, although equally dismayed, was not affrighted. She had seen him thus before; and understood the management of his paroxysm.

'Go, Lois! the sight of thee irritates him, as once that of Faith did. Leave him to me.'

And Lois rushed away to her room, and threw herself on her bed, like a panting, hunted creature. Faith came after her slowly and heavily.

'Lois,' said she, 'wilt thou do me a favour? It is not much to ask. Wilt thou arise before daylight, and bear this letter from me to Pastor Nolan's lodgings? I would have done it myself, but mother has bidden me to come to her, and I may be detained until the time when Hota is to be hung; and the letter tells of matters pertaining to life and death. Seek out Pastor Nolan wherever he may be, and have speech of him after he has read the letter.'

'Cannot Nattee take it?' asked Lois.

'No!' Faith answered, fiercely. 'Why should she?'

But Lois did not reply. A quick suspicion darted through

Faith's mind, sudden as lightning. It had never entered there before.

'Speak, Lois. I read thy thoughts. Thou wouldst fain not be the bearer of this letter?'

'I will take it,' said Lois, meekly. 'It concerns life and death, you say?'

'Yes!' said Faith, in quite a different tone of voice. But, after a pause of thought, she added: 'Then, as soon as the house is still, I will write what I have to say, and leave it here, on this chest; and thou wilt promise me to take it before the day is fully up, while there is yet time for action.'

'Yes! I promise,' said Lois. And Faith knew enough of her to feel sure that the deed would be done, however reluctantly.

The letter was written – laid on the chest; and, ere day dawned, Lois was astir, Faith watching her from between her half-closed eyelids – eyelids that had never been fully closed in sleep the livelong night. The instant Lois, cloaked and hooded, left the room, Faith sprang up, and prepared to go to her mother, whom she heard already stirring. Nearly every one in Salem was awake and up on this awful morning, though few were out of doors, as Lois passed along the streets. Here was the hastily erected gallows, the black shadow of which fell across the street with ghastly significance; now she had to pass the iron-barred gaol, through the unglazed windows of which she heard the fearful cry of a woman, and the sound of many footsteps. On she sped, sick almost to faintness, to the widow woman's where Mr Nolan lodged. He was already up and abroad, gone, his hostess believed, to the gaol. Thither Lois, repeating the words 'for life and for death!' was forced to go. Retracing her steps, she was thankful to see him come out of those dismal portals, rendered more dismal for being in heavy shadow, just as she approached. What his errand had been she knew not; but he looked grave and sad, as she put Faith's letter into his hands, and stood before him quietly waiting until he should read it, and deliver the expected answer. But, instead of opening it, he held it in his hand, apparently absorbed in thought. At last he spoke aloud, but more to himself than to her, –

'My God! and is she then to die in this fearful delirium? It must be – can be – only delirium, that prompts such wild and horrible confessions. Mistress Barclay, I come from the presence of the Indian woman appointed to die. It seems, she considered herself betrayed last evening by her sentence not being respited, even after she had made confession of sin enough to bring down fire from heaven; and, it seems to me, the passionate, impotent anger of this helpless creature has turned to madness, for she appals me by the additional revelations she has made to the keepers during the night – to me this morning. I could almost fancy that she thinks, by deepening the guilt she confesses, to escape this last dread punishment of all, as if, were a tithe of what she says true, one could suffer such a sinner to live. Yet to send her to death in such a state of mad terror! What is to be done?'

'Yet Scripture says that we are not to suffer witches in the land,'* said Lois, slowly.

'True; I would but ask for a respite till the prayers of God's people had gone up for His mercy. Some would pray for her, poor wretch as she is. You would, Mistress Barclay, I am sure?' But he said it in a questioning tone.

'I have been praying for her in the night many a time,' said Lois, in a low voice. 'I pray for her in my heart at this moment; I suppose, they are bidden to put her out of the land, but I would not have her entirely God-forsaken. But, sir, you have not read my cousin's letter. And she bade me bring back an answer with much urgency.'

Still he delayed. He was thinking of the dreadful confession he came from hearing. If it were true, the beautiful earth was a polluted place, and he almost wished to die, to escape from such pollution, into the white innocence of those who stood in the presence of God.

Suddenly his eyes fell on Lois's pure, grave face, upturned and watching his. Faith in earthly goodness came over his soul in that instant, 'and he blessed her unaware'.*

He put his hand on her shoulder, with an action half paternal – although the difference in their ages was not above a dozen years – and, bending a little towards her, whispered, half to himself, 'Mistress Barclay, you have done me good.'

'I!' said Lois, half affrighted, – 'I done you good! How?'

'By being what you are. But, perhaps, I should rather thank

God, who sent you at the very moment when my soul was so disquieted.'

At this instant, they were aware of Faith standing in front of them, with a countenance of thunder. Her angry look made Lois feel guilty. She had not enough urged the pastor to read his letter, she thought; and it was indignation at his delay in what she had been commissioned to do with the urgency of life or death, that made her cousin lower at her so from beneath her straight black brows. Lois explained how she had not found Mr Nolan at his lodgings, and had had to follow him to the door of the gaol. But Faith replied, with obdurate contempt, –

'Spare thy breath, Cousin Lois. It is easy seeing on what pleasant matters thou and the Pastor Nolan were talking. I marvel not at thy forgetfulness. My mind is changed. Give me back my letter, sir; it was about a poor matter – an old woman's life. And what is that compared to a young girl's love?'

Lois heard; but for an instant did not understand that her cousin, in her jealous anger, could suspect the existence of such feeling as love between her and Mr Nolan. No imagination as to its possibility had ever entered her mind; she had respected him, almost revered him – nay, had liked him as the probable husband of Faith. At the thought that her cousin could believe her guilty of such treachery, her grave eyes dilated, and fixed themselves on the flaming countenance of Faith. That serious, unprotesting manner of perfect innocence must have told on her accuser, had it not been that, at the same instant, the latter caught sight of the crimsoned and disturbed countenance of the pastor, who felt the veil rent off the unconscious secret of his heart. Faith snatched her letter out of his hands, and said, –

'Let the witch hang! What care I? She has done harm enough with her charms and her sorcery on Pastor Tappau's girls. Let her die, and let all other witches look to themselves; for there be many kinds of witchcraft abroad. Cousin Lois, thou wilt like best to stop with Pastor Nolan, or I would pray thee to come back with me to breakfast.'

Lois was not to be daunted by jealous sarcasm. She held out her hand to Pastor Nolan, determined to take no heed of her cousin's mad words, but to bid him farewell in her accustomed manner. He hesitated before taking it, and when he did, it was with a convulsive squeeze that almost made her start. Faith waited and watched all, with set lips and vengeful eyes. She bade no farewell; she spake no word; but grasping Lois tightly by the back of the arm, she almost drove her before her down the street till they reached their home.

The arrangement for the morning was this: Grace Hickson and her son Manasseh were to be present at the hanging of the first witch executed in Salem, as pious and godly heads of a family. All the other members were strictly forbidden to stir out, until such time as the low-tolling bell announced that all was over in this world for Hota, the Indian witch. When the execution was ended, there was to be a solemn prayer-meeting of all the inhabitants of Salem; ministers had come from a distance to aid by the efficacy of their prayers in these efforts to purge the land of the devil and his servants. There was reason to think that the great old meeting-house would be crowded, and when Faith and Lois reached home, Grace Hickson was giving her directions to Prudence, urging her to be ready for an early start to that place. The stern old woman was troubled in her mind at the anticipation of the sight she was to see, before many minutes were over, and spoke in a more hurried and incoherent manner than was her wont. She was dressed in her Sunday best; but her face was very grey and colourless, and she seemed afraid to cease speaking about household affairs, for fear she should have time to think. Manasseh stood by her, perfectly, rigidly still; he also was in his Sunday clothes. His face, too, was paler than its wont, but it wore a kind of absent, rapt expression, almost like that of a man who sees a vision. As Faith entered, still holding Lois in her fierce grasp, Manasseh started and smiled; but still dreamily. His manner was so peculiar, that even his mother stayed her talking to observe him more closely; he was in that state of excitement which usually ended in what his mother and certain of her friends esteemed a prophetic revelation. He began to speak, at first very low, and then his voice increased in power.

'How beautiful is the land of Beulah,* far over the sea, beyond the mountains! Thither the angels carry her, lying back in their arms like one fainting. They shall kiss away the black circle of death, and lay her down at the feet of the Lamb.

I hear her pleading there for those on earth who consented to her death. O Lois! pray also for me, pray for me, miserable!'

When he uttered his cousin's name all their eyes turned towards her. It was to her that his vision related! She stood among them, amazed, awe-stricken, but not like one affrighted or dismayed. She was the first to speak.

'Dear friends, do not think of me; his words may or may not be true. I am in God's hands all the same, whether he have the gift of prophecy or not. Besides, hear you not that I end where all would fain end? Think of him, and his needs. Such times as these always leave him exhausted and weary, when he comes out of them.'

And she busied herself in cares for his refreshment, aiding her aunt's trembling hands to set before him the requisite food, as he now sate tired and bewildered, gathering together with difficulty his scattered senses.

Prudence did all she could to assist and speed their departure. But Faith stood apart, watching in silence with her passionate, angry eyes.

As soon as they had set out on their solemn, fatal errand, Faith left the room. She had not tasted food or touched drink. Indeed, they all felt sick at heart. The moment her sister had gone up-stairs, Prudence sprang to the settle on which Lois had thrown down her cloak and hood.

'Lend me your muffles and mantle, Cousin Lois. I never yet saw a woman hanged, and I see not why I should not go. I will stand on the edge of the crowd; no one will know me, and I will be home long before my mother.'

'No!' said Lois, 'that may not be. My aunt would be sore displeased. I wonder at you, Prudence, seeking to witness such a sight.' And as she spoke she held fast her cloak, which Prudence vehemently struggled for.

Faith returned, brought back possibly by the sound of the struggle. She smiled – a deadly smile.

'Give it up, Prudence. Strive no more with her. She has bought success in this world, and we are but her slaves.'

'Oh, Faith!' said Lois, relinquishing her hold of the cloak, and turning round with passionate reproach in her look and voice, 'what have I done that you should speak so of me; you, that I have loved as I think one loves a sister?'

Prudence did not lose her opportunity, but hastily arrayed herself in the mantle, which was too large for her, and which she had, therefore, considered as well adapted for concealment; but, as she went towards the door, her feet became entangled in the unusual length, and she fell, bruising her arm pretty sharply.

'Take care, another time, how you meddle with a witch's things,' said Faith, as one scarcely believing her own words, but at enmity with all the world in her bitter jealousy of heart. Prudence rubbed her arm and looked stealthily at Lois.

'Witch Lois! Witch Lois!' said she at last, softly, pulling a childish face of spite at her.

'Oh, hush, Prudence! Do not bandy such terrible words. Let me look at thine arm. I am sorry for thy hurt, only glad that it has kept thee from disobeying thy mother.'

'Away, away!' said Prudence, springing from her. 'I am afeard of her in very truth, Faith. Keep between me and the witch, or I will throw a stool at her.'

Faith smiled – it was a bad and wicked smile – but she did not stir to calm the fears she had called up in her young sister. Just at this moment, the bell began to toll. Hota, the Indian witch, was dead. Lois covered her face with her hands. Even Faith went a deadlier pale than she had been, and said, sighing, 'Poor Hota! But death is best.'

Prudence alone seemed unmoved by any thoughts connected with the solemn, monotonous sound. Her only consideration was, that now she might go out into the street and see the sights, and hear the news, and escape from the terror which she felt at the presence of her cousin. She flew up-stairs to find her own mantle, ran down again, and past Lois, before the English girl had finished her prayer, and was speedily mingled among the crowd going to the meeting-house. There also Faith and Lois came in due course of time, but separately, not together. Faith so evidently avoided Lois, that she, humbled and grieved, could not force her company upon her cousin, but loitered a little behind, – the quiet tears stealing down her face, shed for the many causes that had occurred this morning.

The meeting-house was full to suffocation; and, as it sometimes happens on such occasions, the greatest crowd was close about the doors, from the fact that few saw, on their first entrance, where there might be possible spaces into which they could wedge themselves. Yet they were impatient of any arrivals from the outside, and pushed and hustled Faith, and after her Lois, till the two were forced on to a conspicuous place in the very centre of the building, where there was no chance of a seat, but still space to stand in. Several stood around, the pulpit being in the middle, and already occupied by two ministers in Geneva bands* and gowns, while other ministers, similarly attired, stood holding on to it, almost as if they were giving support instead of receiving it. Grace Hickson and her son sate decorously in their own pew, thereby showing that they had arrived early from the execution. You might almost have traced out the number of those who had been at the hanging of the Indian witch, by the expression of their countenances. They were awestricken into terrible repose; while the crowd pouring in, still pouring in, of those who had not attended the execution, looked all restless, and excited, and fierce. A buzz went round the meeting, that the stranger minister who stood along with Pastor Tappau in the pulpit was no other than Dr Cotton Mather himself, come all the way from Boston to assist in purging Salem of witches.

And now Pastor Tappau began his prayer, extempore, as was the custom. His words were wild and incoherent, as might be expected from a man who had just been consenting to the bloody death of one who was, but a few days ago, a member of his own family; violent and passionate, as was to be looked for in the father of children, whom he believed to suffer so fearfully from the crime he would denounce before the Lord. He sate down at length from pure exhaustion. Then Dr Cotton Mather stood forward: he did not utter more than a few words of prayer, calm in comparison with what had gone before, and then he went on to address the great crowd before him in a quiet, argumentative way, but arranging what he had to say with something of the same kind of skill which Antony used in his speech to the Romans after Caesar's murder.* Some of Dr Mather's words have been preserved to us, as he afterwards wrote them down in one of his works. Speaking of those 'unbelieving Sadducees' who doubted the existence of such a crime, he said: 'Instead of their apish shouts and jeers at blessed Scripture, and histories which have such undoubted confirmation as that no man that has breeding enough to regard the common laws of human society will offer to doubt of them, it becomes us rather to adore the goodness of God, who from the mouths of babes and sucklings has ordained truth, and by the means of the sore-afflicted children of your godly pastor, has revealed the fact that the devils have with most horrid operations broken in upon your neighbourhood. Let us beseech Him that their power may be restrained, and that they go not so far in their evil machinations as they did but four years ago in the city of Boston, where I was the humble means, under God, of loosing from the power of Satan the four children of that religious and blessed man, Mr Goodwin. These four babes of grace were bewitched by an Irish witch; there is no end to the narration of the torments they had to submit to. At one time they would bark like dogs, at another purr like cats; yea, they would fly like geese, and be carried with an incredible swiftness, having but just their toes now and then upon the ground, sometimes not once in twenty feet, and their arms waved like those of a bird. Yet at other times, by the hellish devices of the woman who had bewitched them, they could not stir without limping, for, by means of an invisible chain, she hampered their limbs, or, sometimes, by means of a noose, almost choked them. One in especial was subjected by this woman of Satan to such heat as of an oven, that I myself have seen the sweat drop from off her, while all around were moderately cold and well at ease. But not to trouble you with more of my stories, I will go on to prove that it was Satan himself that held power over her. For a very remarkable thing it was, that she was not permitted by that evil spirit to read any godly or religious book, speaking the truth as it is in Jesus. She could read Popish books well enough, while both sight and speech seemed to fail her when I gave her the Assembly's Catechism.* Again, she was fond of that prelatical Book of Common Prayer, which is but the Roman mass-book in an English and ungodly shape. In the midst of her sufferings, if one put the Prayer-book into her hands it relieved her. Yet mark you, she could never be brought to read the Lord's Prayer, whatever book she met with it in, proving thereby distinctly that she was in league with the devil. I took her into my own house, that I, even as Dr Martin Luther* did, might wrestle with the devil and have my fling at him. But when I called my household to prayer, the devils that possessed her caused her to whistle, and sing, and yell in a discordant and hellish fashion.'

At this very instant, a shrill, clear whistle pierced all ears. Dr Mather stopped for a moment.

'Satan is among you!' he cried. 'Look to yourselves!' And he prayed with fervour, as if against a present and threatening enemy; but no one heeded him. Whence came that ominous, unearthly whistle? Every man watched his neighbour. Again the whistle, out of their very midst! And then a bustle in a corner of the building, three or four people stirring, without any cause immediately perceptible to those at a distance, the movement spread, and, directly after, a passage even in that dense mass of people was cleared for two men, who bore forwards Prudence Hickson, lying rigid as a log of wood, in the convulsive position of one who suffered from an epileptic fit. They laid her down among the ministers who were gathered round the pulpit. Her mother came to her, sending up a wailing cry at the sight of her distorted child. Dr Mather came down from the pulpit and stood over her, exorcising the devil in possession, as one accustomed to such scenes. The crowd pressed forward in mute horror. At length, her rigidity of form and feature gave way, and she was terribly convulsed – torn by the devil, as they called it. By-and-by the violence of the attack was over, and the spectators began to breathe once more, though still the former horror brooded over them, and they listened as if for the sudden ominous whistle again, and glanced fearfully around, as if Satan were at their backs picking out his next victim.

Meanwhile, Dr Mather, Pastor Tappau, and one or two others were exhorting Prudence to reveal, if she could, the name of the person, the witch, who, by influence over Satan, had subjected the child to such torture as that which they had just witnessed. They bade her speak in the name of the Lord. She whispered a name in the low voice of exhaustion. None of the congregation could hear what it was. But the Pastor

Tappau, when he heard it, drew back in dismay, while Dr Mather, knowing not to whom the name belonged, cried out, in a clear, cold voice, –

'Know ye one Lois Barclay; for it is she who hath bewitched this poor child?'

The answer was given rather by action than by word, although a low murmur went up from many. But all fell back, as far as falling back in such a crowd was possible, from Lois Barclay, where she stood, – and looked on her with surprise and horror. A space of some feet, where no possibility of space had seemed to be not a minute before, left Lois standing alone, with every eye fixed upon her in hatred and dread. She stood like one speechless, tongue-tied, as if in a dream. She a witch! accursed as witches were in the sight of God and man! Her smooth, healthy face became contracted into shrivel and pallor, but she uttered not a word, only looked at Dr Mather with her dilated, terrified eyes.

Some one said, 'She is of the household of Grace Hickson, a God-fearing woman.' Lois did not know if the words were in her favour or not. She did not think about them, even; they told less on her than on any person present. She a witch! and the silver glittering Avon, and the drowning woman she had seen in her childhood at Barford, – at home in England, – were before her, and her eyes fell before her doom. There was some commotion – some rustling of papers; the magistrates of the town were drawing near the pulpit and consulting with the ministers. Dr Mather spoke again.

'The Indian woman, who was hung this morning, named certain people, whom she deposed to having seen at the horrible meetings for the worship of Satan; but there is no name of Lois Barclay down upon the paper, although we are stricken at the sight of the names of some –'

An interruption – a consultation. Again Dr Mather spoke.

'Bring the accusèd witch, Lois Barclay, near to this poor suffering child of Christ.'

They rushed forward to force Lois to the place where Prudence lay. But Lois walked forward of herself.

'Prudence,' she said, in such a sweet, touching voice, that, long afterwards, those who heard it that day, spoke of it to their children, 'have I ever said an unkind word to you, much less done you an ill turn? Speak, dear child. You did not know what you said just now, did you?'

But Prudence writhed away from her approach, and screamed out, as if stricken with fresh agony, –

'Take her away! take her away! Witch Lois, witch Lois, who threw me down only this morning, and turned my arm black and blue.' And she bared her arm, as if in confirmation of her words. It was sorely bruised.

'I was not near you, Prudence!' said Lois, sadly. But that was only reckoned fresh evidence of her diabolical power.

Lois's brain began to get bewildered. Witch Lois! she a witch, abhorred of all men! Yet she would try to think, and make one more effort.

'Aunt Hickson,' she said, and Grace came forwards – 'am I a witch, Aunt Hickson?' she asked; for her aunt, stern, harsh, unloving as she might be, was truth itself, and Lois thought – so near to delirium had she come – if her aunt condemned her, it was possible she might indeed be a witch.

Grace Hickson faced her unwillingly.

'It is a stain upon our family for ever,' was the thought in her mind.

'It is for God to judge whether thou art a witch, or not. Not for me.'

'Alas, alas!' moaned Lois; for she had looked at Faith, and learnt that no good word was to be expected from her gloomy face and averted eyes. The meeting-house was full of eager voices, repressed, out of reverence for the place, into tones of earnest murmuring that seemed to fill the air with gathering sounds of anger, and those who had at first fallen back from the place where Lois stood were now pressing forwards and round about her, ready to seize the young friendless girl, and bear her off to prison. Those who might have been, who ought to have been, her friends, were either averse or indifferent to her; though only Prudence made any open outcry upon her. That evil child cried out perpetually that Lois had cast a devilish spell upon her, and bade them keep the witch away from her; and, indeed, Prudence was strangely convulsed when once or twice Lois's perplexed and wistful eyes were turned in her direction. Here and there girls, women uttering strange cries, and apparently suffering from the same kind of convulsive fit as that which had attacked Prudence, were centres of a group of agitated friends, who muttered much and savagely of witchcraft, and the list which had been taken down only the night before from Hota's own lips. They demanded to have it made public, and objected to the slow forms of the law. Others, not so much or so immediately interested in the sufferers, were kneeling around, and praying aloud for themselves and their own safety, until the excitement should be so much quelled as to enable Dr Cotton Mather to be again heard in prayer and exhortation.

And where was Manasseh? What said he? You must remember, that the stir of the outcry, the accusation, the appeals of the accused, all seemed to go on at once amid the buzz and din of the people who had come to worship God, but remained to judge and upbraid their fellow-creature. Till now Lois had only caught a glimpse of Manasseh, who was apparently trying to push forwards, but whom his mother was holding back with word and action, as Lois knew she would hold him back; for it was not for the first time that she was made aware how carefully her aunt had always shrouded his decent reputation among his fellow-citizens from the least suspicion of his seasons of excitement and incipient insanity. On such days, when he himself imagined that he heard prophetic voices, and saw prophetic visions, his mother would do much to prevent any besides his own family from seeing him; and now Lois, by a process swifter than reasoning, felt certain, from her one look at his face, when she saw it, colourless and deformed by intensity of expression, among a number of others all simply ruddy and angry, that he was in such a state that his mother would in vain do her utmost to prevent his making himself conspicuous. Whatever force or argument Grace used, it was of no avail. In another moment he was by Lois's side, stammering with excitement, and giving vague testimony, which would have been of little value in a calm court of justice, and was only oil to the smouldering fire of that audience.

'Away with her to gaol!' 'Seek out the witches!' 'The sin has spread into all households!' 'Satan is in the very midst of us!' 'Strike and spare not!' In vain Dr Cotton Mather raised his voice in loud prayers, in which he assumed the guilt of the accused girl; no one listened, all were anxious to secure Lois, as if they feared she would vanish from before their very eyes; she, white, trembling, standing quite still in the tight grasp of strange, fierce men, her dilated eyes only wandering a little now and then in search of some pitiful face – some pitiful face that among all those hundreds was not to be found. While some fetched cords to bind her, and others, by low questions, suggested new accusations to the distempered brain of Prudence, Manasseh obtained a hearing once more. Addressing Dr Cotton Mather, he said, evidently anxious to make clear some new argument that had just suggested itself to him: 'Sir, in this matter, be she witch or not, the end has been fore-shown to me by the spirit of prophecy. Now, reverend sir, if the event be known to the spirit, it must have been fore-doomed in the councils of God. If so, why punish her for doing that in which she had no free will?'

'Young man,' said Dr Mather, bending down from the pulpit and looking very severely upon Manasseh, 'take care! you are trenching on blasphemy.'

'I do not care. I say it again. Either Lois Barclay is a witch, or she is not. If she is, it has been foredoomed for her, for I have seen a vision of her death as a condemned witch for many months past – and the voice has told me there was but one escape for her, Lois – the voice you know – ' In his excitement he began to wander a little, but it was touching to see how conscious he was that by giving way he would lose the thread of the logical argument by which he hoped to prove that Lois ought not to be punished, and with what an effort he wrenched his imagination away from the old ideas, and strove to con-centrate all his mind upon the plea that, if Lois was a witch, it had been shown him by prophecy; and if there was prophecy there must be foreknowledge; if foreknowledge, foredoom; if foredoom, no exercise of free will, and, therefore, that Lois was not justly amenable to punishment.

On he went, plunging into heresy, caring not – growing more and more passionate every instant, but directing his passion into keen argument, desperate sarcasm, instead of allowing it to excite his imagination. Even Dr Mather felt himself on the point of being worsted in the very presence of this congregation, who, but a short half-hour ago, looked upon him as all but infallible. Keep a good heart, Cotton

Mather! your opponent's eye begins to glare and flicker with a terrible yet uncertain light – his speech grows less coherent, and his arguments are mixed up with wild glimpses at wilder revelations made to himself alone. He has touched on the limits, – he has entered the borders of blasphemy, and with an awful cry of horror and reprobation the congregation rise up, as one man, against the blasphemer. Dr Mather smiled a grim smile, and the people were ready to stone Manasseh, who went on, regardless, talking and raving.

'Stay, stay!' said Grace Hickson – all the decent family shame which prompted her to conceal the mysterious misfortune of her only son from public knowledge done away with by the sense of the immediate danger to his life. 'Touch him not. He knows not what he is saying. The fit is upon him. I tell you the truth before God. My son, my only son, is mad.'

They stood aghast at the intelligence. The grave young citizen, who had silently taken his part in life close by them in their daily lives – not mixing much with them, it was true, but looked up to, perhaps, all the more – the student of abstruse books on theology, fit to converse with the most learned ministers that ever came about those parts – was he the same with the man now pouring out wild words to Lois the witch, as if he and she were the only two present! A solution of it all occurred to them. He was another victim. Great was the power of Satan! Through the arts of the devil, that white statue of a girl had mastered the soul of Manasseh Hickson. So the word spread from mouth to mouth. And Grace heard it. It seemed a healing balsam for her shame. With wilful, dishonest blindness, she would not see – not even in her secret heart would she acknowledge, that Manasseh had been strange, and moody, and violent long before the English girl had reached Salem. She even found some specious reason for his attempt at suicide long ago. He was recovering from a fever – and though tolerably well in health, the delirium had not finally left him. But since Lois came, how headstrong he had been at times! how unreasonable! how moody! What a strange delusion was that which he was under, of being bidden by some voice to marry her! How he followed her about, and clung to her, as under some compulsion of affection! And over all reigned the idea that, if he were indeed suffering from being bewitched, he

was not mad, and might again assume the honourable position
he had held in the congregation and in the town, when the
spell by which he was held was destroyed. So Grace yielded to
the notion herself, and encouraged it in others, that Lois
Barclay had bewitched both Manasseh and Prudence. And the
consequence of this belief was, that Lois was to be tried, with
little chance in her favour, to see whether she was a witch or
no; and if a witch, whether she would confess, implicate others,
repent, and live a life of bitter shame, avoided by all men, and
cruelly treated by most; or die impenitent, hardened, denying
her crime upon the gallows.

And so they dragged Lois away from the congregation of
Christians to the gaol, to await her trial. I say 'dragged her',
because, although she was docile enough to have followed
them whither they would, she was now so faint as to require
extraneous force – poor Lois! who should have been carried
and tended lovingly in her state of exhaustion, but, instead,
was so detested by the multitude, who looked upon her as an
accomplice of Satan in all his evil doings, that they cared no
more how they treated her than a careless boy minds how he
handles the toad that he is going to throw over the wall.

When Lois came to her full senses, she found herself lying
on a short hard bed in a dark square room, which she at once
knew must be a part of the city gaol. It was about eight feet
square, it had stone walls on every side, and a grated opening
high above her head, letting in all the light and air that could
enter through about a square foot of aperture. It was so lonely,
so dark to that poor girl, when she came slowly and painfully
out of her long faint. She did so want human help in that
struggle which always supervenes after a swoon; when the
effort is to clutch at life, and the effort seems too much for the
will. She did not at first understand where she was; did not
understand how she came to be there, nor did she care to
understand. Her physical instinct was to lie still and let the
hurrying pulses have time to calm. So she shut her eyes once
more. Slowly, slowly the recollection of the scene in the
meeting-house shaped itself into a kind of picture before her.
She saw within her eyelids, as it were, that sea of loathing faces
all turned towards her, as towards something unclean and
hateful. And you must remember, you who in the nineteenth

century read this account, that witchcraft was a real terrible sin to her, Lois Barclay, two hundred years ago. The look on their faces, stamped on heart and brain, excited in her a sort of strange sympathy. Could it, oh God! – could it be true, that Satan had obtained the terrific power over her and her will, of which she had heard and read? Could she indeed be possessed by a demon and be indeed a witch, and yet till now have been unconscious of it? And her excited imagination recalled, with singular vividness, all she had ever heard on the subject – the horrible midnight sacrament, the very presence and power of Satan. Then remembering every angry thought against her neighbour, against the impertinences of Prudence, against the overbearing authority of her aunt, against the persevering crazy suit of Manasseh, the indignation – only that morning, but such ages off in real time – at Faith's injustice; oh, could such evil thoughts have had devilish power given to them by the father of evil, and, all unconsciously to herself, have gone forth as active curses into the world? And so, on the ideas went careering wildly through the poor girl's brain – the girl thrown inward upon herself. At length, the sting of her imagination forced her to start up impatiently. What was this? A weight of iron on her legs – a weight stated afterwards, by the gaoler of Salem prison, to have been 'not more than eight pounds'. It was well for Lois it was a tangible ill, bringing her back from the wild illimitable desert in which her imagination was wandering. She took hold of the iron, and saw her torn stocking, – her bruised ankle, – and began to cry pitifully, out of strange compassion with herself. They feared, then, that even in that cell she would find a way to escape. Why, the utter, ridiculous impossibility of the thing convinced her of her own innocence, and ignorance of all supernatural power; and the heavy iron brought her strangely round from the delusions that seemed to be gathering about her.

No! she never could fly out of that deep dungeon; there was no escape, natural or supernatural, for her, unless by man's mercy. And what was man's mercy in such times of panic? Lois knew that it was nothing; instinct more than reason taught her, that panic calls out cowardice, and cowardice cruelty. Yet she cried, cried freely, and for the first time, when she found herself ironed and chained. It seemed so cruel, so

much as if her fellow-creatures had really learnt to hate and
dread her – her, who had had a few angry thoughts, which God
forgive! but whose thoughts had never gone into words, far
less into actions. Why, even now she could love all the household at home, if they would but let her; yes, even yet, though
she felt that it was the open accusation of Prudence and the
withheld justifications of her aunt and Faith that had brought
her to her present strait. Would they ever come and see her?
Would kinder thoughts of her, – who had shared their daily
bread for months and months, – bring them to see her, and
ask her whether it were really she who had brought on the
illness of Prudence, the derangement of Manasseh's mind?

No one came. Bread and water were pushed in by some one,
who hastily locked and unlocked the door, and cared not to
see if he put them within his prisoner's reach, or perhaps
thought that physical fact mattered little to a witch. It was
long before Lois could reach them; and she had something of
the natural hunger of youth left in her still, which prompted
her, lying her length on the floor, to weary herself with efforts
to obtain the bread. After she had eaten some of it, the day
began to wane, and she thought she would lay her down and
try to sleep. But before she did so, the gaoler heard her singing
the Evening Hymn, –

'Glory to Thee, my God, this night,
For all the blessings of the light.'

And a dull thought came into his dull mind, that she was
thankful for few blessings, if she could tune up her voice to
sing praises after this day of what, if she were a witch, was
shameful detection in abominable practices, and if not —
Well, his mind stopped short at this point in his wondering
contemplation. Lois knelt down and said the Lord's Prayer,
pausing just a little before one clause, that she might be sure
that in her heart of hearts she did forgive. Then she looked at
her ankle, and the tears came into her eyes once again, but not
so much because she was hurt, as because men must have hated
her so bitterly before they could have treated her thus. Then
she lay down, and fell asleep.

The next day, she was led before Mr Hathorn and Mr
Curwin, justices of Salem, to be accused legally and publicly of

witchcraft. Others were with her, under the same charge. And when the prisoners were brought in, they were cried out at by the abhorrent crowd. The two Tappaus, Prudence, and one or two other girls of the same age were there, in the character of victims of the spells of the accused. The prisoners were placed about seven or eight feet from the justices, and the accusers between the justices and them; the former were then ordered to stand right before the justices. All this Lois did at their bidding, with something of the wondering docility of a child, but not with any hope of softening the hard, stony look of detestation that was on all the countenances around her, save those that were distorted by more passionate anger. Then an officer was bidden to hold each of her hands, and Justice Hathorn bade her keep her eyes continually fixed on him, for this reason – which, however, was not told to her – lest, if she looked on Prudence, the girl might either fall into a fit, or cry out that she was suddenly and violently hurt. If any heart could have been touched of that cruel multitude, they would have felt some compassion for the sweet young face of the English girl, trying so meekly to do all that she was ordered, her face quite white, yet so full of sad gentleness, her grey eyes, a little dilated by the very solemnity of her position, fixed with the intent look of innocent maidenhood on the stern face of Justice Hathorn. And thus they stood in silence, one breathless minute. Then they were bidden to say the Lord's Prayer. Lois went through it as if alone in her cell; but, as she had done alone in her cell the night before, she made a little pause, before the prayer to be forgiven as she forgave. And at this instant of hesitation – as if they had been on the watch for it – they all cried out upon her for a witch, and when the clamour ended the justices bade Prudence Hickson come forwards. Then Lois turned a little to one side, wishing to see at least one familiar face; but when her eyes fell upon Prudence, the girl stood stock-still, and answered no questions, nor spoke a word, and the justices declared that she was struck dumb by witchcraft. Then some behind took Prudence under the arms, and would have forced her forwards to touch Lois, possibly esteeming that as a cure for her being bewitched. But Prudence had hardly been made to take three steps before she struggled out of their arms, and fell down writhing as in a fit,

calling out with shrieks, and entreating Lois to help her, and
save her from her torment. Then all the girls began 'to tumble
down like swine' (to use the words of an eye-witness) and to
cry out upon Lois and her fellow-prisoners. These last were
now ordered to stand with their hands stretched out, it being
imagined that if the bodies of the witches were arranged in the
form of a cross they would lose their evil power. By-and-by
Lois felt her strength going, from the unwonted fatigue of such
a position, which she had borne patiently until the pain and
weariness had forced both tears and sweat down her face, and she
asked in a low, plaintive voice, if she might not rest her head
for a few moments against the wooden partition. But Justice
Hathorn told her she had strength enough to torment others,
and should have strength enough to stand. She sighed a little,
and bore on, the clamour against her and the other accused
increasing every moment; the only way she could keep herself
from utterly losing consciousness was by distracting herself
from present pain and danger, and saying to herself verses of
the Psalms as she could remember them, expressive of trust in
God. At length she was orderd back to gaol, and dimly understood that she and others were sentenced to be hanged for
witchcraft. Many people now looked eagerly at Lois, to see if
she would weep at this doom. If she had had strength to cry, it
might – it was just possible that it might – have been considered a plea in her favour, for witches could not shed tears,
but she was too exhausted and dead. All she wanted was to lie
down once more on her prison-bed, out of the reach of men's
cries of abhorrence, and out of shot of their cruel eyes. So they
led her back to prison, speechless and tearless.

But rest gave her back her power of thought and suffering.
Was it, indeed, true that she was to die? She, Lois Barclay,
only eighteen, so well, so young, so full of love and hope as
she had been, till but these little days past! What would they
think of it at home – real, dear home at Barford, in England?
There they had loved her; there she had gone about, singing
and rejoicing all the day long in the pleasant meadows by the
Avon side. Oh, why did father and mother die, and leave her
their bidding to come here to this cruel New England shore,
where no one had wanted her, no one had cared for her, and
where now they were going to put her to a shameful death as

a witch? And there would be no one to send kindly messages by to those she should never see more. Never more! Young Lucy was living, and joyful – probably thinking of her, and of his declared intention of coming to fetch her home to be his wife, this very spring. Possibly he had forgotten her; no one knew. A week before, she would have been indignant at her own distrust in thinking for a minute that he could forget. Now, she doubted all men's goodness for a time; for those around her were deadly, and cruel, and relentless.

Then she turned round, and beat herself with angry blows (to speak in images), for ever doubting her lover. Oh! if she were but with him! Oh! if she might but be with him! He would not let her die; but would hide her in his bosom from the wrath of this people, and carry her back to the old home at Barford. And he might even now be sailing on the wide blue sea, coming nearer, nearer every moment, and yet be too late after all.

So the thoughts chased each other through her head all that feverish night, till she clung almost deliriously to life, and wildly prayed that she might not die; at least, not just yet, and she so young!

Pastor Tappau and certain elders roused her up from a heavy sleep, late on the morning of the following day. All night long she had trembled and cried, till morning light had come peering in through the square grating up above. It soothed her, and she fell asleep, to be awakened, as I have said, by Pastor Tappau.

'Arise!' said he, scrupling to touch her, from his superstitious idea of her evil powers. 'It is noonday.'

'Where am I?' said she, bewildered at this unusual wakening, and the array of severe faces all gazing upon her with reprobation.

'You are in Salem gaol, condemned for a witch.'

'Alas! I had forgotten for an instant,' said she, dropping her head upon her breast.

'She has been out on a devilish ride all night long, doubtless, and is weary and perplexed this morning,' whispered one, in so low a voice that he did not think she could hear; but she lifted up her eyes, and looked at him, with mute reproach.

'We are come,' said Pastor Tappau, 'to exhort you to confess your great and manifold sin.'

'My great and manifold sin!' repeated Lois to herself, shaking her head.

'Yea, your sin of witchcraft. If you will confess, there may yet be balm in Gilead.'*

One of the elders, struck with pity at the young girl's wan, shrunken look, said, that if she confessed, and repented, and did penance, possibly her life might yet be spared.

A sudden flash of light came into her sunk, dulled eye. Might she yet live? Was it yet in her power? Why, no one knew how soon Ralph Lucy might be here, to take her away for ever into the peace of a new home! Life! Oh, then, all hope was not over – perhaps she might still live, and not die. Yet the truth came once more out of her lips, almost without any exercise of her will.

'I am not a witch,' she said.

Then Pastor Tappau blindfolded her, all unresisting, but with languid wonder in her heart as to what was to come next. She heard people enter the dungeon softly, and heard whispering voices; then her hands were lifted up and made to touch some one near, and in an instant she heard a noise of struggling, and the well-known voice of Prudence shrieking out in one of her hysterical fits, and screaming to be taken away and out of that place. It seemed to Lois as if some of her judges must have doubted of her guilt, and demanded yet another test. She sate down heavily on her bed, thinking she must be in a horrible dream, so compassed about with dangers and enemies did she seem. Those in the dungeon – and by the oppression of the air she perceived that they were many – kept on eager talking in low voices. She did not try to make out the sense of the fragments of sentences that reached her dulled brain, till, all at once, a word or two made her understand they were discussing the desirableness of applying the whip or the torture to make her confess, and reveal by what means the spell she had cast upon those whom she had bewitched could be dissolved. A thrill of affright ran through her; and she cried out, beseechingly, –

'I beg you, sirs, for God's mercy's sake, that you do not use such awful means. I may say anything – nay, I may accuse any one if I am subjected to such torment as I have heard tell about. For I am but a young girl, and not very brave, or very good, as some are.'

It touched the hearts of one or two to see her standing there; the tears streaming down from below the coarse handkerchief tightly bound over her eyes; the clanking chain fastening the heavy weight to the slight ankle; the two hands held together as if to keep down a convulsive motion.

'Look!' said one of these. 'She is weeping. They say no witch can weep tears.'

But another scoffed at this test, and bade the first remember how those of her own family, the Hicksons even, bore witness against her.

Once more she was bidden to confess. The charges, esteemed by all men (as they said) to have been proven against her, were read over to her, with all the testimony borne against her in proof thereof. They told her that, considering the godly family to which she belonged, it had been decided by the magistrates and ministers of Salem that she should have her life spared, if she would own her guilt, make reparation, and submit to penance; but that if not, she, and others convicted of witchcraft along with her, were to be hung in Salem marketplace on the next Thursday morning (Thursday being market day). And when they had thus spoken, they waited silently for her answer. It was a minute or two before she spoke. She had sate down again upon the bed meanwhile, for indeed she was very weak. She asked, 'May I have this handkerchief unbound from my eyes, for indeed, sirs, it hurts me?'

The occasion for which she was blindfolded being over, the bandage was taken off, and she was allowed to see. She looked pitifully at the stern faces around her, in grim suspense as to what her answer would be. Then she spoke.

'Sirs, I must choose death with a quiet conscience, rather than life to be gained by a lie. I am not a witch. I know not hardly what you mean when you say I am. I have done many, many things very wrong in my life; but I think God will forgive me them for my Saviour's sake.'

'Take not His name on your wicked lips,' said Pastor Tappau, enraged at her resolution of not confessing, and scarcely able to keep himself from striking her. She saw the desire he had, and shrank away in timid fear. Then Justice Hathorn solemnly read the legal condemnation of Lois Barclay to death by hanging, as a convicted witch. She murmured something which nobody heard fully, but which sounded like a prayer for pity and compassion on her tender years and friendless estate. Then they left her to all the horrors of that solitary, loathsome dungeon, and the strange terror of approaching death.

Outside the prison walls, the dread of the witches, and the excitement against witchcraft, grew with fearful rapidity. Numbers of women, and men, too, were accused, no matter what their station of life and their former character had been. On the other side, it is alleged that upwards of fifty persons were grievously vexed by the devil, and those to whom he had imparted of his power for vile and wicked considerations. How much of malice, distinct, unmistakable personal malice, was mixed up with these accusations, no one can now tell. The dire statistics of this time tell us, that fifty-five escaped death by confessing themselves guilty, one hundred and fifty were in prison, more than two hundred accused, and upwards of twenty suffered death, among whom was the minister I have called Nolan, who was traditionally esteemed to have suffered through hatred of his co-pastor. One old man, scorning the accusation, and refusing to plead at his trial, was, according to the law, pressed to death for his contumacy. Nay, even dogs were accused of witchcraft, suffered the legal penalties, and are recorded among the subjects of capital punishment. One young man found means to effect his mother's escape from confinement, fled with her on horseback, and secreted her in the Blueberry Swamp, not far from Taplay's Brook, in the Great Pasture; he concealed her here in a wigwam which he built for her shelter, provided her with food and clothing, and comforted and sustained her until after the delusion had passed away. The poor creature must, however, have suffered dreadfully, for one of her arms was fractured in the all but desperate effort of getting her out of prison.

But there was no one to try and save Lois. Grace Hickson would fain have ignored her altogether. Such a taint did witchcraft bring upon a whole family, that generations of blameless

life were not at that day esteemed sufficient to wash it out.
Besides, you must remember that Grace, along with most
people of her time, believed most firmly in the reality of the
crime of witchcraft. Poor, forsaken Lois believed in it herself,
and it added to her terror, for the gaoler, in an unusually
communicative mood, told her that nearly every cell was now
full of witches; and it was possible he might have to put one,
if more came, in with her. Lois knew that she was no witch
herself; but not the less did she believe that the crime was
abroad, and largely shared in by evil-minded persons who had
chosen to give up their souls to Satan; and she shuddered with
terror at what the gaoler said, and would have asked him to
spare her this companionship if it were possible. But, somehow, her senses were leaving her, and she could not remember
the right words in which to form her request, until he had left
the place.

The only person who yearned after Lois – who would have
befriended her if he could – was Manasseh: poor, mad
Manasseh. But he was so wild and outrageous in his talk, that
it was all his mother could do to keep his state concealed from
public observation. She had for this purpose given him a
sleeping potion; and, while he lay heavy and inert under the
influence of the poppy-tea, his mother bound him with cords
to the ponderous, antique bed in which he slept. She looked
broken-hearted while she did this office, and thus acknowledged the degradation of her first-born – him of whom she
had ever been so proud.

Late that evening, Grace Hickson stood in Lois's cell,
hooded and cloaked up to her eyes. Lois was sitting quite still,
playing idly with a bit of string which one of the magistrates
had dropped out of his pocket that morning. Her aunt was
standing by her for an instant or two in silence, before Lois
seemed aware of her presence. Suddenly she looked up, and
uttered a little cry, shrinking away from the dark figure. Then,
as if her cry had loosened Grace's tongue, she began, –

'Lois Barclay, did I ever do you any harm?' Grace did not
know how often her want of loving-kindness had pierced the
tender heart of the stranger under her roof; nor did Lois
remember it against her now. Instead, Lois's memory was
filled with grateful thoughts of how much that might have

been left undone, by a less conscientious person, her aunt had done for her, and she half stretched out her arms as to a friend in that desolate place, while she answered, –

'Oh no, no! you were very good! very kind!'

But Grace stood immovable.

'I did you no harm, although I never rightly knew why you came to us.'

'I was sent by my mother on her death-bed,' moaned Lois, covering her face. It grew darker every instant. Her aunt stood, still and silent.

'Did any of mine ever wrong you?' she asked, after a time.

'No, no; never, till Prudence said—Oh, aunt, do you think I am a witch?' And now Lois was standing up, holding by Grace's cloak, and trying to read her face. Grace drew herself, ever so little, away from the girl, whom she dreaded, and yet sought to propitiate.

'Wiser than I, godlier than I, have said it. But, oh, Lois, Lois! he was my first-born. Loose him from the demon, for the sake of Him whose name I dare not name in this terrible building, filled with them who have renounced the hopes of their baptism; loose Manasseh from his awful state, if ever I or mine did you a kindness!'

'You ask me for Christ's sake,' said Lois. 'I can name that holy name – for, oh, aunt! indeed, and in holy truth, I am no witch; and yet I am to die – to be hanged! Aunt, do not let them kill me! I am so young, and I never did any one any harm that I know of.'

'Hush! for very shame! This afternoon I have bound my first-born with strong cords, to keep him from doing himself or us a mischief – he is so frenzied. Lois Barclay, look here!' and Grace knelt down at her niece's feet, and joined her hands as if in prayer, – 'I am a proud woman, God forgive me! and I never thought to kneel to any save to Him. And now I kneel at your feet, to pray you to release my children, more especially my son Manasseh, from the spells you have put upon them. Lois, hearken to me, and I will pray to the Almighty for you, if yet there may be mercy.'

'I cannot do it; I never did you or yours any wrong. How can I undo it? How can I?' And she wrung her hands in intensity of conviction of the inutility of aught she could do.

Here Grace got up, slowly, stiffly, and sternly. She stood aloof from the chained girl, in the remote corner of the prison cell near the door, ready to make her escape as soon as she had cursed the witch, who would not, or could not, undo the evil she had wrought. Grace lifted up her right hand, and held it up on high, as she doomed Lois to be accursed for ever, for her deadly sin, and her want of mercy even at this final hour. And, lastly, she summoned her to meet her at the judgment-seat, and answer for this deadly injury done to both souls and bodies of those who had taken her in, and received her when she came to them an orphan and a stranger.

Until this last summons, Lois had stood as one who hears her sentence and can say nothing against it, for she knows all would be in vain. But she raised her head when she heard her aunt speak of the judgment-seat, and at the end of Grace's speech she, too, lifted up her right hand, as if solemnly pledging herself by that action, and replied, –

'Aunt! I will meet you there. And there you will know my innocence of this deadly thing. God have mercy on you and yours!'

Her calm voice maddened Grace, and making a gesture as if she plucked up a handful of dust off the floor, and threw it at Lois, she cried, –

'Witch! witch! ask mercy for thyself – I need not your prayers. Witches' prayers are read backwards. I spit at thee, and defy thee!' And so she went away.

Lois sate moaning that whole night through. 'God comfort me! God strengthen me!' was all she could remember to say. She just felt that want, nothing more, – all other fears and wants seemed dead within her. And when the gaoler brought in her breakfast the next morning, he reported her as 'gone silly;' for, indeed, she did not seem to know him, but kept rocking herself to and fro, and whispering softly to herself, smiling a little from time to time.

But God did comfort her, and strengthen her too. Late on that Wednesday afternoon, they thrust another 'witch' into her cell, bidding the two, with opprobrious words, keep company together. The newcomer fell prostrate with the push given her from without; and Lois, not recognizing anything

but an old ragged woman lying helpless on her face on the
ground, lifted her up; and lo! it was Nattee – dirty, filthy
indeed, mud-pelted, stone-bruised, beaten, and all astray in
her wits with the treatment she had received from the mob
outside. Lois held her in her arms, and softly wiped the old
brown wrinkled face with her apron, crying over it, as she
had hardly yet cried over her own sorrows. For hours she
tended the old Indian woman – tended her bodily woes; and
as the poor scattered senses of the savage creature came slowly
back, Lois gathered her infinite dread of the morrow, when
she too, as well as Lois, was to be led out to die, in face of all
that infuriated crowd. Lois sought in her own mind for some
source of comfort for the old woman, who shook like one in
the shaking palsy at the dread of death – and such a death.

When all was quiet through the prison, in the deep dead
midnight, the gaoler outside the door heard Lois telling, as if
to a young child, the marvellous and sorrowful story of one
who died on the cross for us and for our sakes. As long as she
spoke, the Indian woman's terror seemed lulled; but the
instant she paused, for weariness, Nattee cried out afresh, as if
some wild beast were following her close through the dense
forests in which she had dwelt in her youth. And then Lois
went on, saying all the blessed words she could remember,
and comforting the helpless Indian woman with the sense of
the presence of a Heavenly Friend. And in comforting her,
Lois was comforted; in strengthening her, Lois was strengthened.

The morning came, and the summons to come forth and
die came. They who entered the cell found Lois asleep, her
face resting on the slumbering old woman, whose head she
still held in her lap. She did not seem clearly to recognize
where she was, when she awakened; the 'silly' look had returned to her wan face; all she appeared to know was, that
somehow or another, through some peril or another, she
had to protect the poor Indian woman. She smiled faintly
when she saw the bright light of the April day; and put her
arm round Nattee, and tried to keep the Indian quiet with
hushing, soothing words of broken meaning, and holy fragments of the Psalms. Nattee tightened her hold upon Lois as

they drew near the gallows, and the outrageous crowd below began to hoot and yell. Lois redoubled her efforts to calm and encourage Nattee, apparently unconscious that any of the opprobrium, the hootings, the stones, the mud, was directed towards her herself. But when they took Nattee from her arms, and led her out to suffer first, Lois seemed all at once to recover her sense of the present terror. She gazed wildly around, stretched out her arms as if to some person in the distance, who was yet visible to her, and cried out once with a voice that thrilled through all who heard it, 'Mother!' Directly afterwards, the body of Lois the Witch swung in the air, and every one stood, with hushed breath, with a sudden wonder, like a fear of deadly crime, fallen upon them.

The stillness and the silence were broken by one crazed and mad, who came rushing up the steps of the ladder, and caught Lois's body in his arms, and kissed her lips with wild passion. And then, as if it were true what the people believed, that he was possessed by a demon, he sprang down, and rushed through the crowd, out of the bounds of the city, and into the dark dense forest, and Manasseh Hickson was no more seen of Christian man.

The people of Salem had awakened from their frightful delusion before the autumn, when Captain Holdernesse and Hugh Lucy came to find out Lois, and bring her home to peaceful Barford, in the pleasant country of England. Instead, they led them to the grassy grave where she lay at rest, done to death by mistaken men. Hugh Lucy shook the dust off his feet in quitting Salem, with a heavy, heavy heart; and lived a bachelor all his life long for her sake.

Long years afterwards, Captain Holdernesse sought him out, to tell him some news that he thought might interest the grave miller of the Avonside. Captain Holdernesse told him that in the previous year (it was then 1713) the sentence of ex-communication against the witches of Salem was ordered, in godly sacramental meeting of the church, to be erased and blotted out, and that those who met together for this purpose 'humbly requested the merciful God would pardon whatso-ever sin, error, or mistake was in the application of justice, through our merciful High Priest, who knoweth how to have compassion on the ignorant, and those that are out of the way.'

He also said that Prudence Hickson – now woman grown – had made a most touching and pungent declaration of sorrow and repentance before the whole church, for the false and mistaken testimony she had given in several instances, among which she particularly mentioned that of her cousin Lois Barclay. To all which Hugh Lucy only answered, –

'No repentance of theirs can bring her back to life.'

Then Captain Holdernesse took out a paper, and read the following humble and solemn declaration of regret on the part of those who signed it, among whom Grace Hickson was one: –

'We, whose names are undersigned, being, in the year 1692, called to serve as jurors in court of Salem, on trial of many who were by some suspected guilty of doing acts of witchcraft upon the bodies of sundry persons; we confess that we ourselves were not capable to understand, nor able to withstand, the mysterious delusions of the powers of darkness, and prince of the air, but were, for want of knowledge in ourselves, and better information from others, prevailed with to take up with such evidence against the accused, as, on further consideration, and better information, we justly fear was insufficient for the touching the lives of any (Deut. xvii. 6), whereby we fear we have been instrumental, with others, though ignorantly and unwittingly, to bring upon ourselves and this people of the Lord the guilt of innocent blood; which sin, the Lord saith in Scripture, he would not pardon (2 Kings, xxiv. 4), that is, we suppose, in regard of his temporal judgments.* We do, therefore, signify to all in general (and to the surviving sufferers in special) our deep sense of, and sorrow for, our errors, in acting on such evidence to the condemning of any person; and do hereby declare, that we justly fear that we were sadly deluded and mistaken, for which we are much disquieted and distressed in our minds, and do therefore humbly beg forgiveness, first of God for Christ's sake, for this our error; and pray that God would not impute the guilt of it to ourselves nor others; and we also pray that we may be considered candidly and aright by the living sufferers, as being then under the power of a strong and general delusion, utterly unacquainted with, and not experienced in, matters of that nature.

'We do heartily ask forgiveness of you all, whom we have

justly offended; and do declare, according to our present minds, we would none of us do such things again on such grounds for the whole world; praying you to accept of this in way of satisfaction for our offence, and that you would bless the inheritance of the Lord, that he may be entreated for the land.

'Foreman, THOMAS FISK, &c.'

To the reading of this paper Hugh Lucy made no reply save this, even more gloomily than before, –

'All their repentance will avail nothing to my Lois, nor will it bring back her life.'

Then Captain Holdernesse spoke once more, and said that on the day of the general fast, appointed to be held all through New England, when the meeting-houses were crowded, an old, old man with white hair had stood up in the place in which he was accustomed to worship, and had handed up into the pulpit a written confession, which he had once or twice essayed to read for himself, acknowledging his great and grievous error in the matter of the witches of Salem, and praying for the forgiveness of God and of his people, ending with an entreaty that all then present would join with him in prayer that his past conduct might not bring down the displeasure of the Most High upon his country, his family, or himself. That old man, who was no other than Justice Sewall, remained standing all the time that his confession was read; and at the end he said, 'The good and gracious God be pleased to save New England and me and my family.' And then it came out that, for years past, Judge Sewall had set apart a day for humiliation and prayer, to keep fresh in his mind a sense of repentance and sorrow for the part he had borne in these trials, and that this solemn anniversary he was pledged to keep as long as he lived, to show his feeling of deep humiliation.

Hugh Lucy's voice trembled as he spoke: 'All this will not bring my Lois to life again, or give me back the hope of my youth.'

But – as Captain Holdernesse shook his head (for what word could he say, or how dispute what was so evidently true?) – Hugh added, 'What is the day, know you, that this justice has set apart?'

'The twenty-ninth of April.'

'Then on that day will I, here at Barford in England, join my prayers as long as I live with the repentant judge, that his sin may be blotted out and no more had in remembrance. She would have willed it so.'

THE CROOKED BRANCH

*

Not many years after the beginning of this century, a worthy couple of the name of Huntroyd occupied a small farm in the North Riding of Yorkshire. They had married late in life, although they were very young when they first began to 'keep company' with each other. Nathan Huntroyd had been farm servant to Hester Rose's father, and had made up to her at a time when her parents thought she might do better; and so, without much consultation of her feelings, they had dismissed Nathan in somewhat cavalier fashion. He had drifted far away from his former connections, when an uncle of his died, leaving Nathan – by this time upwards of forty years of age – enough money to stock a small farm, and yet have something over to put in the bank against bad times. One of the consequences of this bequest was, that Nathan was looking out for a wife and housekeeper, in a kind of discreet and leisurely way, when, one day, he heard that his old love, Hester, was – not married and flourishing, as he had always supposed her to be – but a poor maid-of-all-work, in the town of Ripon. For her father had had a succession of misfortunes, which had brought him in his old age to the workhouse; her mother was dead; her only brother struggling to bring up a large family; and Hester herself, a hard-working, homely-looking (at thirty-seven) servant. Nathan had a kind of growling satisfaction (which only lasted for a minute or two, however) in hearing of these turns of Fortune's wheel. He did not make many intelligible remarks to his informant, and to no one else did he say a word. But, a few days afterwards, he presented himself, dressed in his Sunday best, at Mrs Thompson's back door in Ripon.

Hester stood there, in answer to the good sound knock his good sound oak stick made; she with the light full upon her, he in shadow. For a moment there was silence. He was scanning the face and figure of his old love, for twenty years unseen. The comely beauty of youth had faded away entirely; she was, as I have said, homely-looking, plain-featured, but with a clean skin, and pleasant, frank eyes. Her figure was no longer round, but tidily draped in a blue and white bedgown,* tied round her waist by her white apron-strings, and her short red linsey petticoat showed her tidy feet and ankles. Her former lover fell into no ecstasies. He simply said to himself, 'She'll do'; and forthwith began upon his business.

'Hester, thou dost not mind me. I am Nathan, as thy father turned off at a minute's notice, for thinking of thee for a wife, twenty year come Michaelmas next. I have not thought much upon matrimony since. But Uncle Ben has died, leaving me a small matter in the bank; and I have taken Nab-end Farm, and put in a bit of stock, and shall want a missus to see after it. Wilt like to come? I'll not mislead thee. It's dairy, and it might have been arable. But arable takes more horses nor it suited me to buy, and I'd the offer of a tidy lot of kine. That's all. If thou'lt have me, I'll come for thee as soon as the hay is gotten in.'

Hester only said, 'Come in, and sit thee down.'

He came in, and sate down. For a time, she took no more notice of him than of his stick, bustling about to get dinner ready for the family whom she served. He meanwhile watched her brisk, sharp movements, and repeated to himself, 'She'll do!' After about twenty minutes of silence thus employed, he got up, saying, –

'Well, Hester, I'm going. When shall I come back again?'

'Please thysel', and thou'll please me,' said Hester, in a tone that she tried to make light and indifferent; but he saw that her colour came and went, and that she trembled while she moved about. In another moment Hester was soundly kissed; but when she looked round to scold the middle-aged farmer, he appeared so entirely composed that she hesitated. He said, –

'I have pleased mysel', and thee too, I hope. Is it a month's wage, and a month's warning? To-day is the eighth. July eighth is our wedding-day. I have no time to spend a-wooing before then, and wedding must na take long. Two days is enough to throw away, at our time o' life.'

It was like a dream; but Hester resolved not to think more about it till her work was done. And when all was cleaned up for the evening, she went and gave her mistress warning, telling her all the history of her life in a very few words. That day month she was married from Mrs Thompson's house.

The issue of the marriage was one boy, Benjamin.* A few years after his birth, Hester's brother died at Leeds, leaving ten or twelve children. Hester sorrowed bitterly over this loss; and Nathan showed her much quiet sympathy, although he could not but remember that Jack Rose had added insult to the bitterness of his youth. He helped his wife to make ready to go by the waggon to Leeds. He made light of the household difficulties, which came thronging into her mind after all was fixed for her departure. He filled her purse, that she might have wherewithal to alleviate the immediate wants of her brother's family. And as she was leaving, he ran after the waggon. 'Stop, stop!' he cried. 'Hetty, if thou wilt – if it wunnot be too much for thee – bring back one of Jack's wenches for company, like. We've enough and to spare; and a lass will make the house winsome, as a man may say.'

The waggon moved on; while Hester had such a silent swelling of gratitude in her heart, as was both thanks to her husband, and thanksgiving to God.

And that was the way that little Bessy Rose came to be an inmate of Nab-end Farm.

Virtue met with its own reward in this instance, and in a clear and tangible shape, too, which need not delude people in general into thinking that such is the usual nature of virtue's rewards. Bessy grew up a bright, affectionate, active girl; a daily comfort to her uncle and aunt. She was so much a darling in the household that they even thought her worthy of their only son Benjamin, who was perfection in their eyes. It is not often the case that two plain, homely people have a child of uncommon beauty; but it is so sometimes, and Benjamin Huntroyd was one of these exceptional cases. The hard-working, labour-and-care-marked farmer, and the mother, who could never have been more than tolerably comely in her best days, produced a boy who might have been an earl's son for grace and beauty. Even the hunting squires of the neighbourhood reined up their horses to admire him, as he opened the gates for them. He had no shyness, he was so accustomed to admiration from strangers, and adoration from his parents from his earliest years. As for Bessy Rose, he ruled imperiously over her heart from the time she first set eyes on him. And as she grew older, she grew on in loving, persuading herself that what her uncle and aunt loved so dearly it was her duty to love dearest of all. At every unconscious symptom of the young girl's love for her cousin, his parents smiled and winked: all was going on as they wished, no need to go far afield for Benjamin's wife. The household could go on as it was now; Nathan and Hester sinking into the rest of years, and relinquishing care and authority to those dear ones, who, in process of time, might bring other dear ones to share their love.

But Benjamin took it all very coolly. He had been sent to a day-school in the neighbouring town – a grammar-school, in the high state of neglect in which the majority of such schools were thirty years ago. Neither his father nor his mother knew much of learning. All that they knew (and that directed their choice of a school) was, that they could not, by any possibility, part with their darling to a boarding-school; that some schooling he must have, and that Squire Pollard's son went to Highminster Grammar School. Squire Pollard's son, and many another son destined to make his parents' hearts ache, went to this school. If it had not been so utterly bad a place of education, the simple farmer and his wife might have found it out sooner. But not only did the pupils there learn vice, they also learnt deceit. Benjamin was naturally too clever to remain a dunce, or else, if he had chosen so to be, there was nothing in Highminster Grammar School to hinder his being a dunce of the first water. But, to all appearance, he grew clever and gentlemanlike. His father and mother were even proud of his airs and graces, when he came home for the holidays; taking them for proofs of his refinement, although the practical effect of such refinement was to make him express his contempt for his parents' homely ways and simple ignorance. By the time he was eighteen, an articled clerk in an attorney's office at Highminster, – for he had quite declined becoming a 'mere clodhopper,' that is to say a hard-working, honest farmer like his father – Bessy Rose was the only person who was dissatisfied with him. The little girl of fourteen instinctively felt there was something wrong about him. Alas! two years more, and the girl of sixteen worshipped his very shadow, and would not see that aught could be wrong with one so soft-spoken, so handsome, so kind as Cousin Benjamin. For Benjamin had discovered that the way to cajole his parents out of money for every indulgence he fancied, was to pretend to forward their innocent scheme, and make love to his pretty cousin Bessy Rose. He cared just enough for her to make this work of necessity not disagreeable at the time he was performing it. But he found it tiresome to remember her little claims upon him, when she was no longer present. The letters he had promised her during his weekly absences at Highminster, the trifling commissions she had asked him to do for her, were all considered in the light of troubles; and, even when he was with her, he resented the inquiries she made as to his mode of passing his time, or what female acquaintances he had in Highminster.

When his apprenticeship was ended, nothing would serve him but that he must go up to London for a year or two. Poor Farmer Huntroyd was beginning to repent of his ambition of making his son Benjamin a gentleman. But it was too late to repine now. Both father and mother felt this, and, however sorrowful they might be, they were silent, neither demurring nor assenting to Benjamin's proposition when first he made it. But Bessy, through her tears, noticed that both her uncle and aunt seemed unusually tired that night, and sate hand-in-hand on the fireside settle, idly gazing into the bright flame, as if they saw in it pictures of what they had once hoped their lives would have been. Bessy rattled about among the supper things, as she put them away after Benjamin's departure, making more noise than usual – as if noise and bustle was what she needed to keep her from bursting out crying – and, having at one keen glance taken in the position and looks of Nathan and Hester, she avoided looking in that direction again, for fear the sight of their wistful faces should make her own tears overflow.

'Sit thee down, lass – sit thee down. Bring the creepie-stool* to the fireside, and let's have a bit of talk over the lad's plans,' said Nathan, at last rousing himself to speak. Bessy came and sate down in front of the fire, and threw her apron over her face, as she rested her head on both hands. Nathan felt as if it was a chance which of the two women burst out crying first. So he thought he would speak, in hopes of keeping off the infection of tears.

'Didst ever hear of this mad plan afore, Bessy?'

'No, never!' Her voice came muffled, and changed from under her apron. Hester felt as if the tone, both of question and answer, implied blame, and this she could not bear.

'We should ha' looked to it when we bound him, for of necessity it would ha' come to this. There's examins, and catechizes, and I dunno what all for him to be put through in London. It's not his fault.'

'Which on us said it were?' asked Nathan, rather put out. 'Thof, for that matter, a few weeks would carry him over the mire, and make him as good a lawyer as any judge among 'em. Oud Lawson the attorney told me that, in a talk I had wi' him a bit sin. Na, na! it's the lad's own hankering after London that makes him want for to stay there for a year, let alone two.'

Nathan shook his head.

'And if it be his own hankering,' said Bessy, putting down her apron, her face all aflame, and her eyes swollen up, 'I dunnot see harm in it. Lads aren't like lasses, to be teed to their own fireside like th' crook yonder. It's fitting for a young man to go abroad and see the world afore he settles down.'

Hester's hand sought Bessy's, and the two women sat in sympathetic defiance of any blame that should be thrown on the beloved absent. Nathan only said, –

'Nay, wench, dunna wax up so*; whatten's done's done; and worse, it's my doing. I mun needs make my bairn a gentleman; and we mun pay for it.'

'Dear uncle! he wunna spend much, I'll answer for it; and I'll scrimp and save i' th' house to make it good.'

'Wench!' said Nathan, solemnly, 'it were not paying in cash I were speaking on: it were paying in heart's care, and heaviness of soul. Lunnon is a place where the devil keeps court as well as King George;* and my poor chap has more nor once welly fallen into his clutches here. I dunno what he'll do when he gets close within sniff of him.'

'Don't let him go, father!' said Hester, for the first time taking this view. Hitherto she had only thought of her own grief at parting with him. 'Father, if you think so, keep him here, safe under our own eye.'

'Nay!' said Nathan, 'he's past time o' life for that. Why there's not one on us knows where he is at this present time, and he not gone out of our sight an hour. He's too big to be put back i' th' go-cart, mother, or kept within doors with the chair turned bottom upwards.'*

'I wish he were a wee bairn lying in my arms again. It were a sore day when I weaned him; and I think life's been gettin' sorer and sorer at every turn he's ta'en towards manhood.'

'Coom, lass, that's noan the way to be talking. Be thankful to Marcy that thou'st getten a man for thy son as stands five foot eleven in's stockings, and ne'er a sick piece about him. We wunnot grudge him his fling, will we, Bess, my wench? He'll be coming back in a year, or maybe a bit more; and be a' for settling in a quiet town like, wi' a wife that's noan so fur fra' me at this very minute. An' we oud folk, as we get into years, must gi' up farm, and tak a bit on a house near Lawyer Benjamin.'

And so the good Nathan, his own heart heavy enough, tried to soothe his womenkind. But of the three, his eyes were longest in closing; his apprehensions the deepest founded.

'I misdoubt me I hanna done well by th' lad. I misdoubt me sore,' was the thought that kept him awake till day began to dawn. 'Summat's wrong about him, or folk would na look at me wi' such piteous-like een when they speak on him. I can see th' meaning of it, thof I'm too proud to let on. And Lawson, too, he holds his tongue more nor he should do, when I ax him how my lad's getting on, and whatten sort of a lawyer he'll mak. God be marciful to Hester an' me, if th' lad's gone away! God be marciful! But maybe it's this lying waking a' the night through, that maks me so fearfu'. Why, when I were his age, I daur be bound I should ha' spent money fast enoof, i' I could ha' come by it. But I had to arn it; that maks a great differ'. Well! It were hard to thwart th' child of our old age, and we waitin' so long for to have 'un!'

Next morning, Nathan rode Moggy, the cart horse, into Highminster to see Mr Lawson. Anybody who saw him ride out of his own yard, would have been struck with the change in him which was visible, when he returned; a change, more than a day's unusual exercise should have made in a man of his years. He scarcely held the reins at all. One jerk of Moggy's head would have plucked them out of his hands. His head was bent forward, his eyes looking on some unseen thing, with long unwinking gaze. But as he drew near home on his return, he made an effort to recover himself.

'No need fretting them,' he said; 'lads will be lads. But I didna think he had it in him to be so thowtless, young as he is. Well, well! he'll maybe get more wisdom i' Lunnon. Anyways it's best to cut him off fra such evil lads as Will Hawker, and suchlike. It's they as have led my boy astray. He were a good chap till he knowed them – a good chap till he knowed them.'

But he put all his cares in the background when he came into the house-place, where both Bessy and his wife met him at the door, and both would fain lend a hand to take off his greatcoat.

'Theer, wenches, theer! ye might let a man alone for to get out on's clothes! Why, I might ha' struck thee, lass.' And he went on talking, trying to keep them off for a time from the subject that all had at heart. But there was no putting them off for ever; and, by dint of repeated questioning on his wife's part, more was got out than he had ever meant to tell – enough to grieve both his hearers sorely: and yet the brave old man still kept the worst in his own breast.

The next day Benjamin came home for a week or two, before making his great start to London. His father kept him at a distance, and was solemn and quiet in his manner to the young man. Bessy, who had shown anger enough at first, and had uttered many a sharp speech, began to relent, and then to feel hurt and displeased that her uncle should persevere so long in his cold, reserved manner, and Benjamin just going to leave them. Her aunt went, tremblingly busy, about the clothes-presses* and drawers, as if afraid of letting herself think either of the past or the future; only once or twice, coming behind her son, she suddenly stooped over his sitting figure, and kissed his cheek, and stroked his hair. Bessy remembered after-wards – long years afterwards – how he had tossed his head away with nervous irritability on one of these occasions, and had muttered – her aunt did not hear it, but Bessy did, –

'Can't you leave a man alone?'

Towards Bessy herself he was pretty gracious. No other words express his manner: it was not warm, nor tender, nor cousinly, but there was an assumption of underbred politeness towards her as a young, pretty woman; which politeness was neglected in his authoritative or grumbling manner towards his mother, or his sullen silence before his father. He once or twice ventured on a compliment to Bessy on her personal appearance. She stood still, and looked at him with astonishment.

'How's my eyes changed sin last thou sawst them,' she asked, 'that thou must be telling me about 'em i' that fashion? I'd rayther by a deal see thee helping thy mother when she's dropped her knitting-needle and canna see i' th' dusk for to pick it up.'

But Bessy thought of his pretty speech about her eyes long after he had forgotten making it, and would have been puzzled to tell the colour of them. Many a day, after he was gone, did she look earnestly in the little oblong looking-glass, which hung up against the wall of her little sleeping-chamber, but which she used to take down in order to examine the eyes he had praised, murmuring to herself, 'Pretty soft grey eyes! Pretty soft grey eyes!' until she would hang up the glass again with a sudden laugh and a rosy blush.

In the days when he had gone away to the vague distance and vaguer place – the city called London – Bessy tried to forget all that had gone against her feeling of the affection and duty that a son owed to his parents; and she had many things to forget of this kind that would keep surging up into her mind. For instance, she wished that he had not objected to the home-spun, home-made shirts which his mother and she had had such pleasure in getting ready for him. He might not know, it was true – and so her love urged – how, carefully and evenly the thread had been spun: how not content with bleaching the yarn in the sunniest meadow, the linen, on its return from the weaver's, had been spread out afresh on the sweet summer grass, and watered carefully night after night when there was no dew to perform the kindly office. He did not know – for no one but Bessy herself did – how many false or large stitches, made large and false by her aunt's failing eyes (who yet liked to do the choicest part of the stitching all by herself), Bessy had unpicked at night in her own room, and with dainty fingers had restitched; sewing eagerly in the dead of night. All this he did not know; or he could never have complained of the coarse texture; the old-fashioned make of these shirts; and urged on his mother to give him part of her little store of egg and butter money in order to buy newer-fashioned linen in Highminster.

When once that little precious store of his mother's was discovered, it was well for Bessy's peace of mind that she did not know how loosely her aunt counted up the coins, mistaking guineas for shillings, or just the other way, so that the amount was seldom the same in the old black spoutless teapot. Yet this son, this hope, this love, had still a strange power of fascination over the household. The evening before he left, he sate between his parents, a hand in theirs on either side, and Bessy on the old creepie-stool, her head lying on her aunt's knee, and looking up at him from time to time, as if to learn his face off by heart; till his glances meeting hers, made her drop her eyes, and only sigh.

He stopped up late that night with his father, long after the women had gone to bed. But not to sleep; for I will answer for it the grey-haired mother never slept a wink till the late dawn of the autumn day, and Bessy heard her uncle come up stairs with heavy, deliberate footsteps, and go to the old stocking which served him for bank; and count out golden guineas – once he stopped, but again he went on afresh, as if resolved to crown his gift with liberality. Another long pause – in which she could but indistinctly hear continued words, it might have been advice, it might be a prayer, for it was in her uncle's voice; and then father and son came up to bed. Bessy's room was but parted from her cousin's by a thin wooden partition; and the last sound she distinctly heard, before her eyes, tired out with crying, closed themselves in sleep, was the guineas clinking down upon each other at regular intervals, as if Benjamin were playing at pitch and toss with his father's present.

After he was gone, Bessy wished he had asked her to walk part of the way with him into Highminster. She was all ready, her things laid out on the bed; but she could not accompany him without invitation.

The little household tried to close over the gap as best they might. They seemed to set themselves to their daily work with unusual vigour; but somehow when evening came there had been little done. Heavy hearts never make light work, and there was no telling how much care and anxiety each had had to bear in secret in the field, at the wheel, or in the dairy. Formerly he was looked for every Saturday; looked for, though he might not come, or if he came, there were things to be spoken about, that made his visit anything but a pleasure: still he might come, and all things might go right, and then what sunshine, what gladness to those humble people! But now he was away, and dreary winter was come on; old folks' sight fails, and the evenings were long, and sad, in spite of all Bessy could do or say. And he did not write so often as he might – so every one thought; though every one would have been ready to defend him from either of the others who had expressed such a thought aloud. 'Surely!' said Bessy to herself, when the first primroses peeped out in a sheltered and sunny hedge-bank, and she gathered them as she passed home from afternoon church – 'surely, there never will be such a dreary, miserable winter again as this has been.' There had been a great change in Nathan and Hester Huntroyd during this last year. The spring before, when Benjamin was yet the subject of more hopes than fears, his father and mother looked what I may call an elderly middle-aged couple: people who had a good deal of hearty work in them yet. Now – it was not his absence alone that caused the change – they looked frail and old, as if each day's natural trouble was a burden more than they could bear. For Nathan had heard sad reports about his only child, and had told them solemnly to his wife, as things too bad to be believed, and yet, 'God help us, if indeed he is such a lad as this!' Their eyes were become too dry and hollow for many tears; they sate together, hand in hand; and shivered, and sighed, and did not speak many words, or dare to look at each other: and then Hester had said, –

'We mauna tell th' lass. Young folks' hearts break wi' a little, and she'd be apt to fancy it were true.' Here the old woman's voice broke into a kind of piping cry, but she struggled, and her next words were all right. 'We mauna tell her; he's bound to be fond on her, and may-be, if she thinks well on him, and loves him, it will bring him straight!'

'God grant it!' said Nathan.

'God shall grant it!' said Hester, passionately moaning out her words; and then repeating them, alas! with a vain repetition.

'It's a bad place for lying, is Highminster,' said she at length, as if impatient of the silence. 'I never knowed such a place for getting up stories. But Bessy knows nought on, and nother you nor me belie'es 'em; that's one blessing.'

But if they did not in their hearts believe them, how came they to look so sad, and worn, beyond what mere age could make them?

Then came round another year, another winter, yet more miserable than the last. This year, with the primroses, came Benjamin; a bad, hard, flippant young man, with yet enough of specious manners and handsome countenance to make his appearance striking at first to those to whom the aspect of a London fast young man of the lowest order is strange and new. Just at first, as he sauntered in with a swagger and an air of indifference, which was partly assumed, partly real, his old parents felt a simple kind of awe of him, as if he were not their son, but a real gentleman; but they had too much fine instinct in their homely natures not to know, after a very few minutes had passed, that this was not a true prince.

'Whatten ever does he mean,' said Hester to her niece, as soon as they were alone, 'by a' them maks and wearlocks?* And he minces his words as if his tongue were clipped short, or split like a magpie's. Hech! London is as bad as a hot day i' August for spoiling good flesh; for he were a good-looking lad when he went up; and now, look at him, with his skin gone into lines and flourishes, just like the first page on a copy-book!'*

'I think he looks a good deal better, aunt, for them new-fashioned whiskers!' said Bessy, blushing still at the remembrance of the kiss he had given her on first seeing her – a pledge, she thought, poor girl, that, in spite of his long silence in letter-writing, he still looked upon her as his troth-plight wife. There were things about him which none of them liked,

although they never spoke of them, yet there was also something to gratify them in the way in which he remained quiet at
Nab-end, instead of seeking variety, as he had formerly done,
by constantly stealing off to the neighbouring town. His father
had paid all the debts that he knew of, soon after Benjamin
had gone up to London; so there were no duns that his parents
knew of to alarm him, and keep him at home. And he went
out in the morning with the old man, his father, and lounged
by his side, as Nathan went round his fields, with busy yet
infirm gait, having heart, as he would have expressed it, in all
that was going on, because at length his son seemed to take an
interest in the farming affairs, and stood patiently by his side,
while he compared his own small galloways with the great
short-horns looming over his neighbour's hedge.

'It's a slovenly way, thou seest, that of selling th' milk; folk
don't care whether it's good or not, so that they get their pint-
measure full of stuff that's watered afore it leaves th' beast,
instead o' honest cheating by the help o' th' pump. But look at
Bessy's butter, what skill it shows! part her own manner o'
making, and part good choice o' cattle. It's a pleasure to see
her basket, a' packed ready for to go to market; and it's noan
o' a pleasure for to see the buckets fu' of their blue starch-
water* as yon beasts give. I'm thinking they crossed th' breed
wi' a pump not long sin'. Hech! but our Bessy's a cleaver
canny wench! I sometimes think thou'lt be for gi'eing up th'
law, and taking to th' oud trade, when thou wedst wi' her!'
This was intended to be a skilful way of ascertaining whether
there was any ground for the old farmer's wish and prayer that
Benjamin might give up the law, and return to the primitive
occupation of his father. Nathan dared to hope it now, since
his son had never made much by his profession, owing, as he
had said, to his want of a connexion: and the farm, and the
stock, and the clean wife, too, were ready to his hand; and
Nathan could safely rely on himself never in his most un-
guarded moments to reproach his son with the hardly-earned
hundreds that had been spent on his education. So the old man
listened with painful interest to the answer which his son was
evidently struggling to make; coughing a little, and blowing
his nose before he spoke.

'Well! you see, father, law is a precarious livelihood; a man, as I may express myself, has no chance in the profession unless he is known – known to the judges, and tiptop barristers, and that sort of thing. Now, you see, my mother and you have no acquaintance that you may call exactly in that line. But luckily I have met with a man, a friend, as I may say, who is really a first-rate fellow, knowing everybody, from the Lord Chancellor downwards; and he has offered me a share in his business – a partnership in short – ' He hesitated a little.

'I'm sure that's uncommon kind of the gentleman,' said Nathan. 'I should like for to thank him mysen; for it's not many as would pick up a young chap out o' th' dirt as it were, and say, "Here's hauf my good fortune for you, sir, and your very good health." Most on 'em, when they're gettin' a bit o' luck, run off wi' it to keep it a' to themselves, and gobble it down in a corner. What may be his name, for I should like to know it?'

'You don't quite apprehend me, father. A great deal of what you've said is true to the letter. People don't like to share their good luck, as you say.'

'The more credit to them as does,' broke in Nathan.

'Aye, but, you see, even such a fine fellow as my friend Cavendish does not like to give away half his good practice for nothing. He expects an equivalent.'

'An equivalent,' said Nathan: his voice had dropped down an octave. 'And what may that be? There's always some meaning in grand words, I take it, though I'm not book-larned enough to find it out.'

'Why, in this case the equivalent he demands for taking me into partnership, and afterwards relinquishing the whole business to me, is three hundred pounds down.'

Benjamin looked sideways from under his eyes to see how his father took the proposition. His father struck his stick deep down in the ground, and leaning one hand upon it, faced round at him.

'Then thy fine friend may go and be hanged. Three hunder pound! I'll be darned an' danged too, if I know where to get 'em, e'en if I'd be making a fool o' thee an' mysen too.'

He was out of breath by this time. His son took his father's first words in dogged silence; it was but the burst of surprise he had led himself to expect, and did not daunt him for long.

'I should think, sir – '

' "Sir" – whatten for dost thou "sir" me? Is them your manners? I'm plain Nathan Huntroyd, who never took on to be a gentleman; but I have paid my way up to this time, which I shannot do much longer, if I'm to have a son coming an' asking me for three hunder pound, just meet same* as if I were a cow, and had nothing to do but let down my milk to the first person as strokes me.'

'Well, father,' said Benjamin, with an affectation of frankness, 'then there's nothing for me, but to do as I have often planned before; go and emigrate.'

'And *what?*' said his father, looking sharply and steadily at him.

'Emigrate. Go to America, or India, or some colony where there would be an opening for a young man of spirit.'

Benjamin had reserved this proposition for his trump card, expecting by means of it to carry all before him. But, to his surprise, his father plucked his stick out of the hole he had made when he so vehemently thrust it into the ground, and walked on four or five steps in advance; there he stood still again, and there was a dead silence for a few minutes.

'It 'ud, may-be, be th' best thing thou couldst do,' the father began. Benjamin set his teeth hard to keep in curses. It was well for poor Nathan he did not look round then, and see the look his son gave him. 'But it would come hard like upon us, upon Hester and me, for, whether thou'rt a good 'un or not, thou'rt our flesh and blood, our only bairn, and if thou'rt not all as a man could wish, it's, may-be, been the fault on our pride i' thee. – It 'ud kill the missus if he went off to Amerikay, and Bess, too, the lass as thinks so much on him!' The speech, originally addressed to his son, had wandered off into a monologue – as keenly listened to by Benjamin, however, as if it had all been spoken to him. After a pause of consideration, his father turned round: 'Yon man – I wunnot call him a friend o' yourn, to think of asking you for such a mint o' money – is not th' only one, I'll be bound, as could give ye a start i' the law? Other folks 'ud, may-be, do it for less?'

'Not one of 'em; to give me equal advantages,' said Benjamin, thinking he perceived signs of relenting.

'Well, then, thou mayst tell him, that it's nother he nor

thee as 'll see th' sight o' three hunder pound o' my money. I'll not deny as I've a bit laid up again a rainy day; it's not so much as thatten thouf, and a part on it is for Bessy, as has been like a daughter to us.'

'But Bessy is to be your real daughter some day, when I've a home to take her to,' said Benjamin; for he played very fast and loose, even in his own mind, with his engagement with Bessy. Present with her, when she was looking her brightest and best, he behaved to her as if they were engaged lovers: absent from her, he looked upon her rather as a good wedge, to be driven into his parent's favour on his behalf. Now, however, he was not exactly untrue in speaking as if he meant to make her his wife; for the thought was in his mind, though he made use of it to work upon his father.

'It will be a dree day for us, then,' said the old man. 'But God'll have us in his keeping, and'll may-happen be taking more care on us i' heaven by that time than Bess, good lass as she is, has had on us at Nab-end. Her heart is set on thee, too. But, lad, I hanna gotten the three hunder; I keeps my cash i' th' stocking, thou knowst, till it reaches fifty pound, and then I takes it to Ripon Bank. Now the last scratch they'n gi'en me, made it just two hunder, and I hanna but on to fifteen pound yet i' the stockin', and I meant one hunder an' the red cow's calf to be for Bess, she's ta'en such pleasure like i' rearing it.'

Benjamin gave a sharp glance at his father to see if he was telling the truth; and, that a suspicion of the old man, his father, had entered into the son's head, tells enough of his own character.

'I canna do it – I canna do it, for sure – although I shall like to think as I had helped on the wedding. There's the black heifer to be sold yet, and she'll fetch a matter of ten pound; but a deal on't will be needed for seed-corn, for the arable did but bad last year, and I thought I would try – I'll tell thee what, lad! I'll make it as thouf Bess lent thee her hunder, only thou must give her a writ of hand for it, and thou shalt have a' the money i' Ripon Bank, and see if the lawyer wunnot let thee have a share of what he offered thee at three hunder, for two. I dunnot mean for to wrong him, but thou must get a fair share for the money. At times I think thou'rt done by folk;

now, I wadna have you cheat a bairn of a brass farthing; same time I wadna have thee so soft as to be cheated.'

To explain this, it should be told that some of the bills which Benjamin had received money from his father to pay, had been altered so as to cover other and less creditable expenses which the young man had incurred; and the simple old farmer, who had still much faith left in him for his boy, was acute enough to perceive that he had paid above the usual price for the articles he had purchased.

After some hesitation, Benjamin agreed to receive this two hundred, and promised to employ it to the best advantage in setting himself up in business. He had, nevertheless, a strange hankering after the additional fifteen pounds that was left to accumulate in the stocking. It was his, he thought, as heir to his father; and he soon lost some of his usual complaisance for Bessy that evening, as he dwelt on the idea that there was money being laid by for her, and grudged it to her even in imagination. He thought more of this fifteen pounds that he was not to have, than of all the hardly-earned and humbly-saved two hundred that he was to come into possession of. Meanwhile Nathan was in unusual spirits that evening. He was so generous and affectionate at heart, that he had an unconscious satisfaction in having helped two people on the road to happiness by the sacrifice of the greater part of his property. The very fact of having trusted his son so largely, seemed to make Benjamin more worthy of trust in his father's estimation. The sole idea he tried to banish was, that, if all came to pass as he hoped, both Benjamin and Bessy would be settled far away from Nab-end; but then he had a child-like reliance that 'God would take care of him and his missus, somehow or anodder. It wur o' no use looking too far ahead.'

Bessy had to hear many unintelligible jokes from her uncle that night; for he made no doubt that Benjamin had told her all that had passed, whereas the truth was, his son had said never a word to his cousin on the subject.

When the old couple were in bed, Nathan told his wife of the promise he had made to his son, and the plan in life which the advance of the two hundred was to promote. Poor Hester was a little startled at the sudden change in the destination of the sum, which she had long thought of with secret pride as 'money i' th' bank.' But she was willing enough to part with it, if necessary, for Benjamin. Only, how such a sum could be necessary, was the puzzle. But even this perplexity was jostled out of her mind by the overwhelming idea, not only of 'our Ben' settling in London, but of Bessy going there too as his wife. This great trouble swallowed up all care about money, and Hester shivered and sighed all the night through with distress. In the morning, as Bessy was kneading the bread, her aunt, who had been sitting by the fire in an unusual manner, for one of her active habits, said, –

'I reckon we maun go to th' shop for our bread, an' that's a thing I never thought to come to so long as I lived.'

Bessy looked up from her kneading, surprised.

'I'm sure, I'm noan going to eat their nasty stuff. What for do ye want to get baker's bread, aunt? This dough will rise as high as a kite in a south wind.'

'I'm not up to kneading as I could do once; it welly breaks my back; and when thou'rt off in London, I reckon we maun buy our bread, first time in my life.'

'I'm not a-going to London,' said Bessy, kneading away with fresh resolution, and growing very red, either with the idea or the exertion.

'But our Ben is going partner wi' a great London lawyer, and thou know'st he'll not tarry long but what he'll fetch thee.'

'Now, aunt,' said Bessy, stripping her arms of the dough, but still not looking up, 'if that's all, don't fret yourself. Ben will have twenty minds in his head afore he settles, eyther in business or in wedlock. I sometimes wonder,' she said, with increasing vehemence, 'why I go on thinking on him; for I dunnot think he thinks on me, when I'm out o' sight. I've a month's mind* to try and forget him this time when he leaves us – that I have!'

'For shame, wench! and he to be planning and purposing all for thy sake. It wur only yesterday as he wur talking to thy uncle, and mapping it out so clever; only thou seest, wench, it'll be dree work for us when both thee and him is gone.'

The old woman began to cry the kind of tearless cry of the aged. Bessy hastened to comfort her; and the two talked, and grieved, and hoped, and planned for the days that now were to be, till they ended, the one in being consoled, the other in being secretly happy.

Nathan and his son came back from Highminster that evening, with their business transacted in the roundabout way, which was most satisfactory to the old man. If he had thought it necessary to take half as much pains in ascertaining the truth of the plausible details by which his son bore out the story of the offered partnership, as he did in trying to get his money conveyed to London in the most secure manner, it would have been well for him. But he knew nothing of all this, and acted in the way which satisfied his anxiety best. He came home tired, but content; not in such high spirits as on the night before, but as easy in his mind as he could be on the eve of his son's departure. Bessy, pleasantly agitated by her aunt's tale of the morning of her cousin's true love for her – what ardently we wish we long believe – and the plan which was to end in their marriage – end to her, the woman, at least – Bessy looked almost pretty in her bright, blushing comeliness, and more than once, as she moved about from kitchen to dairy, Benjamin pulled her towards him, and gave her a kiss. To all such proceedings the old couple were wilfully blind; and, as night drew on, every one became sadder and quieter, thinking of the parting that was to be on the morrow. As the hours slipped away, Bessy, too, became subdued; and, by-and-by, her simple cunning was exerted to get Benjamin to sit down next his mother, whose very heart was yearning after him, as Bessy saw. When once her child was placed by her side, and she had got possession of his hand, the old woman kept stroking it, and murmuring long unused words of endearment, such as she had spoken to him while he was yet a little child. But all this was wearisome to him. As long as he might play with, and plague, and caress Bessy, he had not been sleepy; but now he yawned loudly. Bessy could have boxed his ears for not curbing this gaping; at any rate, he need not have done it so openly – so almost ostentatiously. His mother was more pitiful.

'Thou'rt tired, my lad!' said she, putting her hand fondly on his shoulder; but it fell off, as he stood up suddenly, and said, –

'Yes, deuced tired! I'm off to bed.' And with a rough care-less kiss all round, even to Bessy, as if he was 'deuced tired' of playing the lover, he was gone; leaving the three to gather up their thoughts slowly, and follow him up stairs.

He seemed almost impatient at them for rising betimes to see him off the next morning, and made no more of a good-bye than some such speech as this: 'Well, good folk, when next I see you, I hope you'll have merrier faces than you have to-day. Why, you might be going to a funeral; it's enough to scare a man from the place; you look quite ugly to what you did last night, Bess.'

He was gone; and they turned into the house, and settled to the long day's work without many words about their loss. They had no time for unnecessary talking, indeed, for much had been left undone, during his short visit, that ought to have been done; and they had now to work double tides.* Hard work was their comfort for many a long day.

For some time, Benjamin's letters, if not frequent, were full of exultant accounts of his well-doing. It is true that the details of his prosperity were somewhat vague; but the fact was broadly and unmistakably stated. Then came longer pauses; shorter letters, altered in tone. About a year after he had left them, Nathan received a letter, which bewildered and irritated him exceedingly. Something had gone wrong – what, Benjamin did not say – but the letter ended with a request that was almost a demand, for the remainder of his father's savings, whether in the stocking or the bank. Now, the year had not been prosperous with Nathan; there had been an epidemic among cattle, and he had suffered along with his neighbours; and, moreover, the price of cows, when he had bought some to repair his wasted stock, was higher than he had ever re-membered it before. The fifteen pounds in the stocking, which Benjamin left, had diminished to little more than three; and to have that required of him in so peremptory a manner! Before Nathan imparted the contents of this letter to any one (Bessy and her aunt had gone to market on a neighbour's cart that day), he got pen and ink and paper, and wrote back an ill-spelt, but very implicit and stern negative. Benjamin had had his portion; and if he could not make it do, so much the worse for him; his father had no more to give him. That was the substance of the letter.

The letter was written, directed, and sealed, and given to

the country postman, returning to Highminster after his day's distribution and collection of letters, before Hester and Bessy came back from market. It had been a pleasant day of neighbourly meeting and sociable gossip: prices had been high, and they were in good spirits, only agreeably tired, and full of small pieces of news. It was some time before they found out how flatly all their talk fell on the ears of the stay-at-home listener. But, when they saw that his depression was caused by something beyond their powers of accounting for by any little every-day cause, they urged him to tell them what was the matter. His anger had not gone off. It had rather increased by dwelling upon it, and he spoke it out in good resolute terms; and, long ere he had ended, the two women were as sad, if not as angry, as himself. Indeed, it was many days before either feeling wore away in the minds of those who entertained them. Bessy was the soonest comforted, because she found a vent for her sorrow in action; action that was half as a kind of compensation for many a sharp word that she had spoken, when her cousin had done anything to displease her on his last visit, and half because she believed that he never could have written such a letter to his father, unless his want of money had been very pressing and real; though how he could ever have wanted money so soon, after such a heap of it had been given to him, was more than she could justly say. Bessy got out all her savings of little presents of sixpences and shillings, ever since she had been a child, – of all the money she had gained for the eggs of two hens, called her own; she put the whole together, and it was above two pounds – two pound, five and sevenpence, to speak accurately – and, leaving out the penny as a nest-egg for her future savings, she made up the rest in a little parcel, and sent it, with a note, to Benjamin's address in London: –

'From a well-wisher.
Dr. BENJAMIN, – Unkle has lost 2 cows and a vast of monney. He is a good deal Angored, but more Troubled. So no more at present. Hopeing this will finding you well As it leaves us. Tho' lost to Site, To Memory Dear.* Repayment not kneeded.
                    'Your effectonet cousin,
                              'ELIZABETH ROSE.'

When this packet was once fairly sent off, Bessy began to sing again over her work. She never expected the mere form of acknowledgment; indeed, she had such faith in the carrier (who took parcels to York, whence they were forwarded to London by coach), that she felt sure he would go on purpose to London to deliver anything intrusted to him, if he had not full confidence in the person, persons, coach and horses, to whom he committed it. Therefore she was not anxious that she did not hear of its arrival. 'Giving a thing to a man as one knows,' said she to herself, 'is a vast different to poking a thing through a hole into a box,* th' inside of which one has never clapped eyes on; and yet letters get safe some ways or another.' (This belief in the infallibility of the post was destined to a shock before long.) But she had a secret yearning for Benjamin's thanks, and some of the old words of love that she had been without so long. Nay, she even thought – when, day after day, week after week, passed by without a line – that he might be winding up his affairs in that weary, wasteful London, and coming back to Nab-end to thank her in person.

One day – her aunt was up stairs, inspecting the summer's make of cheeses, her uncle out in the fields – the postman brought a letter into the kitchen to Bessy. A country postman, even now, is not much pressed for time, and in those days there were but few letters to distribute, and they were only sent out from Highminster once a week into the district in which Nab-end was situated; and on those occasions, the letter-carrier usually paid morning calls on the various people for whom he had letters. So, half standing by the dresser, half sitting on it, he began to rummage out his bag. 'It's a queer-like thing I've got for Nathan this time. I am afraid it will bear ill news in it, for there's "Dead Letter Office" stamped on the top of it.'

'Lord save us!' said Bessy, and sate down on the nearest chair, as white as a sheet. In an instant, however, she was up, and, snatching the ominous letter out of the man's hands, she pushed him before her out of the house, and said, 'Be off wi' thee, afore aunt comes down;' and ran past him as hard as she could, till she reached the field where she expected to find her uncle.

'Uncle,' said she, breathless, 'what is it? Oh, uncle, speak! Is he dead?'

Nathan's hands trembled, and his eyes dazzled. 'Take it,' he said, 'and tell me what it is.'

'It's a letter – it's from you to Benjamin, it is – and there's words written on it, "Not known at the address given"; so they've sent it back to the writer – that's you, uncle. Oh, it gave me such a start, with them nasty words written outside!'

Nathan had taken the letter back into his own hands, and was turning it over, while he strove to understand what the quick-witted Bessy had picked up at a glance. But he arrived at a different conclusion.

'He's dead!' said he. 'The lad is dead, and he never knowed how as I were sorry I wrote to 'un so sharp. My lad! my lad!' Nathan sate down on the ground where he stood, and covered his face with his old, withered hands. The letter returned to him was one which he had written, with infinite pains and at various times, to tell his child, in kinder words and at greater length than he had done before, the reasons why he could not send him the money demanded. And now Benjamin was dead; nay, the old man immediately jumped to the conclusion that his child had been starved to death, without money, in a wild, wide, strange place. All he could say at first was, –

'My heart, Bess – my heart is broken!' And he put his hand to his side, still keeping his shut eyes covered with the other, as though he never wished to see the light of day again. Bessy was down by his side in an instant, holding him in her arms, chafing and kissing him.

'It's noan so bad, uncle; he's not dead; the letter does not say that, dunnot think it. He's flitted from that lodging, and the lazy tykes dunna know where to find him; and so, they just send y' back th' letter, instead of trying fra' house to house, as Mark Benson would. I've always heerd tell on south country folk for laziness. He's noan dead, uncle; he's just flitted, and he'll let us know afore long where he's getten to, May-be it's a cheaper place, for that lawyer has cheated him. ye reck'let, and he'll be trying to live for as little as he can, that's all, uncle. Dunnot take on so, for it doesna say he's dead.'

By this time, Bessy was crying with agitation, although she firmly believed in her own view of the case, and had felt the opening of the ill-favoured letter as a great relief. Presently she began to urge, both with word and action upon her uncle, that he should sit no longer on the damp grass. She pulled him up, for he was very stiff, and, as he said, 'all shaken to dithers.' She made him walk about, repeating over and over again her solution of the case, always in the same words, beginning again and again, 'He's noan dead; it's just been a flitting,' and so on. Nathan shook his head, and tried to be convinced; but it was a steady belief in his own heart for all that. He looked so deathly ill on his return home with Bessy (for she would not let him go on with his day's work), that his wife made sure he had taken cold, and he, weary and indifferent to life, was glad to subside into bed and the rest from exertion which his real bodily illness gave him. Neither Bessy nor he spoke of the letter again, even to each other, for many days; and she found means to stop Mark Benson's tongue, and satisfy his kindly curiosity, by giving him the rosy side of her own view of the case.

Nathan got up again, an older man in looks and constitution by ten years for that week of bed. His wife gave him many a scolding on his imprudence for sitting down in the wet field, if ever so tired. But now she, too, was beginning to be uneasy at Benjamin's long-continued silence. She could not write herself, but she urged her husband many a time to send a letter to ask for news of her lad. He said nothing in reply for some time: at length, he told her he would write next Sunday afternoon. Sunday was his general day for writing, and this Sunday he meant to go to church for the first time since his illness. On Saturday he was very persistent against his wife's wishes (backed by Bessy as hard as she could), in resolving to go into Highminster to market. The change would do him good, he said. But he came home tired, and a little mysterious in his ways. When he went to the shippon the last thing at night, he asked Bessy to go with him, and hold the lantern, while he looked at an ailing cow; and, when they were fairly out of the earshot of the house, he pulled a little shop-parcel from his pocket and said, –

'Thou'lt put that on ma Sunday hat, wilt'ou, lass? It'll be a bit on a comfort to me; for I know my lad's dead and gone, though I dunna speak on it, for fear o' grieving th' old woman and ye.'

'I'll put it on, uncle, if – But he's noan dead.' (Bessy was sobbing.)

'I know – I know, lass. I dunnot wish other folk to hold my opinion; but I'd like to wear a bit o' crape, out o' respect to my boy. It 'ud have done me good for to have ordered a black coat, but she'd see if I had na on my wedding-coat, Sundays, for a' she's losing her eyesight, poor old wench! But she'll ne'er take notice o' a bit o' crape. Thou'lt put it on all canny and tidy.'

So Nathan went to church with a strip of crape, as narrow as Bessy durst venture to make it, round his hat. Such is the contradictoriness of human nature, that, though he was most anxious his wife should not hear of his conviction that their son was dead, he was half hurt that none of his neighbours noticed his sign of mourning so far as to ask him for whom he wore it.

But after a while, when they never heard a word from or about Benjamin, the household wonder as to what had become of him grew so painful and strong, that Nathan no longer kept his idea to himself. Poor Hester, however, rejected it with her whole will, heart, and soul. She could not and would not believe – nothing should make her believe – that her only child Benjamin had died without some sign of love or farewell to her. No arguments could shake her in this. She believed that, if all natural means of communication between her and him had been cut off at the last supreme moment – if death had come upon him in an instant, sudden and unexpected – her intense love would have been supernaturally made conscious of the blank. Nathan at times tried to feel glad that she could still hope to see the lad again; but at other moments he wanted her sympathy in his grief, his self-reproach, his weary wonder as to how and what they had done wrong in the treatment of their son, that he had been such a care and sorrow to his parents. Bessy was convinced, first by her aunt, and then by her uncle – honestly convinced – on both sides of the argument; and so, for the time, able to sympathise with each. But she lost her youth in a very few months; she looked set and middle-aged long before she ought to have done; and rarely smiled and never sang again.

All sorts of new arrangements were required, by the blow which told so miserably upon the energies of all the household at Nab-end. Nathan could no longer go about and direct his two men, taking a good turn of work himself at busy times. Hester lost her interest in her dairy; for which, indeed, her increasing loss of sight unfitted her. Bessy would either do field work, or attend to the cows and the shippon, or churn, or make cheese; she did all well, no longer merrily, but with something of stern cleverness. But she was not sorry when her uncle, one evening, told her aunt and her that a neighbouring farmer, Job Kirkby, had made him an offer to take so much of his land off his hands as would leave him only pasture enough for two cows, and no arable to attend to; while Farmer Kirkby did not wish to interfere with anything in the house, only would be glad to use some of the outbuildings for his fattening cattle.

'We can do wi' Hawky and Daisy; it'll leave us eight or ten pound o' butter to take to market i' summer time, and keep us fra' thinking too much, which is what I'm dreading on as I get into years.'

'Aye,' said his wife. 'Thou'll not have to go so far afield, if it's only the Aster-Toft as is on thy hands. And Bess will have to gie up her pride i' cheese, and tak' to making cream-butter. I'd allays a fancy for trying at cream-butter, but th' whey had to be used; else, where I come fra', they'd never ha' looked near whey-butter.'

When Hester was left alone with Bessy, she said, in allusion to this change of plan, –

'I'm thankful to the Lord that it is as it is: for I were allays feared Nathan would have to gie up the house and farm altogether, and then the lad would na know where to find us when he came back fra' Merikay. He's gone there for to make his fortune, I'll be bound. Keep up thy heart, lass, he'll be home some day; and have sown his wild oats. Eh! but thatten's a pretty story i' the Gospels about the Prodigal,* who'd to eat the pigs' vittle at one time, but ended i' clover in his father's house. And I'm sure our Nathan 'll be ready to forgive him, and love him, and make much of him, may-be a deal more nor me, who never gave in to's death. It 'll be liken to a resurrection to our Nathan.'

Farmer Kirkby, then, took by far the greater part of the land belonging to Nab-end Farm; and the work about the rest, and about the two remaining cows, was easily done by three pairs of willing hands, with a little occasional assistance. The Kirkby family were pleasant enough to have to deal with. There was a son, a stiff, grave bachelor, who was very particular and methodical about his work, and rarely spoke to any one. But Nathan took it into his head that John Kirkby was looking after Bessy, and was a good deal troubled in his mind in consequence; for it was the first time he had to face the effects of his belief in his son's death; and he discovered, to his own surprise, that he had not that implicit faith, which would make it easy for him to look upon Bessy as the wife of another man, than the one to whom she had been betrothed in her youth. As, however, John Kirkby seemed in no hurry to make his intentions (if indeed he had any) clear to Bessy, it was only now and then that this jealousy on behalf of his lost son seized upon Nathan.

But people, old, and in deep hopeless sorrow, grow irritable at times, however they may repent and struggle against their irritability. There were days when Bessy had to bear a good deal from her uncle; but she loved him so dearly and respected him so much, that, high as her temper was to all other people, she never returned him a rough or impatient word. And she had a reward in the conviction of his deep, true affection for her, and her aunt's entire and most sweet dependence upon her.

One day, however – it was near the end of November – Bessy had had a good deal to bear, that seemed more than usually unreasonable, on behalf of her uncle. The truth was, that one of Kirkby's cows was ill, and John Kirkby was a good deal about in the farmyard; Bessy was interested about the animal, and had helped in preparing a mash over their own fire, that had to be given warm to the sick creature. If John had been out of the way, there would have been no one more anxious about the affair than Nathan; both because he was naturally kind-hearted and neighbourly, and also because he was rather proud of his reputation for knowledge in the diseases of cattle. But because John was about, and Bessy helping a little in what had to be done, Nathan would do nothing, and chose to assume that 'nothing to think on ailed th' beast, but lads and lasses were allays fain to be feared on something'. Now John was upwards of forty, and Bessy nearly eight-and-twenty, so the terms lads and lasses did not exactly apply to their case.

When Bessy brought the milk in from their own cows, towards half-past five o'clock, Nathan bade her make the doors, and not be running out i' the dark and cold about other folk's business; and, though Bessy was a little surprised and a good deal annoyed at his tone, she sate down to her supper without making a remonstrance. It had long been Nathan's custom to look out the last thing at night, to see 'what mak' o' weather it wur'; and when, towards half-past eight, he got his stick and went out – two or three steps from the door, which opened into the house-place where they were sitting – Hester put her hand on her niece's shoulder and said, –

'He's gotten a touch o' the rheumatics, as twinges him and makes him speak so sharp. I didna like to ask thee afore him, but how's yon poor beast?'

'Very ailing, belike. John Kirkby wur off for th' cow-doctor when I cam in. I reckon they'll have to stop up wi't a' night.'

Since their sorrows, her uncle had taken to reading a chapter in the Bible aloud, the last thing at night. He could not read fluently, and often hesitated long over a word, which he miscalled at length; but the very fact of opening the book seemed to soothe those old bereaved parents; for it made them feel quiet and safe in the presence of God, and took them out of the cares and troubles of this world into that futurity which, however dim and vague, was to their faithful hearts as a sure and certain rest.* This little quiet time – Nathan sitting with his horn spectacles; the tallow candle between him and the Bible, and throwing a strong light on his reverent, earnest face; Hester sitting on the other side of the fire, her head bowed in attentive listening, now and then shaking it, and moaning a little, but when a promise came, or any good tidings of great joy, saying 'Amen' with fervour; Bessy by her aunt, perhaps her mind a little wandering to some household cares, or it might be on thoughts of those who were absent – this little quiet pause, I say, was grateful and soothing to this household, as a lullaby to a tired child. But this night, Bessy – sitting opposite to the long low window, only shaded by a few geraniums that grew in the sill, and to the door alongside that window, through which her uncle had passed not a quarter of an hour before – saw the wooden latch of the door gently and almost noiselessly lifted up, as if some one were trying it from the outside.

She was startled; and watched again, intently; but it was perfectly still now. She thought it must have been that it had not fallen into its proper place, when her uncle had come in and locked the door. It was just enough to make her uncomfortable, no more; and she almost persuaded herself it must have been fancy. Before going up stairs, however, she went to the window to look out into the darkness; but all was still. Nothing to be seen; nothing to be heard. So the three went quietly up stairs to bed.

The house was little better than a cottage. The front door opened on a house-place, over which was the old couple's bedroom. To the left, as you entered this pleasant house-place, and at close right angles with the entrance, was a door that led into the small parlour, which was Hester's and Bessy's pride, although not half as comfortable as the house-place, and never on any occasion used as a sitting-room. There were shells and bunches of honesty in the fireplace; the best chest of drawers, and a company-set of gaudy-coloured china, and a bright common carpet on the floor; but all failed to give it the aspect of the homely comfort and delicate cleanliness of the house-place. Over this parlour was the bedroom which Benjamin had slept in when a boy – when at home. It was kept still in a kind of readiness for him. The bed was yet there, in which none had slept since he had last done, eight or nine years ago; and every now and then, the warming-pan was taken quietly and silently up by his old mother, and the bed thoroughly aired. But this she did in her husband's absence, and without saying a word to any one; nor did Bessy offer to help her, though her eyes often filled with tears, as she saw her aunt still going through the hopeless service. But the room had become a receptacle for all unused things; and there was always a corner of it appropriated to the winter's store of apples.

To the left of the house-place, as you stood facing the fire, on the side opposite to the window and outer door, were two other doors; the one on the right led into a kind of back kitchen, and had a lean-to roof, and a door opening on to the farm-yard and back premises; the left-hand door gave on the stairs, underneath which was a closet, in which various household treasures were kept, and beyond that the dairy, over which Bessy slept; her little chamber window opening just above the sloping roof of the back kitchen. There were neither blinds nor shutters to any of the windows, either up stairs or down; the house was built of stone, and there was heavy framework of the same material round the little casement windows, and the long, low window of the house-place was divided by what, in grander dwellings, would be called mullions.

By nine o'clock this night of which I am speaking, all had gone up stairs to bed: it was even later than usual, for the burning of candles was regarded so much in the light of an extravagance, that the household kept early hours even for country-folk. But, somehow, this evening, Bessy could not sleep, although, in general, she was in deep slumber five minutes after her head touched the pillow. Her thoughts ran on the chances for John Kirkby's cow, and a little fear lest the disorder might be epidemic, and spread to their own cattle. Across all these homely cares came a vivid, uncomfortable recollection of the way in which the door-latch went up and down, without any sufficient agency to account for it. She felt more sure now, than she had done down stairs, that it was a real movement and no effect of her imagination. She wished that it had not happened just when her uncle was reading, that she might at once have gone quick to the door, and convinced herself of the cause. As it was, her thoughts ran uneasily on the supernatural; and thence to Benjamin, her dear cousin and play-fellow, her early lover. She had long given him up as lost for ever to her, if not actually dead; but this very giving him up for ever involved a free, full forgiveness of all his wrongs to her. She thought tenderly of him, as of one who might have been led astray in his later years, but who existed rather in her recollection as the innocent child, the spirited lad, the handsome, dashing young man. If John Kirkby's quiet attentions had ever betrayed his wishes to Bessy – if indeed he ever had any wishes on the subject – her first feeling would have been to compare his weather-beaten, middle-aged face and figure with the face and figure she remembered well, but never more expected to see in this life. So thinking, she became very restless, and weary of bed, and, after long tossing and turning, ending in a belief that she should never get to sleep at all that night, she went off soundly and suddenly.

As suddenly was she wide awake, sitting up in bed, listening to some noise that must have awakened her, but which was not repeated for some time. Surely it was in her uncle's room – her uncle was up; but, for a minute or two, there was no further sound. Then she heard him open his door, and go down stairs, with hurried, stumbling steps. She now thought that her aunt must be ill, and hastily sprang out of bed, and was putting on her petticoat with hurried, trembling hands, and had just opened her chamber door, when she heard the front door undone, and a scuffle, as of the feet of several people, and many rude, passionate words, spoken hoarsely below the breath. Quick as thought she understood it all – the house was lonely – her uncle had the reputation of being well-to-do – they had pretended to be belated, and had asked their way or something. What a blessing that John Kirkby's cow was sick, for there were several men watching with him! She went back, opened her window, squeezed herself out, slid down the lean-to roof, and ran barefoot and breathless, to the shippon.

'John, John, for the love of God, come quick; there's robbers in the house, and uncle and aunt'll be murdered!' she whispered, in terrified accents, through the closed and barred shippon door. In a moment it was undone, and John and the cow-doctor stood there, ready to act, if they but understood her rightly. Again she repeated her words, with broken, half-unintelligible explanations of what she as yet did not rightly understand.

'Front door is open, say'st thou?' said John, arming himself with a pitchfork, while the cow-doctor took some other implement. 'Then I reckon we'd best make for that way o' getting into th' house, and catch 'em all in a trap.'

'Run! run!' was all Bessy could say, taking hold of John Kirkby's arm, and pulling him along with her. Swiftly did the three run to the house, round the corner, and in at the open front door. The men carried the horn lantern they had been using in the shippon, and, by the sudden oblong light that it threw, Bessy saw the principal object of her anxiety, her uncle, lying stunned and helpless on the kitchen floor. Her first thought was for him; for she had no idea that her aunt was in any immediate danger, although she heard the noise of feet, and fierce subdued voices up stairs.

'Make th' door* behind us, lass. We'll not let 'em escape!' said brave John Kirkby, dauntless in a good cause, though he knew not how many there might be above. The cow-doctor fastened and locked the door, saying, 'There!' in a defiant tone, as he put the key in his pocket. It was to be a struggle for life or death, or, at any rate, for effectual capture or desperate escape. Bessy kneeled down by her uncle, who did not speak nor give any sign of consciousness. Bessy raised his head by drawing a pillow off the settle and putting it under him; she longed to go for water into the back kitchen, but the sound of a violent struggle, and of heavy blows, and of low, hard curses spoken through closed teeth, and muttered passion, as though breath were too much needed for action to be wasted in speech, kept her still and quiet by her uncle's side in the kitchen, where the darkness might almost be felt, so thick and deep was it. Once – in a pause of her own heart's beating – a sudden terror came over her; she perceived, in that strange way in which the presence of a living creature forces itself on our consciousness in the darkest room, that some one was near her, keeping as still as she. It was not the poor old man's breathing that she heard, nor the radiation of his presence that she felt; some one else was in the kitchen; another robber, perhaps, left to guard the old man, with murderous intent if his consciousness returned. Now, Bessy was fully aware that self-preservation would keep her terrible companion quiet, as there was no motive for his betraying himself stronger than the desire of escape; any effort for which he, the unseen witness, must know would be rendered abortive by the fact of the door being locked. Yet with the knowledge that he was there, close to her, still, silent as the grave, – with fearful, it might be deadly, unspoken thoughts in his heart, – possibly even with keener and stronger sight than hers, as longer accustomed to the darkness, able to discern her figure and posture, and glaring at her like some wild beast, – Bessy could not fail to shrink from the vision that her fancy presented! And still the struggle went on up stairs; feet slipping, blows sounding, and the wrench of intentioned aims, the strong gasps for breath, as the wrestlers paused for an instant. In one of these pauses, Bessy felt conscious of a creeping movement close to her, which ceased when the noise of the strife above died away, and was resumed when it again began. She was aware of it by some subtle vibration of the air, rather than by touch or sound. She was sure that he who had been close to her one minute as she knelt, was, the next, passing stealthily towards the inner door which led to the staircase. She thought he was going to join and strengthen his accomplices, and, with a great cry, she sprang after him; but, just as she came to the doorway, through which some dim portion of light from the upper chambers came, she saw one man thrown down stairs with such violence that he fell almost at her very feet, while the dark, creeping figure glided suddenly away to the left, and as suddenly entered the closet beneath the stairs. Bessy had no time to wonder as to his purpose in so doing, whether he had at first designed to aid his accomplices in their desperate fight or not. He was an enemy, a robber, that was all she knew, and she sprang to the door of the closet, and in a trice had locked it on the outside. And then she stood frightened, panting in that dark corner, sick with terror lest the man who lay before her was either John Kirkby or the cow-doctor. If it were either of those friendly two, what would become of the other – of her uncle, her aunt, herself? But, in a very few minutes, this wonder was ended; her two defenders came slowly and heavily down the stairs, dragging with them a man, fierce, sullen, despairing – disabled with terrible blows, which had made his face one bloody, swollen mass. As for that, neither John nor the cow-doctor were much more presentable. One of them bore the lantern in his teeth, for all their strength was taken up by the weight of the fellow they were bearing.

'Take care,' said Bessy, from her corner; 'there's a chap just beneath your feet. I dunno know if he's dead or alive, and uncle lies on the floor just beyond.'

They stood still on the stairs for a moment. Just then the robber they had thrown down stairs stirred and moaned.

'Bessy,' said John, 'run off to th' stable and fetch ropes and gearing* for to bind 'em, and we'll rid the house on 'em, and thou can'st go see after th' oud folks, who need it sadly.'

Bessy was back in a very few minutes. When she came in, there was more light in the house-place, for some one had stirred up the raked fire.

'That felly makes as though his leg were broken,' said John, nodding towards the man still lying on the ground. Bessy felt almost sorry for him as they handled him – not over gently – and bound him, only half-conscious, as hardly and tightly as they had done his fierce, surly companion. She even felt so sorry for his evident agony, as they turned him over and over, that she ran to get him a cup of water to moisten his lips.

'I'm loth to leave yo' with him alone,' said John, 'though I'm thinking his leg is broken for sartain, and he can't stir, even if he comes to hissel, to do yo' any harm. But we'll just take off this chap, and mak sure of him, and then one on us'll come back to yo', and we can, may-be, find a gate or so for yo' to get shut on him out o' th' house. This felly's made safe enough, I'll be bound,' said he, looking at the burglar, who stood, bloody and black, with fell hatred on his sullen face. His eye caught Bessy's as hers fell on him with dread so evident that it made him smile, and the look and the smile prevented the words from being spoken which were on Bessy's lips. She dared not tell, before him, that an able-bodied accomplice still remained in the house, lest, somehow, the door which kept him a prisoner should be broken open, and the fight renewed. So she only said to John, as he was leaving the house, –

'Thou'll not be long away, for I'm afeard of being left wi' this man.'

'He'll noan do thee harm,' said John.

'No! but I'm feared lest he should die. And there's uncle and aunt. Come back soon, John!'

'Aye, aye!' said he, half-pleased; 'I'll be back, never fear me.'

So Bessy shut the door after them, but did not lock it for fear of mischances in the house, and went once more to her uncle, whose breathing, by this time, was easier than when she had first returned into the house-place with John and the doctor. By the light of the fire, too, she could now see that he had received a blow on the head which was probably the occasion of his stupor. Round this wound, which was bleeding pretty freely, Bessy put cloths dipped in cold water, and then, leaving him for a time, she lighted a candle, and was about to go up stairs to her aunt, when, just as she was passing the bound and disabled robber, she heard her name softly, urgently called, –

'Bessy, Bessy!' At first the voice sounded so close that she thought it must be the unconscious wretch at her feet. But once again that voice thrilled through her, –

'Bessy, Bessy! for God's sake, let me out!'

She went to the stair-closet door, and tried to speak, but could not, her heart beat so terribly. Again, close to her ear, –

'Bessy, Bessy! they'll be back directly; let me out, I say! For God's sake, let me out!' And he began to kick violently against the panels.

'Hush, hush!' she said, sick with a terrible dread, yet with a will strongly resisting her conviction. 'Who are you?' But she knew – knew quite well.

'Benjamin.' An oath. 'Let me out, I say, and I'll be off, and out of England by to-morrow night, never to come back, and you'll have all my father's money.'

'D'ye think I care for that?' said Bessy, vehemently, feeling with trembling hands for the lock; 'I wish there was noan such a thing as money i' the world, afore yo'd come to this. There, yo're free, and I charge yo' never to let me see your face again. I'd ne'er ha' let yo' loose but for fear o' breaking their hearts, if yo' hanna killed them already.' But before she had ended her speech, he was gone – off into the black darkness, leaving the door open wide. With a new terror in her mind, Bessy shut it afresh – shut it and bolted it this time. Then she sate down on the first chair, and relieved her soul by giving a great and exceeding bitter cry. But she knew it was no time for giving way, and, lifting herself up with as much effort as if each of her limbs was a heavy weight, she went into the back kitchen, and took a drink of cold water. To her surprise, she heard her uncle's voice, saying feebly, –

'Carry me up, and lay me by her.'

But Bessy could not carry him: she could only help his faint exertions to walk up stairs; and, by the time he was there, sitting panting on the first chair she could find, John Kirkby and Atkinson returned. John came up now to her aid. Her aunt lay across the bed in a fainting fit, and her uncle sate in so utterly broken-down a state that Bessy feared immediate death for both. But John cheered her up, and lifted the old man into his bed again, and, while Bessy tried to compose poor Hester's limbs into a position of rest, John went down to hunt about for the little store of gin, which was always kept in a corner cupboard against emergencies.

'They've had a sore fright,' said he, shaking his head, as he poured a little gin and hot water into their mouths with a teaspoon, while Bessy chafed their cold feet; 'and it and the cold have been welly too much for 'em, poor old folk!'

He looked tenderly at them, and Bessy blessed him in her heart for that look.

'I maun be off. I sent Atkinson up to th' farm for to bring down Bob, and Jack came wi' him back to th' shippon for to look after t'other man. He began blackguarding us all round, so Bob and Jack were gagging him wi' bridles when I left.'

'Ne'er give heed to what he says,' cried poor Bessy, a new panic besetting her. 'Folks o' his sort are allays for dragging other folks into their mischief. I'm right glad he were well gagged.'

'Well! but what I were saying were this. Atkinson and me will take t'other chap, who seems quiet enough, to th' shippon, and it 'll be one piece o' work for to mind them, and the cow; and I'll saddle old bay mare and ride for constables and doctor fra' Highminster. I'll bring Dr Preston up to see Nathan and Hester first, and then I reckon th' broken-legged chap down below must have his turn, for all as he's met wi' his misfortunes in a wrong line o' life.'

'Aye!' said Bessy. 'We maun ha' the doctor sure enough, for look at them how they lie! like two stone statues on a church monument, so sad and solemn.'

'There's a look o' sense come back into their faces, though, sin' they supped that gin and water. I'd keep on a-bathing his head and giving them a sup on't fra' time to time, if I was you, Bessy.'

Bessy followed him down stairs, and lighted the men out of the house. She dared not light them carrying their burden even, until they passed round the corner of the house; so strong was her fearful conviction that Benjamin was lurking near, seeking again to enter. She rushed back into the kitchen, bolted and barred the door, and pushed the end of the dresser against it, shutting her eyes as she passed the uncurtained window, for fear of catching a glimpse of a white face pressed against the glass, and gazing at her. The poor old couple lay quiet and speechless, although Hester's position had slightly altered: she had turned a little on her side towards her husband, and had laid one shrivelled arm around his neck. But he was just as Bessy had left him, with the wet cloths around his head, his eyes not wanting in a certain intelligence, but solemn, and unconscious to all that was passing around as the eyes of death.

His wife spoke a little from time to time – said a word of thanks, perhaps, or so; but he, never. All the rest of that terrible night, Bessy tended the poor old couple with constant care, her own heart so stunned and bruised in its feelings that she went about her pious duties almost like one in a dream. The November morning was long in coming; nor did she perceive any change, either for the worse or the better, before the doctor came, about eight o'clock. John Kirkby brought him; and was full of the capture of the two burglars.

As far as Bessy could make out, the participation of that unnatural Third was unknown. It was a relief, almost sickening in the revulsion it gave her from her terrible fear, which now she felt had haunted and held possession of her all night long, and had in fact paralysed her from thinking. Now she felt and thought with acute and feverish vividness, owing no doubt, in part, to the sleepless night she had passed. She felt almost sure that her uncle (possibly her aunt too) had recognised Benjamin; but there was a faint chance that they had not done so, and wild horses should never tear the secret from her, nor should any inadvertent word betray the fact that there had been a third person concerned. As to Nathan, he had never uttered a word. It was her aunt's silence that made Bessy fear lest Hester knew, somehow, that her son was concerned.

The doctor examined them both closely; looked hard at the wound on Nathan's head; asked questions which Hester answered shortly and unwillingly, and Nathan not at all: shutting his eyes, as if even the sight of a stranger was pain to him.

Bessy replied in their stead to all that she could answer respecting their state; and followed the doctor down stairs with a beating heart. When they came into the house-place, they found John had opened the outer door to let in some fresh air, had brushed the hearth and made up the fire, and put the chairs and table in their right places. He reddened a little as Bessy's eye fell upon his swollen and battered face, but tried to smile it off in a dry kind of way.

'Yo' see, I'm an ould bachelor, and I just thought as I'd redd up things a bit. How dun yo' find 'em, doctor?'

'Well, the poor old couple have had a terrible shock. I shall send them some soothing medicine to bring down the pulse, and a lotion for the old man's head. It is very well it bled so much; there might have been a good deal of inflammation.' And so he went on, giving directions to Bessy for keeping them quietly in bed through the day. From these directions she gathered that they were not, as she had feared all night long, near to death. The doctor expected them to recover, though they would require care. She almost wished it had been otherwise, and that they, and she too, might have just lain down to their rest in the churchyard – so cruel did life seem to her; so dreadful the recollection of that subdued voice of the hidden robber, smiting her with recognition.

All this time John was getting things ready for breakfast, with something of the handiness of a woman. Bessy half resented his officiousness in pressing Dr Preston to have a cup of tea, she did so want him to be gone and leave her alone with her thoughts. She did not know that all was done for love of her; that the hard-featured, short-spoken John was thinking all the time how ill and miserable she looked, and trying with tender artifices to make it incumbent upon her sense of hospitality to share Dr Preston's meal.

'I've seen as the cows is milked,' said he, 'yourn and all; and Atkinson's brought ours round fine. Whatten a marcy it were as she were sick just this very night! Yon two chaps 'ud ha' made short work on't, if yo' hadna fetched us in; and as it were, we had a sore tussle. One on 'em 'll bear the marks on't to his dying day, wunnot he, doctor?'

'He'll barely have his leg well enough to stand his trial at York Assizes; they're coming off in a fortnight from now.'

'Aye, and that reminds me, Bessy, yo'll have to go witness before Justice Royds. Constables bade me tell yo', and gie yo' this summons. Dunnot be feared; it will not be a long job, though I'm not saying as it 'll be a pleasant one. Yo'll have to answer questions as to how, and all about it; and Jane' (his sister) 'will come and stop wi' th' oud folks; and I'll drive yo' in the shandry.'

No one knew why Bessy's colour blenched, and her eye clouded. No one knew how she apprehended lest she should have to say that Benjamin had been of the gang, if, indeed, in some way, the law had not followed on his heels quick enough to catch him.

But that trial was spared her; she was warned by John to answer questions, and say no more than was necessary, for fear of making her story less clear; and as she was known, by character at least, to Justice Royds and his clerk, they made the examination as little formidable as possible.

When all was over, and John was driving her back again, he expressed his rejoicing that there would be evidence enough to convict the men, without summoning Nathan and Hester to identify them. Bessy was so tired that she hardly understood what an escape it was; how far greater than even her companion understood.

Jane Kirkby stayed with her for a week or more, and was an unspeakable comfort. Otherwise she sometimes thought she should have gone mad, with the face of her uncle always reminding her, in its stony expression of agony, of that fearful night. Her aunt was softer in her sorrow, as became one of her faithful and pious nature; but it was easy to see how her heart bled inwardly. She recovered her strength sooner than her husband; but as she recovered, the doctor perceived the rapid approach of total blindness. Every day, nay, every hour of the day, that Bessy dared, without fear of exciting their suspicions of her knowledge, she told them, as she had anxiously told them at first, that only two men, and those perfect strangers, had been discovered as being concerned in the burglary. Her uncle would never have asked a question about it, even if she had withheld all information respecting the affair; but she noticed the quick, watching, waiting glance of his eye, whenever she returned from any person or place where she might have been supposed to gain intelligence if Benjamin were suspected or caught: and she hastened to relieve the old man's anxiety, by always telling all that she had heard; thankful that as the days passed on the danger she sickened to think of grew less and less.

Day by day, Bessy had ground for thinking that her aunt knew more than she had apprehended at first. There was something so very humble and touching in Hester's blind way of feeling about for her husband – stern, woebegone Nathan – and mutely striving to console him in the deep agony of which Bessy learnt, from this loving, piteous manner, that her aunt was conscious. Her aunt's face looked blankly up into his, tears slowly running down from her sightless eyes, while from time to time, when she thought herself unheard by any save him, she would repeat such texts as she had heard at church in happier days, and which she thought, in her true, simple piety, might tend to console him. Yet, day by day, her aunt grew more and more sad.

Three or four days before assize-time, two summonses to attend the trial at York were sent to the old people. Neither Bessy, nor John, nor Jane, could understand this; for their own notices had come long before, and they had been told that their evidence would be enough to convict.

But alas! the fact was, that the lawyer employed to defend the prisoners had heard from them that there was a third person engaged, and had heard who that third person was; and it was this advocate's business to diminish, if possible, the guilt of his clients, by proving that they were but tools in the hands of one who had, from his superior knowledge of the premises and the daily customs of the inhabitants, been the originator and planner of the whole affair. To do this it was necessary to have the evidence of the parents, who, as the prisoners had said, must have recognized the voice of the young man, their son. For no one knew that Bessy, too, could have borne witness to his having been present; and, as it was supposed that Benjamin had escaped out of England, there was no exact betrayal of him on the part of his accomplices.

Wondering, bewildered, and weary, the old couple reached York, in company with John and Bessy, on the eve of the day of trial. Nathan was still so self-contained, that Bessy could never guess what had been passing in his mind. He was almost passive under his old wife's trembling caresses; he seemed hardly conscious of them, so rigid was his demeanour.

She, Bessy feared at times, was becoming childish; for she had evidently so great and anxious a love for her husband, that her memory seemed going in her endeavours to melt the stonyness of his aspect and manners; she appeared occasionally to have forgotten why he was so changed, in her piteous little attempts to bring him back to his former self.

'They'll, for sure, never torture them when they see what old folks they are!' cried Bessy, on the morning of the trial, a dim fear looming over her mind. 'They'll never be so cruel, for sure!'

But 'for sure' it was so. The barrister looked up at the judge, almost apologetically, as he saw how hoary-headed and woeful an old man was put into the witness-box, when the defence came on, and Nathan Huntroyd was called on for his evidence.

'It is necessary, on behalf of my clients, my lord, that I should pursue a course which, for all other reasons, I deplore.'

'Go on!' said the judge. 'What is right and legal must be done.' But, an old man himself, he covered his quivering mouth with his hand as Nathan, with grey, unmoved face, and solemn, hollow eyes, placing his two hands on each side of the witness-box, prepared to give his answers to questions, the nature of which he was beginning to foresee, but would not shrink from replying to truthfully; 'the very stones' (as he said to himself, with a kind of dulled sense of the Eternal Justice) 'rise up* against such a sinner.'

'Your name is Nathan Huntroyd, I believe?'

'It is.'

'You live at Nab-end Farm?'

'I do.'

'Do you remember the night of November the twelfth?'

'Yes.'

'You were awakened that night by some noise, I believe. What was it?'

The old man's eyes fixed themselves upon his questioner, with the look of a creature brought to bay. That look the barrister never forgets. It will haunt him till his dying day.

'It was a throwing up of stones against our window.'

'Did you hear it at first?'

'No.'

'What awakened you then?'

'She did.'

'And then you both heard the stones. Did you hear nothing else?'

A long pause. Then a low, clear 'Yes.'

'What?'

'Our Benjamin asking us for to let him in. She said as it were him, leastways.'

'And you thought it was him, did you not?'

'I told her' (this time in a louder voice) 'for to get to sleep, and not to be thinking that every drunken chap as passed by were our Benjamin, for that he were dead and gone.'

'And she?'

'She said, as thof she'd heerd our Benjamin, afore she were welly awake, axing for to be let in. But I bade her ne'er heed her dreams, but turn on her other side, and get to sleep again.'

'And did she?'

A long pause, – judge, jury, bar, audience, all held their breath. At length Nathan said, –

'No!'

'What did you do then? (My lord, I am compelled to ask these painful questions.)'

'I saw she wadna be quiet: she had allays thought he would come back to us, like the Prodigal i' th' Gospels.' (His voice choked a little, but he tried to make it steady, succeeded, and went on.) 'She said, if I wadna get up she would; and just then I heerd a voice. I'm not quite mysel', gentlemen – I've been ill and i' bed, an' it makes me trembling-like. Some one said, "Father, mother, I'm here, starving* i' the cold – wunnot yo' get up and let me in?"'

'And that voice was—?'

'It were like our Benjamin's. I see whatten yo're driving at, sir, and I'll tell yo' truth, thof it kills me to speak it. I dunnot say it were our Benjamin as spoke, mind yo' – I only say it were like –'

'That's all I want, my good fellow. And on the strength of that entreaty, spoken in your son's voice, you went down and opened the door to these two prisoners at the bar, and to a third man?'

Nathan nodded assent, and even that counsel was too merciful to force him to put more into words.

'Call Hester Huntroyd.'

An old woman, with a face of which the eyes were evidently blind, with a sweet, gentle, careworn face, came into the witness-box, and meekly curtseyed to the presence of those whom she had been taught to respect – a presence she could not see.

There was something in her humble, blind aspect, as she stood waiting to have something done to her – what, her poor troubled mind hardly knew – that touched all who saw her, inexpressibly. Again the counsel apologized, but the judge could not reply in words; his face was quivering all over, and the jury looked uneasily at the prisoners' counsel. That gentleman saw that he might go too far, and send their sympathies off on the other side; but one or two questions he must ask. So, hastily recapitulating much that he had learned from Nathan, he said, 'You believed it was your son's voice asking to be let in?'

'Aye! Our Benjamin came home, I'm sure; choose where he is gone.'

She turned her head about, as if listening for the voice of her child, in the hushed silence of the court.

'Yes; he came home that night – and your husband went down to let him in?'

'Well! I believe he did. There was a great noise of folk down stair.'

'And you heard your son Benjamin's voice among the others?'

'Is it to do him harm, sir?' asked she, her face growing more intelligent and intent on the business in hand.

'That is not my object in questioning you. I believe he has left England, so nothing you can say will do him any harm. You heard your son's voice, I say?'

'Yes, sir. For sure, I did.'

'And some men came up stairs into your room? What did they say?'

'They axed where Nathan kept his stocking.'

'And you – did you tell them?'

'No, sir, for I knew Nathan would not like me to.'

'What did you do then?'

A shade of reluctance came over her face, as if she began to perceive causes and consequences.

'I just screamed on Bessy – that's my niece, sir.'

'And you heard some one shout out from the bottom of the stairs?'

She looked piteously at him, but did not answer.

'Gentlemen of the jury, I wish to call your particular attention to this fact: she acknowledges she heard some one shout – some third person, you observe – shout out to the two above. What did he say? That is the last question I shall trouble you with. What did the third person, left behind down stairs, say?'

Her face worked – her mouth opened two or three times as if to speak – she stretched out her arms imploringly; but no word came, and she fell back into the arms of those nearest to her. Nathan forced himself forward into the witness-box.

'My Lord Judge, a woman bore ye, as I reckon; it's a cruel shame to serve a mother so. It wur my son, my only child, as called out for us t' open door, and who shouted out for to hold th' oud woman's throat if she did na stop her noise, when hoo'd fain ha' cried for her niece to help. And now yo've truth, and a' th' truth, and I'll leave yo' to th' Judgment o' God for th' way yo've getten at it.'

Before night the mother was stricken with paralysis, and lay on her death-bed. But the broken-hearted go Home, to be comforted of God.

CURIOUS, IF TRUE

(EXTRACT FROM A LETTER FROM RICHARD WHITTINGHAM, ESQ.)

*

You were formerly so much amused at my pride in my descent from that sister of Calvin's, who married a Whittingham, Dean of Durham, that I doubt if you will be able to enter into the regard for my distinguished relation that has led me to France, in order to examine registers and archives, which, I thought, might enable me to discover collateral descendants of the great reformer, with whom I might call cousins. I shall not tell you of my troubles and adventures in this research; you are not worthy to hear of them; but something so curious befel me one evening last August, that if I had not been perfectly certain I was wide awake, I might have taken it for a dream.

For the purpose I have named, it was necessary that I should make Tours my head-quarters for a time. I had traced descendants of the Calvin family out of Normandy into the centre of France; but I found it was necessary to have a kind of permission from the bishop of the diocese before I could see certain family papers, which had fallen into the possession of the Church; and, as I had several English friends at Tours, I awaited the answer to my request to Monseigneur de —, at that town. I was ready to accept any invitation; but I received very few; and was sometimes a little at a loss what to do with my evenings. The *table d'hôte* was at five o'clock; I did not wish to go to the expense of a private sitting-room, disliked the dinnery atmosphere of the *salle à manger*, could not play either at pool or billiards, and the aspect of my fellow guests was unprepossessing enough to make me unwilling to enter into any *tête-à-tête* gamblings with them. So I usually rose from table early, and tried to make the most of the remaining light of the August evenings in walking briskly off to explore the surrounding country; the middle of the day was too hot for this purpose, and better employed in lounging on a bench in the Boulevards, lazily listening to the distant band, and noticing with equal laziness the faces and figures of the women who passed by.

One Thursday evening, the 18th of August it was, I think, I had gone further than usual in my walk, and I found that it was later than I had imagined when I paused to turn back. I fancied I could make a round; I had enough notion of the direction in which I was, to see that by turning up a narrow, straight lane to my left I should shorten my way back to Tours. And so I believe I should have done, could I have found an outlet at the right place, but field-paths are almost unknown in that part of France, and my lane, stiff and straight as any street, and marked into terribly vanishing perspective by the regular row of poplars on each side, seemed interminable. Of course night came on, and I was in darkness. In England I might have had a chance of seeing a light in some cottage only a field or two off, and asking my way from the inhabitants; but here I could see no such welcome sight; indeed, I believe French peasants go to bed with the summer daylight, so if there were any habitations in the neighbourhood I never saw them. At last – I believe I must have walked two hours in the darkness, – I saw the dusky outline of a wood on one side of the weariful lane, and, impatiently careless of all forest laws and penalties for trespassers, I made my way to it, thinking that if the worst came to the worst, I could find some covert – some shelter where I could lie down and rest, until the morning light gave me a chance of finding my way back to Tours. But the plantation, on the outskirts of what appeared to me a dense wood, was of young trees, too closely planted to be more than slender stems growing up to a good height, with scanty foliage on their summits. On I went towards the thicker forest, and once there I slackened my pace, and began to look about me for a good lair. I was as dainty as Lochiel's grandchild, who made his grandsire indignant at the luxury of his pillow of snow:* this brake was too full of brambles, that felt damp with dew; there was no hurry, since I had given up all hope of passing the night between four walls; and I went leisurely groping about, and trusting that there were no wolves to be poked up out of their summer drowsiness by my stick, when all at once I saw a château before me, not a quarter of a mile off, at the end of what seemed to be an ancient avenue (now overgrown and irregular), which I happened to be crossing, when I looked to my right, and saw the welcome sight. Large, stately, and dark was its outline against the dusky night-sky; there were pepper-boxes and tourelles and what-not fantastically going up into the dim starlight. And more to the purpose still, though I could not see the details of the building that I was now facing, it was plain enough that there were lights in many windows, as if some great entertainment was going on.

'They are hospitable people, at any rate,' thought I. 'Perhaps they will give me a bed. I don't suppose French propriétaires have traps and horses quite as plentiful as English gentlemen; but they are evidently having a large party, and some of their guests may be from Tours, and will give me a cast back to the Lion d'Or. I am not proud, and I am dog-tired. I am not above hanging on behind, if need be.'

So, putting a little briskness and spirit into my walk, I went up to the door, which was standing open, most hospitably, showing a large, lighted hall, all hung round with spoils of the chase, armour, &c., the details of which I had not time to notice, for the instant I stood on the threshold a huge porter appeared, in a strange, old-fashioned dress, a kind of livery which well befitted the general appearance of the house. He asked me, in French (so curiously pronounced that I thought I had hit upon a new kind of *patois*), my name, and whence I came. I thought he would not be much the wiser, still it was but civil to give it before I made my request for assistance; so, in reply, I said, –

'My name is Whittingham – Richard Whittingham, an English gentleman, staying at— ' To my infinite surprise, a light of pleased intelligence came over the giant's face; he made me a low bow, and said (still in the same curious dialect) that I was welcome, that I was long expected.

'Long expected!' What could the fellow mean? Had I stumbled on a nest of relations by John Calvin's side, who had heard of my genealogical inquiries, and were gratified and interested by them? But I was too much pleased to be under shelter for the night to think it necessary to account for my agreeable reception before I enjoyed it. Just as he was opening the great, heavy *battants** of the door that led from the hall to the interior, he turned round and said, –

'Apparently Monsieur le Géanquilleur is not come with you.'

'No! I am all alone; I have lost my way,' – and I was going on with my explanation, when he, as if quite indifferent to it, led the way up a great stone staircase, as wide as many rooms, and having on each landing-place massive iron wickets, in a heavy framework; these the porter unlocked with the solemn slowness of age. Indeed, a strange, mysterious awe of the centuries that had passed away since this château was built, came over me as I waited for the turning of the ponderous keys in the ancient locks. I could almost have fancied that I heard a mighty rushing murmur (like the ceaseless sound of a distant sea, ebbing and flowing for ever and for ever), coming forth from the great, vacant galleries that opened out on each side of the broad staircase, and were to be dimly perceived in the darkness above us. It was as if the voices of generations of men yet echoed and eddied in the silent air. It was strange, too, that my friend the porter going before me, ponderously infirm, with his feeble old hands striving in vain to keep the tall flambeau he held steadily before him, – strange, I say, that he was the only domestic I saw in the vast halls and passages, or met with on the grand staircase. At length we stood before the gilded doors that led into the saloon where the family – or it might be the company, so great was the buzz of voices – was assembled. I would have remonstrated when I found he was going to introduce me, dusty and travel-smeared, in a morning costume that was not even my best, into this grand *salon*, with nobody knew how many ladies and gentlemen assembled; but the obstinate old man was evidently bent upon taking me straight to his master, and paid no heed to my words.

The doors flew open, and I was ushered into a saloon curiously full of pale light, which did not culminate on any spot, nor proceed from any centre, nor flicker with any motion of the air, but filled every nook and corner, making all things deliciously distinct; different from our light of gas or candle, as is the difference between a clear southern atmosphere and that of our misty England.

At the first moment, my arrival excited no attention, the apartment was so full of people, all intent on their own conversation. But my friend the porter went up to a handsome lady of middle age, richly attired in that antique manner which fashion has brought round again of late years, and, waiting first in an attitude of deep respect till her attention fell upon him, told her my name and something about me, as far as I could guess from the gestures of the one and the sudden glance of the eye of the other.

She immediately came towards me with the most friendly actions of greeting, even before she had advanced near enough to speak. Then, – and was it not strange? – her words and accent were that of the commonest peasant of the country. Yet she herself looked highbred, and would have been dignified had she been a shade less restless, had her countenance worn a little less lively and inquisitive expression. I had been poking a good deal about the old parts of Tours, and had had to understand the dialect of the people who dwelt in the Marché au Vendredi* and similar places, or I really should not have understood my handsome hostess, as she offered to present me to her husband, a henpecked, gentlemanly man, who was more quaintly attired than she in the very extreme of that style of dress. I thought to myself that in France, as in England, it is the provincials who carry fashion to such an excess as to become ridiculous.

However, he spoke (still in the *patois*) of his pleasure in making my acquaintance, and led me to a strange, uneasy easy-chair, much of a piece with the rest of the furniture, which might have taken its place without any anachronism by the side of that in the Hôtel Cluny.* Then again began the clatter of French voices, which my arrival had for an instant interrupted, and I had leisure to look about me. Opposite to me sat a very sweet-looking lady, who must have been a great beauty in her youth, I should think, and would be charming in old age, from the sweetness of her countenance. She was, however, extremely fat, and on seeing her feet laid up before her on a cushion, I at once perceived that they were so swollen as to render her incapable of walking, which probably brought on her excessive *embonpoint*. Her hands were plump and small, but rather coarse-grained in texture, not quite so clean as they might have been, and altogether not so aristocratic-looking as the charming face. Her dress was of superb black velvet, ermine-trimmed, with diamonds thrown all abroad over it.

Not far from her stood the least little man I had ever seen; of such admirable proportions no one could call him a dwarf, because with that word we usually associate something of deformity; but yet with an elfin look of shrewd, hard, worldly wisdom in his face that marred the impression which his delicate, regular, little features would otherwise have conveyed. Indeed, I do not think he was quite of equal rank with the rest of the company, for his dress was inappropriate to the occasion (and he apparently was an invited, while I was an involuntary guest); and one or two of his gestures and actions were more like the tricks of an uneducated rustic than anything else. To explain what I mean: his boots had evidently seen much service, and had been re-topped, re-heeled, re-soled to the extent of cobbler's powers. Why should he have come in them if they were not his best – his only pair? And what can be more ungenteel than poverty? Then again he had an uneasy trick of putting his hand up to his throat, as if he expected to find something the matter with it; and he had the awkward habit – which I do not think he could have copied from Dr Johnson,* because most probably he had never heard of him – of trying always to retrace his steps on the exact boards on which he had trodden to arrive at any particular part of the room. Besides, to settle the question, I once heard him addressed as Monsieur Poucet, without any aristocratic 'de' for a prefix; and nearly every one else in the room was a marquis, at any rate.

I say, 'nearly every one'; for some strange people had the entrée; unless, indeed, they were, like me, benighted. One of the guests I should have taken for a servant, but for the extraordinary influence he seemed to have over the man I took for his master, and who never did anything without, apparently, being urged thereto by this follower. The master, magnificently dressed, but ill at ease in his clothes, as if they had been made for some one else, was a weak-looking, handsome man, continually sauntering about, and I almost guessed an object of suspicion to some of the gentlemen present, which, perhaps, drove him on the companionship of his follower, who was dressed something in the style of an ambassador's chasseur; yet it was not a chasseur's dress after all; it was something more thoroughly old-world; boots half way up his ridiculously small legs, which clattered as he walked along, as if they were too large for his little feet; and a great quantity of grey fur, as trimming to coat, court-mantle, boots, cap – everything. You know the way in which certain countenances remind you perpetually of some animal, be it bird or beast! Well, this chasseur (as I will call him for want of a better name) was exceedingly like the great Tom-cat that you have seen so often in my chambers, and laughed at almost as often for his uncanny gravity of demeanour. Grey whiskers has my Tom – grey whiskers had the chasseur: grey hair overshadows the upper lip of my Tom – grey mustachios hid that of the chasseur. The pupils of Tom's eyes dilate and contract as I had thought cats' pupils only could do, until I saw those of the chasseur. To be sure, canny as Tom is, the chasseur had the advantage in the more intelligent expression. He seemed to have obtained most complete sway over his master or patron, whose looks he watched, and whose steps he followed, with a kind of distrustful interest that puzzled me greatly.

There were several other groups in the more distant part of the saloon, all of the stately old school, all grand and noble, I conjectured from their bearing. They seemed perfectly well acquainted with each other, as if they were in the habit of meeting. But I was interrupted in my observations by the tiny little gentleman on the opposite side of the room coming across to take a place beside me. It is no difficult matter to a Frenchman to slide into conversation, and so gracefully did my pigmy friend keep up the character of the nation, that we were almost confidential before ten minutes had elapsed.

Now I was quite aware that the welcome which all had extended to me, from the porter up to the vivacious lady and meek lord of the castle, was intended for some other person. But it required either a degree of moral courage, of which I cannot boast, or the self-reliance and conversational powers of a bolder and cleverer man than I, to undeceive people who had fallen into so fortunate a mistake for me. Yet the little man by my side insinuated himself so much into my confidence, that I had half a mind to tell him of my exact situation, and to turn him into a friend and an ally.

'Madame is perceptibly growing older,' said he, in the midst of my perplexity, glancing at our hostess.

'Madame is still a very fine woman,' replied I.

'Now, is it not strange,' continued he, lowering his voice, 'how women almost invariably praise the absent, or departed, as if they were angels of light, while as for the present, or the living' – here he shrugged up his little shoulders, and made an expressive pause. 'Would you believe it! Madame is always praising her late husband to monsieur's face; till, in fact, we guests are quite perplexed how to look: for, you know, the late M. de Retz's character was quite notorious, – everybody has heard of him.' All the world of Touraine, thought I, but I made an assenting noise.

At this instant, monsieur our host came up to me, and with a civil look of tender interest (such as some people put on when they inquire after your mother, about whom they do not care one straw), asked if I had heard lately how my cat was? 'How my cat was!' What could the man mean? My cat! Could he mean the tailless Tom, born in the Isle of Man, and now supposed to be keeping guard against the incursions of rats and mice into my chambers in London? Tom is, as you know, on pretty good terms with some of my friends, using their legs for rubbing-posts without scruple, and highly esteemed by them for his gravity of demeanour, and wise manner of winking his eyes. But could his fame have reached across the Channel? However, an answer must be returned to the inquiry, as monsieur's face was bent down to mine with a look of polite anxiety; so I, in my turn, assumed an expression of gratitude, and assured him that, to the best of my belief, my cat was in remarkably good health.

'And the climate agrees with her?'

'Perfectly,' said I, in a maze of wonder at this deep solicitude in a tailless cat who had lost one foot and half an ear in some cruel trap. My host smiled a sweet smile, and, addressing a few words to my little neighbour, passed on.

'How wearisome those aristocrats are!' quoth my neighbour, with a slight sneer. 'Monsieur's conversation rarely extends to more than two sentences to any one. By that time his faculties are exhausted, and he needs the refreshment of silence. You and I, monsieur, are, at any rate, indebted to our own wits for our rise in the world!'

Here again I was bewildered! As you know, I am rather proud of my descent from families which, if not noble themselves, are allied to nobility, – and as to my 'rise in the world' – if I had risen, it would have been rather for balloon-like qualities than for mother-wit, to being unencumbered with heavy ballast either in my head or my pockets. However, it was my cue to agree: so I smiled again.

'For my part,' said he, 'if a man does not stick at trifles, if he knows how to judiciously add to, or withhold facts, and is not sentimental in his parade of humanity, he is sure to do well; sure to affix a *de* or *von* to his name, and end his days in comfort. There is an example of what I am saying' – and he glanced furtively at the weak-looking master of the sharp, intelligent servant, whom I have called the chasseur.

'Monsieur le Marquis would never have been anything but a miller's son, if it had not been for the talents of his servant. Of course you know his antecedents?'

I was going to make some remarks on the changes in the order of the peerage since the days of Louis XVI – going, in fact, to be very sensible and historical – when there was a slight commotion among the people at the other end of the room. Lacqueys in quaint liveries must have come in from behind the tapestry, I suppose (for I never saw them enter, though I sate right opposite to the doors), and were handing about the slight beverages and slighter viands which are considered sufficient refreshments, but which looked rather meagre to my hungry appetite. These footmen were standing solemnly opposite to a lady, – beautiful, splendid as the dawn, but – sound asleep in a magnificent settee. A gentleman who showed so much irritation at her ill-timed slumbers, that I think he must have been her husband, was trying to awaken her with actions not far removed from shakings. All in vain; she was quite unconscious of his annoyance, or the smiles of the company, or the automatic solemnity of the waiting footman, or the perplexed anxiety of monsieur and madame.

My little friend sat down with a sneer, as if his curiosity was quenched in contempt.

'Moralists would make an infinity of wise remarks on that scene,' said he. 'In the first place, note the ridiculous position into which their superstitious reverence for rank and title puts all these people. Because monsieur is a reigning prince over some minute principality, the exact situation of which no one has as yet discovered, no one must venture to take their glass of eau sucré till Madame la Princesse awakens; and, judging from past experience, those poor lacqueys may have to stand for a century before that happens. Next – always speaking as a moralist, you will observe – note how difficult it is to break off bad habits acquired in youth!'

Just then the prince succeeded, by what means I did not see, in awaking the beautiful sleeper. But at first she did not remember where she was, and looking up at her husband with loving eyes, she smiled and said, –

'Is it you, my prince?'

But he was too conscious of the suppressed amusement of the spectators and his own consequent annoyance, to be reciprocally tender, and turned away with some little French expression, best rendered into English by 'Pooh, pooh, my dear!'

After I had had a glass of delicious wine of some unknown quality, my courage was in rather better plight than before, and I told my cynical little neighbour – whom I must say I was beginning to dislike – that I had lost my way in the wood, and had arrived at the château quite by mistake.

He seemed mightily amused at my story; said that the same thing had happened to himself more than once; and told me that I had better luck than he had on one of these occasions, when, from his account, he must have been in considerable danger of his life. He ended his story by making me admire his boots, which he said he still wore, patched though they were, and all their excellent quality lost by patching, because they were of such a first-rate make for long pedestrian excursions. 'Though, indeed,' he wound up by saying, 'the new fashion of railroads would seem to supersede the necessity for this description of boots.'

When I consulted him as to whether I ought to make myself known to my host and hostess as a benighted traveller, instead of the guest whom they had taken me for, he exclaimed, 'By no means! I hate such squeamish morality.' And he seemed much offended by my innocent question, as if it seemed by implication to condemn something in himself. He was offended and silent; and just at this moment I caught the sweet, attractive eyes of the lady opposite – that lady whom I named at first as being no longer in the bloom of youth, but as being somewhat infirm about the feet, which were supported on a raised cushion before her. Her looks seemed to say, 'Come here, and let us have some conversation together'; and, with a bow of silent excuse to my little companion, I went across to the lame old lady. She acknowledged my coming with the prettiest gesture of thanks possible; and, half apologetically, said, 'It is a little dull to be unable to move about on such evenings as this; but it is a just punishment to me for my early vanities. My poor feet, that were by nature so small, are now taking their revenge for my cruelty in forcing them into such little slippers. . . . Besides, monsieur,' with a pleasant smile, 'I thought it was possible you might be weary of the malicious sayings of your little neighbour. He has not borne the best character in his youth, and such men are sure to be cynical in their old age.'

'Who is he?' asked I, with English abruptness.

'His name is Poucet, and his father was, I believe, a woodcutter, or charcoal burner, or something of the sort. They do tell sad stories of connivance at murder, ingratitude, and obtaining money on false pretences – but you will think me as bad as he if I go on with my slanders. Rather let us admire the lovely lady coming up towards us, with the roses in her hand – I never see her without roses, they are so closely connected with her past history, as you are doubtless aware. Ah, beauty!' said my companion to the lady drawing near to us, 'it is like you to come to me, now that I can no longer go to you.' Then turning to me, and gracefully drawing me into the conversation, she said, 'You must know that, although we never met until we were both married, we have been almost like sisters ever since. There have been so many points of resemblance in our circumstances, and I think I may say in our characters. We had each two elder sisters – mine were but half-sisters, though – who were not so kind to us as they might have been.'

'But have been sorry for it since,' put in the other lady.

'Since we have married princes,' continued the same lady, with an arch smile that had nothing of unkindness in it, 'for we both have married far above our original stations in life; we are both unpunctual in our habits, and, in consequence of this failing of ours, we have both had to suffer mortification and pain.'

'And both are charming,' said a whisper close behind me. 'My lord the marquis, say it – say, "And both are charming." '

'And both are charming,' was spoken aloud by another voice. I turned, and saw the wily, cat-like chasseur, prompting his master to make civil speeches.

The ladies bowed with that kind of haughty acknowledgment which shows that compliments from such a source are distasteful. But our trio of conversation was broken up, and I was sorry for it. The marquis looked as if he had been stirred up to make that one speech, and hoped that he would not be expected to say more; while behind him stood the chasseur, half impertinent and half servile in his ways and attitudes. The ladies, who were real ladies, seemed to be sorry for the awkwardness of the marquis, and addressed some trifling questions to him, adapting themselves to the subjects on which he could have no trouble in answering. The chasseur, meanwhile, was talking to himself in a growling tone of voice. I had fallen a little into the background at this interruption in a conversation which promised to be so pleasant, and I could not help hearing his words.

'Really, De Carabas grows more stupid every day. I have a great mind to throw off his boots, and leave him to his fate. I was intended for a court, and to a court I will go, and make my own fortune as I have made his. The emperor will appreciate my talents.'

And such are the habits of the French, or such his forgetfulness of good manners in his anger, that he spat right and left on the parquetted floor.

Just then a very ugly, very pleasant-looking man, came towards the two ladies to whom I had lately been speaking, leading up to them a delicate, fair woman, dressed all in the softest white, as if she were *vouée au blanc*.* I do not think there was a bit of colour about her. I thought I heard her making, as she came along, a little noise of pleasure, not exactly like the singing of a tea-kettle, nor yet like the cooing of a dove, but reminding me of each sound.

'Madame de Mioumiou was anxious to see you,' said he, addressing the lady with the roses, 'so I have brought her across to give you a pleasure!' What an honest, good face! but oh! how ugly! And yet I liked his ugliness better than most persons' beauty. There was a look of pathetic acknowledgment of his ugliness, and a deprecation of your too hasty judgment, in his countenance that was positively winning. The soft, white lady kept glancing at my neighbour the chasseur, as if they had had some former acquaintance, which puzzled me very much, as they were of such different rank. However, their nerves were evidently strung to the same tune, for at a sound behind the tapestry, which was more like the scuttering of rats and mice than anything else, both Madame de Mioumiou and the chasseur started with the most eager look of anxiety on their countenances, and by their restless movements – madame's panting, and the fiery dilation of his eyes – one might see that commonplace sounds affected them both in a manner very different to the rest of the company. The ugly husband of the lovely lady with the roses now addressed himself to me.

'We are much disappointed,' he said, 'in finding that monsieur is not accompanied by his countryman – le grand Jean d'Angleterre; I cannot pronounce his name rightly' – and he looked at me to help him out.

'Le grand Jean d'Angleterre!' Now who was le grand Jean d'Angleterre? John Bull? John Russell? John Bright?*

'Jean – Jean' – continued the gentleman, seeing my embarrassment. 'Ah, these terrible English names – "Jean de Géanquilleur!" '

I was as wise as ever. And yet the name struck me as familiar, but slightly disguised. I repeated it to myself. It was mighty like John the Giant-killer, only his friends always call that worthy, ' Jack'. I said the name aloud.

'Ah, that is it!' said he. 'But why has he not accompanied you to our little reunion to-night?'

I had been rather puzzled once or twice before, but this serious question added considerably to my perplexity. Jack the Giant-killer had once, it is true, been rather an intimate friend of mine, as far as (printer's) ink and paper can keep up a friendship, but I had not heard his name mentioned for years; and for aught I knew he lay enchanted with King Arthur's knights, who lie entranced until the blast of the trumpets of four mighty kings shall call them to help at England's need. But the question had been asked in serious earnest by that gentleman, whom I more wished to think well of me than I did any other person in the room. So I answered respectfully that it was long since I had heard anything of my countryman; but that I was sure it would have given him as much pleasure as it was doing myself to have been present at such an agreeable gathering of friends. He bowed, and then the lame lady took up the word.

'To-night is the night when, of all the year, this great old forest surrounding the castle is said to be haunted by the phantom of a little peasant girl who once lived hereabouts; the tradition is that she was devoured by a wolf. In former days I have seen her on this night out of yonder window at the end of the gallery. Will you, ma belle, take monsieur to see the view outside by the moonlight (you may possibly see the phantom-child); and leave me to a little *tête-à-tête* with your husband?'

With a gentle movement the lady with the roses complied with the other's request, and we went to a great window, looking down on the forest, in which I had lost my way. The tops of the far-spreading and leafy trees lay motionless beneath us in that pale, wan light, which shows objects almost as distinct in form, though not in colour, as by day. We looked down on the countless avenues, which seemed to converge from all quarters to the great old castle; and suddenly across one, quite near to us, there passed the figure of a little girl, with the 'capuchon' on, that takes the place of a peasant girl's bonnet in France. She had a basket on one arm, and by her, on the side to which her head was turned, there went a wolf. I could almost have said it was licking her hand, as if in penitent love, if either penitence or love had ever been a quality of wolves, – but though not of living, perhaps it may be of phantom wolves.

'There, we have seen her!' exclaimed my beautiful companion. 'Though so long dead, her simple story of household goodness and trustful simplicity still lingers in the hearts of all who have ever heard of her; and the country-people about here say that seeing that phantom-child on this anniversary brings good luck for the year. Let us hope that we shall share in the traditionary good fortune. Ah! here is Madame de Retz – she retains the name of her first husband, you know, as he was of higher rank than the present.' We were joined by our hostess.

'If monsieur is fond of the beauties of nature and art,' said she, perceiving that I had been looking at the view from the great window, 'he will perhaps take pleasure in seeing the picture.' Here she sighed, with a little affectation of grief. 'You know the picture I allude to,' addressing my companion, who bowed assent, and smiled a little maliciously, as I followed the lead of madame.

I went after her to the other end of the saloon, noting by the way with what keen curiosity she caught up what was passing either in word or action on each side of her. When we stood opposite to the end wall, I perceived a full-length picture of a handsome, peculiar-looking man, with – in spite of his good looks – a very fierce and scowling expression. My hostess clasped her hands together as her arms hung down in front, and sighed once more. Then, half in soliloquy, she said, –

'He was the love of my youth; his stern yet manly character first touched this heart of mine. When – when shall I cease to deplore his loss!'

Not being acquainted with her enough to answer this question (if, indeed, it were not sufficiently answered by the fact of her second marriage), I felt awkward; and, by way of saying something, I remarked, –

'The countenance strikes me as resembling something I have seen before – in an engraving from an historical picture, I think; only, it is there the principal figure in a group: he is holding a lady by her hair, and threatening her with his scimitar, while two cavaliers are rushing up the stairs, apparently only just in time to save her life.'

'Alas, alas!' said she, 'you too accurately describe a miserable passage in my life, which has often been represented in a false light. The best of husbands' – here she sobbed, and became slightly inarticulate with her grief – 'will sometimes be displeased. I was young and curious, he was justly angry with my disobedience – my brothers were too hasty – the consequence is, I became a widow!'

After due respect for her tears, I ventured to suggest some commonplace consolation. She turned round sharply.

'No, monsieur: my only comfort is that I have never forgiven the brothers who interfered so cruelly, in such an uncalled-for manner, between my dear husband and myself. To quote my friend Monsieur Sganarelle – "Ce sont petites choses qui sont de temps en temps nécessaires dans l'amitié; et cinq ou six coups d'épée entre gens qui s'aiment ne font que ragaillardir l'affection."* You observe the colouring is not quite what it should be?'

'In this light the beard is of rather a peculiar tint,' said I.

'Yes: the painter did not do it justice. It was most lovely, and gave him such a distinguished air, quite different from the common herd. Stay, I will show you the exact colour, if you will come near this flambeau!' And going near the light, she took off a bracelet of hair, with a magnificent clasp of pearls. It was peculiar, certainly. I did not know what to say. 'His precious lovely beard!' said she. 'And the pearls go so well with the delicate blue!'

Her husband, who had come up to us, and waited till her eye fell upon him before venturing to speak, now said, 'It is strange Monsieur Ogre is not yet arrived!'

'Not at all strange,' said she, tartly. 'He was always very stupid, and constantly falls into mistakes, in which he comes worse off; and it is very well he does, for he is a credulous and cowardly fellow. Not at all strange! If you will' – turning to her husband, so that I hardly heard her words, until I caught – 'Then everybody would have their rights, and we should have no more trouble. Is it not, monsieur?' addressing me.

'If I were in England, I should imagine madame was speaking of the reform bill, or the millennium, – but I am in ignorance.'

And just as I spoke, the great folding-doors were thrown open wide, and every one started to their feet to greet a little old lady, leaning on a thin, black wand – and –

'Madame la Féemarraine,'* was announced by a chorus of sweet shrill voices.

And in a moment I was lying in the grass close by a hollow oak-tree, with the slanting glory of the dawning day shining full in my face, and thousands of little birds and delicate insects piping and warbling out their welcome to the ruddy splendour.

COUSIN PHILLIS

*

PART I

IT is a great thing for a lad when he is first turned into the
independence of lodgings. I do not think I ever was so
satisfied and proud in my life as when, at seventeen, I sate
down in a little three-cornered room above a pastry-cook's
shop in the county town of Eltham. My father had left me that
afternoon, after delivering himself of a few plain precepts,
strongly expressed, for my guidance in the new course of life
on which I was entering. I was to be a clerk under the engineer
who had undertaken to make the little branch line from
Eltham to Hornby. My father had got me this situation, which
was in a position rather above his own in life; or perhaps I
should say, above the station in which he was born and bred;
for he was raising himself every year in men's consideration
and respect. He was a mechanic by trade, but he had some
inventive genius, and a great deal of perseverance, and had
devised several valuable improvements in railway machinery.
He did not do this for profit, though, as was reasonable, what
came in the natural course of things was acceptable; he worked
out his ideas, because, as he said, 'until he could put them into
shape, they plagued him by night and by day.' But this is
enough about my dear father; it is a good thing for a country
where there are many like him. He was a sturdy Independent
by descent and conviction;* and this it was, I believe, which
made him place me in the lodgings at the pastry-cook's. The
shop was kept by the two sisters of our minister at home; and
this was considered as a sort of safeguard to my morals, when
I was turned loose upon the temptations of the county town,
with a salary of thirty pounds a year.

My father had given up two precious days, and put on his
Sunday clothes, in order to bring me to Eltham, and accompany me first to the office, to introduce me to my new master
(who was under some obligations to my father for a sugges-

tion), and next to take me to call on the Independent minister
of the little congregation at Eltham. And then he left me; and
though sorry to part with him, I now began to taste with relish
the pleasure of being my own master. I unpacked the hamper
that my mother had provided me with, and smelt the pots of
preserve with all the delight of a possessor who might break
into their contents at any time he pleased. I handled and
weighed in my fancy the home-cured ham, which seemed to
promise me interminable feasts; and, above all, there was the
fine savour of knowing that I might eat of these dainties when
I liked, at my sole will, not dependent on the pleasure of any
one else, however indulgent. I stowed my eatables away in the
little corner cupboard – that room was all corners, and everything was placed in a corner, the fire-place, the window, the
cupboard; I myself seemed to be the only thing in the middle,
and there was hardly room for me. The table was made of a
folding leaf under the window, and the window looked out
upon the market-place; so the studies for the prosecution of
which my father had brought himself to pay extra for a sitting-
room for me, ran a considerable chance of being diverted from
books to men and women. I was to have my meals with the
two elderly Miss Dawsons in the little parlour behind the
three-cornered shop downstairs; my breakfasts and dinners at
least, for, as my hours in an evening were likely to be uncertain,
my tea or supper was to be an independent meal.

Then, after this pride and satisfaction, came a sense of
desolation. I had never been from home before, and I was an
only child; and though my father's spoken maxim had been,
'Spare the rod, and spoil the child', yet, unconsciously, his
heart had yearned after me, and his ways towards me were
more tender than he knew, or would have approved of in himself could he have known. My mother, who never professed
sternness, was far more severe than my father: perhaps my
boyish faults annoyed her more; for I remember, now that I
have written the above words, how she pleaded for me once
in my riper years, when I had really offended against my
father's sense of right.

But I have nothing to do with that now. It is about cousin
Phillis that I am going to write, and as yet I am far enough
from even saying who cousin Phillis was.

For some months after I was settled in Eltham, the new employment in which I was engaged – the new independence of my life – occupied all my thoughts. I was at my desk by eight o'clock, home to dinner at one, back at the office by two. The afternoon work was more uncertain than the morning's; it might be the same, or it might be that I had to accompany Mr Holdsworth, the managing engineer, to some point on the line between Eltham and Hornby. This I always enjoyed, because of the variety, and because of the country we traversed (which was very wild and pretty), and because I was thrown into companionship with Mr Holdsworth, who held the position of hero in my boyish mind. He was a young man of five-and-twenty or so, and was in a station above mine, both by birth and education; and he had travelled on the Continent, and wore mustachios and whiskers of a somewhat foreign fashion. I was proud of being seen with him. He was really a fine fellow in a good number of ways, and I might have fallen into much worse hands.

Every Saturday I wrote home, telling of my weekly doings – my father had insisted upon this; but there was so little variety in my life that I often found it hard work to fill a letter. On Sundays I went twice to chapel, up a dark narrow entry, to hear droning hymns, and long prayers, and a still longer sermon, preached to a small congregation, of which I was, by nearly a score of years, the youngest member. Occasionally, Mr Peters, the minister, would ask me home to tea after the second service. I dreaded the honour, for I usually sate on the edge of my chair all the evening, and answered solemn questions, put in a deep bass voice, until household prayer-time came, at eight o'clock, when Mrs Peters came in, smoothing down her apron, and the maid-of-all-work followed, and first a sermon, and then a chapter was read, and a long impromptu prayer followed, till some instinct told Mr Peters that supper-time had come, and we rose from our knees with hunger for our predominant feeling. Over supper the minister did unbend a little into one or two ponderous jokes, as if to show me that ministers were men, after all. And then at ten o'clock I went home, and enjoyed my long-repressed yawns in the three-cornered room before going to bed.

Dinah and Hannah Dawson, so their names were put on the

board above the shop-door – I always called them Miss
Dawson and Miss Hannah – considered these visits of mine to
Mr Peters as the greatest honour a young man could have; and
evidently thought that if, after such privileges, I did not work
out my salvation, I was a sort of modern Judas Iscariot. On
the contrary, they shook their heads over my intercourse with
Mr Holdsworth. He had been so kind to me in many ways,
that when I cut into my ham, I hovered over the thought of
asking him to tea in my room, more especially as the annual
fair was being held in Eltham market-place, and the sight of
the booths, the merry-go-rounds, the wild-beast shows, and
such country pomps, was (as I thought at seventeen) very
attractive. But when I ventured to allude to my wish in even
distant terms, Miss Hannah caught me up, and spoke of the
sinfulness of such sights, and something about wallowing in
the mire, and then vaulted into France, and spoke evil of the
nation, and all who had ever set foot therein, till, seeing that
her anger was concentrating itself into a point, and that that
point was Mr Holdsworth, I thought it would be better to
finish my breakfast, and make what haste I could out of the
sound of her voice. I rather wondered afterwards to hear her
and Miss Dawson counting up their weekly profits with glee,
and saying that a pastry-cook's shop in the corner of the
market-place, in Eltham fair week, was no such bad thing.
However, I never ventured to ask Mr Holdsworth to my
lodgings.

There is not much to tell about this first year of mine at
Eltham. But when I was nearly nineteen, and beginning to
think of whiskers on my own account, I came to know cousin
Phillis, whose very existence had been unknown to me till
then. Mr Holdsworth and I had been out to Heathbridge for a
day, working hard. Heathbridge was near Hornby, for our
line of railway was above half finished. Of course, a day's
outing was a great thing to tell about in my weekly letters; and
I fell to describing the country – a fault I was not often guilty
of. I told my father of the bogs, all over wild myrtle and soft
moss, and shaking ground over which we had to carry our
line; and how Mr Holdsworth and I had gone for our mid-day
meals – for we had to stay here for two days and a night – to a
pretty village hard by, Heathbridge proper; and how I hoped

we should often have to go there, for the shaking, uncertain ground was puzzling our engineers – one end of the line going up as soon as the other was weighted down. (I had no thought for the shareholders' interests, as may be seen; we had to make a new line on firmer ground before the junction railway was completed.) I told all this at great length, thankful to fill up my paper. By return letter, I heard that a second-cousin of my mother's was married to the Independent minister of Hornby, Ebenezer Holman by name, and lived at Heathbridge proper; the very Heathbridge I had described, or so my mother believed, for she had never seen her cousin Phillis Green, who was something of an heiress (my father believed), being her father's only child, and old Thomas Green had owned an estate of near upon fifty acres, which must have come to his daughter. My mother's feeling of kinship seemed to have been strongly stirred by the mention of Heathbridge; for my father said she desired me, if ever I went thither again, to make inquiry for the Reverend Ebenezer Holman; and if indeed he lived there, I was further to ask if he had not married one Phillis Green; and if both these questions were answered in the affirmative, I was to go and introduce myself as the only child of Margaret Manning, born Moneypenny. I was enraged at myself for having named Heathbridge at all, when I found what it was drawing down upon me. One Independent minister, as I said to myself, was enough for any man; and here I knew (that is to say, I had been catechized on Sabbath mornings by) Mr Dawson, our minister at home; and I had had to be civil to old Peters at Eltham, and behave myself for five hours running whenever he asked me to tea at his house; and now, just as I felt the free air blowing about me up at Heathbridge, I was to ferret out another minister, and I should perhaps have to be catechized by him, or else asked to tea at his house. Besides, I did not like pushing myself upon strangers, who perhaps had never heard of my mother's name, and such an odd name as it was – Moneypenny; and if they had, had never cared more for her than she had for them, apparently, until this unlucky mention of Heathbridge.

Still, I would not disobey my parents in such a trifle, however irksome it might be. So the next time our business took me to Heathbridge, and we were dining in the little sanded inn-parlour, I took the opportunity of Mr Holdsworth's being out of the room, and asked the questions which I was bidden to ask of the rosy-cheeked maid. I was either unintelligible or she was stupid; for she said she did not know, but would ask master; and of course the landlord came in to understand what it was I wanted to know; and I had to bring out all my stammering inquiries before Mr Holdsworth, who would never have attended to them, I dare say, if I had not blushed, and blundered, and made such a fool of myself.

'Yes,' the landlord said, 'the Hope Farm was in Heathbridge proper, and the owner's name was Holman, and he was an Independent minister, and, as far as the landlord could tell, his wife's Christian name was Phillis, anyhow her maiden name was Green.'

'Relations of yours?' asked Mr Holdsworth.

'No, sir – only my mother's second-cousins. Yes, I suppose they are relations. But I never saw them in my life.'

'The Hope Farm is not a stone's throw from here,' said the officious landlord, going to the window. 'If you carry your eye over yon bed of hollyhocks, over the damson-trees in the orchard yonder, you may see a stack of queer-like stone chimneys. Them is the Hope Farm chimneys; it's an old place, though Holman keeps it in good order.'

Mr Holdsworth had risen from the table with more promptitude than I had, and was standing by the window, looking. At the landlord's last words, he turned round, smiling, – 'It is not often that parsons know how to keep land in order, is it?'

'Beg pardon, sir, but I must speak as I find; and Minister Holman – we call the Church clergyman here "parson," sir; he would be a bit jealous if he heard a Dissenter called parson – Minister Holman knows what he's about as well as e'er a farmer in the neighbourhood. He gives up five days a week to his own work, and two to the Lord's; and it is difficult to say which he works hardest at. He spends Saturday and Sunday a-writing sermons and a-visiting his flock at Hornby; and at five o'clock on Monday morning he'll be guiding his plough in the Hope Farm yonder just as well as if he could neither read nor write. But your dinner will be getting cold, gentlemen.'

So we went back to table. After a while, Mr Holdsworth broke the silence: – 'If I were you, Manning, I'd look up these relations of yours. You can go and see what they're like while we're waiting for Dobson's estimates, and I'll smoke a cigar in the garden meanwhile.'

'Thank you, sir. But I don't know them, and I don't think I want to know them.'

'What did you ask all those questions for, then?' said he, looking quickly up at me. He had no notion of doing or saying things without a purpose. I did not answer, so he continued, – 'Make up your mind, and go off and see what this farmer-minister is like, and come back and tell me – I should like to hear.'

I was so in the habit of yielding to his authority, or influence, that I never thought of resisting, but went on my errand, though I remember feeling as if I would rather have had my head cut off. The landlord, who had evidently taken an interest in the event of our discussion in a way that country landlords have, accompanied me to the house-door, and gave me repeated directions, as if I was likely to miss my way in two hundred yards. But I listened to him, for I was glad of the delay, to screw up my courage for the effort of facing unknown people and introducing myself. I went along the lane, I recollect, switching at all the taller roadside weeds, till, after a turn or two, I found myself close in front of the Hope Farm. There was a garden between the house and the shady, grassy lane; I afterwards found that this garden was called the court; perhaps because there was a low wall round it, with an iron railing on the top of the wall, and two great gates between pillars crowned with stone balls for a state entrance to the flagged path leading up to the front door. It was not the habit of the place to go in either by these great gates or by the front door; the gates, indeed, were locked, as I found, though the door stood wide open. I had to go round by a side-path lightly worn on a broad grassy way, which led past the court-wall, past a horse-mount, half covered with stone-crop and the little wild yellow fumitory, to another door – 'the curate', as I found it was termed by the master of the house, while the front door, 'handsome and all for show', was termed the 'rector'. I knocked with my hand upon the 'curate' door; a tall girl, about my own age, as I thought, came and opened it, and stood there silent, waiting to know my errand. I see her now – cousin Phillis. The westering sun shone full upon her, and made a slanting stream of light into the room within. She was dressed in dark blue cotton of some kind; up to her throat, down to her wrists, with a little frill of the same wherever it touched her white skin. And such a white skin as it was! I have never seen the like. She had light hair, nearer yellow than any other colour. She looked me steadily in the face with large, quiet eyes, wondering, but untroubled by the sight of a stranger. I thought it odd that so old, so full-grown as she was, she should wear a pinafore over her gown.

Before I had quite made up my mind what to say in reply to her mute inquiry of what I wanted there, a woman's voice called out, 'Who is it, Phillis? If it is any one for butter-milk send them round to the back door.'

I thought I could rather speak to the owner of that voice than to the girl before me; so I passed her, and stood at the entrance of a room, hat in hand, for this side-door opened straight into the hall or house-place where the family sate when work was done. There was a brisk little woman of forty or so ironing some huge muslin cravats under the light of a long vine-shaded casement window. She looked at me distrustfully till I began to speak. 'My name is Paul Manning,' said I; but I saw she did not know the name. 'My mother's name was Moneypenny,' said I, – 'Margaret Moneypenny.'

'And she married one John Manning, of Birmingham,' said Mrs Holman, eagerly. 'And you'll be her son. Sit down! I am right glad to see you. To think of your being Margaret's son! Why, she was almost a child not so long ago. Well, to be sure, it is five-and-twenty years ago. And what brings you into these parts?'

She sate down herself, as if oppressed by her curiosity as to all the five-and-twenty years that had passed by since she had seen my mother. Her daughter Phillis took up her knitting – a long grey worsted man's stocking, I remember – and knitted away without looking at her work. I felt that the steady gaze of those deep grey eyes was upon me, though once, when I stealthily raised mine to hers, she was examining something on the wall above my head.

When I had answered all my cousin Holman's questions, she heaved a long breath, and said, 'To think of Margaret Money-penny's boy being in our house! I wish the minister was here. Phillis, in what field is thy father to-day?'

'In the five-acre; they are beginning to cut the corn.'

'He'll not like being sent for, then, else I should have liked you to have seen the minister. But the five-acre is a good step off. You shall have a glass of wine and a bit of cake before you stir from this house, though. You're bound to go, you say, or else the minister comes in mostly when the men have their four o'clock.'

'I must go – I ought to have been off before now.'

'Here, then, Phillis, take the keys.' She gave her daughter some whispered directions, and Phillis left the room.

'She is my cousin, is she not?' I asked. I knew she was, but somehow I wanted to talk of her, and did not know how to begin.

'Yes – Phillis Holman. She is our only child – now.'

Either from that 'now', or from a strange momentary wistfulness in her eyes, I knew that there had been more children, who were now dead.

'How old is cousin Phillis?' said I, scarcely venturing on the new name, it seemed too prettily familiar for me to call her by it; but cousin Holman took no notice of it, answering straight to the purpose.

'Seventeen last May-day; but the minister does not like to hear me calling it May-day,' said she, checking herself with a little awe. 'Phillis was seventeen on the first day of May last,' she repeated in an emended edition.

'And I am nineteen in another month,' thought I, to myself; I don't know why.

Then Phillis came in, carrying a tray with wine and cake upon it.

'We keep a house-servant,' said cousin Holman, 'but it is churning day, and she is busy.' It was meant as a little proud apology for her daughter's being the handmaiden.

'I like doing it, mother,' said Phillis, in her grave, full voice.

I felt as if I were somebody in the Old Testament – who, I could not recollect – being served and waited upon by the daughter of the host. Was I like Abraham's servant, when

Rebekah gave him to drink at the well? I thought Isaac* had not gone the pleasantest way to work in winning him a wife. But Phillis never thought about such things. She was a stately, gracious young woman, in the dress and with the simplicity of a child.

As I had been taught, I drank to the health of my new-found cousin and her husband; and then I ventured to name my cousin Phillis with a little bow of my head towards her; but I was too awkward to look and see how she took my compliment. 'I must go now,' said I, rising.

Neither of the women had thought of sharing in the wine; cousin Holman had broken a bit of cake for form's sake.

'I wish the minister had been within,' said his wife, rising too. Secretly I was very glad he was not. I did not take kindly to ministers in those days, and I thought he must be a particular kind of man, by his objecting to the term May-day. But before I went, cousin Holman made me promise that I would come back on the Saturday following and spend Sunday with them; when I should see something of 'the minister'.

'Come on Friday, if you can,' were her last words as she stood at the curate-door, shading her eyes from the sinking sun with her hand.

Inside the house sate cousin Phillis, her golden hair, her dazzling complexion, lighting up the corner of the vine-shadowed room. She had not risen when I bade her good-by; she had looked at me straight as she said her tranquil words of farewell.

I found Mr Holdsworth down at the line, hard at work superintending. As soon as he had a pause, he said, 'Well, Manning, what are the new cousins like? How do preaching and farming seem to get on together? If the minister turns out to be practical as well as reverend, I shall begin to respect him.'

But he hardly attended to my answer, he was so much more occupied with directing his work-people. Indeed, my answer did not come very readily; and the most distinct part of it was the mention of the invitation that had been given me.

'Oh, of course you can go – and on Friday, too, if you like; there is no reason why not this week; and you've done a long spell of work this time, old fellow.'

I thought that I did not want to go on Friday; but when the

day came, I found that I should prefer going to staying away, so I availed myself of Mr Holdsworth's permission, and went over to Hope Farm some time in the afternoon, a little later than my last visit. I found the 'curate' open to admit the soft September air, so tempered by the warmth of the sun, that it was warmer out of doors than in, although the wooden log lay smouldering in front of a heap of hot ashes on the hearth. The vine-leaves over the window had a tinge more yellow, their edges were here and there scorched and browned; there was no ironing about, and cousin Holman sate just outside the house, mending a shirt. Phillis was at her knitting indoors: it seemed as if she had been at it all the week. The many-speckled fowls were pecking about in the farmyard beyond, and the milk-cans glittered with brightness, hung out to sweeten. The court was so full of flowers that they crept out upon the low-covered wall and horse-mount, and were even to be found self-sown upon the turf that bordered the path to the back of the house. I fancied that my Sunday coat was scented for days afterwards by the bushes of sweetbriar and the fraxinella that perfumed the air. From time to time cousin Holman put her hand into a covered basket at her feet, and threw handsful of corn down for the pigeons that cooed and fluttered in the air around, in expectation of this treat.

I had a thorough welcome as soon as she saw me. 'Now this is kind – this is right down friendly,' shaking my hand warmly. 'Phillis, your cousin Manning is come!'

'Call me Paul, will you?' said I; 'they call me so at home, and Manning in the office.'

'Well, Paul, then. Your room is all ready for you, Paul, for, as I said to the minister, "I'll have it ready whether he comes o' Friday or not." And the minister said he must go up to the Ashfield whether you were to come or not; but he would come home betimes to see if you were here. I'll show you to your room, and you can wash the dust off a bit.'

After I came down, I think she did not quite know what to do with me; or she might think that I was dull; or she might have work to do in which I hindered her; for she called Phillis, and bade her put on her bonnet, and go with me to the Ashfield, and find father. So we set off, I in a little flutter of a desire to make myself agreeable, but wishing that my companion were not quite so tall; for she was above me in height. While I was wondering how to begin our conversation, she took up the words.

'I suppose, cousin Paul, you have to be very busy at your work all day long in general.'

'Yes, we have to be in the office at half-past eight; and we have an hour for dinner, and then we go at it again till eight or nine.'

'Then you have not much time for reading.'

'No,' said I, with a sudden consciousness that I did not make the most of what leisure I had.

'No more have I. Father always gets an hour before going a-field in the mornings, but mother does not like me to get up so early.'

'My mother is always wanting me to get up earlier when I am at home.'

'What time do you get up?'

'Oh! – ah! – sometimes half-past six: not often though;' for I remembered only twice that I had done so during the past summer.

She turned her head and looked at me.

'Father is up at three; and so was mother till she was ill. I should like to be up at four.'

'Your father up at three! Why, what has he to do at that hour?'

'What has he not to do? He has his private exercise* in his own room; he always rings the great bell which calls the men to milking; he rouses up Betty, our maid; as often as not he gives the horses their feed before the man is up – for Jem, who takes care of the horses, is an old man; and father is always loth to disturb him; he looks at the calves, and the shoulders, heels, traces, chaff, and corn before the horses go a-field; he has often to whip-cord the plough-whips; he sees the hogs fed; he looks into the swill-tubs, and writes his orders for what is wanted for food for man and beast; yes, and for fuel, too. And then, if he has a bit of time to spare, he comes in and reads with me – but only English; we keep Latin for the evenings, that we may have time to enjoy it; and then he calls in the men to breakfast, and cuts the boys' bread and cheese; and sees their wooden bottles filled, and sends them off to their work; – and by this time it is half-past six, and we have our breakfast. There is father,' she exclaimed, pointing out to me a man in his shirt-sleeves, taller by the head than the other two with whom he was working. We only saw him through the leaves of the ash-trees growing in the hedge, and I thought I must be confusing the figures, or mistaken: that man still looked like a very powerful labourer, and had none of the precise demureness of appearance which I had always imagined was the characteristic of a minister. It was the Reverend Ebenezer Holman, however. He gave us a nod as we entered the stubble-field; and I think he would have come to meet us but that he was in the middle of giving some directions to his men. I could see that Phillis was built more after his type than her mother's. He, like his daughter, was largely made, and of a fair, ruddy complexion, whereas hers was brilliant and delicate. His hair had been yellow or sandy, but now was grizzled. Yet his grey hairs betokened no failure in strength. I never saw a more powerful man – deep chest, lean flanks, well-planted head. By this time we were nearly up to him; and he interrupted himself and stepped forwards; holding out his hand to me, but addressing Phillis.

'Well, my lass, this is cousin Manning, I suppose. Wait a minute, young man, and I'll put on my coat, and give you a decorous and formal welcome. But – Ned Hall, there ought to be a water-furrow across this land: it's a nasty, stiff, clayey, dauby bit of ground, and thou and I must fall to, come next Monday – I beg your pardon, cousin Manning – and there's old Jem's cottage wants a bit of thatch; you can do that job tomorrow while I am busy.' Then, suddenly changing the tone of his deep bass voice to an odd suggestion of chapels and preachers, he added. 'Now, I will give out the psalm, "Come all harmonious tongues", to be sung to "Mount Ephraim"* tune.'

He lifted his spade in his hand, and began to beat time with it; the two labourers seemed to know both words and music, though I did not; and so did Phillis: her rich voice followed her father's as he set the tune; and the men came in with more uncertainty, but still harmoniously. Phillis looked at me once or twice with a little surprise at my silence; but I did not know the words. There we five stood, bareheaded, excepting Phillis, in the tawny stubble-field, from which all the shocks of corn had not yet been carried – a dark wood on one side, where the woodpigeons were cooing; blue distance seen through the ash-trees on the other. Somehow, I think that if I had known the words, and could have sung, my throat would have been choked up by the feeling of the unaccustomed scene.

The hymn was ended, and the men had drawn off before I could stir. I saw the minister beginning to put on his coat, and looking at me with friendly inspection in his gaze, before I could rouse myself.

'I dare say you railway gentlemen don't wind up the day with singing a psalm together,' said he; 'but it is not a bad practice – not a bad practice. We have had it a bit earlier to-day for hospitality's sake – that's all.'

I had nothing particular to say to this, though I was thinking a great deal. From time to time I stole a look at my companion. His coat was black, and so was his waistcoat; neck-cloth he had none, his strong full throat being bare above the snow-white shirt. He wore drab-coloured knee-breeches, grey worsted stockings (I thought I knew the maker), and strong-nailed shoes. He carried his hat in his hand, as if he liked to feel the coming breeze lifting his hair. After a while, I saw that the father took hold of the daughter's hand, and so, they holding each other, went along towards home. We had to cross a lane. In it were two little children, one lying prone on the grass in a passion of crying, the other standing stock still, with its finger in its mouth, the large tears slowly rolling down its cheeks for sympathy. The cause of their distress was evident; there was a broken brown pitcher, and a little pool of spilt milk on the road.

'Hollo! Hollo! What's all this?' said the minister. 'Why, what have you been about, Tommy,' lifting the little petti-coated lad, who was lying sobbing, with one vigorous arm. Tommy looked at him with surprise in his round eyes, but no affright – they were evidently old acquaintances.

'Mammy's jug!' said he, at last, beginning to cry afresh.

'Well! and will crying piece mammy's jug, or pick up spilt milk? How did you manage it, Tommy?'

'He' (jerking his head at the other) 'and me was running races.'

'Tommy said he could beat me,' put in the other.

'Now, I wonder what will make you two silly lads mind, and not run races again with a pitcher of milk between you,' said the minister, as if musing. 'I might flog you, and so save mammy the trouble; for I dare say she'll do it if I don't.' The fresh burst of whimpering from both showed the probability of this. 'Or I might take you to the Hope Farm, and give you some more milk; but then you'd be running races again, and my milk would follow that to the ground, and make another white pool. I think the flogging would be best – don't you?'

'We would never run races no more,' said the elder of the two.

'Then you'd not be boys; you'd be angels.'

'No, we shouldn't.'

'Why not?'

They looked into each other's eyes for an answer to this puzzling question. At length, one said, 'Angels is dead folk.'

'Come; we'll not get too deep into theology. What do you think of my lending you a tin can with a lid to carry the milk home in? That would not break, at any rate; though I would not answer for the milk not spilling if you ran races. That's it!'

He had dropped his daughter's hand, and now held out each of his to the little fellows. Phillis and I followed, and listened to the prattle which the minister's companions now poured out to him, and which he was evidently enjoying. At a certain point, there was a sudden burst of the tawny, ruddy-evening landscape. The minister turned round and quoted a line or two of Latin.

'It's wonderful,' said he, 'how exactly Virgil* has hit the enduring epithets, nearly two thousand years ago, and in Italy; and yet how it describes to a T what is now lying before us in the parish of Heathbridge, county – , England.'

'I dare say it does,' said I, all aglow with shame, for I had forgotten the little Latin I ever knew.

The minister shifted his eyes to Phillis's face; it mutely gave him back the sympathetic appreciation that I, in my ignorance, could not bestow.

'Oh! this is worse than the catechism,' thought I; 'that was only remembering words.'

'Phillis, lass, thou must go home with these lads, and tell

their mother all about the race and the milk. Mammy must always know the truth,' now speaking to the children. 'And tell her, too, from me that I have got the best birch rod in the parish; and that if she ever thinks her children want a flogging she must bring them to me, and, if I think they deserve it, I'll give it them better than she can.' So Phillis led the children towards the dairy, somewhere in the back yard, and I followed the minister in through the 'curate' into the house-place.

'Their mother,' said he, 'is a bit of a vixen, and apt to punish her children without rhyme or reason. I try to keep the parish rod as well as the parish bull.'*

He sate down in the three-cornered chair by the fire-side, and looked around the empty room.

'Where's the missus?' said he to himself. But she was there in a minute; it was her regular plan to give him his welcome home – by a look, by a touch, nothing more – as soon as she could after his return, and he had missed her now. Regardless of my presence, he went over the day's doings to her; and then, getting up, he said he must go and make himself 'reverend', and that then we would have a cup of tea in the parlour. The parlour was a large room with two casemented windows on the other side of the broad flagged passage leading from the rector-door to the wide staircase, with its shallow, polished oaken steps, on which no carpet was ever laid. The parlour-floor was covered in the middle by a home-made carpeting of needlework and list. One or two quaint family pictures of the Holman family hung round the walls; the fire-grate and irons were much ornamented with brass; and on a table against the wall between the windows, a great beau-pot of flowers was placed upon the folio volumes of Matthew Henry's Bible.* It was a compliment to me to use this room, and I tried to be grateful for it; but we never had our meals there after that first day, and I was glad of it; for the large house-place, living-room, dining-room, whichever you might like to call it, was twice as comfortable and cheerful. There was a rug in front of the great large fire-place, and an oven by the grate, and a crook, with the kettle hanging from it, over the bright wood-fire; everything that ought to be black and polished in that room was black and polished; and the flags, and window-curtains, and such things as were to be white and clean, were just spotless in their purity. Opposite to the fire-place, extending the whole length of the room, was an oaken shovel-board, with the right incline for a skilful player to send the weights into the prescribed space. There were baskets of white work about, and a small shelf of books hung against the wall, books used for reading, and not for propping up a beau-pot of flowers. I took down one or two of those books once when I was left alone in the house-place on the first evening – Virgil, Caesar, a Greek grammar – oh, dear! ah, me! and Phillis Holman's name in each of them! I shut them up, and put them back in their places, and walked as far away from the bookshelf as I could. Yes, and I gave my cousin Phillis a wide berth, although she was sitting at her work quietly enough, and her hair was looking more golden, her dark eyelashes longer, her round pillar of a throat whiter than ever. We had done tea, and we had returned into the house-place that the minister might smoke his pipe without fear of contaminating the drab damask window-curtains of the parlour. He had made himself 'reverend' by putting on one of the voluminous white muslin neckcloths that I had seen cousin Holman ironing that first visit I had paid to the Hope Farm, and by making one or two other unimportant changes in his dress. He sate looking steadily at me, but whether he saw me or not I cannot tell. At the time I fancied that he did, and was gauging me in some unknown fashion in his secret mind. Every now and then he took his pipe out of his mouth, knocked out the ashes, and asked me some fresh question. As long as these related to my acquirements or my reading, I shuffled uneasily and did not know what to answer. By-and-by he got round to the more practical subject of railroads, and on this I was more at home. I really had taken an interest in my work; nor would Mr Holdsworth, indeed, have kept me in his employment if I had not given my mind as well as my time to it; and I was, besides, full of the difficulties which beset us just then, owing to our not being able to find a steady bottom on the Heathbridge moss, over which we wished to carry our line. In the midst of all my eagerness in speaking about this, I could not help being struck with the extreme pertinence of his questions. I do not mean that he did not show ignorance of many of the details of engineering: that was to have been expected; but on the premises he had got hold of, he thought clearly and reasoned logically. Phillis – so like him as she was both in body and mind – kept stopping at her work and looking at me, trying to fully understand all that I said. I felt she did; and perhaps it made me take more pains in using clear expressions, and arranging my words, than I otherwise should.

'She shall see I know something worth knowing, though it mayn't be her dead-and-gone languages,' thought I.

'I see,' said the minister, at length. 'I understand it all. You've a clear, good head of your own, my lad, – choose how you came by it.'

'From my father,' said I, proudly. 'Have you not heard of his discovery of a new method of shunting? It was in the *Gazette*. It was patented. I thought every one had heard of Manning's patent winch.'

'We don't know who invented the alphabet,' said he, half smiling, and taking up his pipe.

'No, I dare say not, sir,' replied I, half offended; 'that's so long ago.'

Puff – puff – puff.

'But your father must be a notable man. I heard of him once before; and it is not many a one fifty miles away whose fame reaches Heathbridge.'

'My father is a notable man, sir. It is not me that says so; it is Mr Holdsworth, and – and everybody.'

'He is right to stand up for his father,' said cousin Holman, as if she were pleading for me.

I chafed inwardly, thinking that my father needed no one to stand up for him. He was man sufficient for himself.

'Yes – he is right,' said the minister, placidly. 'Right, because it comes from his heart – right, too, as I believe, in point of fact. Else there is many a young cockerel that will stand upon a dunghill and crow about his father, by way of making his own plumage to shine. I should like to know thy father,' he went on, turning straight to me, with a kindly, frank look in his eyes.

But I was vexed, and would take no notice. Presently, having finished his pipe, he got up and left the room. Phillis put her work hastily down, and went after him. In a minute or two she returned, and sate down again. Not long after, and before

I had quite recovered my good temper, he opened the door out of which he had passed, and called to me to come to him. I went across a narrow stone passage into a strange, many-cornered room, not ten feet in area, part study, part counting-house, looking into the farm-yard; with a desk to sit at, a desk to stand at, a spittoon, a set of shelves with old divinity books upon them; another, smaller, filled with books on farriery, farming, manures, and such subjects, with pieces of paper containing memoranda stuck against the whitewashed walls with wafers, nails, pins, anything that came readiest to hand; a box of carpenter's tools on the floor, and some manu-scripts in short-hand on the desk.

He turned round, half laughing. 'That foolish girl of mine thinks I have vexed you' – putting his large, powerful hand on my shoulder. ' "Nay," says I, "kindly meant is kindly taken" – is it not so?'

'It was not quite, sir,' replied I, vanquished by his manner; 'but it shall be in future.'

'Come, that's right. You and I shall be friends. Indeed, it's not many a one I would bring in here. But I was reading a book this morning, and I could not make it out; it is a book that was left here by mistake one day; I had subscribed to Brother Robinson's sermons; and I was glad to see this in-stead of them, for sermons though they be, they're . . . well, never mind! I took 'em both, and made my old coat do a bit longer; but all's fish that comes to my net. I have fewer books than leisure to read them, and I have a prodigious big appetite. Here it is.'

It was a volume of stiff mechanics, involving many technical terms, and some rather deep mathematics. These last, which would have puzzled me, seemed easy enough to him; all that he wanted was the explanations of the technical words, which I could easily give.

While he was looking through the book to find the places where he had been puzzled, my wandering eye caught on some of the papers on the wall, and I could not help reading one, which has stuck by me ever since. At first, it seemed a kind of weekly diary; but then I saw that the seven days were portioned out for special prayers and intercessions: Monday for his family, Tuesday for enemies, Wednesday for the

Independent churches, Thursday for all other churches, Friday for persons afflicted, Saturday for his own soul, Sunday for all wanderers and sinners, that they might be brought home to the fold.

We were called back into the house-place to have supper. A door opening into the kitchen was opened; and all stood up in both rooms, while the minister, tall, large, one hand resting on the spread table, the other lifted up, said, in the deep voice that would have been loud had it not been so full and rich, but without the peculiar accent or twang that I believe is considered devout by some people, 'Whether we eat or drink, or whatsoever we do, let us do all to the glory of God.'

The supper was an immense meat-pie. We of the house-place were helped first; then the minister hit the handle of his buck-horn carving-knife on the table once, and said, –

'Now or never,' which meant, did any of us want any more; and when we had all declined, either by silence or by words, he knocked twice with his knife on the table, and Betty came in through the open door, and carried off the great dish to the kitchen, where an old man and a young one, and a help-girl, were awaiting their meal.

'Shut the door, if you will,' said the minister to Betty.

'That's in honour of you,' said cousin Holman, in a tone of satisfaction, as the door was shut. 'When we've no stranger with us, the minister is so fond of keeping the door open, and talking to the men and maids, just as much as to Phillis and me.'

'It brings us all together like a household just before we meet as a household in prayer,' said he, in explanation. 'But to go back to what we were talking about – can you tell me of any simple book on dynamics that I could put in my pocket, and study a little at leisure times in the day?'

'Leisure times, father?' said Phillis, with a nearer approach to a smile than I had yet seen on her face.

'Yes; leisure times, daughter. There is many an odd minute lost in waiting for other folk; and now that railroads are coming so near us, it behoves us to know something about them.'

I thought of his own description of his 'prodigious big appetite' for learning. And he had a good appetite of his own for the more material victual before him. But I saw, or fancied

I saw, that he had some rule for himself in the matter both of food and drink.

As soon as supper was done the household assembled for prayer. It was a long impromptu evening prayer; and it would have seemed desultory enough had I not had a glimpse of the kind of day that preceded it, and so been able to find a clue to the thoughts that preceded the disjointed utterances; for he kept there kneeling down in the centre of a circle, his eyes shut, his outstretched hands pressed palm to palm – sometimes with a long pause of silence, as if waiting to see if there was anything else he wished to 'lay before the Lord' (to use his own expression) – before he concluded with the blessing. He prayed for the cattle and live creatures, rather to my surprise; for my attention had begun to wander, till it was recalled by the familiar words.

And here I must not forget to name an odd incident at the conclusion of the prayer, and before we had risen from our knees (indeed before Betty was well awake, for she made a nightly practice of having a sound nap, her weary head lying on her stalwart arms); the minister, still kneeling in our midst, but with his eyes wide open, and his arms dropped by his side, spoke to the elder man, who turned round on his knees to attend. 'John, didst see that Daisy had her warm mash to-night; for we must not neglect the means, John – two quarts of gruel, a spoonful of ginger, and a gill of beer – the poor beast needs it, and I fear it slipped out of my mind to tell thee; and here was I asking a blessing and neglecting the means, which is a mockery,' said he, droppi ng his voice.

Before we went to bed he told me he should see little or nothing more of me during my visit, which was to end on Sunday evening, as he always gave up both Saturday and Sabbath to his work in the ministry. I remembered that the landlord at the inn had told me this on the day when I first inquired about these new relations of mine; and I did not dislike the opportunity which I saw would be afforded me of becoming more acquainted with cousin Holman and Phillis, though I earnestly hoped that the latter would not attack me on the subject of the dead languages.

I went to bed, and dreamed that I was as tall as cousin Phillis, and had a sudden and miraculous growth of whisker, and a still more miraculous acquaintance with Latin and Greek. Alas! I wakened up still a short, beardless lad, with '*tempus fugit*'* for my sole remembrance of the little Latin I had once learnt. While I was dressing, a bright thought came over me: I could question cousin Phillis, instead of her questioning me, and so manage to keep the choice of the subjects of conversation in my own power.

Early as it was, every one had breakfasted, and my basin of bread and milk was put on the oven-top to await my coming down. Every one was gone about their work. The first to come into the house-place was Phillis with a basket of eggs. Faithful to my resolution, I asked, –

'What are those?'

She looked at me for a moment, and then said gravely, –

'Potatoes!'

'No! they are not,' said I. 'They are eggs. What do you mean by saying they are potatoes?'

'What do you mean by asking me what they were, when they were plain to be seen?' retorted she.

We were both getting a little angry with each other.

'I don't know. I wanted to begin to talk to you; and I was afraid you would talk to me about books as you did yesterday. I have not read much; and you and the minister have read so much.'

'I have not,' said she. 'But you are our guest; and mother says I must make it pleasant to you. We won't talk of books. What must we talk about?'

'I don't know. How old are you?'

'Seventeen last May. How old are you?'

'I am nineteen. Older than you by nearly two years,' said I, drawing myself up to my full height.

'I should not have thought you were above sixteen,' she replied, as quietly as if she were not saying the most provoking thing she possibly could. Then came a pause.

'What are you going to do now?' asked I.

'I should be dusting the bed-chambers; but mother said I had better stay and make it pleasant to you,' said she, a little plaintively, as if dusting rooms was far the easiest task.

'Will you take me to see the live-stock? I like animals, though I don't know much about them.'

'Oh, do you? I am so glad! I was afraid you would not like animals, as you did not like books.'

I wondered why she said this. I think it was because she had begun to fancy all our tastes must be dissimilar. We went together all through the farm-yard; we fed the poultry, she kneeling down with her pinafore full of corn and meal, and tempting the little timid, downy chickens upon it, much to the anxiety of the fussy ruffled hen, their mother. She called to the pigeons, who fluttered down at the sound of her voice. She and I examined the great sleek cart-horses; sympathized in our dislike of pigs; fed the calves; coaxed the sick cow, Daisy; and admired the others out at pasture; and came back tired and hungry and dirty at dinner-time, having quite forgotten that there were such things as dead languages, and consequently capital friends.

PART II

COUSIN HOLMAN gave me the weekly county newspaper to read aloud to her, while she mended stockings out of a high piled-up basket, Phillis helping her mother. I read and read, unregardful of the words I was uttering, thinking of all manner of other things; of the bright colour of Phillis's hair, as the afternoon sun fell on her bending head; of the silence of the house, which enabled me to hear the double tick of the old clock which stood half-way up the stairs; of the variety of inarticulate noises which cousin Holman made while I read, to show her sympathy, wonder, or horror at the newspaper intelligence. The tranquil monotony of that hour made me feel as if I had lived for ever, and should live for ever droning out paragraphs in that warm sunny room, with my two quiet hearers, and the curled-up pussy cat sleeping on the hearth-rug, and the clock on the house-stairs perpetually clicking out the passage of the moments. By-and-by Betty the servant came to the door into the kitchen, and made a sign to Phillis, who put her half-mended stocking down, and went away to the kitchen without a word. Looking at cousin Holman a minute or two afterwards, I saw that she had dropped her chin upon her breast, and had fallen fast asleep. I put the newspaper down, and was nearly following her example, when a waft of air from some unseen source, slightly opened the door of communication with the kitchen, that Phillis must have left unfastened; and I saw part of her figure as she sate by the dresser, peeling apples with quick dexterity of finger, but with repeated turnings of her head towards some book lying on the dresser by her. I softly rose, and as softly went into the kitchen, and looked over her shoulder; before she was aware of my neighbourhood, I had seen that the book was in a language unknown to me, and the running title was *L'Inferno*. Just as I was making out the relationship of this word to 'infernal', she started and turned round, and, as if continuing her thought as she spoke, she sighed out, –

'Oh! it is so difficult! Can you help me?' putting her finger below a line.

'Me! I! Not I! I don't even know what language it is in!'

'Don't you see it is Dante?' she replied, almost petulantly; she did so want help.

'Italian, then?' said I, dubiously; for I was not quite sure.

'Yes. And I do so want to make it out. Father can help me a little, for he knows Latin; but then he has so little time.'

'You have not much, I should think, if you have often to try and do two things at once, as you are doing now.'

'Oh! that's nothing! Father bought a heap of old books cheap. And I knew something about Dante before; and I have always liked Virgil so much. Paring apples is nothing, if I could only make out this old Italian. I wish you knew it.'

'I wish I did,' said I, moved by her impetuosity of tone. 'If, now, only Mr Holdsworth were here; he can speak Italian like anything, I believe.'

'Who is Mr Holdsworth?' said Phillis, looking up.

'Oh, he's our head engineer. He's a regular first-rate fellow! He can do anything;' my hero-worship and my pride in my chief all coming into play. Besides, if I was not clever and book-learned myself, it was something to belong to some one who was.

'How is it that he speaks Italian?' asked Phillis.

'He had to make a railway through Piedmont, which is in Italy, I believe; and he had to talk to all the workmen in Italian; and I have heard him say that for nearly two years he had only Italian books to read in the queer outlandish places he was in.'

'Oh, dear!' said Phillis; 'I wish – ' and then she stopped. I was not quite sure whether to say the next thing that came into my mind; but I said it.

'Could I ask him anything about your book, or your difficulties?'

She was silent for a minute or so, and then she made reply, –

'No! I think not. Thank you very much, though. I can generally puzzle a thing out in time. And then, perhaps, I remember it better than if some one had helped me. I'll put it away now, and you must move off, for I've got to make the paste for the pies; we always have a cold dinner on Sabbaths.'

'But I may stay and help you, mayn't I?'

'Oh, yes; not that you can help at all, but I like to have you with me.'

I was both flattered and annoyed at this straightforward avowal. I was pleased that she liked me; but I was young coxcomb enough to have wished to play the lover, and I was quite wise enough to perceive that if she had any idea of the kind in her head she would never have spoken out so frankly. I comforted myself immediately, however, by finding out that the grapes were sour. A great tall girl in a pinafore, half a head taller than I was, reading books that I had never heard of, and talking about them too, as of far more interest than any mere personal subjects; that was the last day on which I ever thought of my dear cousin Phillis as the possible mistress of my heart and life. But we were all the greater friends for this idea being utterly put away and buried out of sight.

Late in the evening the minister came home from Hornby. He had been calling on the different members of his flock; and unsatisfactory work it had proved to him, it seemed from the fragments that dropped out of his thoughts into his talk.

'I don't see the men; they are all at their business, their shops, or their warehouses; they ought to be there. I have no fault to find with them; only if a pastor's teaching or words of admonition are good for anything, they are needed by the men as much as by the women.'

'Cannot you go and see them in their places of business, and remind them of their Christian privileges and duties, minister?' asked cousin Holman, who evidently thought that her husband's words could never be out of place.

'No!' said he, shaking his head. 'I judge them by myself. If there are clouds in the sky, and I am getting in the hay just ready for loading, and rain sure to come in the night, I should look ill upon brother Robinson if he came into the field to speak about serious things.'

'But, at any rate, father, you do good to the women, and perhaps they repeat what you have said to them to their husbands and children?'

'It is to be hoped they do, for I cannot reach the men directly; but the women are apt to tarry before coming to me, to put on ribbons and gauds; as if they could hear the message I bear to them best in their smart clothes. Mrs Dobson to-day – Phillis, I am thankful thou dost not care for the vanities of dress!'

Phillis reddened a little as she said, in a low humble voice, –

'But I do, father, I'm afraid. I often wish I could wear pretty-coloured ribbons round my throat like the squire's daughters.'

'It's but natural, minister!' said his wife; 'I'm not above liking a silk gown better than a cotton one myself!'

'The love of dress is a temptation and a snare,' said he, gravely. 'The true adornment is a meek and quiet spirit. And, wife,' said he, as a sudden thought crossed his mind, 'in that matter I, too, have sinned. I wanted to ask you, could we not sleep in the grey room, instead of our own?'

'Sleep in the grey room? – change our room at this time o' day?' cousin Holman asked, in dismay.

'Yes,' said he. 'It would save me from a daily temptation to anger. Look at my chin!' he continued; 'I cut it this morning – I cut it on Wednesday when I was shaving; I do not know how many times I have cut it of late, and all from impatience at seeing Timothy Cooper at his work in the yard.'

'He's a downright lazy tyke!' said cousin Holman. 'He's not worth his wage. There's but little he can do, and what he can do, he does badly.'

'True,' said the minister. 'He is but, so to speak, a half-wit; and yet he has got a wife and children.'

'More shame for him!'

'But that is past change. And if I turn him off, no one else will take him on. Yet I cannot help watching him of a morning as he goes sauntering about his work in the yard; and I watch, and I watch, till the old Adam rises strong within me at his lazy ways, and some day, I am afraid, I shall go down and send him about his business – let alone the way in which he makes me cut myself while I am shaving – and then his wife and children will starve. I wish we could move to the grey room.'

I do not remember much more of my first visit to the Hope Farm. We went to chapel in Heathbridge, slowly and decorously walking along the lanes, ruddy and tawny with the colouring of the coming autumn. The minister walked a little before us, his hands behind his back, his head bent down, thinking about the discourse to be delivered to his people, cousin Holman said; and we spoke low and quietly, in order not to interrupt his thoughts. But I could not help noticing the respectful greetings which he received from both rich and poor as we went along; greetings which he acknowledged with a kindly wave of his hand, but with no words of reply. As we drew near the town, I could see some of the young fellows we met cast admiring looks on Phillis; and that made me look too. She had on a white gown, and a short black silk cloak, according to the fashion of the day. A straw bonnet with brown ribbon strings; that was all. But what her dress wanted in colour, her sweet bonny face had. The walk made her cheeks bloom like the rose; the very whites of her eyes had a blue tinge in them, and her dark eyelashes brought out the depth of the blue eyes themselves. Her yellow hair was put away as straight as its natural curliness would allow. If she did not perceive the admiration she excited, I am sure cousin Holman did; for she looked as fierce and as proud as ever her quiet face could look, guarding her treasure, and yet glad to perceive that others could see that it was a treasure. That afternoon I had to return to Eltham to be ready for the next day's work. I found out afterwards that the minister and his family were all 'exercised in spirit,' as to whether they did well in asking me to repeat my visits at the Hope Farm, seeing that of necessity I must return to Eltham on the Sabbath-day. However, they did go on asking me, and I went on visiting them, whenever my other engagements permitted me, Mr Holdsworth being in this case, as in all, a kind and indulgent friend. Nor did my new acquaintances oust him from my strong regard and admiration. I had room in my heart for all, I am happy to say, and as far as I can remember, I kept praising each to the other in a manner which, if I had been an older man, living more amongst people of the world, I should have thought unwise, as well as a little ridiculous. It was unwise, certainly, as it was almost sure to cause disappointment if ever they did become acquainted; and perhaps it was ridiculous, though I do not think we any of us thought it so at the time. The minister used to listen to my accounts of Mr Holdsworth's many accomplishments and various adventures in travel with the truest interest, and most kindly good faith; and Mr Holdsworth in return liked to hear about my visits to the farm, and description of my cousin's life there – liked it, I mean, as much as he liked anything that was merely narrative, without leading to action.

So I went to the farm certainly, on an average, once a month during that autumn; the course of life there was so peaceful and quiet, that I can only remember one small event, and that was one that I think I took more notice of than any one else: Phillis left off wearing the pinafores that had always been so obnoxious to me; I do not know why they were banished, but on one of my visits I found them replaced by pretty linen aprons in the morning, and a black silk one in the afternoon. And the blue cotton gown became a brown stuff one as winter drew on; this sounds like some book I once read, in which a migration from the blue bed to the brown was spoken of as a great family event.*

Towards Christmas my dear father came to see me, and to consult Mr Holdsworth about the improvement which has since been known as 'Manning's driving wheel'. Mr Holdsworth, as I think I have before said, had a very great regard for my father, who had been employed in the same great machine-shop in which Mr Holdsworth had served his apprenticeship; and he and my father had many mutual jokes about one of these gentlemen-apprentices who used to set about his smith's work in white wash-leather gloves, for fear of spoiling his hands. Mr Holdsworth often spoke to me about my father as having the same kind of genius for mechanical invention as that of George Stephenson, and my father had come over now to consult him about several improvements, as well as an offer of partnership. It was a great pleasure to me to see the mutual regard of these two men. Mr Holdsworth, young, handsome, keen, well-dressed, an object of admiration to all the youth of Eltham; my father, in his decent but un-fashionable Sunday clothes, his plain, sensible face full of hard lines, the marks of toil and thought, – his hands, blackened beyond the power of soap and water by years of labour in the foundry; speaking a strong Northern dialect, while Mr Holdsworth had a long soft drawl in his voice, as many of the Southerners have, and was reckoned in Eltham to give him-self airs.

Although most of my father's leisure time was occupied with conversations about the business I have mentioned, he felt that he ought not to leave Eltham without going to pay his respects to the relations who had been so kind to his son. So he and I ran up on an engine along the incomplete line as far as Heathbridge, and went, by invitation, to spend a day at the farm.

It was odd and yet pleasant to me to perceive how these two men, each having led up to this point such totally dissimilar lives, seemed to come together by instinct, after one quiet straight look into each other's faces. My father was a thin, wiry man of five foot seven; the minister was a broad-shouldered, fresh-coloured man of six foot one; they were neither of them great talkers in general – perhaps the minister the most so – but they spoke much to each other. My father went into the fields with the minister; I think I see him now, with his hands behind his back, listening intently to all explanations of tillage, and the different processes of farming; occasionally taking up an implement, as if unconsciously, and examining it with a critical eye, and now and then asking a question, which I could see was considered as pertinent by his companion. Then we returned to look at the cattle, housed and bedded in expectation of the snow-storm hanging black on the western horizon, and my father learned the points of a cow with as much attention as if he meant to turn farmer. He had his little book that he used for mechanical memoranda and measurements in his pocket, and he took it out to write down 'straight back', 'small muzzle', 'deep barrel', and I know not what else, under the head 'cow'. He was very critical on a turnip-cutting machine, the clumsiness of which first incited him to talk; and when we went into the house he sate thinking and quiet for a bit, while Phillis and her mother made the last preparations for tea, with a little unheeded apology from cousin Holman, because we were not sitting in the best parlour, which she thought might be chilly on so cold a night. I wanted nothing better than the blazing, crackling fire that sent a glow over all the house-place, and warmed the snowy flags under our feet till they seemed to have more heat than the crimson rug right in front of the fire. After tea, as Phillis and I were talking together very happily, I heard an irrepressible exclamation from cousin Holman, –

'Whatever is the man about!'

And on looking round, I saw my father taking a straight burning stick out of the fire, and, after waiting for a minute, and examining the charred end to see if it was fitted for his purpose, he went to the hard-wood dresser, scoured to the last pitch of whiteness and cleanliness, and began drawing with the stick; the best substitute for chalk or charcoal within his reach, for his pocket-book pencil was not strong or bold enough for his purpose. When he had done, he began to explain his new model of a turnip-cutting machine to the minister, who had been watching him in silence all the time. Cousin Holman had, in the meantime, taken a duster out of a drawer, and, under pretence of being as much interested as her husband in the drawing, was secretly trying on an outside mark how easily it would come off, and whether it would leave her dresser as white as before. Then Phillis was sent for the book on dynamics, about which I had been consulted during my first visit, and my father had to explain many difficulties, which he did in language as clear as his mind, making drawings with his stick wherever they were needed as illustrations, the minister sitting with his massive head resting on his hands, his elbows on the table, almost unconscious of Phillis, leaning over and listening greedily, with her hand on his shoulder, sucking in information like her father's own daughter. I was rather sorry for cousin Holman; I had been so once or twice before; for do what she would, she was completely unable even to understand the pleasure her husband and daughter took in intellectual pursuits, much less to care in the least herself for the pursuits themselves, and was thus unavoidably thrown out of some of their interests. I had once or twice thought she was a little jealous of her own child, as a fitter companion for her husband than she was herself; and I fancied the minister himself was aware of this feeling, for I had noticed an occasional sudden change of subject, and a tenderness of appeal in his voice as he spoke to her, which always made her look contented and peaceful again. I do not think that Phillis ever perceived these little shadows; in the first place, she had such complete reverence for her parents that she listened to them both as if they had been St Peter and St Paul; and besides, she was always too much engrossed with any matter in hand to think about other people's manners and looks.

This night I could see, though she did not, how much she was winning on my father. She asked a few questions which showed that she had followed his explanations up to that point; possibly, too, her unusual beauty might have something to do with his favourable impression of her; but he made no scruple of expressing his admiration of her to her father and mother in her absence from the room; and from that evening I date a project of his which came out to me a day or two afterwards, as we sate in my little three-cornered room in Eltham.

'Paul,' he began, 'I never thought to be a rich man; but I think it's coming upon me. Some folk are making a deal of my new machine (calling it by its technical name), and Ellison, of the Borough Green Works, has gone so far as to ask me to be his partner.'

'Mr Ellison the Justice! – who lives in King Street? why, he drives his carriage!' said I, doubting, yet exultant.

'Aye, lad, John Ellison. But that's no sign that I shall drive my carriage. Though I should like to save thy mother walking, for she's not so young as she was. But that's a long way off, anyhow. I reckon I should start with a third profit. It might be seven hundred, or it might be more. I should like to have the power to work out some fancies o' mine. I care for that much more than for th' brass. And Ellison has no lads; and by nature the business would come to thee in course o' time. Ellison's lasses are but bits o' things, and are not like to come by husbands just yet; and when they do, maybe they'll not be in the mechanical line. It will be an opening for thee, lad, if thou art steady. Thou'rt not great shakes, I know, in th' inventing line; but many a one gets on better without having fancies for something he does not see and never has seen. I'm right down glad to see that mother's cousins are such uncommon folk for sense and goodness. I have taken the minister to my heart like a brother; and she is a womanly quiet sort of a body. And I'll tell you frank, Paul, it will be a happy day for me if ever you can come and tell me that Phillis Holman is like to be my daughter. I think if that lass had not a penny, she would be the making of a man; and she'll have yon house and lands, and you may be her match yet in fortune if all goes well.'

I was growing as red as fire; I did not know what to say, and yet I wanted to say something; but the idea of having a wife of my own at some future day, though it had often floated about in my own head, sounded so strange when it was thus first spoken about by my father. He saw my confusion, and half smiling said, –

'Well, lad, what dost say to the old father's plans? Thou art but young, to be sure; but when I was thy age, I would ha' given my right hand if I might ha' thought of the chance of wedding the lass I cared for – '

'My mother?' asked I, a little struck by the change of his tone of voice.

'No! not thy mother. Thy mother is a very good woman – none better. No! the lass I cared for at nineteen ne'er knew how I loved her, and a year or two after and she was dead, and ne'er knew. I think she would ha' been glad to ha' known it, poor Molly; but I had to leave the place where we lived for to try to earn my bread – and I meant to come back – but before ever I did, she was dead and gone: I ha' never gone there since. But if you fancy Phillis Holman, and can get her to fancy you, my lad, it shall go different with you, Paul, to what it did with your father.'

I took counsel with myself very rapidly, and I came to a clear conclusion.

'Father,' said I, 'if I fancied Phillis ever so much, she would never fancy me. I like her as much as I could like a sister; and she likes me as if I were her brother – her younger brother.'

I could see my father's countenance fall a little.

'You see she's so clever – she's more like a man than a woman – she knows Latin and Greek.'

'She'd forget 'em, if she'd a houseful of children,' was my father's comment on this.

'But she knows many a thing besides, and is wise as well as learned; she has been so much with her father. She would never think much of me, and I should like my wife to think a deal of her husband.'

'It is not just book-learning or the want of it as makes a wife think much or little of her husband,' replied my father, evidently unwilling to give up a project which had taken deep root in his mind. 'It's a something – I don't rightly know how to call it – if he's manly, and sensible, and straightforward; and I reckon you're that, my boy.'

'I don't think I should like to have a wife taller than I am, father,' said I, smiling; he smiled too, but not heartily.

'Well,' said he, after a pause. 'It's but a few days I've been thinking of it, but I'd got as fond of my notion as if it had been a new engine as I'd been planning out. Here's our Paul, thinks I to myself, a good sensible breed o' lad, as has never vexed or troubled his mother or me; with a good business opening out before him, age nineteen, not so bad-looking, though perhaps not to call handsome, and here's his cousin, not too near a cousin, but just nice, as one may say; aged seventeen, good and true, and well brought up to work with her hands as well as her head; a scholar – but that can't be helped, and is more her misfortune than her fault, seeing she is the only child of a scholar – and as I said afore, once she's a wife and a mother she'll forget it all, I'll be bound – with a good fortune in land and house when it shall please the Lord to take her parents to himself; with eyes like poor Molly's for beauty, a colour that comes and goes on a milk-white skin, and as pretty a mouth – '

'Why, Mr Manning, what fair lady are you describing?' asked Mr Holdsworth, who had come quickly and suddenly upon our *tête-à-tête*, and had caught my father's last words as he entered the room.

Both my father and I felt rather abashed; it was such an odd subject for us to be talking about; but my father, like a straightforward simple man as he was, spoke out the truth.

'I've been telling Paul of Ellison's offer, and saying how good an opening it made for him –'

'I wish I'd as good,' said Mr Holdsworth. 'But has the business a "pretty mouth"?'

'You're always so full of your joking, Mr Holdsworth,' said my father. 'I was going to say that if he and his cousin Phillis Holman liked to make it up between them, I would put no spoke in the wheel.'

'Phillis Holman!' said Mr Holdsworth. 'Is she the daughter of the minister-farmer out at Heathbridge? Have I been helping on the course of true love by letting you go there so often? I knew nothing of it.'

'There is nothing to know,' said I, more annoyed than I

chose to show. 'There is no more true love in the case than
may be between the first brother and sister you may choose to
meet. I have been telling father she would never think of me;
she's a great deal taller and cleverer; and I'd rather be taller
and more learned than my wife when I have one.'

'And it is she, then, that has the pretty mouth your father
spoke about? I should think that would be an antidote to the
cleverness and learning. But I ought to apologize for breaking
in upon your last night; I came upon business to your father.'

And then he and my father began to talk about many things
that had no interest for me just then, and I began to go over
again my conversation with my father. The more I thought
about it, the more I felt that I had spoken truly about my
feelings towards Phillis Holman. I loved her dearly as a sister,
but I could never fancy her as my wife. Still less could I think
of her ever – yes, *condescending*, that is the word – condescending to marry me. I was roused from a reverie on what I should
like my possible wife to be, by hearing my father's warm
praise of the minister, as a most unusual character; how they
had got back from the diameter of driving-wheels to the subject
of the Holmans I could never tell; but I saw that my father's
weighty praises were exciting some curiosity in Mr Holdsworth's mind; indeed, he said, almost in a voice of reproach, –

'Why, Paul, you never told me what kind of a fellow this
minister-cousin of yours was!'

'I don't know that I found out, sir,' said I. 'But if I had, I
don't think you'd have listened to me, as you have done to my
father.'

'No! most likely not, old fellow,' replied Mr Holdsworth,
laughing. And again and afresh I saw what a handsome pleasant clear face his was; and though this evening I had been a
bit put out with him – through his sudden coming, and his
having heard my father's open-hearted confidence – my hero
resumed all his empire over me by his bright merry laugh.

And if he had not resumed his old place that night, he
would have done so the next day, when, after my father's
departure, Mr Holdsworth spoke about him with such just
respect for his character, such ungrudging admiration of his
great mechanical genius, that I was compelled to say, almost
unawares, –

'Thank you, sir. I am very much obliged to you.'

'Oh, you're not at all. I am only speaking the truth. Here's a Birmingham workman, self-educated, one may say – having never associated with stimulating minds, or had what advantages travel and contact with the world may be supposed to afford – working out his own thoughts into steel and iron, making a scientific name for himself – a fortune, if it pleases him to work for money – and keeping his singleness of heart, his perfect simplicity of manner; it puts me out of patience to think of my expensive schooling, my travels hither and thither, my heaps of scientific books, and I have done nothing to speak of. But it's evidently good blood; there's that Mr Holman, that cousin of yours, made of the same stuff.'

'But he's only cousin because he married my mother's second cousin,' said I.

'That knocks a pretty theory on the head, and twice over, too. I should like to make Holman's acquaintance.'

'I am sure they would be so glad to see you at Hope Farm,' said I, eagerly. 'In fact, they've asked me to bring you several times: only I thought you would find it dull.'

'Not at all. I can't go yet though, even if you do get me an invitation; for the —— —— Company want me to go to the —— Valley, and look over the ground a bit for them, to see if it would do for a branch line; it's a job which may take me away for some time; but I shall be backwards and forwards, and you're quite up to doing what is needed in my absence; the only work that may be beyond you is keeping old Jevons from drinking.'

He went on giving me directions about the management of the men employed on the line, and no more was said then, or for several months, about his going to Hope Farm. He went off into —— Valley, a dark overshadowed dale, where the sun seemed to set behind the hills before four o'clock on midsummer afternoon.

Perhaps it was this that brought on the attack of low fever which he had soon after the beginning of the new year; he was very ill for many weeks, almost many months; a married sister – his only relation, I think – came down from London to nurse him, and I went over to him when I could, to see him, and give him 'masculine news,' as he called it; reports of the progress of the line, which, I am glad to say, I was able to carry on in his absence, in the slow gradual way which suited the company best, while trade was in a languid state, and money dear in the market. Of course, with this occupation for my scanty leisure, I did not often go over to Hope Farm. Whenever I did go, I met with a thorough welcome; and many inquiries were made as to Holdsworth's illness, and the progress of his recovery.

At length, in June I think it was, he was sufficiently recovered to come back to his lodgings at Eltham, and resume part at least of his work. His sister, Mrs Robinson, had been obliged to leave him some weeks before, owing to some epidemic amongst her own children. As long as I had seen Mr Holdsworth in the rooms at the little inn at Hensleydale, where I had been accustomed to look upon him as an invalid, I had not been aware of the visible shake his fever had given to his health. But, once back in the old lodgings, where I had always seen him so buoyant, eloquent, decided, and vigorous in former days, my spirits sank at the change in one whom I had always regarded with a strong feeling of admiring affection. He sank into silence and despondency after the least exertion; he seemed as if he could not make up his mind to any action, or else that, when it was made up, he lacked strength to carry out his purpose. Of course, it was but the natural state of slow convalescence, after so sharp an illness; but, at the time, I did not know this, and perhaps I represented his state as more serious than it was to my kind relations at Hope Farm; who, in their grave, simple, eager way, immediately thought of the only help they could give.

'Bring him out here,' said the minister. 'Our air here is good to a proverb; the June days are fine; he may loiter away his time in the hay-field, and the sweet smells will be a balm in themselves – better than physic.'

'And,' said cousin Holman, scarcely waiting for her husband to finish his sentence, 'tell him there is new milk and fresh eggs to be had for the asking; it's lucky Daisy has just calved, for her milk is always as good as other cows' cream; and there is the plaid room with the morning sun all streaming in.'

Phillis said nothing, but looked as much interested in the project as any one. I took it upon myself. I wanted them to see him; him to know them. I proposed it to him when I got home. He was too languid after the day's fatigue, to be willing to make the little exertion of going amongst strangers; and disappointed me by almost declining to accept the invitation I brought. The next morning it was different; he apologized for his ungraciousness of the night before; and told me that he would get all things in train, so as to be ready to go out with me to Hope Farm on the following Saturday.

'For you must go with me, Manning,' said he; 'I used to be as impudent a fellow as need be, and rather liked going amongst strangers, and making my way; but since my illness I am almost like a girl, and turn hot and cold with shyness, as they do, I fancy.'

So it was fixed. We were to go out to Hope Farm on Saturday afternoon; and it was also understood that if the air and the life suited Mr Holdsworth, he was to remain there for a week or ten days, doing what work he could at that end of the line, while I took his place at Eltham to the best of my ability. I grew a little nervous, as the time drew near, and wondered how the brilliant Holdsworth would agree with the quiet quaint family of the minister; how they would like him, and many of his half-foreign ways. I tried to prepare him, by telling him from time to time little things about the goings-on at Hope Farm.

'Manning,' said he, 'I see you don't think I am half good enough for your friends. Out with it, man.'

'No,' I replied, boldly. 'I think you are good; but I don't know if you are quite of their kind of goodness.'

'And you've found out already that there is greater chance of disagreement between two "kinds of goodness", each having its own idea of right, than between a given goodness and a moderate degree of naughtiness – which last often arises from an indifference to right?'

'I don't know. I think you're talking metaphysics, and I am sure that is bad for you.'

' "When a man talks to you in a way that you don't understand about a thing which he does not understand, them's metaphysics." You remember the clown's definition, don't you, Manning?'

'No, I don't,' said I. 'But what I do understand is, that you must go to bed; and tell me at what time we must start to-morrow, that I may go to Hepworth, and get those letters written we were talking about this morning.'

'Wait till to-morrow, and let us see what the day is like,' he answered, with such languid indecision as showed me he was over-fatigued. So I went my way.

The morrow was blue and sunny, and beautiful; the very perfection of an early summer's day. Mr Holdsworth was all impatience to be off into the country; morning had brought back his freshness and strength, and consequent eagerness to be doing. I was afraid we were going to my cousin's farm rather too early, before they would expect us; but what could I do with such a restless vehement man as Holdsworth was that morning? We came down upon the Hope Farm before the dew was off the grass on the shady side of the lane; the great house-dog was loose, basking in the sun, near the closed side door. I was surprised at this door being shut, for all summer long it was open from morning to night; but it was only on latch. I opened it, Rover watching me with half-suspicious, half-trustful eyes. The room was empty.

'I don't know where they can be,' said I. 'But come in and sit down while I go and look for them. You must be tired.'

'Not I. This sweet balmy air is like a thousand tonics. Besides, this room is hot, and smells of those pungent wood-ashes. What are we to do?'

'Go round to the kitchen. Betty will tell us where they are.'

So we went round into the farmyard, Rover accompanying us out of a grave sense of duty. Betty was washing out her milk-pans in the cold bubbling spring-water that constantly trickled in and out of a stone trough. In such weather as this most of her kitchen-work was done out of doors.

'Eh, dear!' said she, 'the minister and missus is away at Hornby! They ne'er thought of your coming so betimes! The missus had some errands to do, and she thought as she'd walk with the minister and be back by dinner-time.'

'Did not they expect us to dinner?' said I.

'Well, they did, and they did not, as I may say. Missus said to me the cold lamb would do well enough if you did not come; and if you did I was to put on a chicken and some bacon to boil; and I'll go do it now, for it is hard to boil bacon enough.'

'And is Phillis gone, too?' Mr Holdsworth was making friends with Rover.

'No! She's just somewhere about. I reckon you'll find her in the kitchen-garden, getting peas.'

'Let us go there,' said Holdsworth, suddenly leaving off his play with the dog.

So I led the way into the kitchen-garden. It was in the first promise of a summer profuse in vegetables and fruits. Perhaps it was not so much cared for as other parts of the property; but it was more attended to than most kitchen-gardens belonging to farm-houses. There were borders of flowers along each side of the gravel walks; and there was an old sheltering wall on the north side covered with tolerably choice fruit-trees; there was a slope down to the fish-pond at the end, where there were great strawberry-beds; and raspberry-bushes and rose-bushes grew wherever there was a space; it seemed a chance which had been planted. Long rows of peas stretched at right angles from the main walk, and I saw Phillis stooping down among them, before she saw us. As soon as she heard our cranching steps on the gravel, she stood up, and shading her eyes from the sun, recognized us. She was quite still for a moment, and then came slowly towards us, blushing a little from evident shyness. I had never seen Phillis shy before.

'This is Mr Holdsworth, Phillis,' said I, as soon as I had shaken hands with her. She glanced up at him, and then looked down, more flushed than ever at his grand formality of taking his hat off and bowing; such manners had never been seen at Hope Farm before.

'Father and mother are out. They will be so sorry; you did not write, Paul, as you said you would.'

'It was my fault,' said Holdsworth, understanding what she meant as well as if she had put it more fully into words. 'I have not yet given up all the privileges of an invalid; one of which is indecision. Last night, when your cousin asked me at what time we were to start, I really could not make up my mind.'

Phillis seemed as if she could not make up her mind as to what to do with us. I tried to help her, –

'Have you finished getting peas?' taking hold of the half-filled basket she was unconsciously holding in her hand; 'or may we stay and help you?'

'If you would. But perhaps it will tire you, sir?' added she, speaking now to Holdsworth.

'Not a bit,' said he. 'It will carry me back twenty years in my life, when I used to gather peas in my grandfather's garden. I suppose I may eat a few as I go along?'

'Certainly, sir. But if you went to the strawberry-beds you would find some strawberries ripe, and Paul can show you where they are.'

'I am afraid you distrust me. I can assure you I know the exact fulness at which peas should be gathered. I take great care not to pluck them when they are unripe. I will not be turned off, as unfit for my work.'

This was a style of half-joking talk that Phillis was not accustomed to. She looked for a moment as if she would have liked to defend herself from the playful charge of distrust made against her, but she ended by not saying a word. We all plucked our peas in busy silence for the next five minutes. Then Holdsworth lifted himself up from between the rows, and said, a little wearily, –

'I am afraid I must strike work. I am not as strong as I fancied myself.'

Phillis was full of penitence immediately. He did, indeed, look pale; and she blamed herself for having allowed him to help her.

'It was very thoughtless of me. I did not know – I thought, perhaps, you really liked it. I ought to have offered you something to eat, sir! Oh, Paul, we have gathered quite enough; how stupid I was to forget that Mr Holdsworth had been ill!' And in a blushing hurry she led the way towards the house. We went in, and she moved a heavy cushioned chair forwards, into which Holdsworth was only too glad to sink. Then with deft and quiet speed she brought in a little tray, wine, water, cake, home-made bread, and newly-churned butter. She stood by in some anxiety till, after bite and sup, the colour returned to Mr Holdsworth's face, and he would fain have made us some laughing apologies for the fright he had given us. But then Phillis drew back from her innocent show of care and interest, and relapsed into the cold shyness habitual to her when she was first thrown into the company of strangers. She brought out the last week's county paper (which Mr Holdsworth had read five days ago), and then quietly withdrew; and then he subsided into languor, leaning back and shutting his eyes as if he would go to sleep. I stole into the kitchen after Phillis; but she had made the round of the corner of the house outside, and I found her sitting on the horse-mount, with her basket of peas, and a basin into which she was shelling them. Rover lay at her feet, snapping now and then at the flies. I went to her, and tried to help her, but somehow the sweet crisp young peas found their way more frequently into my mouth than into the basket, while we talked together in a low tone, fearful of being overheard through the open casements of the house-place in which Holdsworth was resting.

'Don't you think him handsome?' asked I.

'Perhaps – yes – I have hardly looked at him,' she replied. 'But is not he very like a foreigner?'

'Yes, he cuts his hair foreign fashion,' said I.

'I like an Englishman to look like an Englishman.'

'I don't think he thinks about it. He says he began that way when he was in Italy, because everybody wore it so, and it is natural to keep it on in England.'

'Not if he began it in Italy because everybody there wore it so. Everybody here wears it differently.'

I was a little offended with Phillis's logical fault-finding with my friend; and I determined to change the subject.

'When is your mother coming home?'

'I should think she might come any time now; but she had to go and see Mrs Morton, who was ill, and she might be kept, and not be home till dinner. Don't you think you ought to go and see how Mr Holdsworth is going on, Paul? He may be faint again.'

I went at her bidding; but there was no need for it. Mr Holdsworth was up, standing by the window, his hands in his pockets; he had evidently been watching us. He turned away as I entered.

'So that is the girl I found your good father planning for your wife, Paul, that evening when I interrupted you! Are you of the same coy mind still? It did not look like it a minute ago.'

'Phillis and I understand each other,' I replied, sturdily. 'We are like brother and sister. She would not have me as a husband if there was not another man in the world; and it would take a deal to make me think of her – as my father wishes' (somehow I did not like to say 'as a wife'), 'but we love each other dearly.'

'Well, I am rather surprised at it – not at your loving each other in a brother-and-sister kind of way – but at your finding it so impossible to fall in love with such a beautiful woman.'

Woman! beautiful woman! I had thought of Phillis as a comely but awkward girl; and I could not banish the pinafore from my mind's eye when I tried to picture her to myself. Now I turned, as Mr Holdsworth had done, to look at her again out of the window: she had just finished her task, and was standing up, her back to us, holding the basket, and the basin in it, high in air, out of Rover's reach, who was giving vent to his delight at the probability of a change of place by glad leaps and barks, and snatches at what he imagined to be a withheld prize. At length she grew tired of their mutual play, and with a feint of striking him, and a 'Down, Rover! do hush!' she looked towards the window where we were standing, as if to reassure herself that no one had been disturbed by the noise, and seeing us, she coloured all over, and hurried away, with Rover still curving in sinuous lines about her as she walked.

'I should like to have sketched her,' said Mr Holdsworth, as he turned away. He went back to his chair, and rested in silence for a minute or two. Then he was up again.

'I would give a good deal for a book,' he said. 'It would keep me quiet.' He began to look round; there were a few volumes at one end of the shovel-board.

'Fifth volume of Matthew Henry's *Commentary*,'* said he, reading their titles aloud. ' *Housewife's complete Manual*; *Berridge on Prayer*; *L'Inferno* – Dante!' in great surprise. 'Why, who reads this?'

'I told you Phillis read it. Don't you remember? She knows Latin and Greek, too.'

'To be sure! I remember! But somehow I never put two and two together. That quiet girl, full of household work, is the wonderful scholar, then, that put you to rout with her questions when you first began to come here. To be sure, "Cousin Phillis!" What's here: a paper with the hard, obsolete words written out. I wonder what sort of a dictionary she has got. Baretti* won't tell her all these words. Stay! I have got a pencil here. I'll write down the most accepted meanings, and save her a little trouble.'

So he took her book and the paper back to the little round table, and employed himself in writing explanations and definitions of the words which had troubled her. I was not sure if he was not taking a liberty: it did not quite please me, and yet I did not know why. He had only just done, and replaced the paper in the book, and put the latter back in its place, when I heard the sound of wheels stopping in the lane, and looking out, I saw cousin Holman getting out of a neighbour's gig, making her little curtsey of acknowledgment, and then coming towards the house. I went to meet her.

'Oh, Paul!' said she, 'I am so sorry I was kept; and then Thomas Dobson said if I would wait a quarter of an hour he would – But where's your friend Mr Holdsworth? I hope he is come?'

Just then he came out, and with his pleasant cordial manner took her hand, and thanked her for asking him to come out here to get strong.

'I'm sure I am very glad to see you, sir. It was the minister's thought. I took it into my head you would be dull in our quiet house, for Paul says you've been such a great traveller; but the minister said that dulness would perhaps suit you while you were but ailing, and that I was to ask Paul to be here as much as he could. I hope you'll find yourself happy with us, I'm sure, sir. Has Phillis given you something to eat and drink, I wonder? there's a deal in eating a little often, if one has to get strong after an illness.' And then she began to question him as to the details of his indisposition in her simple, motherly way. He seemed at once to understand her, and to enter into friendly relations with her. It was not quite the same in the evening when the minister came home. Men have always a little natural antipathy to get over when they first meet as strangers. But in this case each was disposed to make an effort to like the other; only each was to each a specimen of an unknown class. I had to leave the Hope Farm on Sunday afternoon, as I had Mr Holdsworth's work as well as my own to look to in Eltham; and I was not at all sure how things would go on during the week that Holdsworth was to remain on his visit; I had been once or twice in hot water already at the near clash of opinions between the minister and my much-vaunted friend. On the Wednesday I received a short note from Holdsworth; he was going to stay on, and return with me on the following Sunday, and he wanted me to send him a certain list of books, his theodolite, and other surveying instruments, all of which could easily be conveyed down the line to Heathbridge. I went to his lodgings and picked out the books. Italian, Latin, trigonometry; a pretty considerable parcel they made, besides the implements. I began to be curious as to the general progress of affairs at Hope Farm, but I could not go over till the Saturday. At Heathbridge I found Holdsworth, come to meet me. He was looking quite a different man to what I had left him; embrowned, sparkles in his eyes, so languid before. I told him how much stronger he looked.

'Yes!' said he. 'I am fidging fain* to be at work again. Last week I dreaded the thoughts of my employment: now I am full of desire to begin. This week in the country has done wonders for me.'

'You have enjoyed yourself, then?'

'Oh! it has been perfect in its way. Such a thorough country life! and yet removed from the dulness which I always used to fancy accompanied country life, by the extraordinary intelligence of the minister. I have fallen into calling him "the minister", like every one else.'

'You get on with him, then?' said I. 'I was a little afraid.'

'I was on the verge of displeasing him once or twice, I fear, with random assertions and exaggerated expressions, such as one always uses with other people, and thinks nothing of; but I tried to check myself when I saw how it shocked the good man; and really it is very wholesome exercise, this trying to make one's words represent one's thoughts, instead of merely looking to their effect on others.'

'Then you are quite friends now?' I asked.

'Yes, thoroughly; at any rate as far as I go. I never met with a man with such a desire for knowledge. In information, as far as it can be gained from books, he far exceeds me on most subjects; but then I have travelled and seen – Were not you surprised at the list of things I sent for?'

'Yes; I thought it did not promise much rest.'

'Oh! some of the books were for the minister, and some for

his daughter. (I call her Phillis to myself, but I use euphuisms*
in speaking about her to others. I don't like to seem familiar,
and yet Miss Holman is a term I have never heard used.)'

'I thought the Italian books were for her.'

'Yes! Fancy her trying at Dante for her first book in Italian!
I had a capital novel by Manzoni, *I Promessi Sposi,** just the
thing for a beginner; and if she must still puzzle out Dante,
my dictionary is far better than hers.'

'Then she found out you had written those definitions on
her list of words?'

'Oh! yes' – with a smile of amusement and pleasure. He was
going to tell me what had taken place, but checked himself.

'But I don't think the minister will like your having given
her a novel to read?'

'Pooh! What can be more harmless? Why make a bugbear
of a word? It is as pretty and innocent a tale as can be met with.
You don't suppose they take Virgil for gospel?'

By this time we were at the farm. I think Phillis gave me a
warmer welcome than usual, and cousin Holman was kindness
itself. Yet somehow I felt as if I had lost my place, and that
Holdsworth had taken it. He knew all the ways of the house;
he was full of little filial attentions to cousin Holman; he
treated Phillis with the affectionate condescension of an elder
brother; not a bit more; not in any way different. He questioned
me about the progress of affairs in Eltham with eager interest.

'Ah!' said cousin Holman, 'you'll be spending a different kind
of time next week to what you have done this! I can see how
busy you'll make yourself! But if you don't take care you'll be
ill again, and have to come back to our quiet ways of going on.'

'Do you suppose I shall need to be ill to wish to come back
here?' he answered, warmly. 'I am only afraid you have treated
me so kindly that I shall always be turning up on your hands.'

'That's right,' she replied. 'Only don't go and make yourself ill by over-work. I hope you'll go on with a cup of new
milk every morning, for I am sure that is the best medicine;
and put a teaspoonful of rum in it, if you like; many a one
speaks highly of that, only we had no rum in the house.'

I brought with me an atmosphere of active life which I
think he had begun to miss; and it was natural that he should
seek my company, after his week of retirement. Once I saw

Phillis looking at us as we talked together with a kind of wistful curiosity; but as soon as she caught my eye, she turned away, blushing deeply.

That evening I had a little talk with the minister. I strolled along the Hornby road to meet him; for Holdsworth was giving Phillis an Italian lesson, and cousin Holman had fallen asleep over her work.

Somehow, and not unwillingly on my part, our talk fell on the friend whom I had introduced to the Hope Farm.

'Yes! I like him!' said the minister, weighing his words a little as he spoke. 'I like him. I hope I am justified in doing it, but he takes hold of me, as it were; and I have almost been afraid lest he carries me away, in spite of my judgment.'

'He is a good fellow; indeed he is,' said I. 'My father thinks well of him; and I have seen a deal of him. I would not have had him come here if I did not know that you would approve of him.'

'Yes,' (once more hesitating,) 'I like him, and I think he is an upright man; there is a want of seriousness in his talk at times, but, at the same time, it is wonderful to listen to him! He makes Horace and Virgil living, instead of dead, by the stories he tells me of his sojourn in the very countries where they lived, and where to this day, he says – But it is like dram-drinking. I listen to him till I forget my duties, and am carried off my feet. Last Sabbath evening he led us away into talk on profane subjects ill befitting the day.'

By this time we were at the house, and our conversation stopped. But before the day was out, I saw the unconscious hold that my friend had got over all the family. And no wonder: he had seen so much and done so much as compared to them, and he told about it all so easily and naturally, and yet as I never heard any one else do; and his ready pencil was out in an instant to draw on scraps of paper all sorts of illustrations – modes of drawing up water in Northern Italy, wine-carts, buffaloes, stone-pines, I know not what. After we had all looked at these drawings, Phillis gathered them together, and took them.

It is many years since I have seen thee, Edward Holdsworth, but thou wast a delightful fellow! Aye, and a good one too; though much sorrow was caused by thee!

Part iii

Just after this I went home for a week's holiday. Everything was prospering there; my father's new partnership gave evident satisfaction to both parties. There was no display of increased wealth in our modest household; but my mother had a few extra comforts provided for her by her husband. I made acquaintance with Mr and Mrs Ellison, and first saw pretty Margaret Ellison, who is now my wife. When I returned to Eltham, I found that a step was decided upon, which had been in contemplation for some time; that Holdsworth and I should remove our quarters to Hornby; our daily presence, and as much of our time as possible, being required for the completion of the line at that end.

Of course this led to greater facility of intercourse with the Hope Farm people. We could easily walk out there after our day's work was done, and spend a balmy evening hour or two, and yet return before the summer's twilight had quite faded away. Many a time, indeed, we would fain have stayed longer – the open air, the fresh and pleasant country, made so agreeable a contrast to the close, hot town lodgings which I shared with Mr Holdsworth; but early hours, both at eve and morn, were an imperative necessity with the minister, and he made no scruple at turning either or both of us out of the house directly after evening prayer, or 'exercise', as he called it. The remembrance of many a happy day, and of several little scenes, comes back upon me as I think of that summer. They rise like pictures to my memory, and in this way I can date their succession; for I know that corn harvest must have come after hay-making, apple-gathering after corn-harvest.

The removal to Hornby took up some time, during which we had neither of us any leisure to go out to the Hope Farm. Mr Holdsworth had been out there once during my absence at home. One sultry evening, when work was done, he proposed our walking out and paying the Holmans a visit. It so happened that I had omitted to write my usual weekly letter home in our press of business, and I wished to finish that before going out. Then he said that he would go, and that I could follow him if I liked. This I did in about an hour; the weather was so oppressive, I remember, that I took off my coat as I walked, and hung it over my arm. All the doors and windows at the farm were open when I arrived there, and every tiny leaf on the trees was still. The silence of the place was profound; at first I thought that it was entirely deserted; but just as I drew near the door I heard a weak sweet voice begin to sing; it was cousin Holman, all by herself in the house-place, piping up a hymn, as she knitted away in the clouded light. She gave me a kindly welcome, and poured out all the small domestic news of the fortnight past upon me, and, in return, I told her about my own people and my visit at home.

'Where were the rest?' at length I asked.

Betty and the men were in the field helping with the last load of hay, for the minister said there would be rain before the morning. Yes, and the minister himself, and Phillis, and Mr Holdsworth, were all there helping. She thought that she herself could have done something; but perhaps she was the least fit for hay-making of any one; and somebody must stay at home and take care of the house, there were so many tramps about; if I had not had something to do with the rail-road she would have called them navvies.* I asked her if she minded being left alone, as I should like to go and help; and having her full and glad permission to leave her alone, I went off, following her directions: through the farmyard, past the cattle-pond, into the ashfield, beyond into the higher field with two holly-bushes in the middle. I arrived there: there was Betty with all the farming men, and a cleared field, and a heavily laden cart; one man at the top of the great pile ready to catch the fragrant hay which the others threw up to him with their pitchforks; a little heap of cast-off clothes in a corner of the field (for the heat, even at seven o'clock, was insufferable), a few cans and baskets, and Rover lying by them panting, and keeping watch. Plenty of loud, hearty, cheerful talking; but no minister, no Phillis, no Mr Holdsworth. Betty saw me first, and understanding who it was that I was in search of, she came towards me.

'They're out yonder – agait wi' them things o' Measter Holdsworth's.'

So 'out yonder' I went; out on to a broad upland common, full of red sand-banks, and sweeps and hollows; bordered by dark firs, purple in the coming shadows, but near at hand all ablaze with flowering gorse, or, as we call it in the south, furze-bushes, which, seen against the belt of distant trees, appeared brilliantly golden. On this heath, a little way from the field-gate, I saw the three. I counted their heads, joined together in an eager group over Holdsworth's theodolite. He was teaching the minister the practical art of surveying and taking a level. I was wanted to assist, and was quickly set to work to hold the chain. Phillis was as intent as her father; she had hardly time to greet me, so desirous was she to hear some answer to her father's question.

So we went on, the dark clouds still gathering, for perhaps five minutes after my arrival. Then came the blinding lightning and the rumble and quick-following rattling peal of thunder right over our heads. It came sooner than I expected, sooner than they had looked for: the rain delayed not; it came pouring down; and what were we to do for shelter? Phillis had nothing on but her indoor things – no bonnet, no shawl. Quick as the darting lightning around us, Holdsworth took off his coat and wrapped it round her neck and shoulders, and, almost without a word, hurried us all into such poor shelter as one of the overhanging sand-banks could give. There we were, cowered down, close together, Phillis innermost, almost too tightly packed to free her arms enough to divest herself of the coat, which she, in her turn, tried to put lightly over Holdsworth's shoulders. In doing so she touched his shirt.

'Oh, how wet you are!' she cried, in pitying dismay; 'and you've hardly got over your fever! Oh, Mr Holdsworth, I am so sorry!' He turned his head a little, smiling at her.

'If I do catch cold, it is all my fault for having deluded you into staying out here!' but she only murmured again, 'I am so sorry.'

The minister spoke now. 'It is a regular downpour. Please God that the hay is saved! But there is no likelihood of its ceasing, and I had better go home at once, and send you all some wraps; umbrellas will not be safe with yonder thunder and lightning.'

Both Holdsworth and I offered to go instead of him; but he was resolved, although perhaps it would have been wiser if Holdsworth, wet as he already was, had kept himself in exercise. As he moved off, Phillis crept out, and could see on to the storm-swept heath. Part of Holdsworth's apparatus still remained exposed to all the rain. Before we could have any warning, she had rushed out of the shelter and collected the various things, and brought them back in triumph to where we crouched. Holdsworth had stood up, uncertain whether to go to her assistance or not. She came running back, her long lovely hair floating and dripping, her eyes glad and bright, and her colour freshened to a glow of health by the exercise and the rain.

'Now, Miss Holman, that's what I call wilful,' said Holdsworth, as she gave them to him. 'No, I won't thank you' (his looks were thanking her all the time). 'My little bit of dampness annoyed you, because you thought I had got wet in your service; so you were determined to make me as uncomfortable as you were yourself. It was an unchristian piece of revenge!'

His tone of badinage (as the French call it) would have been palpable enough to any one accustomed to the world; but Phillis was not, and it distressed or rather bewildered her. 'Unchristian' had to her a very serious meaning; it was not a word to be used lightly; and though she did not exactly understand what wrong it was that she was accused of doing, she was evidently desirous to throw off the imputation. At first her earnestness to disclaim unkind motives amused Holdsworth; while his light continuance of the joke perplexed her still more; but at last he said something gravely, and in too low a tone for me to hear, which made her all at once become silent, and called out her blushes. After a while, the minister came back, a moving mass of shawls, cloaks, and umbrellas. Phillis kept very close to her father's side on our return to the farm. She appeared to me to be shrinking away from Holdsworth, while he had not the slightest variation in his manner from what it usually was in his graver moods; kind, protecting, and thoughtful towards her. Of course, there was a great commotion about our wet clothes; but I name the little events of that evening now because I wondered at the time what he had said in that low voice to silence Phillis so effectually, and because, in thinking of their intercourse by the light of future events, that evening stands out with some prominence.

I have said that after our removal to Hornby our communications with the farm became almost of daily occurrence. Cousin Holman and I were the two who had least to do with this intimacy. After Mr Holdsworth regained his health, he too often talked above her head in intellectual matters, and too often in his light bantering tone for her to feel quite at her ease with him. I really believe that he adopted this latter tone in speaking to her because he did not know what to talk about to a purely motherly woman, whose intellect had never been cultivated, and whose loving heart was entirely occupied with her husband, her child, her household affairs and, perhaps, a little with the concerns of the members of her husband's congregation, because they, in a way, belonged to her husband. I had noticed before that she had fleeting shadows of jealousy even ot Phillis, when her daughter and her husband appeared to have strong interests and sympathies in things which were quite beyond her comprehension. I had noticed it in my first acquaintance with them, I say, and had admired the delicate tact which made the minister, on such occasions, bring the conversation back to such subjects as those on which his wife, with her practical experience of every-day life, was an authority; while Phillis, devoted to her father, unconsciously followed his lead, totally unaware, in her filial reverence, of his motive for doing so.

To return to Holdsworth. The minister had at more than one time spoken of him to me with slight distrust, principally occasioned by the suspicion that his careleᶜs words were not always those of soberness and truth. But it was more as a protest against the fascination which the younger man evidently exercised over the elder one – more as it were to strengthen himself against yielding to this fascination – that the minister spoke out to me about this failing of Holdsworth's, as it appeared to him. In return Holdsworth was subdued by the minister's uprightness and goodness, and delighted with his clear intellect – his strong healthy craving after further knowledge. I never met two men who took more thorough pleasure and relish in each other's society. To Phillis his relation continued that of an elder brother: he directed her studies into new paths, he patiently drew out the expression of many of her thoughts, and perplexities, and unformed theories – scarcely ever now falling into the vein of banter which she was so slow to understand.

One day – harvest-time – he had been drawing on a loose piece of paper – sketching ears of corn, sketching carts drawn by bullocks and laden with grapes – all the time talking with Phillis and me, cousin Holman putting in her not pertinent remarks, when suddenly he said to Phillis, –

'Keep your head still; I see a sketch! I have often tried to draw your head from memory, and failed; but I think I can do it now. If I succeed I will give it to your mother. You would like a portrait of your daughter as Ceres, would you not, ma'am?'

'I should like a picture of her; yes, very much, thank you, Mr Holdsworth; but if you put that straw in her hair,' (he was holding some wheat ears above her passive head, looking at the effect with an artistic eye,) 'you'll ruffle her hair. Phillis, my dear, if you're to have your picture taken, go up-stairs, and brush your hair smooth.'

'Not on any account. I beg your pardon, but I want hair loosely flowing.'

He began to draw, looking intently at Phillis; I could see this stare of his discomposed her – her colour came and went, her breath quickened with the consciousness of his regard; at last, when he said, 'Please look at me for a minute or two, I want to get in the eyes,' she looked up at him, quivered, and suddenly got up and left the room. He did not say a word, but went on with some other part of the drawing; his silence was unnatural, and his dark cheek blanched a little. Cousin Holman looked up from her work, and put her spectacles down.

'What's the matter? Where is she gone?'

Holdsworth never uttered a word, but went on drawing. I felt obliged to say something; it was stupid enough, but stupidity was better than silence just then.

'I'll go and call her,' said I. So I went into the hall, and to the bottom of the stairs; but just as I was going to call Phillis, she came down swiftly with her bonnet on, and saying, 'I'm going to father in the five-acre,' passed out by the open 'rector,' right in front of the house-place windows, and out at the little white side-gate. She had been seen by her mother and

Holdsworth, as she passed; so there was no need for explanation, only cousin Holman and I had a long discussion as
to whether she could have found the room too hot, or what
had occasioned her sudden departure. Holdsworth was very
quiet during all the rest of that day; nor did he resume the
portrait-taking by his own desire, only at my cousin Holman's
request the next time that he came; and then he said he should
not require any more formal sittings for only such a slight
sketch as he felt himself capable of making. Phillis was just the
same as ever the next time I saw her after her abrupt passing
me in the hall. She never gave any explanation of her rush out
of the room.

So all things went on, at least as far as my observation
reached at the time, or memory can recall now, till the great
apple-gathering of the year. The nights were frosty, the
mornings and evenings were misty, but at mid-day all was
sunnyand bright, and it was one mid-day that both of us being
on the line near Heathbridge, and knowing that they were
gathering apples at the farm, we resolved to spend the men's
dinner-hour in going over there. We found the great clothes-
baskets full of apples, scenting the house, and stopping up the
way; and an universal air of merry contentment with this the
final produce of the year. The yellow leaves hung on the trees
ready to flutter down at the slightest puff of air; the great
bushes of Michaelmas daisies in the kitchen-garden were making their last show of flowers. We must needs taste the fruit off
the different trees, and pass our judgment as to their flavour;
and we went away with our pockets stuffed with those that we
liked best. As we had passed to the orchard, Holdsworth had
admired and spoken about some flower which he saw; it so
happened he had never seen this old-fashioned kind since the
days of his boyhood. I do not know whether he had thought
anything more about this chance speech of his, but I know I
had not – when Phillis, who had been missing just at the last
moment of our hurried visit, re-appeared with a little nosegay
of this same flower, which she was tying up with a blade of
grass. She offered it to Holdsworth as he stood with her father
on the point of departure. I saw their faces. I saw for the first
time an unmistakable look of love in his black eyes; it was
more than gratitude for the little attention; it was tender and

beeseching – passionate. She shrank from it in confusion, her glance fell on me; and, partly to hide her emotion, partly out of real kindness at what might appear ungracious neglect of an older friend, she flew off to gather me a few late-blooming China roses. But it was the first time she had ever done any-thing of the kind for me.

We had to walk fast to be back on the line before the men's return, so we spoke but little to each other, and of course the afternoon was too much occupied for us to have any talk. In the evening we went back to our joint lodgings in Hornby. There, on the table, lay a letter for Holdsworth, which had been forwarded to him from Eltham. As our tea was ready, and I had had nothing to eat since morning, I fell to directly without paying much attention to my companion as he opened and read his letter. He was very silent for a few minutes; at length he said, –

'Old fellow! I'm going to leave you!'

'Leave me!' said I. 'How? When?'

'This letter ought to have come to hand sooner. It is from Greathed the engineer' (Greathed was well known in those days; he is dead now, and his name half-forgotten); 'he wants to see me about some business; in fact, I may as well tell you, Paul, this letter contains a very advantageous proposal for me to go out to Canada, and superintend the making of a line there.'

I was in utter dismay.

'But what will our company say to that?'

'Oh, Greathed has the superintendence of this line, you know; and he is going to be engineer in chief to this Canadian line; many of the shareholders in this company are going in for the other, so I fancy they will make no difficulty in follow-ing Greathed's lead. He says he has a young man ready to put in my place.'

'I hate him,' said I.

'Thank you,' said Holdsworth, laughing.

'But you must not,' he resumed; 'for this is a very good thing for me, and, of course, if no one can be found to take my inferior work, I can't be spared to take the superior. I only wish I had received this letter a day sooner. Every hour is of consequence, for Greathed says they are threatening a rival line. Do you know, Paul, I almost fancy I must go up to-night? I can take an engine back to Eltham, and catch the night train. I should not like Greathed to think me luke-warm.'

'But you'll come back?' I asked, distressed at the thought of this sudden parting.

'Oh, yes! At least I hope so. They may want me to go out by the next steamer, that will be on Saturday.' He began to eat and drink standing, but I think he was quite unconscious of the nature of either his food or his drink.

'I will go to-night. Activity and readiness go a long way in our profession. Remember that, my boy! I hope I shall come back, but if I don't, be sure and recollect all the words of wisdom that have fallen from my lips. Now where's the portmanteau? If I can gain half an hour for a gathering up of my things in Eltham, so much the better. I'm clear of debt anyhow; and what I owe for my lodgings you can pay for me out of my quarter's salary, due November 4th.'

'Then you don't think you will come back?' I said, despondingly.

'I will come back some time, never fear,' said he, kindly. 'I may be back in a couple of days, having been found incompetent for the Canadian work; or I may not be wanted to go out so soon as I now anticipate. Anyhow you don't suppose I am going to forget you, Paul – this work out there ought not to take me above two years, and, perhaps, after that, we may be employed together again.'

Perhaps! I had very little hope. The same kind of happy days never returns. However, I did all I could in helping him: clothes, papers, books, instruments; how we pushed and struggled – how I stuffed. All was done in a much shorter time than we had calculated upon, when I had run down to the sheds to order the engine. I was going to drive him to Eltham. We sate ready for a summons. Holdsworth took up the little nosegay that he had brought away from the Hope Farm, and had laid on the mantel-piece on first coming into the room. He smelt at it, and caressed it with his lips.

'What grieves me is that I did not know – that I have not said good-bye to – to them.'

He spoke in a grave tone, the shadow of the coming separation falling upon him at last.

'I will tell them,' said I. 'I am sure they will be very sorry.'
Then we were silent.

'I never liked any family so much.'

'I knew you would like them.'

'How one's thoughts change, – this morning I was full of a
hope, Paul.' He paused, and then he said, –

'You put that sketch in carefully?'

'That outline of a head?' asked I. But I knew he meant an
abortive sketch of Phillis, which had not been successful
enough for him to complete it with shading or colouring.

'Yes. What a sweet innocent face it is! and yet so – Oh, dear!'

He sighed and got up, his hands in his pockets, to walk up
and down the room in evident disturbance of mind. He
suddenly stopped opposite to me.

'You'll tell them how it all was. Be sure and tell the good
minister that I was so sorry not to wish him good-bye, and to
thank him and his wife for all their kindness. As for Phillis, –
please God in two years I'll be back and tell her myself all in
my heart.'

'You love Phillis, then?' said I.

'Love her! Yes, that I do. Who could help it, seeing her as I
have done? Her character as unusual and rare as her beauty!
God bless her! God keep her in her high tranquillity, her pure
innocence. – Two years! It is a long time. – But she lives in
such seclusion, almost like the sleeping beauty, Paul,' – (he
was smiling now, though a minute before I had thought him
on the verge of tears,) – 'but I shall come back like a prince
from Canada, and waken her to my love. I can't help hoping
that it won't be difficult, eh, Paul?'

This touch of coxcombry displeased me a little, and I made
no answer. He went on, half apologetically, –

'You see, the salary they offer me is large; and beside that,
this experience will give me a name which will entitle me to
expect a still larger in any future undertaking.'

'That won't influence Phillis.'

'No! but it will make me more eligible in the eyes of her
father and mother.'

I made no answer.

'You give me your best wishes, Paul,' said he, almost
pleading. 'You would like me for a cousin?'

I heard the scream and whistle of the engine ready down at the sheds.

'Aye, that I should,' I replied, suddenly softened towards my friend now that he was going away. 'I wish you were to be married to-morrow, and I were to be best man.'

'Thank you, lad. Now for this cursed portmanteau (how the minister would be shocked); but it is heavy!' and off we sped into the darkness.

He only just caught the night train at Eltham, and I slept, desolately enough, at my old lodgings at Miss Dawsons', for that night. Of course the next few days I was busier than ever, doing both his work and my own. Then came a letter from him, very short and affectionate. He was going out in the Saturday steamer, as he had more than half expected; and by the following Monday the man who was to succeed him would be down at Eltham. There was a P.S., with only these words: –

'My nosegay goes with me to Canada, but I do not need it to remind me of Hope Farm.'

Saturday came; but it was very late before I could go out to the farm. It was a frosty night, the stars shone clear above me, and the road was crisping beneath my feet. They must have heard my footsteps before I got up to the house. They were sitting at their usual employments in the house-place when I went in. Phillis's eyes went beyond me in their look of welcome, and then fell in quiet disappointment on her work.

'And where's Mr Holdsworth?' asked cousin Holman, in a minute or two. 'I hope his cold is not worse, – I did not like his short cough.'

I laughed awkwardly; for I felt that I was the bearer of unpleasant news.

'His cold had need be better – for he's gone – gone away to Canada!'

I purposely looked away from Phillis, as I thus abruptly told my news.

'To Canada!' said the minister.

'Gone away!' said his wife.

But no word from Phillis.

'Yes!' said I. 'He found a letter at Hornby when we got home the other night – when we got home from here; he

ought to have got it sooner; he was ordered to go up to
London directly, and to see some people about a new line in
Canada, and he's gone to lay it down; he has sailed to-day. He
was sadly grieved not to have time to come out and wish you
all good-by; but he started for London within two hours after
he got that letter. He bade me thank you most gratefully for
all your kindnesses; he was very sorry not to come here once
again.'

Phillis got up and left the room with noiseless steps.

'I am very sorry,' said the minister.

'I am sure so am I!' said cousin Holman. 'I was real fond of
that lad ever since I nursed him last June after that bad fever.'

The minister went on asking me questions respecting
Holdsworth's future plans; and brought out a large old-
fashioned atlas, that he might find out the exact places between
which the new railroad was to run. Then supper was ready; it
was always on the table as soon as the clock on the stairs struck
eight, and down came Phillis – her face white and set, her dry
eyes looking defiance to me, for I am afraid I hurt her maidenly
pride by my glance of sympathetic interest as she entered the
room. Never a word did she say – never a question did she ask
about the absent friend, yet she forced herself to talk.

And so it was all the next day. She was as pale as could be,
like one who has received some shock; but she would not let
me talk to her, and she tried hard to behave as usual. Two or
three times I repeated, in public, the various affectionate
messages to the family with which I was charged by Holdsworth; but she took no more notice of them than if my words
had been empty air. And in this mood I left her on the Sabbath
evening.

My new master was not half so indulgent as my old one. He
kept up strict discipline as to hours, so that it was some time
before I could again go out, even to pay a call at the Hope
Farm.

It was a cold misty evening in November. The air, even
indoors, seemed full of haze; yet there was a great log burning
on the hearth, which ought to have made the room cheerful.
Cousin Holman and Phillis were sitting at the little round
table before the fire, working away in silence. The minister

had his books out on the dresser, seemingly deep in study, by the light of his solitary candle; perhaps the fear of disturbing him made the unusual stillness of the room. But a welcome was ready for me from all; not noisy, not demonstrative – that it never was; my damp wrappers were taken off, the next meal was hastened, and a chair placed for me on one side of the fire, so that I pretty much commanded a view of the room. My eye caught on Phillis, looking so pale and weary, and with a sort of aching tone (if I may call it so) in her voice. She was doing all the accustomed things – fulfilling small household duties, but somehow differently – I can't tell you how, for she was just as deft and quick in her movements, only the light spring was gone out of them. Cousin Holman began to question me; even the minister put aside his books, and came and stood on the opposite side of the fire-place, to hear what waft of intelligence I brought. I had first to tell them why I had not been to see them for so long – more than five weeks. The answer was simple enough; business and the necessity of attending strictly to the orders of a new superintendent, who had not yet learned trust, much less indulgence. The minister nodded his approval of my conduct, and said, –

'Right, Paul! "Servants, obey in all things your master according to the flesh."* I have had my fears lest you had too much licence under Edward Holdsworth.'

'Ah,' said cousin Holman, 'poor Mr Holdsworth, he'll be on the salt seas by this time!'

'No, indeed,' said I, 'he's landed. I have had a letter from him from Halifax.'

Immediately a shower of questions fell thick upon me. When? How? What was he doing? How did he like it? What sort of a voyage? &c.

'Many is the time we have thought of him when the wind was blowing so hard; the old quince-tree is blown down, Paul, that on the right-hand of the great pear-tree; it was blown down last Monday week, and it was that night that I asked the minister to pray in an especial manner for all them that went down in ships upon the great deep, and he said then, that Mr Holdsworth might be already landed; but I said, even if the prayer did not fit him, it was sure to be fitting somebody out at sea, who would need the Lord's care. Both Phillis and I thought he would be a month on the seas.'

Phillis began to speak, but her voice did not come rightly at first. It was a little higher pitched than usual, when she said, –

'We thought he would be a month if he went in a sailing-vessel, or perhaps longer. I suppose he went in a steamer?'

'Old Obadiah Grimshaw was more than six weeks in getting to America,' observed cousin Holman.

'I presume he cannot as yet tell how he likes his new work?' asked the minister.

'No! he is but just landed; it is but one page long. I'll read it to you, shall I? –

'DEAR PAUL, –
  'WE are safe on shore, after a rough passage. Thought you would like to hear this, but homeward-bound steamer is making signals for letters. Will write again soon. It seems a year since I left Hornby. Longer since I was at the farm. I have got my nosegay safe. Remember me to the Holmans.

'Yours,   'E. H.'

'That's not much, certainly,' said the minister. 'But it's a comfort to know he's on land these blowy nights.'

Phillis said nothing. She kept her head bent down over her work; but I don't think she put a stitch in, while I was reading the letter. I wondered if she understood what nosegay was meant; but I could not tell. When next she lifted up her face, there were two spots of brilliant colour on the cheeks that had been so pale before. After I had spent an hour or two there, I was bound to return back to Hornby. I told them I did not know when I could come again, as we – by which I mean the company – had undertaken the Hensleydale line; that branch for which poor Holdsworth was surveying when he caught his fever.

'But you'll have a holiday at Christmas,' said my cousin. 'Surely they'll not be such heathens as to work you then?'

'Perhaps the lad will be going home,' said the minister, as if to mitigate his wife's urgency; but for all that, I believe he wanted me to come. Phillis fixed her eyes on me with a wistful expression, hard to resist. But, indeed, I had no thought of resisting. Under my new master I had no hope of a holiday long enough to enable me to go to Birmingham and see my parents with any comfort; and nothing could be pleasanter to me than to find myself at home at my cousins' for a day or two, then. So it was fixed that we were to meet in Hornby Chapel on Christmas Day, and that I was to accompany them home after service, and if possible to stay over the next day.

I was not able to get to chapel till late on the appointed day, and so I took a seat near the door in considerable shame, although it really was not my fault. When the service was ended, I went and stood in the porch to await the coming out of my cousins. Some worthy people belonging to the congregation clustered into a group just where I stood, and exchanged the good wishes of the season. It had just begun to snow, and this occasioned a little delay, and they fell into further conversation. I was not attending to what was not meant for me to hear, till I caught the name of Phillis Holman. And then I listened; where was the harm?

'I never saw any one so changed!'

'I asked Mrs Holman,' quoth another, ' "Is Phillis well?" and she just said she had been having a cold which had pulled her down; she did not seem to think anything of it.'

'They had best take care of her,' said one of the oldest of the good ladies; 'Phillis comes of a family as is not long-lived. Her mother's sister, Lydia Green, her own aunt as was, died of a decline just when she was about this lass's age.'

This ill-omened talk was broken in upon by the coming out of the minister, his wife and daughter, and the consequent interchange of Christmas compliments. I had had a shock, and felt heavy-hearted and anxious, and hardly up to making the appropriate replies to the kind greetings of my relations. I looked askance at Phillis. She had certainly grown taller and slighter, and was thinner; but there was a flush of colour on her face which deceived me for a time, and made me think she was looking as well as ever. I only saw her paleness after we had returned to the farm, and she had subsided into silence and quiet. Her grey eyes looked hollow and sad; her complexion was of a dead white. But she went about just as usual; at least, just as she had done the last time I was there, and seemed to have no ailment; and I was inclined to think that my cousin was right when she had answered the inquiries of the good-natured gossips, and told them that Phillis was suffering from the consequences of a bad cold, nothing more.

I have said that I was to stay over the next day; a great deal of snow had come down, but not all, they said, though the ground was covered deep with the white fall. The minister was anxiously housing his cattle, and preparing all things for a long continuance of the same kind of weather. The men were chopping wood, sending wheat to the mill to be ground before the road should become impassable for a cart and horse. My cousin and Phillis had gone up-stairs to the apple-room to cover up the fruit from the frost. I had been out the greater part of the morning, and came in about an hour before dinner. To my surprise, knowing how she had planned to be engaged, I found Phillis sitting at the dresser, resting her head on her two hands and reading, or seeming to read. She did not look up when I came in, but murmured something about her mother having sent her down out of the cold. It flashed across me that she was crying, but I put it down to some little spirt of temper; I might have known better than to suspect the gentle, serene Phillis of crossness, poor girl; I stooped down, and began to stir and build up the fire, which appeared to have been neglected. While my head was down I heard a noise which made me pause and listen – a sob, an unmistakable, irrepressible sob. I started up.

'Phillis!' I cried, going towards her, with my hand out, to take hers for sympathy with her sorrow, whatever it was. But she was too quick for me, she held her hand out of my grasp, for fear of my detaining her; as she quickly passed out of the house, she said, –

'Don't, Paul! I cannot bear it!' and passed me, still sobbing, and went out into the keen, open air.

I stood still and wondered. What could have come to Phillis? The most perfect harmony prevailed in the family, and Phillis especially, good and gentle as she was, was so beloved that if they had found out that her finger ached, it would have cast a shadow over their hearts. Had I done anything to vex her? No: she was crying before I came in. I went to look at her book – one of those unintelligible Italian books.

I could make neither head nor tail of it. I saw some pencil-notes on the margin, in Holdsworth's handwriting.

Could that be it? Could that be the cause of her white looks, her weary eyes, her wasted figure, her struggling sobs? This idea came upon me like a flash of lightning on a dark night, making all things so clear we cannot forget them afterwards when the gloomy obscurity returns. I was still standing with the book in my hand when I heard cousin Holman's footsteps on the stairs, and as I did not wish to speak to her just then, I followed Phillis's example, and rushed out of the house. The snow was lying on the ground; I could track her feet by the marks they had made; I could see where Rover had joined her. I followed on till I came to a great stack of wood in the orchard – it was built up against the back wall of the outbuildings, – and I recollected then how Phillis had told me, that first day when we strolled about together, that underneath this stack had been her hermitage, her sanctuary, when she was a child; how she used to bring her book to study there, or her work, when she was not wanted in the house; and she had now evidently gone back to this quiet retreat of her childhood, forgetful of the clue given me by her footmarks on the new-fallen snow. The stack was built up very high; but through the interstices of the sticks I could see her figure, although I did not all at once perceive how I could get to her. She was sitting on a log of wood, Rover by her. She had laid her cheek on Rover's head, and had her arm round his neck, partly for a pillow, partly from an instinctive craving for warmth on that bitter cold day. She was making a low moan, like an animal in pain, or perhaps more like the sobbing of the wind. Rover, highly flattered by her caress, and also, perhaps, touched by sympathy, was flapping his heavy tail against the ground, but not otherwise moving a hair, until he heard my approach with his quick erected ears. Then, with a short, abrupt bark of distrust, he sprang up as if to leave his mistress. Both he and I were immovably still for a moment. I was not sure if what I longed to do was wise: and yet I could not bear to see the sweet serenity of my dear cousin's life so disturbed by a suffering which I thought I could assuage. But Rover's ears were sharper than my breathing was noiseless: he heard me, and sprang out from under Phillis's restraining hand.

'Oh, Rover, don't you leave me, too,' she plained out.

'Phillis!' said I, seeing by Rover's exit that the entrance to where she sate was to be found on the other side of the stack. 'Phillis, come out! You have got a cold already; and it is not fit for you to sit there on such a day as this. You know how displeased and anxious it would make them all.'

She sighed, but obeyed; stooping a little, she came out, and stood upright, opposite to me in the lonely, leafless orchard. Her face looked so meek and so sad that I felt as if I ought to beg her pardon for my necessarily authoritative words.

'Sometimes I feel the house so close,' she said; 'and I used to sit under the wood-stack when I was a child. It was very kind of you, but there was no need to come after me. I don't catch cold easily.'

'Come with me into this cow-house, Phillis. I have got something to say to you; and I can't stand this cold, if you can.'

I think she would have fain run away again; but her fit of energy was all spent. She followed me unwillingly enough – that I could see. The place to which I took her was full of the fragrant breath of the cows, and was a little warmer than the outer air. I put her inside, and stood myself in the doorway, thinking how I could best begin. At last I plunged into it.

'I must see that you don't get cold for more reasons than one; if you are ill, Holdsworth will be so anxious and miserable out there' (by which I meant Canada) –

She shot one penetrating look at me, and then turned her face away with a slightly impatient movement. If she could have run away then she would, but I held the means of exit in my own power. 'In for a penny, in for a pound,' thought I, and I went on rapidly, anyhow.

'He talked so much about you, just before he left – that night after he had been here, you know – and you had given him those flowers.' She put her hands up to hide her face, but she was listening now – listening with all her ears.

'He had never spoken much about you before, but the sudden going away unlocked his heart, and he told me how he loved you, and how he hoped on his return that you might be his wife.'

'Don't,' said she, almost gasping out the word, which she

had tried once or twice before to speak; but her voice had been choked. Now she put her hand backwards; she had quite turned away from me, and felt for mine. She gave it a soft lingering pressure; and then she put her arms down on the wooden division, and laid her head on it, and cried quiet tears. I did not understand her at once, and feared lest I had mistaken the whole case, and only annoyed her. I went up to her. 'Oh, Phillis! I am so sorry – I thought you would, perhaps, have cared to hear it; he did talk so feelingly, as if he did love you so much, and somehow I thought it would give you pleasure.'

She lifted up her head and looked at me. Such a look! Her eyes, glittering with tears as they were, expressed an almost heavenly happiness; her tender mouth was curved with rapture – her colour vivid and blushing; but as if she was afraid her face expressed too much, more than the thankfulness to me she was essaying to speak, she hid it again almost immediately. So it was all right then, and my conjecture was well-founded! I tried to remember something more to tell her of what he had said, but again she stopped me.

'Don't,' she said. She still kept her face covered and hidden. In half a minute she added, in a very low voice, 'Please, Paul, I think I would rather not hear any more – I don't mean but what I have – but what I am very much obliged – Only – only, I think I would rather hear the rest from himself when he comes back.'

And then she cried a little more, in quite a different way. I did not say any more, I waited for her. By-and-by she turned towards me – not meeting my eyes, however; and putting her hand in mine just as if we were two children, she said, –

'We had best go back now – I don't look as if I had been crying, do I?'

'You look as if you had a bad cold,' was all the answer I made.

'Oh! but I am quite well, only cold; and a good run will warm me. Come along, Paul.'

So we ran, hand in hand, till, just as we were on the threshold of the house, she stopped, –

'Paul, please, we won't speak about *that* again.'

PART IV

WHEN I went over on Easter Day I heard the chapel-gossips complimenting cousin Holman on her daughter's blooming looks, quite forgetful of their sinister prophecies three months before. And I looked at Phillis, and did not wonder at their words. I had not seen her since the day after Christmas Day. I had left the Hope Farm only a few hours after I had told her the news which had quickened her heart into renewed life and vigour. The remembrance of our conversation in the cow-house was vividly in my mind as I looked at her when her bright healthy appearance was remarked upon. As her eyes met mine our mutual recollections flashed intelligence from one to the other. She turned away, her colour heightening as she did so. She seemed to be shy of me for the first few hours after our meeting, and I felt rather vexed with her for her conscious avoidance of me after my long absence. I had stepped a little out of my usual line in telling her what I did; not that I had received any charge of secrecy, or given even the slightest promise to Holdsworth that I would not repeat his words. But I had an uneasy feeling sometimes when I thought of what I had done in the excitement of seeing Phillis so ill and in so much trouble. I meant to have told Holdsworth when I wrote next to him; but when I had my half-finished letter before me I sate with my pen in my hand hesitating. I had more scruple in revealing what I had found out or guessed at of Phillis's secret than in repeating to her his spoken words. I did not think I had any right to say out to him what I believed – namely, that she loved him dearly, and had felt his absence even to the injury of her health. Yet to explain what I had done in telling her how he had spoken about her that last night, it would be necessary to give my reasons, so I had settled within myself to leave it alone. As she had told me she should like to hear all the details and fuller particulars and more explicit declarations first from him, so he should have the pleasure of extracting the delicious tender secret from her maidenly lips. I would not betray my guesses, my surmises, my all but certain knowledge of the state of her heart. I had

received two letters from him after he had settled to his business; they were full of life and energy; but in each there had
been a message to the family at the Hope Farm of more than
common regard; and a slight but distinct mention of Phillis
herself, showing that she stood single and alone in his memory.
These letters I had sent on to the minister, for he was sure to
care for them, even supposing he had been unacquainted with
their writer, because they were so clever and so picturesquely
worded that they brought, as it were, a whiff of foreign
atmosphere into his circumscribed life. I used to wonder what
was the trade or business in which the minister would not
have thriven, mentally I mean, if it had so happened that he
had been called into that state. He would have made a capital
engineer, that I know; and he had a fancy for the sea, like
many other land-locked men to whom the great deep is a
mystery and a fascination. He read law-books with relish; and,
once happening to borrow *De Lolme on the British Constitution**
(or some such title), he talked about jurisprudence till he was
far beyond my depth. But to return to Holdsworth's letters.
When the minister sent them back he also wrote out a list of
questions suggested by their perusal, which I was to pass on
in my answers to Holdsworth, until I thought of suggesting
direct correspondence between the two. That was the state of
things as regarded the absent one when I went to the farm for
my Easter visit, and when I found Phillis in that state of shy
reserve towards me which I have named before. I thought she
was ungrateful; for I was not quite sure if I had done wisely in
having told her what I did. I had committed a fault, or a folly,
perhaps, and all for her sake; and here was she, less friends
with me than she had even been before. This little estrangement only lasted a few hours. I think that as soon as she felt
pretty sure of there being no recurrence, either by word, look,
or allusion, to the one subject that was predominant in her
mind, she came back to her old sisterly ways with me. She had
much to tell me of her own familiar interests; how Rover had
been ill, and how anxious they had all of them been, and how,
after some little discussion between her father and her, both
equally grieved by the sufferings of the old dog, he had been
'remembered in the household prayers', and how he had begun
to get better only the very next day, and then she would have

led me into a conversation on the right ends of prayer, and on special providences, and I know not what; only I 'jibbed' like their old cart-horse, and refused to stir a step in that direction. Then we talked about the different broods of chickens, and she showed me the hens that were good mothers, and told me the characters of all the poultry with the utmost good faith; and in all good faith I listened, for I believe there was a good deal of truth in all she said. And then we strolled on into the wood beyond the ash-meadow, and both of us sought for early primroses, and the fresh green crinkled leaves. She was not afraid of being alone with me after the first day. I never saw her so lovely, or so happy. I think she hardly knew why she was so happy all the time. I can see her now, standing under the budding branches of the grey trees, over which a tinge of green seemed to be deepening day after day, her sun-bonnet fallen back on her neck, her hands full of delicate wood-flowers, quite unconscious of my gaze, but intent on sweet mockery of some bird in neighbouring bush or tree. She had the art of warbling, and replying to the notes of different birds, and knew their song, their habits and ways, more accurately than any one else I ever knew. She had often done it at my request the spring before; but this year she really gurgled, and whistled, and warbled just as they did, out of the very fulness and joy of her heart. She was more than ever the very apple of her father's eye; her mother gave her both her own share of love, and that of the dead child who had died in infancy. I have heard cousin Holman murmur, after a long dreamy look at Phillis, and tell herself how like she was growing to Johnnie, and soothe herself with plaintive inarticulate sounds, and many gentle shakes of the head, for the aching sense of loss she would never get over in this world. The old servants about the place had the dumb loyal attachment to the child of the land, common to most agricultural labourers; not often stirred into activity or expression. My cousin Phillis was like a rose that had come to full bloom on the sunny side of a lonely house, sheltered from storms. I have read in some book of poetry, –

> A maid whom there were none to praise,
>   And very few to love.*

And somehow those lines always reminded me of Phillis; yet they were not true of her either. I never heard her praised; and out of her own household there were very few to love her; but though no one spoke out their approbation, she always did right in her parents' eyes out of her natural simple goodness and wisdom. Holdsworth's name was never mentioned between us when we were alone; but I had sent on his letters to the minister, as I have said; and more than once he began to talk about our absent friend, when he was smoking his pipe after the day's work was done. Then Phillis hung her head a little over her work, and listened in silence.

'I miss him more than I thought for; no offence to you, Paul. I said once his company was like dram-drinking; that was before I knew him; and perhaps I spoke in a spirit of judgment. To some men's minds everything presents itself strongly, and they speak accordingly; and so did he. And I thought in my vanity of censorship that his were not true and sober words; they would not have been if I had used them, but they were so to a man of his class of perceptions. I thought of the measure with which I had been meting* to him when Brother Robinson was here last Thursday, and told me that a poor little quotation I was making from the *Georgics* savoured of vain babbling and profane heathenism. He went so far as to say that by learning other languages than our own, we were flying in the face of the Lord's purpose when He had said, at the building of the Tower of Babel, that He would confound their languages* so that they should not understand each other's speech. As Brother Robinson was to me, so was I to the quick wits, bright senses, and ready words of Holdsworth.'

The first little cloud upon my peace came in the shape of a letter from Canada, in which there were two or three sentences that troubled me more than they ought to have done, to judge merely from the words employed. It was this: – 'I should feel dreary enough in this out-of-the-way place if it were not for a friendship I have formed with a French Canadian of the name of Ventadour. He and his family are a great resource to me in the long evenings. I never heard such delicious vocal music as the voices of these Ventadour boys and girls in their part songs; and the foreign element retained in their characters and manner of living reminds me of some of the happiest days of my life. Lucille, the second daughter, is curiously like Phillis Holman.' In vain I said to myself that it was probably this likeness that made him take pleasure in the society of the Ventadour family. In vain I told my anxious fancy that nothing could be more natural than this intimacy, and that there was no sign of its leading to any consequence that ought to disturb me. I had a presentiment, and I was disturbed; and I could not reason it away. I dare say my presentiment was rendered more persistent and keen by the doubts which would force themselves into my mind, as to whether I had done well in repeating Holdsworth's words to Phillis. Her state of vivid happiness this summer was markedly different to the peaceful serenity of former days. If in my thoughtfulness at noticing this I caught her eye, she blushed and sparkled all over, guessing that I was remembering our joint secret. Her eyes fell before mine, as if she could hardly bear me to see the revelation of their bright glances. And yet I considered again, and comforted myself by the reflection that, if this change had been anything more than my silly fancy, her father or her mother would have perceived it. But they went on in tranquil unconsciousness and undisturbed peace.

A change in my own life was quickly approaching. In the July of this year my occupation on the —— railway and its branches came to an end. The lines were completed, and I was to leave ——shire, to return to Birmingham, where there was a niche already provided for me in my father's prosperous business. But before I left the north it was an understood thing amongst us all that I was to go and pay a visit of some weeks at the Hope Farm. My father was as much pleased at this plan as I was; and the dear family of cousins often spoke of things to be done, and sights to be shown me, during this visit. My want of wisdom in having told 'that thing' (under such ambiguous words I concealed the injudicious confidence I had made to Phillis) was the only drawback to my anticipations of pleasure.

The ways of life were too simple at the Hope Farm for my coming to them to make the slightest disturbance. I knew my room, like a son of the house. I knew the regular course of their days, and that I was expected to fall into it, like one of the

family. Deep summer peace brooded over the place; the warm
golden air was filled with the murmur of insects near at hand,
the more distant sound of voices out in the fields, the clear far-
away rumble of carts over the stone-paved lanes miles away.
The heat was too great for the birds to be singing; only now
and then one might hear the wood-pigeons in the trees beyond the Ashfield. The cattle stood knee-deep in the pond,
flicking their tails about to keep off the flies. The minister
stood in the hay-field, without hat or cravat, coat or waistcoat,
panting and smiling. Phillis had been leading the row of farm-
servants, turning the swathes of fragrant hay with measured
movement. She went to the end – to the hedge, and then,
throwing down her rake, she came to me with her free sisterly
welcome. 'Go, Paul!' said the minister. 'We need all hands to
make use of the sunshine to-day. "Whatsoever thine hand
findeth to do, do it with all thy might."'* It will be a healthy
change of work for thee, lad; and I find best rest in change of
work.' So off I went, a willing labourer, following Phillis's
lead; it was the primitive distinction of rank; the boy who
frightened the sparrows off the fruit was the last in our rear.
We did not leave off till the red sun was gone down behind the
fir-trees bordering the common. Then we went home to
supper – prayers – to bed; some bird singing far into the night,
as I heard it through my open window, and the poultry beginning their clatter and cackle in the earliest morning. I had
carried what luggage I immediately needed with me from my
lodgings, and the rest was to be sent by the carrier. He brought
it to the farm betimes that morning, and along with it he
brought a letter or two that had arrived since I had left. I was
talking to cousin Holman – about my mother's ways of making bread, I remember; cousin Holman was questioning me,
and had got me far beyond my depth – in the house-place,
when the letters were brought in by one of the men, and I had
to pay the carrier for his trouble before I could look at them. A
bill – a Canadian letter! What instinct made me so thankful
that I was alone with my dear unobservant cousin? What made
me hurry them away into my coat-pocket? I do not know. I
felt strange and sick, and made irrelevant answers, I am
afraid. Then I went to my room, ostensibly to carry up my
boxes. I sate on the side of my bed and opened my letter from

Holdsworth. It seemed to me as if I had read its contents before, and knew exactly what he had got to say. I knew he was going to be married to Lucille Ventadour; nay, that he *was* married; for this was the 5th of July, and he wrote word that his marriage was fixed to take place on the 29th of June. I knew all the reasons he gave, all the raptures he went into. I held the letter loosely in my hands, and looked into vacancy, yet I saw the chaffinch's nest on the lichen-covered trunk of an old apple-tree opposite my window, and saw the mother-bird come fluttering in to feed her brood, – and yet I did not see it, although it seemed to me afterwards as if I could have drawn every fibre, every feather. I was stirred up to action by the merry sound of voices and the clamp of rustic feet coming home for the mid-day meal. I knew I must go down to dinner; I knew, too, I must tell Phillis; for in his happy egotism, his new-fangled foppery, Holdsworth had put in a P.S., saying that he should send wedding-cards* to me and some other Hornby and Eltham acquaintances, and 'to his kind friends at Hope Farm'. Phillis had faded away to one among several 'kind friends'. I don't know how I got through dinner that day. I remember forcing myself to eat, and talking hard; but I also recollect the wondering look in the minister's eyes. He was not one to think evil without cause; but many a one would have taken me for drunk. As soon as I decently could I left the table, saying I would go out for a walk. At first I must have tried to stun reflection by rapid walking, for I had lost myself on the high moorlands far beyond the familiar gorse-covered common, before I was obliged for very weariness to slacken my pace. I kept wishing – oh! how fervently wishing I had never committed that blunder; that the one little half-hour's indiscretion could be blotted out. Alternating with this was anger against Holdsworth; unjust enough, I dare say. I suppose I stayed in that solitary place for a good hour or more, and then I turned homewards, resolving to get over the telling Phillis at the first opportunity, but shrinking from the fulfilment of my resolution so much that when I came into the house and saw Phillis (doors and windows open wide in the sultry weather) alone in the kitchen, I became quite sick with apprehension. She was standing by the dresser, cutting up a great household loaf into hunches of bread for the hungry labourers who might come in any minute, for the heavy thunder-clouds were overspreading the sky. She looked round as she heard my step.

'You should have been in the field, helping with the hay,' said she, in her calm, pleasant voice. I had heard her as I came near the house softly chanting some hymn-tune, and the peacefulness of that seemed to be brooding over her now.

'Perhaps I should. It looks as if it was going to rain.'

'Yes; there is thunder about. Mother has had to go to bed with one of her bad headaches. Now you are come in –'

'Phillis,' said I, rushing at my subject and interrupting her, 'I went a long walk to think over a letter I had this morning – a letter from Canada. You don't know how it has grieved me.' I held it out to her as I spoke. Her colour changed a little, but it was more the reflection of my face, I think, than because she formed any definite idea from my words. Still she did not take the letter. I had to bid her to read it, before she quite understood what I wished. She sate down rather suddenly as she received it into her hands; and, spreading it on the dresser before her, she rested her forehead on the palms of her hands, her arms supported on the table, her figure a little averted, and her countenance thus shaded. I looked out of the open window; my heart was very heavy. How peaceful it all seemed in the farmyard! Peace and plenty. How still and deep was the silence of the house! Tick-tick went the unseen clock on the wide staircase. I had heard the rustle once, when she turned over the page of thin paper. She must have read to the end. Yet she did not move, or say a word, or even sigh. I kept on looking out of the window, my hands in my pockets. I wonder how long that time really was? It seemed to me interminable – unbearable. At length I looked round at her. She must have felt my look, for she changed her attitude with a quick sharp movement, and caught my eyes.

'Don't look so sorry, Paul,' she said. 'Don't, please. I can't bear it. There is nothing to be sorry for. I think not, at least. You have not done wrong, at any rate.' I felt that I groaned, but I don't think she heard me. 'And he, – there's no wrong in his marrying, is there? I'm sure I hope he'll be happy. Oh! how I hope it!' These last words were like a wail; but I believe she was afraid of breaking down, for she changed the key in which she spoke, and hurried on. 'Lucille – that's our English Lucy, I suppose? Lucille Holdsworth! It's a pretty name; and I hope – I forget what I was going to say. Oh! it was this. Paul, I think we need never speak about this again; only remember you are not to be sorry. You have not done wrong; you have been very, *very* kind; and if I see you looking grieved I don't know what I might do; – I might break down, you know.'

I think she was on the point of doing so then, but the dark storm came dashing down, and the thunder-cloud broke right above the house, as it seemed. Her mother, roused from sleep, called out for Phillis; the men and women from the hay-field came running into shelter, drenched through. The minister followed, smiling, and not unpleasantly excited by the war of elements; for, by dint of hard work through the long summer's day, the greater part of the hay was safely housed in the barn in the field. Once or twice in the succeeding bustle I came across Phillis, always busy, and, as it seemed to me, always doing the right thing. When I was alone in my own room at night I allowed myself to feel relieved; and to believe that the worst was over, and was not so very bad after all. But the succeeding days were very miserable. Sometimes I thought it must be my fancy that falsely represented Phillis to me as strangely changed, for surely, if this idea of mine was well-founded, her parents – her father and mother – her own flesh and blood – would have been the first to perceive it. Yet they went on in their household peace and content; if anything, a little more cheerfully than usual, for the 'harvest of the first-fruits', as the minister called it, had been more bounteous than usual, and there was plenty all around in which the humblest labourer was made to share. After the one thunderstorm, came one or two lovely serene summer days, during which the hay was all carried; and then succeeded long soft rains filling the ears of corn, and causing the mown grass to spring afresh. The minister allowed himself a few more hours of relaxation and home enjoyment than usual during this wet spell: hard earth-bound frost was his winter holiday; these wet days, after the hay harvest, his summer holiday. We sate with open windows, the fragrance and the freshness called out by the soft-falling rain filling the house-place; while the quiet ceaseless patter among the leaves outside ought to have had the same lulling effect as all other gentle perpetual sounds, such as mill-wheels and bubbling springs, have on the nerves of happy people. But two of us were not happy. I was sure enough of myself, for one. I was worse than sure, – I was wretchedly anxious about Phillis. Ever since that day of the thunderstorm there had been a new, sharp, discordant sound to me in her voice, a sort of jangle in her tone; and her restless eyes had no quietness in them; and her colour came and went without a cause that I could find out. The minister, happy in ignorance of what most concerned him, brought out his books; his learned volumes and classics. Whether he read and talked to Phillis, or to me, I do not know; but feeling by instinct that she was not, could not be, attending to the peaceful details, so strange and foreign to the turmoil in her heart, I forced myself to listen, and if possible to understand.

'Look here!' said the minister, tapping the old vellum-bound book he held; 'in the first *Georgic* he speaks of rolling and irrigation, a little further on he insists on choice of the best seed, and advises us to keep the drains clear. Again, no Scotch farmer could give shrewder advice than to cut light meadows while the dew is on, even though it involve night-work. It is all living truth in these days.' He began beating time with a ruler upon his knee, to some Latin lines he read aloud just then. I suppose the monotonous chant irritated Phillis to some irregular energy, for I remember the quick knotting and breaking of the thread with which she was sewing. I never hear that snap repeated now, without suspecting some sting or stab troubling the heart of the worker. Cousin Holman, at her peaceful knitting, noticed the reason why Phillis had so constantly to interrupt the progress of her seam.

'It is bad thread, I'm afraid,' she said, in a gentle sympathetic voice. But it was too much for Phillis.

'The thread is bad – everything is bad – I am so tired of it all!' And she put down her work, and hastily left the room. I do not suppose that in all her life Phillis had ever shown so much temper before. In many a family the tone, the manner, would not have been noticed; but here it fell with a sharp surprise upon the sweet, calm atmosphere of home. The minister put down ruler and book, and pushed his spectacles up to his forehead. The mother looked distressed for a moment, and then smoothed her features and said in an explanatory tone, – 'It's the weather, I think. Some people feel it different to others. It always brings on a headache with me.' She got up to follow her daughter, but half-way to the door she thought better of it, and came back to her seat. Good mother! she hoped the better to conceal the unusual spirt of temper, by pretending not to take much notice of it. 'Go on, minister,' she said; 'it is very interesting what you are reading about, and when I don't quite understand it, I like the sound of your voice.' So he went on, but languidly and irregularly, and beat no more time with his ruler to any Latin lines. When the dusk came on, early that July night because of the cloudy sky, Phillis came softly back, making as though nothing had happened. She took up her work, but it was too dark to do many stitches; and she dropped it soon. Then I saw how her hand stole into her mother's, and how this latter fondled it with quiet little caresses, while the minister, as fully aware as I was of this tender pantomime, went on talking in a happier tone of voice about things as uninteresting to him, at the time, I very believe, as they were to me; and that is saying a good deal, and shows how much more real what was passing before him was, even to a farmer, than the agricultural customs of the ancients.

I remember one thing more, – an attack which Betty the servant made upon me one day as I came in through the kitchen where she was churning, and stopped to ask her for a drink of buttermilk.

'I say, cousin Paul,' (she had adopted the family habit of addressing me generally as cousin Paul, and always speaking of me in that form,) 'something's amiss with our Phillis, and I reckon you've a good guess what it is. She's not one to take up wi' such as you,' (not complimentary, but that Betty never was, even to those for whom she felt the highest respect,) 'but I'd as lief yon Holdsworth had never come near us. So there you've a bit o' my mind.'

And a very unsatisfactory bit it was. I did not know what to answer to the glimpse at the real state of the case implied in the shrewd woman's speech; so I tried to put her off by assuming surprise at her first assertion.

'Amiss with Phillis! I should like to know why you think anything is wrong with her. She looks as blooming as any one can do.'

'Poor lad! you're but a big child after all; and you've likely never heared of a fever-flush. But you know better nor that, my fine fellow! so don't think for to put me off wi' blooms and blossoms and such-like talk. What makes her walk about for hours and hours o' nights when she used to be abed and asleep? I sleep next room to her, and hear her plain as can be. What makes her come in panting and ready to drop into that chair,' – nodding to one close to the door, – 'and it's "Oh! Betty, some water, please"? That's the way she comes in now, when she used to come back as fresh and bright as she went out. If yon friend o' yours has played her false, he's a deal for t' answer for; she's a lass who's as sweet and as sound as a nut, and the very apple of her father's eye, and of her mother's too, only wi' her she ranks second to th' minister. You'll have to look after yon chap, for I, for one, will stand no wrong to our Phillis.'

What was I to do, or to say? I wanted to justify Holdsworth, to keep Phillis's secret, and to pacify the woman all in the same breath. I did not take the best course, I'm afraid.

'I don't believe Holdsworth ever spoke a word of – of love to her in all his life. I'm sure he didn't.'

'Aye, aye! but there's eyes, and there's hands, as well as tongues; and a man has two o' th' one and but one o' t'other.'

'And she's so young; do you suppose her parents would not have seen it?'

'Well! if you axe me that, I'll say out boldly, "No". They've called her "the child" so long – "the child" is always their name for her when they talk on her between themselves, as if never anybody else had a ewe-lamb before them – that she's grown up to be a woman under their very eyes, and they look on her still as if she were in her long clothes. And you ne'er heard on a man falling in love wi' a babby in long clothes!'

'No!' said I, half laughing. But she went on as grave as a judge.

'Aye! you see you'll laugh at the bare thought on it – and I'll be bound th' minister, though he's not a laughing man, would ha' sniggled at th' notion of falling in love wi' the child. Where's Holdsworth off to ?'

'Canada,' said I, shortly.

'Canada here, Canada there,' she replied, testily. 'Tell me how far he's off, instead of giving me your gibberish. Is he a two days' journey away ? or a three ? or a week ?'

'He's ever so far off – three weeks at the least,' cried I in despair. 'And he's either married, or just going to be. So there!' I expected a fresh burst of anger. But no; the matter was too serious. Betty sate down, and kept silence for a minute or two. She looked so miserable and downcast, that I could not help going on, and taking her a little into my confidence.

'It is quite true what I said. I know he never spoke a word to her. I think he liked her, but it's all over now. The best thing we can do – the best and kindest for her – and I know you love her, Betty—'

'I nursed her in my arms; I gave her little brother his last taste o' earthly food,' said Betty, putting her apron up to her eyes.

'Well! don't let us show her we guess that she is grieving; she'll get over it the sooner. Her father and mother don't even guess at it, and we must make as if we didn't. It's too late now to do anything else.'

'I'll never let on; I know nought. I've known true love mysel', in my day. But I wish he'd been farred* before he ever came near this house, with his "Please Betty" this, and "Please Betty" that, and drinking up our new milk as if he'd been a cat. I hate such beguiling ways.'

I thought it was as well to let her exhaust herself in abusing the absent Holdsworth; if it was shabby and treacherous in me, I came in for my punishment directly.

'It's a caution to a man how he goes about beguiling. Some men do it as easy and innocent as cooing doves. Don't you be none of 'em, my lad. Not that you've got the gifts to do it, either; you're no great shakes to look at, neither for figure, nor yet for face, and it would need be a deaf adder to be taken in wi' your words, though there may be no great harm in 'em.' A lad of nineteen or twenty is not flattered by such an outspoken opinion even from the oldest and ugliest of her sex; and I was only too glad to change the subject by my repeated injunctions to keep Phillis's secret. The end of our conversation was this speech of hers, –

'You great gaupus, for all you're called cousin o' th' minister – many a one is cursed wi' fools for cousins – d'ye think I can't see sense except through your spectacles? I give you leave to cut out my tongue, and nail it up on th' barn-door for a caution to magpies, if I let out on that poor wench, either to herself, or any one that is hers, as the Bible says. Now you've heard me speak Scripture language, perhaps you'll be content, and leave me my kitchen to myself.'

During all these days, from the 5th of July to the 17th, I must have forgotten what Holdsworth had said about sending cards. And yet I think I could not have quite forgotten; but, once having told Phillis about his marriage, I must have looked upon the after consequence of cards as of no importance. At any rate they came upon me as a surprise at last. The penny-post reform,* as people call it, had come into operation a short time before; but the never-ending stream of notes and letters which seem now to flow in upon most households had not yet begun its course; at least in those remote parts. There was a post-office at Hornby; and an old fellow, who stowed away the few letters in any or all his pockets, as it best suited him, was the letter-carrier to Heathbridge and the neighbourhood. I have often met him in the lanes thereabouts, and asked him for letters. Sometimes I have come upon him, sitting on the hedge-bank resting; and he has begged me to read him an address, too illegible for his spectacled eyes to decipher. When I used to inquire if he had anything for me, or for Holdsworth (he was not particular to whom he gave up the letters, so that he got rid of them somehow, and could set off homewards), he would say he thought that he had, for such was his invariable safe form of answer; and would fumble in breast-pockets, waistcoat-pockets, breeches-pockets, and, as a last resource, in coat-tail pockets; and at length try to comfort me, if I looked disappointed, by telling me, 'Hoo had missed this toime, but was sure to write to-morrow;' 'Hoo' representing an imaginary sweetheart.

Sometimes I had seen the minister bring home a letter which

he had found lying for him at the little shop that was the post-office at Heathbridge, or from the grander establishment at Hornby. Once or twice Josiah, the carter, remembered that the old letter-carrier had trusted him with an epistle to 'Measter', as they had met in the lanes. I think it must have been about ten days after my arrival at the farm, and my talk to Phillis cutting bread-and-butter at the kitchen dresser, before the day on which the minister suddenly spoke at the dinner-table, and said, –

'By-the-by, I've got a letter in my pocket. Reach me my coat here, Phillis.' The weather was still sultry, and for coolness and ease the minister was sitting in his shirt-sleeves. 'I went to Heathbridge about the paper they had sent me, which spoils all the pens – and I called at the post-office, and found a letter for me, unpaid, – and they did not like to trust it to old Zekiel. Aye! here it is! Now we shall hear news of Holdsworth, – I thought I'd keep it till we were all together.' My heart seemed to stop beating, and I hung my head over my plate, not daring to look up. What would come of it now? What was Phillis doing? How was she looking? A moment of suspense, – and then he spoke again. 'Why! what's this? Here are two visiting tickets with his name on, no writing at all. No! it's not his name on both. Mrs Holdsworth! The young man has gone and got married.' I lifted my head at these words; I could not help looking just for one instant at Phillis. It seemed to me as if she had been keeping watch over my face and ways. Her face was brilliantly flushed; her eyes were dry and glittering; but she did not speak; her lips were set together almost as if she was pinching them tight to prevent words or sounds coming out. Cousin Holman's face expressed surprise and interest.

'Well!' said she, 'who'd ha' thought it! He's made quick work of his wooing and wedding. I'm sure I wish him happy. Let me see' – counting on her fingers, – 'October, November, December, January, February, March, April, May, June, July, – at least we're at the 28th, – it is nearly ten months after all, and reckon a month each way off—'

'Did you know of this news before?' said the minister, turning sharp round on me, surprised, I suppose, at my silence, – hardly suspicious, as yet.

'I knew – I had heard – something. It is to a French Canadian young lady,' I went on, forcing myself to talk. 'Her name is Ventadour.'

'Lucille Ventadour!' said Phillis, in a sharp voice, out of tune.

'Then you knew too!' exclaimed the minister.

We both spoke at once. I said, 'I heard of the probability of——, and told Phillis.' She said, 'He is married to Lucille Ventadour, of French descent; one of a large family near St. Meurice; am not I right?' I nodded. 'Paul told me, – that is all we know, is not it? Did you see the Howsons, father, in Heathbridge?' and she forced herself to talk more than she had done for several days, asking many questions, trying, as I could see, to keep the conversation off the one raw surface, on which to touch was agony. I had less self-command; but I followed her lead. I was not so much absorbed in the conversation but what I could see that the minister was puzzled and uneasy; though he seconded Phillis's efforts to prevent her mother from recurring to the great piece of news, and uttering continual exclamations of wonder and surprise. But with that one exception we were all disturbed out of our natural equanimity, more or less. Every day, every hour, I was reproaching myself more and more for my blundering officiousness. If only I had held my foolish tongue for that one half-hour; if only I had not been in such impatient haste to do something to relieve pain! I could have knocked my stupid head against the wall in my remorse. Yet all I could do now was to second the brave girl in her efforts to conceal her disappointment and keep her maidenly secret. But I thought that dinner would never, never come to an end. I suffered for her, even more than for myself. Until now everything which I had heard spoken in that happy household were simple words of true meaning. If we had aught to say, we said it; and if any one preferred silence, nay if all did so, there would have been no spasmodic, forced efforts to talk for the sake of talking, or to keep off intrusive thoughts or suspicions.

At length we got up from our places, and prepared to disperse; but two or three of us had lost our zest and interest in the daily labour. The minister stood looking out of the window in silence, and when he roused himself to go out to the fields where his labourers were working, it was with a sigh; and he tried to avert his troubled face as he passed us on his way to the door. When he had left us, I caught sight of Phillis's face, as, thinking herself unobserved, her countenance relaxed for a moment or two into sad, woeful weariness. She started into briskness again when her mother spoke, and hurried away to do some little errand at her bidding. When we two were alone, cousin Holman recurred to Holdsworth's marriage. She was one of those people who like to view an event from every side of probability, or even possibility; and she had been cut short from indulging herself in this way during dinner.

'To think of Mr Holdsworth's being married! I can't get over it, Paul. Not but what he was a very nice young man! I don't like her name, though; it sounds foreign. Say it again, my dear. I hope she'll know how to take care of him, English fashion. He is not strong, and if she does not see that his things are well aired, I should be afraid of the old cough '

'He always said he was stronger than he had ever been before, after that fever.'

'He might think so, but I have my doubts. He was a very pleasant young man, but he did not stand nursing very well. He got tired of being coddled, as he called it. I hope they'll soon come back to England, and then he'll have a chance for his health. I wonder now, if she speaks English; but, to be sure, he can speak foreign tongues like anything, as I've heard the minister say.'

And so we went on for some time, till she became drowsy over her knitting, on the sultry summer afternoon; and I stole away for a walk, for I wanted some solitude in which to think over things, and, alas! to blame myself with poignant stabs of remorse.

I lounged lazily as soon as I got to the wood. Here and there the bubbling, brawling brook circled round a great stone, or a root of an old tree, and made a pool; otherwise it coursed brightly over the gravel and stones. I stood by one of these for more than half an hour, or, indeed, longer, throwing bits of wood or pebbles into the water, and wondering what I could do to remedy the present state of things. Of course all my meditation was of no use; and at length the distant sound of the horn employed to tell the men far afield to leave off work, warned me that it was six o'clock, and time for me to go home. Then I caught wafts of the loud-voiced singing of the evening psalm. As I was crossing the Ashfield, I saw the minister at some distance talking to a man. I could not hear what they were saying, but I saw an impatient or dissentient (I could not tell which) gesture on the part of the former, who walked quickly away, and was apparently absorbed in his thoughts, for though he passed within twenty yards of me, as both our paths converged towards home, he took no notice of me. We passed the evening in a way which was even worse than dinner-time. The minister was silent, depressed, even irritable. Poor cousin Holman was utterly perplexed by this unusual frame of mind and temper in her husband; she was not well herself, and was suffering from the extreme and sultry heat, which made her less talkative than usual. Phillis, usually so reverently tender to her parents, so soft, so gentle, seemed now to take no notice of the unusual state of things, but talked to me – to any one, on indifferent subjects, regardless of her father's gravity, of her mother's piteous looks of bewilderment. But once my eyes fell upon her hands, concealed under the table, and I could see the passionate, convulsive manner in which she laced and interlaced her fingers perpetually, wringing them together from time to time, wringing till the compressed flesh became perfectly white. What could I do? I talked with her, as I saw she wished; her grey eyes had dark circles round them. and a strange kind of dark light in them; her cheeks were flushed, but her lips were white and wan. I wondered that others did not read these signs as clearly as I did. But perhaps they did; I think, from what came afterwards, the minister did.

Poor cousin Holman! she worshipped her husband; and the outward signs of his uneasiness were more patent to her simple heart than were her daughter's. After a while she could bear it no longer. She got up, and, softly laying her hand on his broad stooping shoulder, she said, –

'What is the matter, minister? Has anything gone wrong?'

He started as if from a dream. Phillis hung her head, and caught her breath in terror at the answer she feared. But he, looking round with a sweeping glance, turned his broad, wise face up to his anxious wife, and forced a smile, and took her hand in a reassuring manner.

'I am blaming myself, dear. I have been overcome with anger this afternoon. I scarcely knew what I was doing, but I turned away Timothy Cooper. He has killed the Ribstone pippin at the corner of the orchard; gone and piled the quicklime for the mortar for the new stable wall against the trunk of the tree – stupid fellow! killed the tree outright – and it loaded with apples!'

'And Ribstone pippins are so scarce,' said sympathetic cousin Holman.

'Aye! But Timothy is but a half-wit; and he has a wife and children. He had often put me to it sore, with his slothful ways, but I had laid it before the Lord, and striven to bear with him. But I will not stand it any longer, it's past my patience. And he has notice to find another place. Wife, we won't talk more about it.' He took her hand gently off his shoulder, touched it with his lips; but relapsed into a silence as profound, if not quite so morose in appearance, as before. I could not tell why, but this bit of talk between her father and mother seemed to take all the factitious spirits out of Phillis. She did not speak now, but looked out of the open casement at the calm large moon, slowly moving through the twilight sky. Once I thought her eyes were filling with tears; but, if so, she shook them off, and arose with alacrity when her mother, tired and dispirited, proposed to go to bed immediately after prayers. We all said good-night in our separate ways to the minister, who still sate at the table with the great Bible open before him, not much looking up at any of our salutations, but returning them kindly. But when I, last of all, was on the point of leaving the room, he said, still scarcely looking up, –

'Paul, you will oblige me by staying here a few minutes. I would fain have some talk with you.'

I knew what was coming, all in a moment. I carefully shut-to the door, put out my candle, and sate down to my fate. He seemed to find some difficulty in beginning, for, if I had not heard that he wanted to speak to me, I should never have guessed it, he seemed so much absorbed in reading a chapter to the end. Suddenly he lifted his head up and said, –

'It is about that friend of yours, Holdsworth! Paul, have you any reason for thinking he has played tricks upon Phillis?'

I saw that his eyes were blazing with such a fire of anger at the bare idea, that I lost all my presence of mind, and only repeated, –

'Played tricks on Phillis!'

'Aye! you know what I mean: made love to her, courted her, made her think that he loved her, and then gone away and left her. Put it as you will, only give me an answer of some kind or another – a true answer, I mean – and don't repeat my words, Paul.'

He was shaking all over as he said this. I did not delay a moment in answering him, –

'I do not believe that Edward Holdsworth ever played tricks on Phillis, ever made love to her; he never, to my knowledge, made her believe that he loved her.'

I stopped; I wanted to nerve up my courage for a confession, yet I wished to save the secret of Phillis's love for Holdsworth as much as I could; that secret which she had so striven to keep sacred and safe; and I had need of some reflection before I went on with what I had to say.

He began again before I had quite arranged my manner of speech. It was almost as if to himself, – 'She is my only child; my little daughter! She is hardly out of childhood; I have thought to gather her under my wings for years to come; her mother and I would lay down our lives to keep her from harm and grief.' Then, raising his voice, and looking at me, he said, 'Something has gone wrong with the child; and it seemed to me to date from the time she heard of that marriage. It is hard to think that you may know more of her secret cares and sorrows than I do, – but perhaps you do, Paul, perhaps you do, – only, if it be not a sin, tell me what I can do to make her happy again; tell me.'

'It will not do much good, I am afraid,' said I, 'but I will own how wrong I did; I don't mean wrong in the way of sin, but in the way of judgment. Holdsworth told me just before he went that he loved Phillis, and hoped to make her his wife, and I told her.'

There! it was out; all my part in it, at least; and I set my lips tight together, and waited for the words to come. I did not see his face; I looked straight at the wall opposite; but I heard him once begin to speak, and then turn over the leaves in the book before him. How awfully still that room was! The air outside,

how still it was! The open windows let in no rustle of leaves,
no twitter or movement of birds – no sound whatever. The
clock on the stairs – the minister's hard breathing – was it to
go on for ever? Impatient beyond bearing at the deep quiet, I
spoke again, –

'I did it for the best, as I thought.'

The minister shut the book to hastily, and stood up. Then I
saw how angry he was.

'For the best, do you say? It was best, was it, to go and tell a
young girl what you never told a word of to her parents, who
trusted you like a son of their own?'

He began walking about, up and down the room close under
the open windows, churning up his bitter thoughts of me.

'To put such thoughts into the child's head,' continued he;
'to spoil her peaceful maidenhood with talk about another
man's love; and such love, too,' he spoke scornfully now –
'a love that is ready for any young woman. Oh, the misery in
my poor little daughter's face to-day at dinner – the misery,
Paul! I thought you were one to be trusted – your father's son
too, to go and put such thoughts into the child's mind; you
two talking together about that man wishing to marry her.'

I could not help remembering the pinafore, the childish
garment which Phillis wore so long, as if her parents were unaware of her progress towards womanhood. Just in the same
way the minister spoke and thought of her now, as a child,
whose innocent peace I had spoiled by vain and foolish talk. I
knew that the truth was different, though I could hardly have
told it now; but, indeed, I never thought of trying to tell; it
was far from my mind to add one iota to the sorrow which I
had caused. The minister went on walking, occasionally
stopping to move things on the table, or articles of furniture,
in a sharp, impatient, meaningless way, then he began again, –

'So young, so pure from the world! how could you go and
talk to such a child, raising hopes, exciting feelings – all to end
thus; and best so, even though I saw her poor piteous face
look as it did. I can't forgive you, Paul; it was more than
wrong – it was wicked – to go and repeat that man's words.'

His back was now to the door, and, in listening to his low
angry tones, he did not hear it slowly open, nor did he see
Phillis, standing just within the room, until he turned round;

then he stood still. She must have been half undressed; but she had covered herself with a dark winter cloak, which fell in long folds to her white, naked, noiseless feet. Her face was strangely pale: her eyes heavy in the black circles round them. She came up to the table very slowly, and leant her hand upon it, saying mournfully, –

'Father, you must not blame Paul. I could not help hearing a great deal of what you were saying. He did tell me, and perhaps it would have been wiser not, dear Paul! But – oh, dear! oh, dear! I am so sick with shame! He told me out of his kind heart, because he saw – that I was so very unhappy at *his* going away.'

She hung her head, and leant more heavily than before on her supporting hand.

'I don't understand,' said her father; but he was beginning to understand. Phillis did not answer till he asked her again. I could have struck him now for his cruelty; but then I knew all.

'I loved him, father!' she said at length, raising her eyes to the minister's face.

'Had he ever spoken of love to you? Paul says not!'

'Never.' She let fall her eyes, and drooped more than ever. I almost thought she would fall.

'I could not have believed it,' said he, in a hard voice, yet sighing the moment he had spoken. A dead silence for a moment. 'Paul! I was unjust to you. You deserved blame, but not all that I said.' Then again a silence. I thought I saw Phillis's white lips moving, but it might have been the flickering of the candlelight – a moth had flown in through the open casement, and was fluttering round the flame; I might have saved it, but I did not care to do so, my heart was too full of other things. At any rate, no sound was heard for long endless minutes. Then he said, – 'Phillis! did we not make you happy here? Have we not loved you enough?'

She did not seem to understand the drift of this question; she looked up as if bewildered, and her beautiful eyes dilated with a painful, tortured expression. He went on, without noticing the look on her face; he did not see it, I am sure.

'And yet you would have left us, left your home, left your father and your mother, and gone away with this stranger, wandering over the world.'

He suffered, too; there were tones of pain in the voice in which he uttered this reproach. Probably the father and daughter were never so far apart in their lives, so unsympathetic. Yet some new terror came over her, and it was to him she turned for help. A shadow came over her face, and she tottered towards her father; falling down, her arms across his knees, and moaning out, –

'Father, my head! my head!' and then slipped through his quick-enfolding arms, and lay on the ground at his feet.

I shall never forget his sudden look of agony while I live; never! We raised her up; her colour had strangely darkened; she was insensible. I ran through the back-kitchen to the yard pump, and brought back water. The minister had her on his knees, her head against his breast, almost as though she were a sleeping child. He was trying to rise up with his poor precious burden, but the momentary terror had robbed the strong man of his strength, and he sank back in his chair with sobbing breath.

'She is not dead, Paul! is she?' he whispered, hoarse, as I came near him.

I, too, could not speak, but I pointed to the quivering of the muscles round her mouth. Just then cousin Holman, attracted by some unwonted sound, came down. I remember I was surprised at the time at her presence of mind, she seemed to know so much better what to do than the minister, in the midst of the sick affright which blanched her countenance, and made her tremble all over. I think now that it was the recollection of what had gone before; the miserable thought that possibly his words had brought on this attack, whatever it might be, that so unmanned the minister. We carried her upstairs, and while the women were putting her to bed, still unconscious, still slightly convulsed, I slipped out, and saddled one of the horses, and rode as fast as the heavy-trotting beast could go, to Hornby, to find the doctor there, and bring him back. He was out, might be detained the whole night. I remember saying, 'God help us all!' as I sate on my horse, under the window, through which the apprentice's head had appeared to answer my furious tugs at the night-bell. He was a good-natured fellow. He said, –

'He may be home in half an hour, there's no knowing; but I

daresay he will. I'll send him out to the Hope Farm directly he comes in. It's that good-looking young woman, Holman's daughter, that's ill, isn't it?'

'Yes.'

'It would be a pity if she was to go. She's an only child, isn't she? I'll get up, and smoke a pipe in the surgery, ready for the governor's coming home. I might go to sleep if I went to bed again.'

'Thank you, you're a good fellow!' and I rode back almost as quickly as I came.

It was a brain fever. The doctor said so, when he came in the early summer morning. I believe we had come to know the nature of the illness in the night-watches that had gone before. As to hope of ultimate recovery, or even evil prophecy of the probable end, the cautious doctor would be entrapped into neither. He gave his directions, and promised to come again; so soon, that this one thing showed his opinion of the gravity of the case.

By God's mercy she recovered, but it was a long, weary time first. According to previously made plans, I was to have gone home at the beginning of August. But all such ideas were put aside now, without a word being spoken. I really think that I was necessary in the house, and especially necessary to the minister at this time; my father was the last man in the world, under such circumstances, to expect me home.

I say, I think I was necessary in the house. Every person (I had almost said every creature, for all the dumb beasts seemed to know and love Phillis) about the place went grieving and sad, as though a cloud was over the sun. They did their work, each striving to steer clear of the temptation to eye-service,* in fulfilment of the trust reposed in them by the minister. For the day after Phillis had been taken ill, he had called all the men employed on the farm into the empty barn; and there he had entreated their prayers for his only child; and then and there he had told them of his present incapacity for thought about any other thing in this world but his little daughter, lying nigh unto death, and he had asked them to go on with their daily labours as best they could, without his direction. So, as I say, these honest men did their work to the best of their ability, but they slouched along with sad and careful faces, coming one by one in the dim mornings to ask news of the sorrow that overshadowed the house; and receiving Betty's intelligence, always rather darkened by passing through her mind, with slow shakes of the head, and a dull wistfulness of sympathy. But, poor fellows, they were hardly fit to be trusted with hasty messages, and here my poor services came in. One time I was to ride hard to Sir William Bentinck's, and petition for ice out of his ice-house, to put on Phillis's head. Another it was to Eltham I must go, by train, horse, anyhow, and bid the doctor there come for a consultation, for fresh symptoms had appeared, which Mr Brown, of Hornby, considered unfavourable. Many an hour have I sate on the window-seat, half-way up the stairs, close by the old clock, listening in the hot stillness of the house for the sounds in the sick-room. The minister and I met often, but spoke together seldom. He looked so old – so old! He shared the nursing with his wife; the strength that was needed seemed to be given to them both in that day. They required no one else about their child. Every office about her was sacred to them; even Betty only went into the room for the most necessary purposes. Once I saw Phillis through the open door; her pretty golden hair had been cut off long before; her head was covered with wet cloths, and she was moving it backwards and forwards on the pillow, with weary, never-ending motion, her poor eyes shut, trying in the old accustomed way to croon out a hymn tune, but perpetually breaking it up into moans of pain. Her mother sate by her, tearless, changing the cloths upon her head with patient solicitude. I did not see the minister at first, but there he was in a dark corner, down upon his knees, his hands clasped together in passionate prayer. Then the door shut, and I saw no more.

One day he was wanted; and I had to summon him. Brother Robinson and another minister, hearing of his 'trial', had come to see him. I told him this upon the stair-landing in a whisper. He was strangely troubled.

'They will want me to lay bare my heart. I cannot do it. Paul, stay with me. They mean well; but as for spiritual help at such a time – it is God only, God only, who can give it.'

So I went in with him. They were two ministers from the neighbourhood; both older than Ebenezer Holman; but evidently inferior to him in education and worldly position. I thought they looked at me as if I were an intruder, but remembering the minister's words I held my ground, and took up one of poor Phillis's books (of which I could not read a word) to have an ostensible occupation. Presently I was asked to 'engage in prayer', and we all knelt down; Brother Robinson 'leading', and quoting largely as I remember from the Book of Job. He seemed to take for his text, if texts are ever taken for prayers, 'Behold thou hast instructed many; but now it is come upon thee, and thou faintest, it toucheth thee and thou art troubled.'* When we others rose up, the minister continued for some minutes on his knees. Then he too got up, and stood facing us, for a moment, before we all sate down in conclave. After a pause Robinson began, –

'We grieve for you, Brother Holman, for your trouble is great. But we would fain have you remember you are as a light set on a hill; and the congregations are looking at you with watchful eyes. We have been talking as we came along on the two duties required of you in this strait; Brother Hodgson and me. And we have resolved to exhort you on these two points. First, God has given you the opportunity of showing forth an example of resignation.' Poor Mr Holman visibly winced at this word. I could fancy how he had tossed aside such brotherly preachings in his happier moments; but now his whole system was unstrung, and 'resignation' seemed a term which presupposed that the dreaded misery of losing Phillis was inevitable. But good stupid Mr Robinson went on. 'We hear on all sides that there are scarce any hopes of your child's recovery; and it may be well to bring you to mind of Abraham;* and how he was willing to kill his only child when the Lord commanded. Take example by him, Brother Holman. Let us hear you say, "The Lord giveth and the Lord taketh away. Blessed be the name of the Lord!" '

There was a pause of expectancy. I verily believe the minister tried to feel it; but he could not. Heart of flesh was too strong. Heart of stone he had not.

'I will say it to my God, when He gives me strength, – when the day comes,' he spoke at last.

The other two looked at each other, and shook their heads. I think the reluctance to answer as they wished was not quite unexpected. The minister went on: 'There are hopes yet,' he said, as if to himself. 'God has given me a great heart for hoping, and I will not look forward beyond the hour.' Then turning more to them, and speaking louder, he added: 'Brethren, God will strengthen me when the time comes, when such resignation as you speak of is needed. Till then I cannot feel it; and what I do not feel I will not express; using words as if they were a charm.' He was getting chafed, I could see.

He had rather put them out by these speeches of his; but after a short time and some more shakes of the head, Robinson began again, –

'Secondly, we would have you listen to the voice of the rod, and ask yourself for what sins this trial has been laid upon you; whether you may not have been too much given up to your farm and your cattle; whether this world's learning has not puffed you up to vain conceit and neglect of the things of God; whether you have not made an idol of your daughter?'

'I cannot answer – I will not answer!' exclaimed the minister. 'My sins I confess to God. But if they were scarlet (and they are so in His sight),' he added, humbly, 'I hold with Christ that afflictions are not sent by God in wrath as penalties for sin.'

'Is that orthodox, Brother Robinson?' asked the third minister, in a deferential tone of inquiry.

Despite the minister's injunction not to leave him, I thought matters were getting so serious that a little homely interruption would be more to the purpose than my continued presence, and I went round to the kitchen to ask for Betty's help.

' 'Od rot 'em!' said she; 'they're always a-coming at ill-convenient times; and they have such hearty appetites, they'll make nothing of what would have served master and you since our poor lass has been ill. I've but a bit of cold beef in th' house; but I'll do some ham and eggs, and that 'll rout 'em from worrying the minister. They're a deal quieter after they've had their victual. Last time as old Robinson came, he was very reprehensible upon master's learning, which he couldn't compass to save his life, so he needn't have been afeard of that temptation, and used words long enough to have knocked a body down; but after me and missus had given him his fill of victual, and he'd had some good ale and a pipe, he spoke just like any other man, and could crack a joke with me.'

Their visit was the only break in the long weary days and nights. I do not mean that no other inquiries were made. I believe that all the neighbours hung about the place daily till they could learn from some out-comer how Phillis Holman was. But they knew better than to come up to the house, for the August weather was so hot that every door and window was kept constantly open, and the least sound outside penetrated all through. I am sure the cocks and hens had a sad time of it; for Betty drove them all into an empty barn, and kept them fastened up in the dark for several days, with very little effect as regarded their crowing and clacking. At length came a sleep which was the crisis, and from which she wakened up with a new faint life. Her slumber had lasted many, many hours. We scarcely dared to breathe or move during the time; we had striven to hope so long, that we were sick at heart, and durst not trust in the favourable signs: the even breathing, the moistened skin, the slight return of delicate colour into the pale, wan lips. I recollect stealing out that evening in the dusk, and wandering down the grassy lane, under the shadow of the over-arching elms to the little bridge at the foot of the hill, where the lane to the Hope Farm joined another road to Hornby. On the low parapet of that bridge I found Timothy Cooper, the stupid, half-witted labourer, sitting, idly throwing bits of mortar into the brook below. He just looked up at me as I came near, but gave me no greeting, either by word or gesture. He had generally made some sign of recognition to me, but this time I thought he was sullen at being dismissed. Nevertheless I felt as if it would be a relief to talk a little to some one, and I sate down by him. While I was thinking how to begin, he yawned wearily.

'You are tired, Tim?' said I.

'Aye,' said he. 'But I reckon I may go home now.'

'Have you been sitting here long?'

'Welly all day long. Leastways sin' seven i' th' morning.'

'Why, what in the world have you been doing?'

'Nought.'

'Why have you been sitting here, then?'

'T' keep carts off.' He was up now, stretching himself, and shaking his lubberly limbs.

'Carts! what carts?'

'Carts as might ha' wakened yon wench! It's Hornby market-day. I reckon yo're no better nor a half-wit yoursel'.' He cocked his eye at me as if he were gauging my intellect.

'And have you been sitting here all day to keep the lane quiet?'

'Aye. I've nought else to do. Th' minister has turned me adrift. Have yo' heard how th' lass is faring to-night?'

'They hope she'll waken better for this long sleep. Good-night to you, and God bless you, Timothy,' said I.

He scarcely took any notice of my words, as he lumbered across a stile that led to his cottage. Presently I went home to the farm. Phillis had stirred, had spoken two or three faint words. Her mother was with her, dropping nourishment into her scarce conscious mouth. The rest of the household were summoned to evening prayer for the first time for many days. It was a return to the daily habits of happiness and health. But in these silent days our very lives had been an unspoken prayer. Now we met in the house-place, and looked at each other with strange recognition of the thankfulness on all our faces. We knelt down; we waited for the minister's voice. He did not begin as usual. He could not; he was choking. Presently we heard the strong man's sob. Then old John turned round on his knees, and said, –

'Minister, I reckon we have blessed the Lord wi' all our souls, though we've ne'er talked about it; and maybe He'll not need spoken words this night. God bless us all, and keep our Phillis safe from harm! Amen.'

Old John's impromptu prayer was all we had that night.

'Our Phillis,' as he called her, grew better day by day from that time. Not quickly; I sometimes grew desponding, and feared that she would never be what she had been before; no more she has, in some ways.

I seized an early opportunity to tell the minister about Timothy Cooper's unsolicited watch on the bridge during the long summer's day.

'God forgive me!' said the minister. 'I have been too proud

in my own conceit. The first steps I take out of this house shall be to Cooper's cottage.'

I need hardly say Timothy was reinstated in his place on the farm; and I have often since admired the patience with which his master tried to teach him how to do the easy work which was henceforward carefully adjusted to his capacity.

Phillis was carried down-stairs, and lay for hour after hour quite silent on the great sofa, drawn up under the windows of the house-place. She seemed always the same, gentle, quiet, and sad. Her energy did not return with her bodily strength. It was sometimes pitiful to see her parents' vain endeavours to rouse her to interest. One day the minister brought her a set of blue ribbons, reminding her with a tender smile of a former conversation in which she had owned to a love of such feminine vanities. She spoke gratefully to him, but when he was gone she laid them on one side, and languidly shut her eyes. Another time I saw her mother bring her the Latin and Italian books that she had been so fond of before her illness – or, rather, before Holdsworth had gone away. That was worst of all. She turned her face to the wall, and cried as soon as her mother's back was turned. Betty was laying the cloth for the early dinner. Her sharp eyes saw the state of the case.

'Now, Phillis!' said she, coming up to the sofa; 'we ha' done a' we can for you, and th' doctors has done a' they can for you, and I think the Lord has done a' He can for you, and more than you deserve, too, if you don't do something for yourself. If I were you, I'd rise up and snuff the moon, sooner than break your father's and your mother's hearts wi' watching and waiting till it pleases you to fight your own way back to cheerfulness. There, I never favoured long preachings, and I've said my say.'

A day or two after Phillis asked me, when we were alone, if I thought my father and mother would allow her to go and stay with them for a couple of months. She blushed a little as she faltered out her wish for change of thought and scene.

'Only for a short time, Paul. Then – we will go back to the peace of the old days. I know we shall; I can, and I will!'

EXPLANATORY NOTES

LIZZIE LEIGH

Published *Household Words*, 1850, Vol. 1, 30 March–13 April (3 episodes). Reprinted in *Lizzie Leigh and other Tales*, 1855 (text from Cheap edition, 1855).

1. *Milton's famous line:* 'God is thy law, thou mine: to know no more/Is woman's happiest knowledge and her praise' (Eve to Adam, *Paradise Lost*, Book IV, ll. 637–8).
2. *house-place:* a farm living-room.
3. *the Prodigal Son:* Luke 15: 11–32.
4. *sadly pottered:* extremely vexed, bothered.
5. *chaffering:* haggling, bargaining.
5. *shippon:* cowshed, byre.
7. *sided:* put in order.
10. *made good his footing:* established his right to be there, established the terms on which he would be welcome.
12. *threep it up:* press the point, insist upon discussing it.
12. *speered:* questioned.
14. *loosed:* let out, dismissed.
14. *right gradely things:* very handsome, splendid.
15. *frab:* worry, disturb.
17. *flyted:* scolded, found fault.
22. *lost and is found:* the Prodigal Son.
26. *Not all the scalding tears of care:* not traced.
26. *a-this-ons:* like this.
30. *as-that-as:* like that.
32. *the lost piece of silver:* Luke 15: 8–10.

THE OLD NURSE'S STORY

Published *Household Words*, 1852, Christmas Number ('A Round of Stories by the Christmas Fire'), 18 December. Reprinted in *Lizzie Leigh and other Tales*, 1855 (text from Cheap edition, 1855).

40. *the younger sister:* by custom an elder sister was addressed by her surname alone, preceded by 'Miss'; any subsequent sisters by Christian name alone, preceded by 'Miss'.
42. *Crosthwaite Church:* just outside Keswick, Cumberland; the nurse comes from adjoining Westmoreland.
45. *perished:* frozen, near dead with cold.
45. *maud:* shepherd's plaid, shawl.
51. *army in America:* presumably during the War of American Independence, 1775–1783.

HALF A LIFE-TIME AGO

Originally published as 'Martha Preston' in *Sartain's Union Magazine*, 1850, Vol. 6; rewritten and published under present title in *Household Words*, 1855, Vol. 12, 6–20 October (3 episodes). Reprinted in *Round the Sofa*, 2 Vols., 1859 (present text).

61. *'Paradise Lost'* . . . *'The Pilgrim's Progress'*: Milton's two epics; Solomon Gessner's (1730–88) prose epic, *The Death of Abel* (1758); Richard Graves's (1715–1804) comic novel, *The Spiritual Quixote* (1773), a satire on Methodism, hardly grave or solid; Bunyan's *The Pilgrim's Progress* (Part 1, 1672; part 2, 1678).
63. *a dree bit:* dangerous, hazardous place.
63. *take tent:* take care of.
67. *lungeous:* rough.
78. *shandry:* light cart or trap on springs.
80. *the good penny:* wedding portion, dowry.
81. *part thee and me:* Ruth 1:16.
92. *redded up:* tidied, cleared up.
93. vis inertiae: dead force.
94. *attempted to jockey:* tried to cheat or overreach.
95. *lift:* sky.
96. *doddered:* having lost the top or branches.

LOIS THE WITCH

Published *All the Year Round*, 1859, Vol. 1, 8–22 October (3 episodes). Reprinted in *Right at Last and other Tales*, 1860 (present text).

Gaskell drew historical material from the Rev. Charles W. Upham's *Lectures on Witchcraft* (Boston, 1831). He provides details of life in the colony and Salem; of the English Crown's withdrawal of the Massachusetts State Charter in 1685; and of the threats from the French in Canada and from the Indians, whether on their own initiative or stirred up by the French – in 1675 Thomas Lothrop was ambushed by Indians and destroyed with his men ('Lothrop's business'), while in 1690 attacks on Canada, varyingly successful, brought no permanent peace: the unsettled state of things, with no permanent army, meant that all men were expected to be ready for service as militia at a moment's notice (hence 'minute-men'). The witch scare began amongst the Rev. Samuel Parris's household (Rev. Tappau here) and one of the eventual victims was the Rev. George Burroughs (drawn on for Rev. Nolan). Upham mentions the historical figures of the drama: John Hathorne and Jonathan Corwin were both Salem magistrates, while Cotton Mather (1633–1728), minister at Boston, was convinced of the reality of witchcraft and eager in its prosecution. The story of Mr Goodwin's family is in Mather's *Magnalia Christi Americana* (a history of Christianity in the

American Colonies). Upham also provides details of the victims and their fates, including the allusion to Giles Corey, pressed to death for refusing to plead: since condemnation was all but certain, refusal to plead meant no trial and no shame of witchcraft, but the law allowed persuasion by loading weights on the accused's chest until he pleaded – or died. The eye-witness who refers to the girls tumbling like swine was Nathaniel Cary, describing the trial of his wife, who eventually escaped. The aftermath included the public confession of error by Justice Samuel Sewall (1652–1730) and by the people of Salem. Gaskell deftly weaves this information into a story original to herself.

107. *Edgehill:* first battle (1642) of the Civil War.
107. *schismatic:* separated from the Church of England, an Independent or Presbyterian, roughly the Puritan of the Civil War.
109. *great bough of a tree:* commonly displayed to indicate an inn.
110. *wampum-beads:* made from shells and strung for money or decoration.
111. *punken-pie:* i.e. pumpkin-pie.
111. *brandered:* cooked over hot coals or ashes.
111. *Jacobite:* usually applied after 1688 to supporters of the exiled male line of the Stuart kings.
111. *Archbishop Laud:* 1573–1645: under Charles I vigorously supported the King and the Anglican Church, attempting to impose uniformity or religion upon the Schismatics or Puritans.
113. *Butler . . . through the nose:* Samuel Butler (1612–80) satirized the Puritans in his poem *Hudibras* (1663–78): Part 1, Canto 1, l.230.
114. *like a roaring lion:* I Peter 5:8.
119. *the oaths to Charles Stuart:* after Charles II's Restoration holders of Anglican livings were required to swear to the Act of Uniformity; those who failed to do so by St. Bartholemew's Day 1662 were ejected from the churches: these were mainly Puritans. Calling the King 'Charles Stuart' is deliberately denigrating.
122. *on Aaron's beard:* Psalm 132.
125. *Church and State:* i.e. the Establishment, the union of Anglican Church and the British Government.
125. *Popish rubric:* the details laid down for the conduct of religious ceremonies by the Book of Common Prayer, felt by Puritans to be a Roman Catholic document.
125. *irreligious King:* Charles I.
131. *apple eaten . . . ways of divination:* When the apple is eaten in front of a mirror and held over the left shoulder, it will be taken from behind by an unseen supernatural being and the girl see her future husband in the mirror; drops from the sheet form patterns or letters that indicate the lover or else the sheet when dropped gives the outline or features of the man; basins of water serve as mirrors to show the image of the lover or else

the solidified shapes of molten wax or lead dropped in them are interpreted as letters of names or signs of the lover's profession; the nuts are named for possible men and when burnt the brighter flame indicates which will be the lover or else one nut is named for the girl and one for the possible husband, the behaviour of the burning nuts indicating the course of the marriage.

137. *even as Samuel did:* I Samuel 3.

137. *Hazael:* II Kings 8: 7–15; Manasseh is convinced his marriage with Lois is as surely ordained, despite what she says, as Hazael's wickedness was ordained, despite what *he* said.

139. *evening hymn:* by Bishop Thomas Ken (1637–1711).

146. *elect . . . Free-Will . . . Fore-Knowledge:* Puritans believe God has already chosen those who are to be saved and that this is revealed to those so 'elected'. This would seem to determine man's fate and so give him no part in his own salvation; but others argue that while God in eternity knows what will happen, man in time has free choice.

148. *the general court:* originally a mass meeting of the colony's freemen, it became an elective body, with some of the powers and authority of the state government: later, its revival of the law making witchcraft a capital offence meant that not just Salem but the country at large was responsible for the witch-trials.

149. *possessed by him in Judea:* e.g. Matthew 4:24, 8:28–33, 17: 14–21.

150. *herd of swine:* Matthew 8:28–33.

153. *Master Matthew Hopkinson:* properly 'Hopkins'; died 1647. Procured special commission to search for witches (1644–7) and hanged many old women. Published *Discovery of Witches* (1647). Himself executed as a sorcerer.

159. *the right hand . . . the right eye:* Matthew 18:9.

160. *against the Holy Ghost:* Matthew 12:31–2.

162. *shepherd David . . . king Saul:* I Samuel 16:14–23.

164. *not to suffer witches in the land:* Exodus 22:18.

164. *'and he blessed her unaware':* adapted from Coleridge's *The Ancient Mariner.*

166. *the land of Beulah:* Isaiah 62:4.

169. *Geneva bands:* clerical collar, with two strips of linen hanging down, a form originated by Calvin at Geneva.

169. *after Caesar's murder:* Antony's oration, *Julius Caesar*, III, ii.

170. *the Assembly's Catechism:* a book setting out basic Christian doctrine in question and answer form, approved by the church assembly of the Puritans.

171. *as Dr. Martin Luther:* traditionally, Luther was distracted by the devil and flung his ink-pot to drive him off.

183. *balm in Gilead:* i.e. forgiveness, Jeremiah 8:22.

191. *in regard of his temporal judgements:* judgements made and carried out on earth, as opposed to the eternal judgements of the dead by God.

THE CROOKED BRANCH

Published *All the Year Round*, 1859, Christmas Number ('The Haunted House'), December, as *The Ghost in the Garden Room*. Reprinted with new title in *Right at Last and other Tales*, 1860 (present text).

196. *bedgown:* informal dress worn when first getting out of bed (but more than a dressing-gown).

197. *one boy, Benjamin:* named (ironically in the event) after the best loved son of Jacob.

199. *creepie-stool:* low, three-legged stool.

200. *wax up so:* flare up so, grow so excited.

200. *King George:* George IV (reigned 1820–1830).

201. *turned bottom upwards:* as a fence or guard round the child or to bar the door.

202. *clothes-presses:* cupboards, wardrobes.

206. *maks and wearlocks:* fashions and quantities of clothes.

206. *copy-book:* a book to learn writing from, the first pages with a variety of stylish pen strokes for imitation.

207. *blue starch-water:* the blue colour of watered milk, like that of liquid starch.

209. *just meet same:* exactly the same.

212. *a month's mind:* a strong inclination.

214. *to work double tides:* to work twice as hard.

215. *To Memory Dear:* formula commonly used on tombstones; it gives an ominous ring to subsequent events.

216. *a hole into a box:* the reference seems to be to a pillarbox, strictly an anachronism at this date.

220. *about the Prodigal:* Luke 15:11–32.

222. *a sure and certain rest:* echoes successive passages of the Book of Common Prayer's Burial Service.

226. *Make th' door:* shut the door securely, fasten it.

228. *gearing:* trappings and harness of a horse.

235. *the very stones . . . rise up:* Luke 19:40 (the context is a choice between speaking and bidding silence).

236. *starving:* freezing.

CURIOUS, IF TRUE

Published *Cornhill Magazine*, 1860, Vol. 1, February (one episode). Reprinted in *The Grey Woman and other Tales*, 1865 (present text).

The characters, except Whittingham, come from well known English and French versions of fairy tales. The chief French sources are Charles Perrault (1628–1703), *Tales of Mother Goose* (1697; translated G. Brereton, 1957, and Angela Carter, 1977), and Marie-Catherine Le Jumel de Barneville, baronne d'Aulnoy (1650/1–1705): her *Blanchette* or *The White Cat* is in Andrew Lang's *Blue Fairy Book* (1889; often reprinted). For the first English appearance of many of the tales see Iona and Peter Opie, *The Classic Fairy Tales*, 1974.

242. *Lochiel's grandchild . . . pillow of snow:* Sir Evan Cameron of Lochiel (1629–1719) is reported to have kicked away such a pillow from his son's or nephew's head, seeing it as a sign of degeneracy (Walter Scott, *Tales of a Grandfather*, 1836, III, 119–20).

244. battants: wooden bars to secure a door.

245. *Marché au Vendredi:* literally, the Friday Market, the area of the town where it was held.

245. *the Hôtel Cluny:* in Paris, with extensive collections of the sixteenth and seventeenth centuries.

246. *copied from Dr. Johnson:* James Boswell, *Life of Samuel Johnson* World's Classics, p. 342. tells of the Doctor's anxious cares to take a fixed number of steps from a certain point and if necessary to go back and go over the ground according to his ritual.

252. vouée au blanc: dedicated or pledged to white things.

253. *John Russell? John Bright?:* Russell (1792–1878), twice Prime Minister, Foreign Minister at time of publication; Bright (1811–89), Parliamentarian and leading Anti-Corn Law Reformer. Both are of Whittingham's world of concrete realities.

256. *Monsieur Sganarelle . . . ragaillardir l'affection:* in *The Doctor Despite Himself* by Molière (1622–73), Sganarelle, making up with his wife after a quarrel, tries to pass off what has happened: 'There are some little things that are occasionally necessary in a friendship; and five or six blows of a sword between folk that love one another only revive their tenderness.'

256. *la Féemarraine:* the Fairy Godmother.

COUSIN PHILLIS

Published *Cornhill Magazine*, 1863–4, Vols. 8–9, November–February (4 episodes). Reprinted in *Cousin Phillis and other Tales*, 1865 (present text).

259. *Independent by descent and conviction:* 'Independent' was the name given to those Protestants who rejected the Anglican Church in the seventeenth century (roughly the Puritans) and who survive as the Baptists, Congregationalists and Unitarians. Holman, though it is never explicitly stated, has many Unitarian characteristics.

268. *in the Old Testament . . . Abraham's servant . . . Isaac:* Genesis, 24. Abraham sent his servant in search of a wife for Isaac his son; the servant met Rebekah, Isaac's cousin, and when she gave him water it was a sign from God that she was to be Isaac's bride. Paul's doubts arise because the parallel cuts him off from marrying Phillis, while he feels Isaac could have chosen for himself rather than relying on another man.

270. *private exercise:* prayers, devotions (*not* physical exercise).

271. *the psalm . . . to 'Mount Ephraim'*: not a psalm but a hymn by Isaac Watts (1674–1748), the tune by Benjamin Milgrove (1769).

273. *Virgil*: Roman poet (70–19 B.C.); besides his epic, the *Aeneid*, which Gaskell possibly draws on for parallels between the love of Aeneas and Dido and that of Holdsworth and Phillis, he wrote pastoral poems (*Eclogues*) and poems on agricultural matters (*Georgics*). These last clearly interest Holman most and he specifically refers to them later. Perhaps Holman here has in mind the passage in the first *Georgic* of weather signs at sunset.

274. *parish rod . . . parish bull*: it was common for a parish to have a single bull, hired out by its owner to impregnate the parish's cows. Holman suggests that just as people come to him as a farmer for the bull's services, he wants them to come to him also as their spiritual minister rather than take punishments into their own hands, so that he may mingle mercy and justice – his reference to the parish rod is of course figurative rather than literal.

274. *Matthew Henry's Bible*: Henry (1662–1714), non-conformist divine: his Commentaries on the Bible (or *Exposition*), mentioned below, appeared 1708–10 (5 vols.) and were often reprinted. Here the Bible text and commentaries are combined.

280. tempus fugit: 'time flies'; the simplest of tags, a dire reflection on the remains of Paul's classical knowledge.

287. *some book . . . great family event*: see Oliver Goldsmith, *The Vicar of Wakefield* (1766), Chapter 1.

301. *Henry's . . . Manual . . . Berridge . . . Dante . . . Baretti*: for Henry, see above; the Housewife's Manual would be typical of such practical handbooks and guides, and stresses the household routine; John Berridge (1716–93), evangelical clergyman; *L'Inferno* (Hell) is the first section of Dante's poem, *The Divine Comedy* (c. 1300); Guiseppi Baretti (1717–89) published a Standard Italian/English Dictionary (1760).

303. *fidging fain*: restlessly anxious, eager.

304. *I use euphuisms*: Euphuisms are ornate rhetorical descriptions (the term derives from the style used by the Elizabethan author John Lyly in his prose tale, *Euphues*). The term as used here is not very precise: Gaskell seems to mean that Holdsworth only uses the intimate 'Phillis' to himself, since his relationship with her does not entitle him to use it in ordinary conversation; but since no one refers to her as 'Miss Holman', he has to find elaborate or periphrastic ways of referring to her in public (e.g. 'the daughter of the minister').

304. *Manzoni, I Promessi Sposi*: historical novel (1825–7; *The Betrothed*) by Alessandro Manzoni (1785–1873): important in the growth of Italian self-identification that led to eventual political unity.

307. *navvies*: name originally for labourers digging canals (short-

ened from 'navigators'), thence applied to any such workers: often rough and creators of trouble, their presence indicates other changes brought by the railway.

318. *according to the flesh:* Ephesians 6:5.

326. *De Lolme . . . Constitution:* Jean Louis de Lolme (1740–1806), of Geneva, published *The Constitution of England* (1771; trans. 1775).

327. *And very few to love:* Wordsworth, 'She dwelt among th' untrodden ways'.

328. *measure . . . meting:* Mark 4:24.

328. *Babel . . . confound their languages:* Genesis 11:7.

330. *do it with all thy might:* Ecclesiastes 9:10.

331. *wedding-cards:* two cards sent after a wedding, each with the name of one of the couple, often linked with a silk thread: the custom was common during the nineteenth century.

337. *he'd been farred:* he had been removed, at a long distance.

338. *penny-post reform:* instituted 1840; dates the action to the early 1840's.

348. *eye-service:* work only performed properly when the employer has an eye on proceedings.

350. *thou art troubled:* Job 4:3.

350. *Abraham:* Genesis 22.

J. A. V. Chapple, in 'Elizabeth Gaskell: Two Unpublished Letters to George Smith', *Études Anglaises*, XXXIII (1980), 183–187, prints a letter (10 December 1863) in which Gaskell sketches two endings for 'Cousin Phillis', one abrupt and crude, the other taking Phillis beyond the present end of the story. The minister now dead and her mother bed-ridden, Phillis supervises the levelling and draining of the undrained village, from what she has learned from Holdsworth, and adopts two children whose parents are dead of fever.